Y008381

D1356856

BERTA ISLA

By the same author

All Souls

A Heart So White

Tomorrow in the Battle Think on Me

When I was Mortal

Dark Back of Time

The Man of Feeling

Your Face Tomorrow 1: Fever and Spear

Voyage along the Horizon

Written Lives

Your Face Tomorrow 2: Dance and Dream

Your Face Tomorrow 3: Poison, Shadow and Farewell

Bad Nature, or with Elvis in Mexico

While the Women are Sleeping

The Infatuations

Thus Bad Begins

Venice, An Interior

Between Eternities

BERTA ISLA

Javier Marías

TRANSLATED BY
MARGARET JULL COSTA

HAMISH HAMILTON
an imprint of
PENGUIN BOOKS

HAMISH HAMILTON

UK | USA | Canada | Ireland | Australia
India | New Zealand | South Africa

Hamish Hamilton is part of the Penguin Random House group of companies
whose addresses can be found at global.penguinrandomhouse.com

First published in Spain by Alfaguara, Penguin Random House Grupo Editorial S.A.U. 2017
First published in Great Britain by Hamish Hamilton 2018

001

Copyright © Javier Marías, 2017
Translation copyright © Margaret Jull Costa, 2018

Extracts taken from 'Little Gidding', 'The Dry Salvages' and 'The Love Song
of J. Alfred Prufrock', copyright © Estate of T. S. Eliot, from *Collected Poems 1909–62*.
Reproduced by permission of Faber & Faber Ltd

The moral right of the author and translator has been asserted

Set in 12.5/16 pt Fournier MT Std
Typeset by Jouve (UK), Milton Keynes
Printed and bound in Great Britain by Clays Ltd, Elcograf S.p.A.

A CIP catalogue record for this book is available from the British Library

HARDBACK ISBN: 978–0–241–34371–5
TRADE PAPERBACK ISBN: 978–0–241–34372–2

www.greenpenguin.co.uk

For Carme López Mercader,
the attentive eyes that see,
the attentive ears that hear,
and the voice that offers the best advice

And for Eric Southworth,
still unwittingly providing me with
fruitful quotations,
after half a lifetime of friendship

I

For a while, she wasn't sure her husband was her husband, much as, when you're dozing, you're not sure whether you're thinking or dreaming, whether you're actually in charge of your own thoughts or have completely lost track of them out of sheer exhaustion. Sometimes she thought he was, sometimes not, and at other times, she decided to believe nothing and simply continue living her life with him, or with that man so similar to him, albeit older. But then she, too, had grown older in his absence; she was very young when they married.

Those other times were the best times, the calmest, gentlest, most satisfactory times, but they never lasted very long, it's not easy to shrug off such a doubt. She would manage to set it aside for weeks at a time and immerse herself in unconsidered daily life, which most of the Earth's inhabitants have no difficulty in enjoying, those who merely watch the days begin and see how they trace an arc as they pass and then end. Then they imagine there's some sort of closure, a pause, a division or a frontier, marked by falling asleep, but no such thing exists: time continues to advance and to work, not only on our body, but on our consciousness too, time doesn't care whether we're deep asleep or wide awake or unable to sleep at all or if our eyes unwittingly close as if we were raw recruits on night duty, what in Spanish we call *la imaginaria*, literally, something that exists only in the imagination, perhaps because, afterwards, to the person standing guard while the rest of the world sleeps, it does seem as if that period of time hadn't really happened – always assuming the soldier did manage to stay awake and wasn't subsequently confined to barracks or, in time of war, executed. One irresistible slide into sleep and you find yourself dead, asleep for ever. How very dangerous everything is.

When she believed that her husband was her husband, she felt less at ease and found it harder to get out of bed and begin the day, she felt a prisoner of what she had so long been waiting for and which had now happened and for which she no longer waited, because anyone who has grown used to waiting never entirely consents to that waiting coming to a close, it's like having half the air you breathe snatched from you. And when she believed that he wasn't her husband, then she would spend the night feeling agitated and guilty, and hope not to wake up so as not to have to face her own suspicions about him or the reproaches with which she chastised herself. She hated to see herself becoming this hard-hearted wretch. On the other hand, during the times when she decided, or was able, to believe nothing, she felt the lure of the hidden doubt, the postponed uncertainty, which, sooner or later, would inevitably return. She had discovered how boring it was to live with absolute certainty and how it condemned you to just a single existence, or to experiencing the real and the imaginary as one and the same, but then none of us ever quite escapes that. She discovered, too, that a state of permanent suspicion is equally unbearable, because it's exhausting to be constantly observing yourself and others, especially if that other is the person closest to you, always comparing him with your memories of him, for memories can never be relied upon. No one can see clearly what is no longer there before them, even if it's only just happened, even if the aroma or discontent left behind by someone is still hanging there in the room. Someone only has to go through a door and disappear for their image to begin to fade, you only have to stop seeing something to stop seeing it clearly or at all; the same happens with hearing and, of course, with touch. How, then, can one remember clearly and in its proper sequence something that happened long ago? How could she faithfully recall the husband of fifteen or twenty years ago, the husband who, when she had already been asleep for a while, would slip into bed and, without a word, penetrate her? Maybe all these things vanish and blur, just as happens perhaps with those soldiers on night duty, *la imaginaria*. Perhaps they are precisely the things that fade most rapidly.

Her simultaneously Spanish and English husband, Tom or Tomás Nevinson by name, hadn't always been gripped by discontent. He hadn't always exuded a kind of all-pervading irritation, a deep-seated annoyance, which he dragged with him around the apartment, so that it managed to be both deep-seated and superficial at the same time. It came with him into the living room, the bedroom, the kitchen, like an emanation, or as if it were a storm hanging over his head, following him everywhere and rarely leaving him. This caused him to be somewhat abrupt and to answer very few questions, regardless of whether these were compromising or entirely inoffensive. He took shelter from the first kind by saying that he was not authorised to reveal anything, always taking the opportunity to remind his wife, Berta Isla, that he never would be given such authorisation, that even if whole decades passed and he were about to die, he would never be able to tell her about his current exploits or his past assignments or missions, about the life he lived when he was away from her. Berta had to accept this and she did: there was a zone or a dimension of her husband that would remain for ever in darkness, always just beyond her field of vision and her hearing, the untold tale, the half-closed or myopic or, rather, blind eye; a life she could only imagine or speculate about.

'Besides, it's best you don't know,' he told her on one occasion, for his enforced hermeticism did not prevent him from occasionally talking about it, in the abstract and without making any specific reference to places or individuals. 'It's often unpleasant, and contains some very sad stories, all doomed to end unhappily for one party or the other; sometimes it's amusing, but it's nearly always ugly or, worse, depressing. And I often emerge from it with a bad conscience. Fortunately, that soon passes, it doesn't last. And fortunately, too, I forget what I've done, which is the advantage of such pretend situations, you're not the one experiencing it, or only as if you were an actor. Actors return to their own selves once the film or the play is over, and films and plays eventually fade. In the long term, they leave only a vague memory, as if they were something dreamed and improbable and definitely dubious. Or else are so out of keeping with yourself, that you think: "No, I couldn't possibly have behaved like that, my memory's playing tricks on me, that was another me, it never happened." Or as if you were a sleepwalker unaware of what you did.'

Berta Isla knew she was living partially with a stranger. And anyone who is barred from explaining whole months of his existence ends up feeling he has the right not to explain anything ever. On the other hand, Tom was, again partially, someone she had known all her life, someone she took as much for granted as the air she breathed. And no one interrogates the air.

They had known each other almost since they were children, when Tomás Nevinson was cheerful and frivolous, and free of mists and shadows. The British Institute in Calle Martínez Campos – next to the Museo Sorolla and where he had always studied – abandoned or released its students when they were thirteen or fourteen, after the fourth year of baccalaureate. The fifth, sixth and pre-university years, the three years preceding university, had to be taken elsewhere, and quite a few students moved to Berta's school, the Studio, even if only because it was also co-educational and secular, which was not at all the norm in Franco's Spain, and because it meant not having to travel to a different neighbourhood, since the Studio was based in nearby Calle Miguel Ángel.

Unless they were completely hideous or dull as ditchwater, the 'new boys' usually enjoyed great success with the opposite sex, precisely because they were 'new', and Berta soon fell primitively and obsessively in love with young Nevinson. There is much that is arbitrary and instinctive about such young loves, not to say aesthetic or presumptuous (you look around and say to yourself: 'I'll have him or her'), loves that, inevitably, begin timidly, with shy glances, smiles and inconsequential conversations that nevertheless conceal a passion that instantly puts down roots and seems guaranteed to last until the end of time. It is, of course, an entirely theoretical and untested passion, learned from novels and films, a fantasy in which a single image predominates: the girl imagines herself married to her chosen one and he to her, like a painting with no history, that never changes or develops, and the vision ends there, because both lack the ability to go any further, to see themselves at some remote age that does not concern them and which they fancy to be unreachable, or to imagine anything more than that culminating moment, beyond which everything is vague, everything stops; or which the more clear-sighted or stubborn see as consummation. In an age when it was expected that women, when they married, would add a 'de' to their family name, followed by that of their husband, Berta was even influenced in her choice by the look and sound of her far-off future name: to become Berta Isla de Nevinson, so evocative of adventures and exotic places (one day, she would have a business card on which precisely those names would appear, alongside who knows what other facts or titles), was simply not the same as becoming Berta Isla de Suárez, the surname of the classmate she had liked until Tom turned up.

8

She wasn't the only girl in her class who had noticed Tom in that vehement, resolute way, and who nursed certain aspirations. Indeed, his arrival caused a general stir in the microcosmos, which lasted for two whole terms, until he was claimed by his rightful owner. Tomás Nevinson was quite good-looking and somewhat taller than most of the other boys, he wore his fairish hair rather old-fashionedly combed back (like a bomber pilot from the 1940s, or like a railway worker when he wore it shorter, or a musician when he wore it longer, although never very long, contrary to the coming trend; for the benefit of the visually curious or those with a good memory, when his hair was short, he resembled the B-movie actor Dan Duryea, and, when it reached its maximum length, he resembled leading actor Gérard Philipe); and his whole person radiated the solidity of someone immune to fashion and, therefore, to the insecurities that, when you're fifteen, take so many forms, and from which almost no one escapes. He gave the impression of not being subject to the age he lived in, or of skimming over its surface, as if he cared nothing for chance circumstances, for example, the date you were born and even the century you were born into. His looks were, in fact, no more than agreeable, and he certainly wasn't an example of sublime youthful beauty; indeed, his looks bordered on the insipid, and would be undeniably so about twenty years later. For the moment, what saved them were his full, shapely lips (which made you feel like running a finger over them, touching rather than kissing them) and his eyes, which were either a dull or a bright, tormented grey, depending on the light or the incipient torment gathering within them: penetrating, restless eyes, and rather more almond-shaped than usual, eyes that rarely rested and that contradicted his otherwise serene appearance. You could sense something anomalous in those eyes or perhaps a warning of anomalies to come, which were there crouched and watching, as if it were not yet their moment to wake and they needed to ripen or incubate in order to reach their full potency. His nose was undistinguished, rather broad and unfinished-looking or, rather, ending without a flourish. His chin was strong, almost square and slightly prominent, which gave him a determined air. It was the whole that was attractive and charming, and what prevailed was not his appearance, but his frivolous, ironic personality, always ready with a sly quip, and as unconcerned with what was going on in the outside world as he was with what was happening inside his own head, which was never easy to divine, not by himself and certainly not by those close to him; Nevinson avoided introspection and spoke little about his own personality or beliefs, as if he thought both things childish and a waste of time. He was the very opposite of the adolescent discovering himself and analysing and observing and trying to understand himself, impatient to find out what kind of person he is, not realising that such inquiries are pointless because he is not yet complete and, besides, such knowledge does not come – if it ever does, and is not constantly being modified and negated – until he has to make some really difficult decisions and act on the spur of the moment, and when that happens, it's too late to change and be a different kind of person. Anyway, Tomás Nevinson was not particularly interested in being known and certainly not interested in knowing himself, or perhaps he had already completed the latter process and considered the former to be a job for narcissists. This could perhaps be attributed to his English ancestry, but, ultimately, no one really knew what he was like. Beneath his friendly, diaphanous, even affable appearance there was a frontier of opacity and reserve. And the greatest opacity lay in the fact that others were unaware of that impenetrable layer or else barely noticed it.

He was completely bilingual, speaking English like his father and Spanish like his mother, and the fact that he had lived principally in Madrid since before he could utter a single word, or only very few, did nothing to diminish his fluency or his eloquence in the first of those languages: he had been brought up in it as a child, it was the dominant language at home, and for as long as he could remember, he had spent every summer in England. Added to this was the facility with which he could learn a third or fourth language, and his extra-ordinary talent for imitating voice and cadence and diction and accent, for he had only to listen to someone for a short while to be able to mimic him or her to perfection, with no previous practice or effort. This won him the sympathy and laughter of his classmates, who would end up asking him to give them his very best impressions. He was skilled at disguising his own voice and so could easily repro-duce those of the people he imitated, especially – in his schooldays – the people he saw on television, especially Franco, of course, and the occasional minister who appeared on the news slightly more often than others. He kept any parodies in his paternal tongue for when he stayed in London or near Oxford, for his friends and relatives there (Mr Nevinson was originally from Oxford); at school, no one would have understood or encouraged him, apart, that is, from a couple of ex-classmates from the British Institute, who were equally bilingual. When he expressed himself in one or other language, there was not a hint of foreignness, he spoke both languages like a native, and so never had any problem in being accepted in Madrid as another *madrileño*, despite his surname; he knew all the latest turns of phrase and all the slang, and if he chose, he could be as foul-mouthed as the most foul-mouthed boy in all of Madrid, not including the outer reaches. In short, he was one of the lads, although more like your average Spaniard than your average Englishman. He had not ruled out doing his university studies in his father's country, indeed his father urged him to do so, but life, for him, was in Madrid, as it always had been, and, very soon, life became wherever Berta was. If he was offered a place at Oxford, he might well go there, but he was sure that, once he finished his education, he would return to Madrid to stay.

His father, Jack Nevinson, had lived in Spain for many years, initially by chance, and later, inevitably, because he fell in love and married. Tom could not remember his father living anywhere else, he simply knew that he had, but then we tend not to know much about the lives lived by our parents before we were born, and they are often a matter of no interest to us until we are grown-ups ourselves and then it's sometimes too late to ask. Mr Nevinson combined his work at the British embassy with his duties at the British Council, a job he had found thanks to the man who had been the Council's representative for nearly fifteen years, Walter Starkie, the Irishman who, in 1940, had founded the British Institute, where for many years he was the director, as well as being an enthusiastic, adventurous Hispanist and the author of various books about gypsies, including one that bore the slightly ridiculous title of *Don Gypsy*. Jack Nevinson had found it very difficult to master his wife's language, and although he had, ultimately, succeeded syntactically and grammatically, with a wide, if somewhat antiquated and bookish, vocabulary, he had never rid himself of his strong English accent, which made his children see him, partly, as an intruder in the house, and meant that they always addressed him in English, to avoid blushes and irrepressible fits of the giggles. They felt embarrassed when there were Spanish visitors in the house and when he had no alternative but to speak Spanish; in his mouth it sounded almost like a joke, as if they were listening to the versions of the old movies that Laurel and Hardy themselves dubbed into Spanish (Stan Laurel was, in fact, English, not American, and his and Hardy's accents were very different when they ventured into a language not their own). Perhaps his father's oral insecurity in his adopted country explains why Tom tended to view him with a somewhat incongruous paternalism, as if his own great gifts for learning other languages and imitating other ways of speaking led him to believe that he could cope much better out in the world – could embrace it or make more of it – than Jack Nevinson ever would, for he was not exactly an authoritarian or decisive figure within the family, although one assumes he was more so outside it.

Tom did not allow himself the same air of premature superiority with his mother, Mercedes, an affectionate, very bright woman, whom he'd had to respect and suffer as a teacher for a couple of courses at the British Institute, where she was one of the teaching staff. 'Miss Mercedes', as the students called her, knew her husband's language very well and spoke it more confidently than he did hers, although she, too, had a foreign accent. The only ones who didn't were the four children: Tom, his brother and his two sisters.

Berta Isla, on the other hand, was pure *madrileña* (of the fourth or fifth generation, which was not that common at the time), a dark-haired beauty, a serene or restrained and imperfect beauty. If you analysed her features, none was exactly striking, but the combination of face and figure proved deeply alluring, for she was as irresistibly attractive as are all cheerful, smiling women prone to bursts of laughter; she appeared to be always contented, or contented with very little or determined to be so at all costs, and there are many men for whom this becomes a desirable characteristic: it's as if they want to master that laughter – or suppress it if they're of a malicious bent – or to have that laughter directed at them or to be the ones to provoke it, not realising that the toothsome smile permanently illuminating her face, and which proves a strong magnet to whoever sees it, would appear anyway, with no need for it to be summoned up, as invariable a feature as nose, forehead or ears. This cheerful side of Berta indicated a kind, almost obliging nature, but this was slightly misleading: her good cheer came naturally, easily and readily, although if she could find no reason to be cheerful, she didn't squander that good cheer or pretend to be happy when she wasn't; she could, it's true, always find many reasons to be cheerful, but if there *was* no reason, she could become very serious or sad or even irritable. This never lasted long, though, as if she grew bored with those glum, surly states of mind, as if she could see that they would bring her no reward nor evolve in any interesting way, and that to prolong them would be monotonous and unenlightening, an insistent drip-drip-drip that succeeded only in raising the level of the liquid without in any way changing it, but neither did she blithely shrug them off when they occurred. Beneath her appearance of harmony, almost of bonhomie, she was a young woman with very clear, almost stubborn ideas. If she wanted something, she went for it, not head-on, not by instilling fear or imposing herself or hurrying, but by being persuasive, intelligent and kind, by making herself indispensable, although always with great determination, as though she saw no need to hide her desires as long as they were not grubby or malign. She had an ability to delude her acquaintances, friends and boyfriends – insofar as the chosen ones of her adolescence could be called boyfriends – she managed to convince them all that the worst thing that could possibly happen to them would be to lose her or her friendship or her jovial company; in the same way, she convinced them that there was no greater blessing on Earth than her companionship, than the chance to share with her classes, games, plans, amusements, conversation or existence itself. Not that she was crafty, a kind of Iago figure who directs and manipulates and deceives by constantly whispering in her victim's ear, far from it. She herself must have spontaneously and proudly believed all this herself, and so she carried the belief with her, painted on her forehead or on her smile or on her pink cheeks, unwittingly infecting others with that same belief. She was not only successful with boys, but with her girlfriends too: to become her friend was like a badge of honour, as it was to be part of her circle; strangely, she did not arouse envy or jealousy, or very little, it was as if the genuine affection she showed to almost everyone shielded her from the grudges and pitiless malevolence of that fickle and arbitrary age. Berta, like Tomás, seemed to know very early on what kind of person she was, what kind of girl and future woman, as if she had never doubted that she would play a lead role rather than a supporting one, at least in her own life. For some people have a dread of becoming mere supporting actors even in their own story, as if they had been born knowing that, regardless of the uniqueness of each individual life, their story did not merit being told by anyone, or only as a fleeting reference when recounting someone else's more eventful and interesting life. Not even as a way of passing the time during some prolonged after-dinner conversation, or sitting beside the fire one sleepless night.

It was the third term of the fifth year of baccalaureate when Berta and Tom paired up as openly as one can at that age, and his other suitors accepted this with a sigh of resignation and forbearance: if Berta truly was interested in Tom, then it was hardly surprising that he should prefer her; after all, the whole masculine half of the Studio would turn to stare at her, and had done for the last couple of years, whenever they passed her on the vast marble staircase or in the playground at break time. She drew the gazes of all the boys in the school, the older ones and the younger ones, and there were several boys of ten or eleven for whom Berta Isla was their first distant, dazzling love – a love that did not as yet bear that name – which is why they never forgot her, in youth or maturity or old age, even though they had never so much as exchanged a word with her and even though, as far as she was concerned, they did not exist. Even boys from other schools would hang around outside to see her leave and follow her, and the Studio boys, with an exaggerated sense of ownership, rebelled against these intruders and kept a careful watch to ensure that she did not fall into the nets of someone who was not 'one of us'.

Neither Tom nor Berta, who had been born in August and September respectively, had turned fifteen when they agreed to 'go out' or 'be sweethearts', as people used to say then, and revealed their feelings to each other. She had revealed her feelings a long time before, but had taken pains to disguise her primitive, obsessive passion – or to contain it – at least enough so as not to appear too pushy or too brazen, enough to appear proper – in the terms of the mid-1960s – and so that he would have a sense, once he did decide to make a move, that he had not merely been chosen and led, but had himself taken the initiative.

Couples who meet very early on are condemned to develop a vaguely fraternal relationship, even if only during the initial phase – the inaugural phase, which is such an indicator of the direction things will take in the future – when they know that they must wait to fulfil their loves and ardours. In that social class and at that time, and despite the urgings of an untried and often explosive sexuality, they deemed it imprudent and disrespectful to force things once they were serious about each other, and Tomás and Berta knew at once that theirs was a serious relationship and not a brief flirtation that would end along with the term, or even two years later, when school came to an end and abandoned them. There was in Tom Nevinson, as well as his complete lack of experience in the field, a kind of timidity, and, besides, he felt as many boys do: they feel too much respect for the girl they have chosen as the love of their present, future and eternal life, and so they avoid overstepping the mark with her as they certainly don't with other girls, and often become overly protective and cautious because they see her as an ideal despite her being a creature of curious, healthy flesh and blood and inquisitive sexual desires, for fear of profaning her and making her almost untouchable. And Berta experienced what many other girls experience: knowing that their true love is free to touch them and eager to profane them, they do not want to be seen to be impatient, still less overkeen. So much so that it is not unusual – after so much restraint and passionate looks and tentative kisses, excluding all other areas of the body – that, after so many deferential caresses and holding back when they sense that same deference giving way, the first time they do consummate their love, they do so separately and vicariously, that is, with chance third parties.

They both lost their virginity during their first year at university, and neither of them told the other. They spent that year relatively far apart, or, rather, comparatively speaking, much further apart. Tom was given a place at Oxford, in large measure due to the good offices of his father and Walter Starkie, but thanks also to his own extraordinary linguistic abilities, and Berta began her course in the Faculty of Arts at the Complutense University in Madrid. The vacation periods at Oxford are very long, a little over a month between Michaelmas and Hilary, the same again between Hilary and Trinity, and three whole months between Trinity and the next Michaelmas, which meant that Tomás was able to return to Madrid after his eight or nine weeks of hard study away, and thus have time to resume his Madrid life, or at least not to lose sight of it entirely, to cut himself off from it or replace it, or to forget anything. However, during those eight or nine weeks, they could both put the other person on hold, in parentheses. And, at the same time, they knew that what they were placing in parentheses was that period of separation, and that once they were together again, everything would return to normal. Repeated absences allow this, so that neither of those alternating periods is ever really real, so that both seem phantasmagoric, and that while they last, each one blurs and negates and almost erases the other; in short, anything that occurs during them is part of a dream world, and hasn't actually happened and, besides, is of little importance. Tom and Berta did not know that this would be the model for much of their life together – together, but mainly apart and with no normal to return to, or together, but facing away from each other.

In 1969, two fashions were doing the rounds in Europe, both mainly affecting the young: politics and sex. The May 1968 riots in Paris and the Prague Spring crushed by Soviet tanks set half the continent buzzing, at least temporarily. In Spain, a dictatorship that had begun more than three decades earlier was still dragging on. Strikes by workers and students prompted the Francoist regime to declare a state of emergency throughout the country, although this was merely a euphemism for reducing still further our few, feeble rights, increasing the prerogatives and the impunity of the police, and giving them a free hand to do whatever they wanted to whomever they wanted. On 20 January, the law student Enrique Ruano, who, three days before, had been arrested for throwing leaflets at members of the much-feared Brigada Político-Social, died while in custody. The official version, which kept changing and was full of contradictions, was that the twenty-one-year-old had been taken to the seventh floor of a building in what is now Calle Príncipe de Vergara in order to be searched, but that, once there, he broke away from the three policemen guarding him and either fell or threw himself from a window. The Minister of Information, Fraga Iribarne, and the newspaper *ABC* did their best to present his death as a suicide and to suggest that Ruano was mentally frail and unbalanced, publishing on the front page and in instalments a letter he had written to his psychiatrist, which they cut up and manipulated so that it appeared to have been extracted from a supposedly tormented private diary. However, almost no one believed this version and the episode was seen as a political assassination, since the student was a member of the Frente de Liberación Popular, or 'Felipe', a clandestine anti-Franco organisation of little account, as all such organisations inevitably were (of little account and clandestine, that is). The general public disbelief was perfectly justified, and not just because of the deep-seated habit of lying common to all governments under the dictatorship: twenty-seven years later, when Ruano's body was exhumed for the problematic trial of the three policemen involved – Spain was, by then, a democracy – they found that part of his clavicle had been sawn off, because, almost beyond a shadow of a doubt, that bone had been pierced by a bullet. At the time, the autopsy had been falsified, the family were not allowed to see the body or to publish an obituary in the newspaper; and Fraga, in person, phoned Ruano's father to urge him not to protest and to keep quiet, saying words to the effect of: 'Remember you have a daughter to worry about too', referring to Ruano's sister, Margot, who was also involved in politics. After so much time had passed, it was impossible to prove anything, and the three *sociales*, or members of the Brigada Política-Social, were found not guilty of murder – Colino, Galván and Simón were their names – but the young man had probably been tortured while under arrest, including on the final day, when they took him to that seventh-floor room in Príncipe de Vergara, shot him and threw him out into the street. That is what his companions believed in 1969.

So great was the anger among students that, during the demonstrations that followed, even students like Berta Isla took part, students who had previously been either apolitical or unwilling to take risks or to court trouble. Some university friends persuaded her to join them on a demonstration arranged one evening in Plaza de Manuel Becerra, not far from Las Ventas bullring. Such demonstrations, all of which were illegal, never lasted very long: the armed police, the *grises* – so-called because of their grey uniforms – would know about them beforehand and would disperse any group by using physical force, and, if a group did manage to gather in strength and march a few metres, chanting slogans, not to mention throwing stones at shops and banks, they would immediately set upon them, either on foot or on horseback, with their long, black, flexible truncheons (the ones wielded by the mounted police were longer and even more flexible, rather like short, fat whips), and there would always be one particularly cocky or nervous individual among them who would get out his pistol so as to instil more fear or in order to feel less afraid himself.

As soon as the scuffle began, Berta found herself running ahead of the police, along with a number of friends and strangers. Each one raced off in a different direction, in the hope that their pursuers wouldn't choose them as their target but would beat up someone else instead. She was a novice at such insurrections and had no idea what to do for the best, whether to go down into the metro or take refuge in a bar and mingle with the other customers or stay out in the street, where there was always the possibility of escaping and not being trapped in one place. She knew that being arrested at some political rally would mean, at best, a night and a beating in the Dirección General de Seguridad – where the security police had their headquarters – and, at worst, a trial and a prison sentence of months or even a couple of years, depending on how malevolent the judge was feeling, as well as immediate expulsion from the university. She also knew that being a woman and very young (she was in her first year at university) was no safeguard against whatever punishment might befall her.

She soon lost sight of her friends, and in the dark night, only dimly lit by the rather feeble street lamps, she began to panic, running aimlessly this way and that – the January chill soon disappearing beneath the burning sensation of dangers unknown – instinctively breaking away from the rest of the crowd and distancing herself from the Plaza, racing off down a rather narrow nearby street, which was fairly empty of other demonstrators, the rest of the stampede having opted for other paths or doing their best not to get too dispersed, in the hope that they might regroup and vainly try again, their fear and fury only growing, their courage high, pulses racing and all well-laid plans banished. She was running as if the devil himself were after her, absolutely terrified, glimpsing no one either to left or right out of the corners of her eyes as she flew along, intending never to stop or not until she thought she was safe, until she had left the city behind her or reached home, and then, without in the least diminishing her speed, it occurred to her to look back – perhaps she heard a strange noise, the sound of snorting or trotting, a summer sound, a village or rustic sound, a sound from childhood – and almost immediately behind her she saw the huge figure of a *gris* on horseback, his truncheon already raised, about to unleash a blow on the back of her neck or on her buttocks or her back, one that would doubtless knock her over, probably leaving her unconscious or dazed, unable to fight back or keep running, fated to receive a second and a third blow if the policeman was in a particularly vicious mood, or, if he wasn't, being dragged off in handcuffs and thrown into a police van and, in just a few rash, unlucky moments, seeing her present utterly altered and her future ruined. She saw the face of the black horse and thought she also saw that of the man in grey, even though his forehead was

22

covered by his helmet, and his chin by the rather thick, sturdy strap. Berta didn't stumble nor was she paralysed with fright, instead, quite pointlessly, she ran still faster, fuelled by the final impetus of despair, which is what we always do even when we're doomed; after all, what chance do a young woman's legs have against the legs of a swift quadruped, and yet those legs nonetheless quickened their pace, like those of an ignorant beast still convinced it can escape. Then an arm appeared from an alleyway, and a hand tugged hard at her, making her lose her balance and fall flat on her face, but snatching her away from horse and rider and the inevitable blow from that truncheon. Horse and rider continued on past, at least for a few metres, out of sheer inertia, it's very hard to rein in a horse at full gallop, and, she hoped, horse and rider would lose interest and go in search of other subversives to punish, for there were hundreds of them around. With another tug the hand helped her to her feet, and Berta found herself looking at a rather handsome young man, who didn't appear to be a student or the type to take part in protests: agitators don't usually wear a tie or a hat, and this young man did, as well as an overcoat that had aspirations to elegance, being long and navy blue and with the collar turned up. He was an old-fashioned sort, and the hat had a rather narrow brim, as if it were a hand-me-down.

'Come on, girl, let's go,' he said. 'We need to leg it – now.' And he again tugged at her hand, trying to get her to move, to guide her, save her.

However, before they could disappear down the alleyway, the mounted policeman reappeared, having hastened back for his prey. He had turned his mount round and resumed his pursuit, as if annoyed not to have caught a specimen he had already picked out and which he had (almost) in his bag. Now he would have to choose between two, Berta and the young man who had dared to whisk her away, or, if he was quick and took careful aim, he could catch them both, especially if some fellow policemen came to his aid, although there were none in sight, most of them would be happily labouring away in the Plaza, lashing out blindly to left and right, in case one of their superiors saw them holding back and then they'd be in trouble later on. The young man in the hat squeezed Berta's hand, but he didn't seem alarmed; rather, he stood there defiantly and coolly erect, scornful of the danger and refusing to reveal any fear. The *gris* was still holding his truncheon in one hand, but not in any threatening way, he was resting it on the wrist of the hand holding the reins, as if it were a fishing rod or a flexible reed. He was very young too, he had blue eyes and very thick, dark eyebrows, at least those were the features most visible beneath his helmet, pleasant features that spoke of the countryside, of the south, probably Andalusia. Berta and the old-fashioned youth stood watching him, not moving, not daring to race off down the alleyway, from which it might or might not be easy to escape. In fact, they knew at once there was no need to run away from that particular horseman.

'I wasn't going to hit you, girl. What do you take me for?' he said to Berta; both men had addressed her as 'girl', a term not much used in the Madrid of the time, especially among young men. 'I just wanted to get you away from the mob at all costs. You're very young to be caught up in things like that. Go on, go home. And as for you,' he said, addressing the old-fashioned youth, 'don't get in my way again, or you'll pay for it with a beating and a month or two in the clink. Not this time though. Anyway, scram, both of you. You've already taken up quite enough of my time.'

The other young man, with his neatly knotted tie and his long overcoat, was quite unfazed by this future threat. He remained erect, with his cold, alert eyes fixed on those of the horseman, as if he were

24

divining his intentions and was convinced that, if it came to it, he would be able to unseat him from where he stood. And contrary to what he had said, the policeman did not leave at once, as if he were waiting for them to apologise first, or wanted to gaze his fill on the young woman and not lose sight of her until she had vanished from his field of vision and his eyes could no longer see her, however hard they tried. Neither she nor the young man said anything, and, later on, Berta Isla regretted not thanking him. In those days, though, no one could bring themselves to thank a *gris*, one of Franco's police-men, even if they deserved thanks. Most people considered them to be utterly despicable, the enemy, the ones who pursued and beat and arrested, ruining lives only just begun.

Berta had torn her stockings, one knee was bleeding and she was still very frightened; seeing that horse just behind her and the policeman's truncheon raised and about to come down on her neck or her back had left her a bundle of nerves, despite the benign outcome, which had also left her feeling strangely weak. These mixed emotions momentarily exhausted her, she felt disoriented and will-less, and wouldn't have known where to go just at that moment. The old-fashioned young man, still holding her by the hand as if she were a child, hurriedly led her away from the most dangerous zone and headed towards Las Ventas, saying:

'I live right near here. Come in and I'll clean that wound and let you calm down a bit. Come on. You can't go back home looking like that, woman. You need to rest and get cleaned up a bit.' He no longer called her 'girl'. 'What's your name? Are you a student?'

'Yes. My first name's Berta. Berta Isla. What's yours?'

'Esteban. Esteban Yanes. I'm a banderillero.'

Berta was surprised. She had never met anyone involved in bull-fighting, nor had she ever imagined the bit-part players of that world outside the ring and in civvies.

'A banderillero of bulls, you mean?'

'No, rhinoceroses, what do you think? What other animal do they stick darts in?'

This distracted her for a few seconds from her agitated, exhausted state; she would have smiled if she hadn't been so dazed. It gave her time to think: 'He's used to dealing with animals far more dangerous than a highly trained horse; that's why he wasn't frightened and didn't turn a hair, because he would have known how to dodge it, perhaps even draw it away from me.' And she eyed him with growing curiosity. All it occurred to her to say, though, and at the risk of seeming impertinent, was: 'I don't know if you realise it, but that hat really doesn't suit you.' This had been her initial thought when she saw him in the alleyway, one of those superfluous but persistent thoughts that remains floating around in your head, waiting to find its moment, in the midst of other more urgent tasks.

He let go of her hand, immediately removed his hat and looked at it with interest, turning it round and round in his hands; standing in the middle of the street, he asked in a disappointed tone of voice:

'Really? You're kidding. What's wrong with it? Do you honestly think it doesn't suit me? It's good quality, you know.'

He had a thick thatch of hair, parted on the left, so that the right-hand side almost formed a fringe; indeed, it was hard to understand how all that hair had fitted so neatly underneath the hat. He was more attractive like that, his now liberated hair setting his features in their proper place or giving them more definition. His very wide-set, brown, almost plum-coloured eyes lent a clarity and candour to his face, it was a face entirely without duplicity, not in the least self-absorbed or evasive or embarrassed, the kind of face of which people used to say you could read it like a book (although some books, of course, are totally impenetrable and unreadable), a face that seems to conceal nothing beyond what it actually expresses. He had a large, straight nose, and strong, slightly prominent teeth, the sort that appear to have a life of their own when revealed by a generous smile, an African smile that lit up his other features, so that his whole face invited one to trust its owner. The kind of teeth that would make certain people think: 'If I could just borrow those teeth, things would be very different, especially when I went out on the pull.'

'No, it doesn't suit you at all. The brim's too narrow for the crown. It's just not you. It makes your head look much smaller than it is, almost like a pinhead, and you haven't got a small head.'

'There's nothing more to be said, then. To hell with the hat. I certainly don't want to be a pinhead,' said the banderillero Esteban Yanes, and he blithely tossed the hat into a nearby litter bin. Then he smiled and gave a wave of his hand, as if he had just successfully skewered a bull with a couple of banderillas.

Berta gave a start and felt guilty, not expecting that her comments would condemn the hat to death. (Or to being left to adorn the dishevelled locks of the beggar who would doubtless retrieve it.) He might not have inherited the hat, but he had paid good money for it. He was a few years older than her, about twenty-three or twenty-four, not an age to be exactly swimming in money, certainly not in those days.

'Look, take no notice of me. If you like the hat, what does it matter what I think? You don't even know me. There's no need to be quite so drastic.'

'One look at you was enough for me to do whatever you tell me, regardless of its drasticity.' This sounded like a compliment if one judged it solely by the words used (although she doubted if that last word actually existed, but then those who care little about such things are often more cheerfully and adroitly inventive than those who do). Neither his tone of voice nor his expression, however, seemed like mere gallantry. Or perhaps gallantry was such an antiquated concept that Berta failed to recognise it: none of her male friends, not even those who fancied her, not even Tom, would ever have said such a thing (the age of surliness was just beginning, in which good manners were seen as a fault and bad manners a mark of honour). 'Come on, we need to clean that wound if you don't want it to get infected.'

When she saw his apartment, Berta decided that he wasn't badly off at all. The furniture was new and barely used (although admittedly there wasn't much of it) and the apartment itself was quite a lot bigger than the ones rented by the few students who could afford it and which were nearly always shared by at least two people, if not four or five. This was a proper apartment, although clearly inhabited by a bachelor, a single man, and one who had only recently moved in. Everything seemed orderly, even deliberate, and yet still had an air of provisionality. A few photos of bullfights adorned the walls, as well as some posters advertising corridas, on one of which she spotted names that even she recognised as being famous: Santiago Martín, 'El Viti', and Gregorio Sánchez. Fortunately, there was no bull's head hung up and framed like some exaggeratedly high-relief sculpture; perhaps they were only given to matadors, not to subalterns, but then Berta knew nothing about the subject.

'Do you live alone?' she asked. 'Is all this just for you?'

'Yes, I've been renting it for a few months now. I won't be using it much during the season, because I'm hardly ever in Madrid, and it costs me an arm and a leg. But lately, things have worked out pretty well for me as a *suelto*, and we all need somewhere to lay our head when there's nothing going on. And I've never had a contract to work the winter season in Latin America. And the fact is you get sick to death of guesthouses and hotels.'

'A *suelto*?'

'I'll explain in a minute, while I'm cleaning that wound. Come on, sit down over there,' he pointed to an armchair with a rug underneath

it, 'and take off your stockings. They're no good for anything anyway. If you haven't got a spare pair with you, I'll pop out later and
buy you some, although you'll have to tell me where to buy them,
because I haven't the faintest. I'll go and fetch the first-aid box.'

He left the room, and Berta could hear him in the distance, rummaging around, opening and closing cabinets and drawers,
presumably in the bathroom. She took off her overcoat and put it
down on the sofa nearby, then sat in the armchair he had indicated
and took off her boots – knee-high zip-up boots – along with her
dark stockings that were, in fact, tights, which were already the norm
then. She had to pull her skirt up quite some way to get them off,
because it was a straight, almost tight-fitting skirt, and rather short –
it covered about two-thirds of her thighs, possibly less – as was also
the fashion at the time. Her decision to join the demonstration had
been so spur-of-the-moment that she had left home dressed to go to
her classes, and certainly not suitably attired to flee down the streets
pursued by a mounted policeman. While she was removing them, she
glanced a couple of times at the door through which her host had
disappeared, in case he should reappear in the midst of her partial
disrobing (she hadn't counted, of course, but she had already taken
off four items, if you included her scarf, that is, so half of her clothes:
she was left wearing only her skirt, a soft V-necked sweater, her
knickers and her bra). She looked for looking's sake really, because
she realised that she didn't much care if he did catch a glimpse of her
with her skirt hitched up; the combination of a very recent shock and
a very present weariness does tend to lower a person's guard, and she
was overcome by a kind of indifference, almost complacency, after
having emerged unscathed from that predicament and feeling able,
at last, to begin to relax. Besides, she trusted young Yanes, she felt
comfortable in his company. Once she had finished that rapid

shedding of clothes (her tights lay in tatters on the floor, but she didn't have the energy to pick them up), she sat back in the chair, her legs bare and her bare feet resting on the rug; she glanced casually at the blood on her knee, and felt suddenly rather sleepy, but there wasn't time for that feeling to take proper hold because the banderillero returned, having already removed overcoat, jacket and tie and rolled up his sleeves. In one hand he was holding a glass of Coca-Cola with ice, which he gave to her, and in the other, a small white first-aid box complete with handle, perhaps all bullfighters had one at home, just in case they needed to change bandages. A precaution. Yanes picked up a low stool and sat down in front of her.

'Right,' he said. 'First, I'll clean the wound a little, and that won't hurt much.' Berta instinctively crossed her legs, partly to make things easier and to bring her knee closer to him, and partly to make things more difficult (more difficult for him to see up her skirt). 'No, don't cross your legs, that won't help. Rest your calf on my thigh, it will be easier like that.' He carefully washed the wound with a small sponge and some soap and water, then he dabbed it dry with a little towel, as if the last thing he wanted was to hurt her or rub too hard. Then he blew on the wound, keeping his breath cool, or trying to. From his low position, Yanes could now clearly see up her short, tight skirt (with her legs uncrossed the fabric was pulled taut), the crotch of her knickers would have entered his field of vision, and if he needed a better angle, he would only have to move his thigh to the left, and Berta's calf, resting on top of his thigh, would have to obey. And that is exactly what he did, he shifted his thigh imperceptibly to one side, and the desired image was revealed to him by her parted legs, from ankle to groin, so to speak (from bare feet to groin); they were strong legs, sturdy but not fat, American legs, firm and muscular and quite long, legs that invited one to linger and go higher, and there is always

31

a slight mound visible at the end (or, rather, a small hillock, a swelling, a throbbing). 'I'm going to apply a little alcohol now, and that will sting at first, but not for long.' He poured some alcohol onto a piece of cotton wool, and when it was well soaked, so that no fibres would stick to the wound, he ran it over the cut, delicately, tenderly. And then he blew again; well, he actually blew on an area just above the knee, as if his aim had failed him, or perhaps he was trying to soothe a place that did not yet sting or burn.

The stinging sensation immediately became evident on Berta's face (she clenched her teeth and drew her lips back), but the pain was short-lived. She felt as she had when she was a child and some adult was cleaning a cut or a scratch. It was pleasant to feel herself once again in someone else's hands, to have someone touch her and do useful things with his hands, it didn't much matter what: at first, it probably wasn't so very different from the sensation caused by a barber when he passes the razor or the shaver over the neck of a man, who then almost falls asleep, or even that provoked by the dentist when he only probes or causes some vibration, but no pain; and it was even more reminiscent of when the doctor listens and palpates and drums with one finger, the middle finger, then presses and asks: 'Does it hurt here? And here? And here?' There is an element of pleasure in allowing oneself to be handled and touched, even for unpleasant reasons, even when it verges on discomfort or even fear (a barber could always accidentally cut you, a doctor's expression could change to one of deep concern, a man could inflict pain on a woman, especially if she's inexperienced). Berta Isla felt easy and lazy and cared for, and that languor increased as Yanes finished his labours by putting a large plaster on the wound. Once he had done this, he did not immediately remove his hands, but rather rested both of them, still gently, on top of her thighs, like someone laying his hands

32

protectively on someone's shoulders or in a gesture meaning: 'Right, that's done now.' But thighs are not shoulders, not even the top of the thighs, not at all. Berta did not react, she sat looking at him, her eyes slightly glazed because she was both sleepy and intrigued, her eyes half-closed, trying to feel alarmed and failing, wanly summoning up the blush that usually came to her so easily, like someone waiting and not knowing if she wants those hands to be removed, and even feeling a certain curiosity as to whether they would change position or move elsewhere, for example to the inner thighs, which are still less like shoulders, where the protective gesture can become menacing for the person being touched or even provoke anger, it all depends on the day and on whose thighs and whose hands they are. For a whole minute – a long minute of absolute silence, because neither spoke – Yanes's hands did not move one millimetre, but stayed where they were, utterly still, neither caressing nor pressing, just there, almost inert; those palms would leave a red mark if they lingered much longer, and it might even be slightly difficult to unstick them from the skin. The banderillero withstood the gaze of those misty eyes fixed on his own wide-set eyes, with their air of clarity and ingenuousness. They themselves gave nothing away, did not anticipate the next step, but exuded only serenity. And yet his face could be read, and Berta knew what that stranger – because he was a stranger – would try sooner or later, she knew this with such certainty that she would have been disappointed had he acted otherwise. She forced herself to think of Tomás Nevinson, whom she loved with such conviction, with such deliberate, stubborn unconditionality; but it seemed to her that that particular evening – or, rather, night – had nothing to do with him nor would it impinge on him in any way, she could see no link between her distant, half-English boyfriend and that situation in an apartment close to the bullring with a young man who doubtless performed or had ambitions to perform there, and who had failed to explain to her what *suelto* meant. She hadn't, she thought, recovered either her sense of place or her will; she was still troubled or numbed by the shock of that equine or clandestine adventure, by that encounter with the policeman, or all those things at once. Nothing beats believing you've lost your will, feeling you're at the mercy of the come-and-go of the waves and can abandon yourself and allow yourself to be rocked; even better is believing that you've handed your will over to someone else, who must now decide what happens next.

Then, his expression unchanged, and keeping his eyes trained on hers as if to remain alert to the slightest hint of disapproval or rejection so that he could always take a step back, Esteban Yanes, bold and resolute, did, after that minute, go too far. However, as soon as he made this perilous move, Berta laughed out loud – the ready laugh that had won over so many people – perhaps because she found the whole situation hilarious, a situation that would have been unimaginable an hour earlier, and perhaps, too, out of an unexpected feeling of contentment, which is usually aroused by the fulfilment of a desire that is as yet unformulated or confessed and only reveals itself as a desire when it is already being fulfilled. Berta's laugh triggered the banderillero's African smile, which seemed to invite immediate confidence and dispel all danger, and which immediately became a laugh too. And so both were laughing at the very moment when Yanes slowly, and without further warning, placed one hand on the charming swelling or charming hillock – namely, the crotch of the knickers he had already observed with such pleasure – and then gently slipped one finger beneath the damp fabric. Tom Nevinson had never gone that far, even at his most daring, his index finger had always stopped at that cloth barrier and never ventured any further, out of respect or dread, or because he was overly conscious of their youth, or out of a wish to postpone the moment, a fear of the irreversible. Berta, however, was made of more interrogative stuff and, noting this more forward approach, she embraced the novelty of it. Of the four items of clothing that remained, she soon lost another three, by which time she was lying on the sofa; she retained only one, which there was no need to remove, and which, besides, she preferred not to take off.

II

Berta would sometimes think of Esteban Yanes, both during the predictable, normal start of her married life and during the anomalous time that followed, when she didn't know what to believe, when she had no idea if her husband, Tom Nevinson, had or had not joined the company of the dead, if he still breathed the same air as her in some distant, hidden-away place or if, for some time, he had not breathed at all, exiled from the Earth or welcomed into it, that is, buried under its surface only a few metres beneath our feet, where we nonchalantly walk with not a thought as to what the earth might conceal. Or possibly thrown into the sea or into an estuary or a lake, or a large river: when you have no control over the fate of a body, the most absurd conjectures appear and reappear, and it's not so very hard to imagine its return. The return of the living body, you understand, not of the corpse or the ghost. They neither console nor are they of any interest, or only to minds troubled by intense uncertainty or dissatisfaction.

After that January evening, she never again saw that banderillero *suelto*. He did finally explain that *suelto* was the name given to banderilleros who work independently, not as part of any one matador's team (or only occasionally, as a substitute) but as a freelance, accepting whatever offers come their way and best suit them, four fights here, a couple there, another one over there, or a whole summer here.

That's why he didn't usually cover the season in Latin America, the winter season, and remained unemployed from the end of October to March, more or less. Esteban Yanes would spend those months training and practising for a few hours each day, and live a life of leisure the rest of the time, going to the bars and restaurants frequented by his colleagues and by the big names and agents who stayed behind on this side of the Atlantic, being seen and hoping to be remembered by those who might take him on in the future. This worked well for him, he had enough work and earned enough to be able to 'hibernate', as he put it, that is, to eke out his savings and not have to earn a penny until the season began again around mid-March or so.

While they were chatting after the untraumatic and rather unspectacular loss of her virginity – a little blood, a brief pain, minimal and unexpected pleasure – Berta Isla knew at once that, whatever Yanes's physical and personal attractions – he was a calm, confident man, funny and pleasant and no fool either, an inveterate reader, albeit unmethodical and disorganised, and an interesting conversationalist to boot – their worlds were too far apart and there was no way to reconcile them, or even have them coincide in time and space. She found the idea of reducing their relationship to sporadic sexual encounters unacceptable, not just because such reductions are impossible to control and you can end up faced with tacit obligations and timetables and demands, but also because, after that inaugural evening when two lots of blood had been shed, her feelings for Tomás Nevinson had not changed one jot, nor had her certainty that her place was at his side, once he finished his studies in England and everything returned to normal, that is, to Madrid. For her, Tom was what many people describe to themselves as 'the love of my life' – although they might never say this out loud – and which is often used to designate a chosen one when your life has only just begun and when you still have no idea how many chosen ones there will be nor how long that life will be.

Berta, though, never forgot that first time; however evanescent, no one does. She didn't give Esteban Yanes her number and he didn't give her his. She didn't let him accompany her home in a taxi, as he wanted to do, even though it was fairly late by the time Berta recovered nearly all her clothes and set off to a metro station, with a plaster on her knee and with no tights, because the young man had not, in the end, gone out to buy her a new pair. Thus Yanes didn't know where she lived, and although her surname was not that common, it only appeared fifty or so times in the telephone book, there was no question of him ringing all the Islas in the book just to try his luck. She alone could re-establish contact by presenting herself at his apartment or sending him a note, and although it was pleasant to know that this was a possibility and that she could take that initiative, she did neither. After a few years, she assumed that he would no longer live there, that he would have moved and perhaps married, or even left for another city. And so she merely kept that memory as a refuge, as an ever more distant and nebulous place – a rather special place that she vaguely missed – to which she could go in her mind whenever she wanted, like someone consoling herself by saying that if there had once been a time of insouciance and spontaneity, of frivolity and caprice, it must still exist somewhere, although it would be difficult to return to that time except in her slowly dissolving memory and in her frozen thoughts that neither advanced nor retreated, but kept revisiting the same scene that repeated itself over and over from the first to the last detail, until it took on the characteristics of a painting, always identical, infuriatingly fixed and unaltered. That is how she saw that youthful encounter, as a painting. The odd thing is that, as time passed and all trace of him faded in his absence, the features of the young banderillero whom she had only seen on that one occasion became blurred and confused with those of the equally young mounted policeman, whose features she had merely glimpsed for a moment as he rode after her and perhaps studied briefly while he remained still – his flexible truncheon resting on his wrist – and there were moments when she wasn't sure which one she'd had sex with, the *gris* or the banderillero. Or, rather, she knew perfectly well that the beginning of her consummated sexual life had occurred with the latter, but she found it harder and harder to remember his face, or else his face and that of the policeman overlapped or became juxtaposed like interchangeable masks: the blue eyes and the wide-set, almost plum-coloured eyes, those teeth with a life of their own and the Andalusian peasant face, the thick eyebrows and the large, straight nose, the helmet and the narrow-brimmed hat concealing that abundance of hair, all formed a whole that was contained within the same venturesome day.

What never faded was the memory of that finger slipping beneath the thin fabric of her knickers and the exploratory caresses that followed, the kisses that were more hurried or impatient than passionate, the rapid disappearance of all the man's clothes and of hers, apart from her skirt, which did not constitute an obstacle; the strangely welcome sensation that a man's penis – any man; after all, she had only met that man little more than an hour before – could, after an initial struggle, enter her and stay there for a while at its ease, and with scarcely any resistance from the protective membrane that proved more tenuous than its reputation. Although, by then, its reputation was already much diminished, and nowadays it has none at all.

For his part, Tomás Nevinson made his debut in the usual way these things happened in England in 1969, casually and without a second thought – almost like someone going through a formality whose importance he prefers not to exaggerate by postponing it – first, with a fellow undergraduate about whom he had no qualms and who was swiftly followed by a girl who worked locally, and both he and they were determined not to lend these effusions any importance and not to be affected by them either for good or for ill; those were the days of so-called sexual liberation, which was permeated by the idea that there was barely any difference between having sex with someone and having a cup of coffee with them, as if they were equivalent activities, and as if neither should leave behind any trace or sense of unease. (Even if no memory remains of the one, and of the other it eternally does – however vague and pale that memory may become – the event does at least leave a trace, or perhaps only in our knowledge and awareness that it did occur.) Nor did he see these between-the-sheets encounters and his immovable love for Berta as contradictory or conflicting. They simply led him to think that on one of his next stays in Madrid, it would be high time that he and she finally had such an encounter, for Spain always lagged a little behind in fashion and in boldness, although less so then: those in the know prided themselves on being up to the minute, and Tom and Berta included themselves in that number. The second of those brief encounters did have some influence on his future, because, while the local girl was never a real presence in his life, she didn't disappear entirely during the years he spent at Oxford, not even when she died: he would see her now and again at the antiquarian bookshop where she worked as an assistant, and whenever he went to the shop, they would end up arranging to meet that night or the next, which is why he preferred to space out his searches for old books, at least in that particular establishment. Tom rarely asked himself what her feelings might be, or what her expectations were of him, if indeed she had any. He tended to think that she didn't, just as he had no expectations of her, of Janet, for that was her name. He knew she had a boyfriend or something in London and that she got together with him at weekends. He took it for granted that, for her, he was as much of a pastime, comfort and compensation for other absences as she was for him; in those places where you're obliged to spend most of your days, even if only temporarily, you have to find some consolation. While he was sure that, sooner or later, he would return to Madrid, at no point during his time there did he see any sign of Janet leaving her job and moving to London to live with her boyfriend or get married. There appeared to be nothing temporary about her stay in Oxford, where she had, after all, been born and brought up and grown into an attractive, sensual woman.

Equally influential for his future were his studies and his relationships with certain professors or dons, especially with the man who was King Alfonso XIII Professor of Spanish Studies – in an American university, he would have been called the head of the Spanish department – appointed to Exeter College after having been a fellow at Queen's, the Hispanist and Lusitanist, Peter Edward Lionel Wheeler, a keen-witted man of growing prestige, by turns affectionate and sardonic, of whom it was rumoured that he had worked for the Secret Service during the war, like many others recruited during those extreme times, and that, afterwards, he had continued to collaborate at a distance – with MI5 or MI6 or with both – in the days of apparent peace, unlike the many people who, once the war was over, had merely returned to their civilian jobs and maintained an enforced silence under oath about any occasional, or perhaps seasonal, crimes they may have committed, crimes made legal and justifiable by the war situation, with wars treated as parentheses, as prolonged, mortally serious carnivals, cruel and almost devoid of farce, during which citizens are given carte blanche, and the most brilliant, the most intelligent, the most able and capable are even taken up and trained – a character-building exercise – to sabotage, betray, deceive, trick, to abolish all feelings, all scruples, and to murder.

It was said that Peter Wheeler had been subjected to a harsh training regime in 1941 at the centre for commandos and special operations at Lochailort, on the west coast of Scotland, and that he suffered a serious car accident there, which partially damaged the bone structure of his face. He underwent reconstructive surgery at Basingstoke Hospital, where he remained for four months, and, as a result of those various operations, he was left with permanent scars (these faded only slowly, pining palely away), one on his chin, the other on his forehead, but these did not in the least diminish his decidedly gallant appearance. It was also said that, even while he was still convalescing, he received a terrible beating, as part of a mock interrogation, at the hands of some ex-policemen from Shanghai at Inverailort House, which had been requisitioned at the time by the Navy and by the SOE, or Special Operations Executive, in order to harden him up were he ever captured by the enemy. The following year, he had been appointed director of security in Jamaica, and later assigned to postings in West Africa – where he took advantage of the RAF's secret surveillance flights to get a bird's-eye view of geographical details that would prove useful in his books *The English Intervention in Spain and Portugal in the Time of Edward III and Richard II*, published in 1955, and *Prince Henry the Navigator: A Life*, first published in 1960 – as well as in Rangoon (Burma), Colombo (Ceylon), where he reached the rank of lieutenant colonel, and Indonesia, after the Japanese surrender in 1945. A lot of stories were told about him, but he himself never told any, doubtless still bound by the oath of confidentiality taken by anyone involved in espionage and undercover work, that is, work whose existence will never be revealed or will always be denied. He knew that various tales and anecdotes about him regularly did the rounds of his colleagues and students, but he let them pass as if they didn't concern him. And if anyone dared to ask him directly, he would immediately make a joke or shoot them a stern look, depending on who it was, and then divert the conversation onto the *Cantar de Mío Cid*, *La Celestina*, Iberian translators of the fifteenth century, or Edward, the Black Prince. All these rumours made him a singularly attractive figure to the few students who heard them, and Tom Nevinson, whose excellent linguistic skills soon aroused the interest of his teachers – even their admiration, to the limited extent that teachers will allow themselves to admire a student – was one of those who most benefitted from the whispers and gossip normally reserved for the clerically named 'members of the Congregation', that is, the faculty. Tom was one of those people to whom others tend to tell things without being asked – he came across as likeable and sympathetic without even trying, and he was a wonderful listener, whose intense attentiveness always flattered and encouraged his interlocutors, unless, that is, he chose not to listen, in which case he would cut the conversation short – making him the repository of their trust without even wondering why they were talking so much about themselves or why the hell they were blithely divulging secrets without having them wheedled or coaxed out of them.

His outstanding linguistic gifts were immediately noticed by his tutors, and, of course, by the former Lieutenant Colonel Peter Wheeler, who, at the time, was not yet sixty and who combined his exceptionally acute antennae – his alert, curious mind – with long years of experience. When he went up to Oxford, Tomás had already mastered to perfection most of the registers, intonations, varieties, dictions and accents of his two family languages; he also spoke almost impeccable French and very respectable Italian. At Oxford, he not only made huge advances in those last two languages, but by the end of his third year, in 1971, when he was almost twenty, after having been persuaded to enrol in Slavonic languages too, he could speak Russian almost flawlessly, with barely any mistakes, and could get by in Polish, Czech and Serbo-Croat. He was clearly extraordinarily gifted in that field, a prodigy, as if he had retained the linguistic malleability of a small child, who can learn however many languages are spoken around him, can master and allow them to become part of his being, because, in his eyes, they are all *his* language, as any language could be, depending on where the wind took him and where he ended up living; who can retain them all and keep them separate, and only rarely confuse or mix them up. His imitative skills also developed and grew as he immersed himself in his studies, and one Easter vacation, when he decided not to go back to Spain, he devoted himself to travelling around Ireland instead, and at the end of that time (the vacation lasted almost five weeks), he had mastered all the island's main dialects. He was already familiar with the accents of Scotland and Wales, of Liverpool, Newcastle, York, Manchester and other places, having heard them here and there, on the radio and television, during his summer holidays as a child. Anything he heard he could learn instantly, could memorise and later reproduce with precision and skill.

Tomás Nevinson stayed on for a fourth year, intending to return to Spain when he was almost twenty-one, having gained the highest marks of his year in his final exams, and with his Bachelor of Arts degree in his pocket. In those days, contrary to popular belief, everything happened more rapidly and was more advanced, people grew up more quickly than they do now, and young men felt they were adults from very early on, ready to tackle whatever tasks were set for them, ready to learn by doing and thus scramble up onto the world's back. There was no reason to wait or shirk, to try and prolong adolescence or childhood; with their placid lack of definition, such actions were for the cowardly and the fearful, with whom the world is now so full that no one even notices. They are the norm, an over-protected, idle humanity, which has sprung up out of nowhere after centuries of exactly the opposite: action, restlessness, boldness and impatience.

Wheeler's Spanish was excellent, as one would expect given his speciality and his eminence in the field, but he was less confident when it came to writing Spanish, and so when he had finished a text that was to be published in that language, he would ask Tom, as a native speaker he trusted, to check over what he had written and point out any possible imperfections or awkwardnesses and get rid of any expressions which, although correct, sounded inelegant or inappropriate in Spanish. Tomás was very proud to be asked and only too happy to help: he would go to Wheeler's house by the River Cherwell, where Wheeler, who had been a widower for many years, lived with a housekeeper who attended to domestic matters, and together they would read through the texts. (His wife, now so remote, had suffered a mysterious death: he mentioned her sometimes, Valerie was her name, but he never said a word about her death, the cause or the circumstances, and no one else knew anything about it either, which was strange in a city as prone to creating and keeping secrets as it was to uncovering and gossiping about them.) Tom would read out loud, and his tutor would listen contentedly, and they, especially Tom, would stop whenever anything grated. Tom felt honoured to be invited to visit him and be alone with him, not to mention being the first to find out about his new discoveries, even though these concerned erudite matters of little interest to him.

On one such occasion, at the beginning of Trinity, or the third short term, they took a break, and Wheeler offered him a drink; despite Tom's youth, Wheeler did not hesitate to pour him a gin and tonic. Wheeler sat for a while rubbing his thumbnail back and forth on the scar on his chin, as if stroking it – something he often did. The scar began near the left-hand corner of his mouth and continued on a slight diagonal as far as the bottom of his chin, which made it look as if that side of his face never smiled (although it did), and gave him a somewhat sullen, sombre look. He was doubtless aware of this, and so, when he could, he tended to offer people his right side. However, on that particular day, he did not bother; he looked straight at Tomás with his blue eyes slightly narrowed, and so penetrating they were like sparks, as if they could not help scrutinising everything with a degree of suspicion, to the point that the blue seemed to metamorphose into yellow, like the eyes of a tired, but very alert, lion, or perhaps some other feline. His abundant wavy hair was now very white, and when he smiled or laughed he revealed teeth that were rather widely set, giving him a mischievous air. And he could be mischievous, there was no doubt about that, the mischievousness of someone who is too intelligent not to notice the often comical side of people – the more solemn or stern or serious they were the more risible – but one that was basically benign. He had probably already inflicted enough harm in his life and wasn't prepared to continue to do so, unless such harm were to prove extremely useful, and that usefulness could compensate for any pain caused, although we never really know if someone has been harmed until their story is complete, and that takes time.

'Have you had any thoughts about what you're going to do, Tomás? When you graduate, I mean. I understand you want to go back to Spain.' He liked to call him by his Spanish name, even though they usually spoke in English. 'You won't have many options there, only teaching, publishing or politics, really. Franco will die eventually, and then, I imagine, various parties will spring up. But with no democratic tradition, it will be very off the cuff and chaotic. Always assuming *no se arma la de San Quintín*, as you Spaniards say.' And that last expression he said in Spanish of course, meaning 'always assuming all hell doesn't break loose'.

'I don't know, Professor.' In Oxford, that is both a form of address and a title, and applied only to those who have reached the highest academic rank, and never to other teachers, however distinguished. 'I wouldn't even consider going into politics, certainly not as long as the dictatorship lasts, what would be the point of being a mere puppet, not to mention soiling my hands. And as for talk of when it will end, well, that's a bit premature, it's still almost unimaginable. When things go on and on like that, they stop you even imagining the future, don't you think? I don't know, I'll talk to my father and to Mr Starkie. He's come back to Madrid after his years in America, and even though he's retired, he still has influence. Something interesting might come up at the British Council, and then we'll see.'

Wheeler's mischievous side immediately made an appearance:

'Ah, poor Starkie,' he said. 'He's probably still casting voodoo spells on me, and sticking pins in a little doll whose hair must be turning grey by now. He and an eminent Hispanist from Glasgow, Atkinson, both applied for my post in 1953, when Entwistle died. They never could accept that the King Alfonso XIII chair should go to a thirty-nine-year-old with hardly any publications, compared with them, that is. And, of course, poor Starkie had wasted so much time on those gypsies of his, and I'm not sure how well that would have gone down in the Oxford of the day, because, as you know, this is a very snobbish place,' he added with a smile, because in the early 1970s, Oxford was only marginally less snobbish than it had been in the eighteenth century or even the fourteenth. 'At least he learned a bit of voodoo, or do gypsies not practise voodoo? Anyway, it didn't help him in my case, neither that nor any curse or whatever it was he put on me. But that looks like a very dull and boring future, Tomás, if you're going to depend on what Don Gypsy has to offer. A waste of your talents.' There was presumably still a degree of mutual resentment between those two former rivals. 'If you were to stay in England, on the other hand, every door would be open to you after doing so brilliantly here: finance, diplomacy, politics, business, even here at the university if you fancied it. Although I can't really see you teaching and doing research. You're a man of action, I would say, keen to influence the world directly or indirectly. You do have dual nationality, don't you? Or not? If not, I hope you're British. You could choose whichever career you wanted. What you actually studied is purely secondary. With your record, you'd be welcomed with open arms anywhere. They'd wait until you'd been trained in whatever field you chose.'

'Thank you for your confidence in me, Professor, but my life is in Spain. I was born there, and that's where I've always imagined myself settling down.'

'Anyone's life can be lived anywhere, wherever you happen to go or end up,' said Wheeler succinctly. 'Let me remind you that I was born in New Zealand, but of what relevance is that, I ask? Given your gift for languages and mimicry,' he went on, 'have you considered becoming an actor? Obviously, you'd need other abilities too, and I can't honestly see you going on stage night after night and repeating the same words in exchange for rapturous applause, which would soon grow monotonous. That doesn't shape the world. Nor would spending your life making films here, there and everywhere, because filming takes for ever. And to what end? To be the idol of the undiscerning, who are as likely to worship Olivier as a Californian dog?' Yes, snobbery in Oxford was clearly a thing of the past. Wheeler belonged to the old school and clung to the idea that Laurence Olivier was still the greatest living actor when no one else thought so, not even in his proud country of birth.

Tom laughed. It was true that he was restless – although his was a rather diffuse kind of restlessness, the sort that abates over time – but not like your average man of action, not in the way we usually understand the expression. He wasn't adventurous enough or ambitious enough, or else didn't yet know how to be either or wasn't tempted to be – nor indeed did he need to be. At the age he was then, he didn't see himself influencing the world, as Wheeler had put it, regardless of what country he lived in. He didn't see anyone doing that, not even the great financiers or scientists or politicians. The first group could face setbacks and brutal competition; the second could make mistakes, and their inevitable fate was, sooner or later, to have their work refuted or superseded; the third group would pass, fall from power and vanish into obscurity (the democratic politicians, that is; even Churchill had lost in 1945, after all his great deeds), and as soon as they vacated their seat, others would come along to erase what they had done, and few would remember them after a matter of years or months (with the odd rare exception, Churchill being a case in point). It amused him that someone as sharp and experienced as Wheeler should use that concept; it revealed a certain innocence on his part, from Tom's youthful point of view, that is, but then the young do tend to believe themselves to be more blasé and more in the know than anyone, including their mentors.

'No, I don't really see myself as an actor. Still less as another Olivier. My generation find him very old-fashioned.'

'Oh, really? So, he's seen as old hat now, is he? Forgive me, I don't go to the cinema or the theatre very much. It doesn't matter, it was just an example.'

'But who does shape the world, Professor?' Tomás asked him, for those words had stuck in his mind; and he was expecting Wheeler to trot out the usual professions, the big financiers, the scientists and politicians, possibly the military, capable of destroying the world with their weapons. 'Certainly not actors or university lecturers,' he added. 'Or philosophers or novelists or singers, I imagine, however many of us young people rush to imitate the latter, and however much they may change certain customs. Just look at what happened with the Beatles. We'll get over that, though. And television is too inane, generally speaking, despite its influence. So who does shape the world, then? Who is in a position to do that?'

Wheeler shifted in his armchair, elegantly crossed his legs (he was very tall and long-limbed), and again stroked the scar on his chin with his nail, as if he enjoyed tracing the furrow that had once been there and no longer was, it must have been rather smooth and polished to the touch, that ancient ghost of a brutal cut or serious wound.

'Well, no one can shape it on his own, Tomás, or even with the help of others. If there's something that characterises and unites most of humanity (and by that I mean all those who have lived on Earth since time immemorial), it's that the universe influences us without us being able to influence it even minimally, if that. We may believe that we form part of the universe, we may exist in the universe and may struggle to change some tiny detail of it during our lifetime, but we are in fact outcasts of the universe, to use an expression from that famous story about the man who erased himself from the world simply by taking lodgings in the next street and not telling anyone.' And he repeated those words 'outcasts of the universe', as if they gave him food for thought and as if this were the first time in ages that he had recalled them. Tomás didn't know the story he was referring to, but preferred not to ask so as not to interrupt him, and was, besides, too interested in what Wheeler was saying. 'Nothing about us changes it, neither our elimination nor our birth, neither our unhurried journey through it, nor our existence or chance appearance nor our inevitable annihilation. Neither does any deed, any crime committed or prevented, any event. In short, it would be exactly the same without Plato or Shakespeare or Newton, without the discovery of America or the French Revolution. Not perhaps without all those things at once, but definitely in the absence of any particular one. Everything that has ever happened could just as well not have happened, and everything would be essentially the same. Or it could have happened differently or with some detour or circumlocution, or at a later date or with different protagonists. It doesn't matter, we can't miss what never happened, I can assure you that the average twelfth-century European did not long for the New World, nor did he feel its non-existence as an amputation or a loss, which is how we would feel after five hundred years of knowing it existed. That would be like a cataclysm.'

'So why talk to me then about shaping the world if nothing and no one can, Professor?'

'No, no one can, apart from mass murderers, but we don't want to be one of them, do we? There are degrees of influence. We are all influenced by the universe, but incapable of influencing it, or even scratching its surface. And as far as nine hundred and ninety-nine people out of a thousand are concerned, the universe jostles and shakes them, treats them or regards them as if they were a package, not even a being with an iota of free will or a tenuous capacity to make decisions. The man in that story opted to become – just that – a package, which he probably was anyway, an insignificant Londoner. Or perhaps he stopped being that, just a little, precisely because he dispensed with witnesses by making himself invisible, by erasing himself: he resolved to disappear, at least as far as his wife and those closest to him were concerned, to leave and withdraw. That's something at least. But there are other, less extreme, less paradoxical ways:

the man who stays at home is more of an outcast than the one who leaves; the man who does something less so than the one who doesn't even move, even if the efforts of the former prove fruitless. An actor or a university teacher is more of an outcast than a politician or a scientist. The latter do at least disturb the universe a little, perhaps tousle its hair, change its expression, make it raise an eyebrow at such impertinence.' And Wheeler raised a peevish eyebrow, as if pretending to be a very cold, slightly offended universe.

'So what are you suggesting? That I go into politics? Or become a scientist? I don't have the training for the latter, as you know, and have neither the necessary talent nor the patience for the former. Besides, in Spain, there is no politics, just orders from the Generalísimo.'

Wheeler laughed, showing his slightly wide-set teeth and narrowing his yellowish eyes, his face filled with a look of amiable mischief.

'Don't be so literal-minded. That's not what I meant at all. They're not the ones who shape the world, to continue using that rather extreme verb. The ones who most shape the world are those who are not exposed, who can't be seen; unknown, opaque beings about whom almost no one knows anything. Like the hidden man in the story, except that instead of living a passive vegetable existence, they plot and weave webs in the shadows. Everyone knows who the rulers are, and could even name some of the super rich and a few military commanders, and the scientists who make astonishing advances in their field. Look at that otherwise unknown South African, Dr Barnard, who became famous throughout the world after carrying out the first human heart transplant. Look at General Dayan of Israel, another country that no one pays much attention to, and yet everyone knows his face, with his eyepatch and his bald head. Eminent people are now so exposed to the public gaze that their over-exposure some-how nullifies them, and, in future, this will become more and more the case. They won't be able to take a step without being followed by journalists and cameras, without being watched, and then they won't be able to shape or mould anything. Nothing has any weight if it lacks mystery, a surrounding mist, and we are heading towards a reality bereft of shadows, bereft almost of light and shade. Every-thing and anything known is destined to become rapidly swallowed up and trivialised, and so to lack any real influence. Anything that is visible, a spectacle in the public domain, can never create change. Contrary to what people think, the shape of the universe hasn't changed one bit just because, a couple of years ago, two astronauts walked on the Moon. Everything continues exactly the same as before, what difference has it made to anyone's life, let alone to the functioning and configuration of the universe? They even broadcast the event on television, which is still further proof of its complete irrelevance. The truly decisive events are never shown or even described, or not at the time they happen; instead, they're always kept hidden away, wrapped in silence, at least for a very long time; at most, we learn about them when they're no longer of any interest, when they already belong to the remote past, and people don't care about the past, they think it doesn't affect them and can't be changed, and in that respect, they're right. For example, the most important operations during the war, the ones that were fundamental to our victory, are those we know nothing about and that have never leaked out, that don't appear in the history books and of which there is no trace. The ones that, with admirable coolness and cynicism, people even deny ever happened if some rumour appears in the press or some vain person talks too much, thus breaking his oath, but that's another matter. Those who act swathed in mist, their backs turned on everyone else, who don't demand or need recognition, they are the ones who most disturb the universe. Albeit very little, it must be said. But at least they make it shift slightly in its armchair and adopt a different posture. That is the most we individuals can hope for, if we are not to be complete and utter outcasts.' And Wheeler again stirred in his armchair and uncrossed his legs and changed his posture, having decided to play the part of his imaginary universe.

'I imagine you're speaking from personal experience,' said Tom Nevinson cautiously. 'As you know, there are all sorts of stories about your past activities, not all of them academic . . .'

'Yes, well, fortunately, not all of them *are* academic. Although the vast majority of those stories are false, you know. Oxbridge legends dreamed up to make our boring high tables more palatable.'

'Yes, but, if I've understood you rightly, you've just given a speech in praise of secrecy as the supreme way of influencing the world. And one of the things that everyone holds to be true is that you worked for the Secret Service.'

Wheeler blew out air between his teeth, with a mixture of sarcasm and impatience, as if to say: 'Oh really' or 'What nonsense'. Or perhaps it was Tom's use of the preterite tense that struck him as inappropriate.

'Who didn't work for them, at a time when every last man counted, and every last woman too, of course. Some paid a very high price.' He fell silent for a moment as if remembering someone. Tom wondered if Valerie, Wheeler's late wife of whom he rarely spoke, had been one of those to pay a high price. 'It's not in the least unusual. Well, when I say "who didn't", I mean those who were better suited to that than piloting planes or being part of a naval crew or fighting at the front. I wouldn't have been much use at any of that. On the other hand, there are people with a special gift for murky, undercover work. A gift, in fact, that most people don't have: they lack the necessary knowledge or can't speak another language, or are too transparent and incapable of pretence, or have too many scruples and lack sangfroid and patience, and in time of war, you can't afford to waste people by sending them off to perform a task for which they're unsuited. That's what you Spaniards have traditionally done.' He suddenly considered Tom to be Spanish, whereas, in general, he thought of him as British. 'You start by handing over command to a total amateur, an old custom that still persists. I mean, that dictator of yours is an utter incompetent, except, like all dictators, he puts on a fierce front. If it hadn't been for the British in the Peninsular War, you would continue to be an occupied country . . .' The Peninsular War is what the British call the War of Independence against Bonaparte. Tom wasn't in the least offended, feeling as he did that he belonged to both countries.

'Ah, yes, Wellington as brilliant strategist and all that,' he said, to avoid an excursus, which he successfully did, because Wheeler immediately returned to what he had been saying before:

'Gifted people like you are still needed today. Even in times of apparent peace. Peace, alas, is only ever apparent and transitory, a pretence. War is the natural state of the world. Often it's open warfare, but when it's not, war is always there in latent or indirect form or is merely a war-in-waiting. There are large portions of humanity who are always trying to harm others, or to take something from them, and rancour and discord reign at all times, and, if not, then they're there in the wings, watching and waiting. When there is no war, there's the threat of war, and what gifted people like you can do is keep it as only a threat. In its infancy, so to speak, not yet unleashed. People like you are capable of avoiding wars, or at least of distracting and delaying them for those living at the time, of making sure they break out later, when others will have to endure them and when there will perhaps be other gifted people who can again avert them. And that is what I mean by intervening in the universe, Tomás. Very subtly. It's more like blocking and containing it . . . temporarily. Which is no small thing, don't you think?'

Tomás Nevinson was a bright, pleasant young man, quick and funny and even genial, but too youthful to be wise, having not as yet had to make any important decisions or felt the need to consider what kind of person he was. The frivolity with which he observed the external world and his own internal world prevented him from doing so, as did the opacity and reserve that his frivolity concealed. As I said before, no one, not even he, could see through him, and no one tried. He was one of those people with great abilities and qualities, but who has no idea what to do with them unless instructed and told what they are for. If guided in his studies, he was an excellent student, and he perhaps needed someone who could perform the same didactic function in other areas of his life, especially as regards the practical and the personal. He realised that Wheeler was playing a similar role that afternoon – perhaps he was trying to see through him, or had already done so and seen his future – and he felt flattered to think that Wheeler might become his guide; however, he could still not understand or guess precisely what he was proposing, what path he was indicating with all those digressions, which door he was inviting him to open.

'I don't quite follow, Professor. I don't know what you're talking about. I know you Oxford people like to hint at things, drop in a few ambiguous words or make allusions whose meaning is immediately grasped. And, yes, I've lived here for years now, coming and going, but bear in mind my origins. In Spain, you have to speak clearly or no one will have a clue what you mean. You're including me among those gifted people, as you call them, but I have no idea what gifts you're referring to, what gifts you imagine I possess. I really don't see myself as someone capable of postponing no less a thing than a war.'

Wheeler gave a deep sigh that seemed to indicate a certain impatience. He doubtless thought he had been crystal clear and explicit in his explanations.

'Let's see, Tom. According to you, I spoke in praise of secrets, and you yourself mentioned the rumours about my past. You have an exceptional gift for mimicry and for languages, more so than anyone I've ever known, and yet you've never received any specific training, unlike many others who've crossed my path, both during the war and afterwards – yes, afterwards too. What do you think I'm suggesting? You would be very useful here. You would be extremely useful to us.'

Tom Nevinson laughed, part incredulous, part genuinely amused and part flattered. Laughter did not favour him, it broadened his already broad nose and made him seem coarser. He lost his usually serene expression, and this accentuated that look in his eyes warning of anomalies to come. It was as if his features lost control of themselves and took on another, perhaps future, life.

'Do you mean you're still in touch with the Secret Service? Are you suggesting I should join them?'

Wheeler regarded him coolly and with a glimmer of displeasure, perhaps because of that laugh, perhaps because of the excessive frankness of his questions. His narrowed eyes regained their original blue colour and lost their leonine look. He took a sip of his drink to calm himself, or perhaps to delay giving an answer. Then he said:

'Once you've been involved with the Secret Service, they're the ones who keep in touch with you. Rarely or frequently, as they choose. You don't abandon them, that would be an act of betrayal.

We always stand and wait.' And those last words sounded like a quotation or a reference to something else. 'They barely ever contact me now, but, yes, there are occasional exchanges. You never completely retire if you can still be of use to them. It's a way of serving your country and not becoming an outcast. It's within your grasp not to become a complete, lifelong outcast. Which is what you will be if you return to Spain. If you go back for good, I mean. Nothing would stop you living there part-time. In fact, that would be the best way, to have a double life, with one life being lived abroad. You wouldn't have to give up much. Or only for short periods, like any businessman, for they all spend time away from their families, travelling or setting up a business in another city or country, they're sometimes absent for months. That's no reason for them not to get married and have children, though. They simply come and go. Like any other man of the world.'

Tomás wasn't laughing now. Wheeler was speaking in a very serious, professional tone of voice. He spoke circumspectly, like someone complying with a formality, like someone explaining what the job involves, the working conditions and possible perks. He had already carried out the task of tempting, or perhaps attracting him. The temptation to intervene in some way in the universe, even if only minimally, and not to pass through it like a suitcase or a rubbish bin or a piece of furniture, which, according to Wheeler, was what all men and women had done since time began: people who laboured away each day and knew no rest from the moment they got up until they went to bed, who had a thousand duties to fulfil and who broke their backs just to put food on the table, or who played at influencing their fellow men and women, controlling them or dazzling them; they were of as little interest as the shopkeeper who spends his entire life opening and closing his business, day after day at the appointed hour, never once varying his routine. They were all out-casts from the moment they were born or from their conception or even before that: from the time when they were merely a twinkle in the eye of their irresponsible or unthinking parents, who were per-haps unaware that, by succumbing to their instincts, they would be creating yet another being surplus to requirements.

'But what would I have to do? What kind of work?'

'Well, whatever they assigned you to do, once you'd been accepted. At first, they wouldn't ask you to do anything you hadn't agreed to beforehand. Sometimes, of course, situations get compli-cated, unexpected things happen, and you'd have to improvise. Then you just have to carry on and do things you hadn't counted on doing. There would be plenty of possible jobs for someone like you, you really could be useful. With your genius for mimicry and your other remarkable talents, you would make an excellent infiltrator. Given the relevant training, you could pass for a native in quite a few places.' Tom Nevinson felt flattered, which was doubtless the intention of those interpolated compliments; young people are very susceptible to flattery. 'No mission would last very long. The great danger isn't that the agent will be unmasked (although that remains a danger, of course), but that he ends up too immersed in the role he's playing, that he loses sight of who he is in reality and who he's working for. You mustn't prolong pretence. It's very hard to be two people at once for any length of time. For someone in his right mind, I mean. We all tend to be just one, exclusive person, and there's always the risk that you'll turn into the person you're pretending to be, with the latter driving out and supplanting the original you. As I said: a few months at the most, like any businessman with various irons in the fire, with branches to visit and supervise and manage. His family or friends wouldn't find this odd or unusual. Everything would carry on as normal when you were in Spain. When you weren't, well, I won't lie to you, you would live fictitious lives, lives not your own, but only temporarily. Sooner or later, you would always leave them and return to your own self, to thy former self.' And he seemed again to be quoting from something, because he used the archaic 'thy', which only survives in prayers. 'You would be helping others and yourself. You would know that your time on Earth had not been entirely in vain. I mean that you would have contributed or removed, added or subtracted something: a blade of grass, a speck of dust, a life, a war, a fragment of ash, a thread, it all depends. But something.'

Tomás couldn't believe what he was hearing, those flattering remarks hadn't been enough for him to accept the implausibility of it all, to transport him into a world of spies, novels and films, even though it was being presented to him in the middle of ordinary everyday life, on a peaceful afternoon by the River Cherwell, where he had expected to be editing a text. An infiltrator into who knows what groups or in what countries? Pretending to be someone else, living various alternative existences, invented, deceitful, corrupt, and, to use Wheeler's word, 'fictitious'? He couldn't understand how Wheeler could have thought of such a thing, how he could even be suggesting such a possibility, how they had ended up having what, for him, was an unreal, fantastical conversation. He felt he must be dreaming, but he wasn't: there was his mentor with the scar on his chin, directing, suggesting, proposing, leading. Showing him a future path, acting as his guide. Which, up to a point, was what he wanted. And yet it all seemed absurd, pie in the sky, impossible. He glanced at Wheeler and saw a look on his face of sudden repudiation, disappointment, almost scorn, as if realising that his arguments and attempts at persuasion had had no effect. He was a very perceptive man, who could read people's faces. The faces of students rarely hold much mystery for their teachers.

'I don't know how such an idea could occur to you, Professor. I really don't deserve such confidence in my abilities. You're quite wrong about them. I'm enormously grateful, but I'm simply not equipped for the kind of work you describe. That would require a sense of adventure and courage and, of course, character. I'm a pretty ordinary, sedentary fellow really, and, quite probably, a coward, although fortunately, in the latter case, I haven't had many occasions to find out. And with luck I won't have any. So the last thing I would do is to encourage such occasions, and expose myself to them voluntarily. Thank you, but please, just forget it. I could never be part of something like that. And I'm not sure I would want to if I could.'

Wheeler fixed him with an intense, almost severe gaze, of a kind rarely found in England, as if he were trying to work out if Tomás was merely being falsely modest and hoping that he, Wheeler, would insist, argue back or heap him with more compliments. He must have decided that this was not the case, because he then waved his hand in a gesture of displeasure or dismissal, as if he were a monarch ordering a minister to leave, or as if he were saying: 'We clearly do not agree. We'll speak no more about it. It's your loss.' Then he brought the pause to an end and suggested they return to his text. Tomás was sorry to have failed him and to have left him feeling disappointed or embarrassed, but he had no alternative. He could not imagine himself living among conspirators, criminals, genuine spies or terrorists, and passing himself off as one of them, if that is what was meant by the word 'infiltrator'. He realised that their discursive chat had ended and that nothing of what had been said would be mentioned again, that it was the kind of conversation that would happen once and once only. He had perhaps not reckoned with the existence of people who, if they see something in you and choose you, never abandon the topic or entirely withdraw, but are like vultures: they move off and circle around and wait, then try their luck again. He had resumed his reading of the text out loud when he heard Wheeler murmur in a ruminative voice, as if the words were emerging from inside a helmet:

'Give it a little more thought. Am I so mistaken? That would only be the second time in many years. I don't think so. I don't usually make such mistakes.'

A week later, when it was not yet halfway through the so-called Trinity term, Tom Nevinson made one of his incursions into Waterfield's, the second-hand bookshop on several floors where Janet worked from Monday to Friday, doubtless always eagerly waiting for the weekend to arrive so that she could get together with her long-term London boyfriend, about whom she had never told him a thing, except to mention his existence and his first name, Hugh, and how long they had been together. He, unlike Tom, was clearly not a way of filling the time but, rather, her objective or reward after those five days of work, that is, the sole goal and reason for her time, the very axis and illumination of its passing. Tom imagined Hugh to be married and older than her, a proper grown-up with responsibilities, but he didn't actually know this. Those five days would pass so slowly that Janet might have to kill time by resorting to some kind of distraction, whole months and years dominated by days that were either empty or parenthetical, days that you long for merely so that they can give way to the next day and thus move on from the despairing 'It's still only Tuesday' to the impatient 'Wednesdays are so long' to the hopeful 'It's Thursday already'. There are far too many such accumulated transitional nights in anyone's life.

This was doubtless why Janet was always pleased to receive Tom's visits, which usually culminated a few hours later in somewhat mechanical, utilitarian sex, and he, as I said, was the one who tried to stagger their meetings, partly so that he would not inadvertently become another, albeit lesser, way of filling her time (of which Janet had so much), for habit can work miracles and confer the rank of necessity on the unpredictable and the superfluous. Whenever he decided to see her, he would usually do so on a Tuesday or a Wednesday, because he had the impression that on Mondays she was still under the spell of her brief London stay and that on Thursdays she was already anticipating the next one; and so he chose the days when she would be at her lowest ebb, the days when she would be feeling most bored or peeved with or even resentful of her lover, preferring to punish him without his knowledge and in silence, keeping that punishment purely to herself.

That Wednesday was no different. They chatted on the third floor of the bookshop, the one with fewest customers, and, concealed behind the bookshelves, they partook of a brief advance payment: Tomás was more experienced now and slipped his hand up her skirt for a good long minute, staring at the spines of some of Kipling's works as he did so, both of them standing, both, as is frequent among the young, primitively excited by that first contact, both storing away those sensations in order to recover and relive them for the rest of the day, until they met up again in the modest flat she occupied in St John Street, near the Ashmolean Museum and the elegant Randolph Hotel. They didn't even go out for supper together, he simply said he would drop around at about nine o'clock, neither of them requiring any deceiving preamble.

They stayed together for less than an hour, shifting, during that time, from the excitement of anticipation to the faint melancholy that always follows what has already happened, leaving no memory or even any imaginary longing; indeed, it had begun to seem superfluous and forgotten even while it was happening: clinical sex with no frills, prescribed sex because you have to have it every few days or, at least, every few weeks and anyone who doesn't is a pariah, but also because you feel the need – a need more of the idea than the actual act – but it's a very half-hearted business once it's over and when viewed in retrospect, and afterwards, the predominant, troubling thought is: 'OK, I felt that urgent need, but I could easily not have bothered, now that it's so joylessly and rather sadly over, it wasn't worth it; if I could go back, I wouldn't bother.' And, at the same time, you know this isn't true: if you could go back, you would feel the same urgency again and proceed, elementally, ahead.

Tomás felt sorry for Janet, and wondered if she might not feel equally sorry for him. They didn't even get undressed, it was just a prolongation of what they had begun that morning in the bookshop, as if the memory of that had lingered on and imposed itself on those new and different circumstances, as if yielding to the thoughts that had filled their minds during the day, in occasional, involuntary waves. Tom did remove her tights and knickers, but only took off his raincoat and jacket, then unzipped his flies, nothing more. When he finished, he went quickly to the bathroom so as not to stain anything, and when he returned to the bedroom, Janet was lying on her side on the bed, her head resting on the pillow and a book in her hands, as though she had moved on to something else or was in a hurry to take up reading where she had left off when he arrived. Her skirt had ridden up to mid-thigh level; she wore a watch on her left wrist and a couple of bracelets on the right one. Tomás had heard the bracelets tinkling – a slight distraction – while he and Janet were busily at it, just as he had noticed her earrings swaying – large hoop earrings – while he pumped away, with her resting her fists on the mattress and him standing behind her, neither of them having bothered to take off anything that did not present an obstacle. Now she was more the image of a woman in a hotel room absorbed in her book, waiting for sleep to come, than that of someone in her own home who has just partaken of a youthful fuck: Janet was three or four years older than him, with very blonde, probably bleached hair; features that were at once delicate, fierce and determined; and very pretty, curved eyebrows, much darker than her hair. She had very red lips and a gap between her front teeth, which lent a childish element to her smile; and inquisitive eyes that were devouring those pages as voraciously as if nothing else mattered in the world. She didn't even look up at him, but, sensing his presence, raised her left hand as if to say: 'Let me just read this bit.' She also hadn't taken off the two rings she wore on that hand, a kind of wedding ring on her ring finger and a discreet onyx ring on her middle finger. Both could have been presents from her lover Hugh, thought Tom, the first as a simulacrum of an engagement, the second a gift.

'How are things with your boyfriend, Hugh? Do you plan to live together? Are you going to move in with him?' he asked. He didn't usually ask anything about Hugh, certainly not so directly, but he found the way Janet was so completely ignoring him both disconcerting and irritating. After one of these sessions, he never expected her to be affectionate or to cuddle up to him; that was the last thing he wanted, but it did seem a bit much for her to immediately immerse herself in a book, as if she were showing him the door, now that he had fulfilled his strictly physical function. He couldn't think of anything else to say, or any other subject that would command her attention.

She closed her book, although not completely, leaving one finger in as a marker, and Tomás could finally see the cover clearly: *The Secret Agent* by Joseph Conrad, a Penguin edition with a grey spine.

He was unjustifiably surprised: he had never seen her reading before, but given that she worked among books, it would have been odd for her not to open and read one now and then.

'There never are any plans with him, just habit and repetition,' she said. 'He's too busy to make plans, or even to stop to think that the future exists beyond the following day or the following week. He's the sort who lives from day to day. As far as he's concerned, things are fine as they are. He doesn't like change.'

'What about you, though? Are things fine for you too?'

'No, they're not. I've been waiting for things to change for years now, but I know that's not going to happen.'

'So what next?' Tomás felt suddenly curious, and reproached himself for not having asked such questions on previous occasions.

Janet removed her finger from its place in the book, turned down the corner of the page and put the closed book on the pillow. She sat up a little, leaning on one elbow, her head resting on one hand, while with the other – with its long, painted nails – she stroked her mane of hair, perhaps considering whether to answer or not. She must have been a natural blonde, although a duller blonde than she was then. Her hair was a positively dazzling, Scandinavian yellow, so intense as to be unmistakable if you happened to see her in the street; sometimes it resembled a golden helmet lit by a hidden sun that fell like a spotlight on her through Oxford's shifting clouds.

'I've given him an ultimatum,' she said coolly, and all her features grew suddenly thinner, as happens to the very old, in whom, however, it's a warning of imminent death; as if nose, eyes and mouth had turned into sharp, cutting ice, even her lovely curved eyebrows and her chin. 'I've given him until next weekend to change the situation.'

'And what will you do if he won't? Will you leave him? I imagine you know that ultimatums nearly always rebound against the people issuing them and usually turn out badly.'

'Of course I do, especially in this particular case. I'm not expecting a response, or not at least the one I'd like.'

'So why wait another week, then?'

She fell silent, then took a large toffee from a glass jar she kept on the bedside table and put it in her mouth. Tom watched as it filled first one cheek, then the other, as if it were too big for either.

'Well, the truth is that you always hope for something, however convinced you are to the contrary. You hope to give the other person a fright, that he'll imagine how much he'll miss you, how difficult it will be to live without you. But that other person never imagines anything or takes such warnings seriously. Besides, he's been used to not seeing me for five days of the week, which is how he wanted it from the start. No, I'm not expecting any surprises. I just thought I owed him a warning, and not to take any steps without telling him beforehand and explaining what those steps would be. Because I won't just leave him. I'll ruin his life first. Leaving him wouldn't be enough after years of broken – not to say, false – promises. False from day one. I'd probably be doing him a favour. No, I've squandered my years, invested an awful lot of time, endured night after lonely night. I've lost all that time now, and no one can give it back to me. Just to leave him wouldn't make up for that. If it's been a complete waste of time for me, if I've lost out, then it should be the same for him.'

'He's married, then,' said Tomás.

Janet changed her position, shaking her bracelets as she did so, to shuffle them further up her arm, and she looked at him, surprised, as if wondering why she was telling him all this for the first time, after their many previous encounters. She bit through the toffee so that it

72

was less uncomfortable and unmanageable in her mouth. Her thighs were slightly parted, and she hadn't put her knickers back on, they were still there on the floor (she may not even have wiped herself clean when he went to the bathroom, possibly a sign of despair, or else carelessness). And although Tom had just visited that part of her anatomy, he felt a sudden impulse to return, an unexpected, irresistible sense of urgency, even though it was doubtless purely visual. She'd been standing with her back to him before, and he hadn't looked. And the fleeting thought occurred to him: 'How is this possible? A moment ago I was thinking I should have saved myself the trouble, and yet here I am wanting it again.'

'You're asking a lot of questions today,' Janet said suspiciously, and added, not so much to satisfy his curiosity as because she couldn't stop herself: 'If you read the papers, you'll find out. Not that it matters. What matters is that he's Someone.' That's how it sounded, as if she had added a capital letter, indicating 'someone important'. 'And I can turn him into Nobody, into a has-been. He knows this, but he doesn't believe it. He thinks I wouldn't dare, or that he'll once again persuade me and placate me, and everything will carry on as before. That I'll get over it. That I'll go and see him next weekend and after a few kisses and caresses and a few jokes, I'll forget all about my ultimatum. That's one of his charms: his incorrigible optimism. He's convinced that everything will always go his way. Always. I wish I were like that.'

'So Hugh is Someone, then?' Tom couldn't resist asking. 'But who is he? Do I know him?'

'That's a question too far. Look, I'm tired. You'd better leave.' She said this without moving, without giving the slightest indication that she might see him out, or even stand up to give him a farewell kiss. Tomás could see what he could see, her still moist, still slightly

73

tumescent cunt; it seemed to him to be pulsating, and he felt it calling to him still more loudly. He wanted to enter it again or take a closer look, and, after all, what was there to stop him? Nothing. He crouched down so as to observe it brazenly and from the appropriate height, and even reached out two fingers, for the visual is often a prelude to the tactile, but not always, some men prefer to look and abhor any contact. 'What are you doing?' Janet interrupted him in a voice that was both incredulous and offended, and quickly brought her thighs together as if a dagger were approaching, thus shutting off the view. 'What's wrong with you tonight? I've just told you that I'm really tired. What were you thinking? Aren't you in a hurry to get away? Well, I'm in a hurry to get to sleep.'

Tomás Nevinson paused, embarrassed, his fingers in mid-air. 'Yes, what *am* I doing?' he asked himself. He improvised a feeble, unconvincing excuse, of the kind you don't expect to be believed, merely heard and ignored:

'You misunderstood, I'm sorry. I thought I'd left my cigarettes on the bed, underneath you. I must have them in my jacket.' He stood up, went over to where his jacket was, put it on, and took out the small metal Marcovitch cigarette case, placed a cigarette between his lips, but didn't light it. Now that he was on his feet, he put his raincoat on as well and prepared to leave, since he had nothing more to do there and there was nothing more he wanted to do. 'Let me know how it goes. With the ultimatum, I mean. I wish you luck.'

'I'll need it.' She fell silent for a few seconds, then added, more to herself than to him, 'I can hardly be bothered to set it all in motion; vengeance is hard work, and stressful too. But I'll do it. I'll do it . . .'

Janet said these last words while staring into space, and almost out of inertia. She did sound genuinely exhausted now. She picked up *The Secret Agent*, opened it and stared at the page. She pretended to be reading, as if she were saying to him: 'As far as I'm concerned, you've left already.' But she wasn't taking in a single word. Tom went over to her, stroked her cheek by way of a goodbye, and she mechanically raised her hand to return his gesture, but without looking up; she miscalculated and scratched him slightly with her long nails and knocked the cigarette from his lips. Tom turned away, but didn't flinch or go and look at his face in the mirror, it could only have been a tiny scratch. He didn't pick up his cigarette either, which must have rolled under the bed. She didn't even notice this minor incident, her eyes fixed on the same page as if she were studying a map she had to memorise.

Tomás went downstairs into the street; it was a chilly night. He walked only as far as the corner of Beaumont Street, took out another Marcovitch cigarette and lit it, deciding to smoke it there, looking up at the lighted windows of Janet's flat, for that second, untimely urgent impulse had not entirely dissipated, despite the rebuff he'd received, but he knew the night was over and that there'd be no point in going up again. Given her sudden tiredness, he was expecting the lights to go out at any moment, and then the temptation would vanish. There was no street lamp on St John Street where he was standing, but there was one near Janet's door. This is why he could see without being seen. He was just about to stub out his cigarette when a well-built man of medium height suddenly appeared. Tom hadn't seen him get out of a car or even heard his footsteps before he entered that pool of light. He had dark, wavy hair, was wearing a long, calf-length over-coat, black or navy blue, as if in the hope that this would make him look taller and slimmer, with a pale grey scarf carefully tucked in at the collar, and matching grey gloves, the kind a racing driver might wear. Tom only glimpsed the man's face, a flash, a blurred snapshot: a nose with large nostrils, small, bright eyes, cleft chin, an attractive combination, at least at first glance, which is all Tom had. He would have been in his forties, and moved with great ease and confidence. He took the three steps up to the door in one agile bound. Tom saw him ring the bell, saw him say something very quickly (something like 'It's me, open up', nothing more), and then he went straight in. He raised the collar of his coat and disappeared behind the door, which immediately closed again. Tomás Nevinson continued looking up at the windows for the time it took to smoke another cigarette. The windows remained lit, but he saw no figure silhouetted in them. The man was clearly visiting someone else, and now he, Tom, really did have nothing more to do there.

The following day, at the end of one of his tutorials in St Peter's College, in the rooms of a newly recruited and still youthful teacher or don, Mr Southworth, a plain-clothes policeman was waiting respectfully and patiently outside for the class to end. He said he wanted to speak to Tom and asked Southworth, quite unnecessarily, if he could come in. Southworth in turn asked if he could stay or if he should leave, to which the police officer replied that this was up to him and Mr Nevinson, and that, for the moment, he merely wanted to check a few facts and ask a few questions. That 'for the moment' did not augur well. He introduced himself as Inspector or Sergeant or whatever it was, and prefixed his name with some initials – DS or DI or CID or DC – none of which meant anything to Tomás, and so he failed to retain them, thus remaining unclear as to the man's rank, and ascertaining only that he was a member of the Thames Valley Constabulary and was called Morse. The three men sat down – Southworth overcome by curiosity, or perhaps a desire to protect his brilliant student – and the policeman, a serious man of thirty or so, with pale, watery-blue eyes, a slightly hooked nose, a wavy mouth that looked as if it had been drawn in pencil, and a vaguely imperious air, said rather than asked:

'Mr Nevinson, last night you were with Janet Jefferys in her flat in St John Street, is that right?'

'Yes, I suppose I was. Why?'

'You suppose?' said Morse, opening his eyes wide in scornful surprise. 'Aren't you sure?'

'What I meant to say was that I realise now that I've never known her surname, or, if she told me what it was some time ago, I've forgotten it. To me, she's just Janet who works at Waterfield's. But it must be her, I imagine, if she lives in St John Street. I've been there several times, of course, and last night too, but why? What's happened? And how do you know?'

Morse did not answer this, but said:

'Doesn't it seem a little odd to you that I, who have only seen her once and when she's no longer alive, should know her surname, but you don't? Was your relationship that superficial?'

'No longer alive? What do you mean, "no longer alive"?' asked Tomás, more uncomprehending than alarmed.

'I assume, naturally, that she was alive when you left? How long were you there? What time did you leave?'

Tomás began to get used to the idea or to assimilate the words as if they were true, because he had heard them clearly and they were clearly true. He turned pale, felt sick and a desire to retch, but controlled himself.

'She's dead? What happened to her? How can that be? I was with her until about ten o'clock, and she was absolutely fine. I spent a whole hour with her, from nine until ten, more or less, and at no point did she feel unwell.'

The policeman said nothing for a few seconds, studying him with an interrogative eye, as if waiting for him to say more or to give something away by his facial expression. This was enough to make Tomás feel uncomfortable and to alarm Mr Southworth, who raised one hand and opened his mouth to intervene. In the end, he didn't, perhaps because he had not yet mentally formulated what he was about to say, and he was always a very precise fellow. Instead, he merely held out the palm of that hand to Morse, as if allowing him to go first or as if urging him to continue. As if he were a theatre director prompting a distracted or forgetful actor to give his response. And he succeeded.

'She had no reason to feel unwell,' said Morse in a voice that was a strange mixture of harsh and gentle. 'Her death was caused by her tights, with which she was strangled. And as far as we can ascertain, this happened at around the time you left her. Either a little before or a little afterwards.'

The sense of danger is as quickly aroused as the survival instinct, and Tom Nevinson was not thinking now about what had happened to Janet, that she was no longer in this world and had been driven from it in the cruellest possible way, without warning and with no chance to prepare herself, vainly resisting someone else's decision and her own extinction, unable to believe what was happening to her, trying to call for help and unable to utter a sound. He did not even ponder how strange it must be to cease to exist, the incredulity of the person who still retains some remnant of consciousness, until that, too, is snuffed out. What he thought was this: 'I casually removed those tights last night and, who knows, maybe I laddered them or accidentally tore them; they were left lying on the floor along with her knickers, no one picked them up, and I, of course, didn't bother, it wasn't my job. Who would have thought they would be put to such use, that someone, some dark, murderous person, saw them there and immediately had that idea, how is that possible? A murderer. Those tights will, therefore, have my fingerprints on them, and not those of the well-built man who arrived after me, he probably kept his grey racing-driver's gloves on, at no point would he have removed them, and so his fingerprints won't even be on the doorbell downstairs, and I was too far away to see if it was Janet's doorbell, although it must have been, even though I didn't see his silhouette or hers later on in the window, the door and the bed were too far away, she would have opened the door perhaps thinking I had come back to try my luck again, she would have interrupted her reading or her absorbed contemplation of those lines in *The Secret Agent*, a novel she will never finish now . . .' Because our thoughts immediately revert to ourselves and our own salvation as soon as we realise we might be in danger, then even the still warm dead are relegated to the background; after all, we can't do anything for them now, nothing for poor Janet with her wasted, truncated time, but, on the other hand, there's Tom to worry about.

'It must have been afterwards,' he said hastily, naïvely. 'I can assure you that she was alive when I left. It must have been the man who arrived immediately after that.'

'What man?' asked Morse.

Tom told him what he had seen from the shadows on the corner of Beaumont Street. He described the man and regretted not having had the time to fix his face in his memory, but only to have had that one glimpse, which became still vaguer the harder he tried to fix it. Southworth very prudently tried to stop him and said to Morse:

'I don't know if my student should be speaking to you without a lawyer present. I understand that, at this point, and given the circumstances, suspicion may fall on him. Is that right?'

But the policeman took no notice. His job was to investigate and to ask questions, and so he responded briefly:

'As long as no one has been arrested, suspicion can fall on anyone. Even on you, Mr Southworth, unless you have a verifiable alibi. One never knows who knows who.' Southworth looked daggers at Morse, pressing his lips together as if preparing to open them again, but then stopped or perhaps decided it was unnecessary; his expression could not have put it more clearly: 'That remark is an impertinence and entirely uncalled for.'

'Please go on, Mr Nevinson. This is all very useful.'

The innocent suspect cannot wait for the eye to stop looking at him, to dispel any doubts, and he collaborates almost too enthusiastically, too eagerly, and will say anything he thinks might shift the spotlight away from him, not realising that spotlights are as mobile as a torch, and come and go. And so Tom kept talking and even mentioned Hugh, the little he had found out over the years and what Janet had confided to him that night. He was Someone, she said. She had given him an ultimatum, to Hugh, that is. She could ruin his life, that's how Janet had put it. And she had used the word 'vengeance': vengeance was hard work and stressful too, and she wasn't sure she could be bothered. But she would do what was necessary in order to harm him. It was a question of fairness. Tomás was surprised to hear himself use that word, which was his own choice, although it in no way contradicted the young woman's intentions; he still found it hard to believe she was no longer alive, that she could no longer breathe or speak as he could. 'She's dead,' he thought, 'and I should no longer feel desire for her, and yet my last memory, my last vision of her, is that of her parted thighs and her cunt that I wanted to enter again. Perhaps once time has passed over her corpse, I'll feel the respect one owes to the dead, and even more so to those who died violently and very young, and I will cancel out the image that did not seem inappropriate yesterday, but is beginning to seem so today. I don't know why, but that's my feeling, as if continuing to feel desire were a kind of profanation, as if it were at odds with the pity or compassion one usually feels. In our minds, we don't really differentiate between the living and the dead, and from now on, Janet, poor Janet, will be just that, nothing but evocation and thought.'

Morse gave a friendly, ironic smile:

'Leave it to me to decide what to do next. These are all conjectures, but very useful. We will probably have to question you again, but tell me three things . . . Do you smoke?'

'Yes.'

'May I see what brand you smoke, if you have them on you, of course.'

Tomás took out his oblong metal Marcovitch cigarette case: on the left, vertical black and white lines, on the right, a small vignette of a man in a black top hat lighting a cigarette, his grey-gloved hands cupping the flame, and, snug around his neck, a white scarf; his convex nose was as sharp as the blade of a tomahawk; his thin, intensely red lips seemed about to smile; and he had very thick eyebrows and rather murky, painted eyes, more mask than face, a little sinister really. Tall flames rose up behind him, perhaps the flames of hell. He held the case out to Morse:

'Why do you want to see it?'

The policeman looked at it for a moment, then handed it back.

'What a shame,' he said. 'If you didn't smoke that brand, we'd have to find someone else who did. It's not that common. But I see that you do. And tell me, how did you get that scratch on your chin?' And he pointed to the precise spot on his own chin (more or less where Wheeler's scar was), to show Tomás what he meant.

Morse was very observant. Tomás had completely forgotten about the scratch until he saw it that morning in the mirror, and, by then, it had already begun to form a slight scab, and he had carefully shaved around it.

'This?' He touched it. 'Oh, Janet did that accidentally. She was

82

lying on the bed, and, without looking, she raised her hand to stroke my cheek, miscalculated and scratched me. As you may have noticed, she had very long nails. I hope you're not thinking anything untoward.'

'I'm thinking all kinds of things,' said Morse. 'It may not always seem so at times, but that's partly what my colleagues and I are paid for. So I think everything, insofar as I can. Lastly, what exactly was your relationship with Janet Jefferys?'

Tom shot an interrogative glance at Southworth. Despite the latter's youth, he was still his tutor, or one of them. Southworth nodded more with his lips – which he pressed together – than with his chin, as if giving him his approval or confirming that he was indeed being asked about the degree of physical intimacy between him and Janet.

'We had sex occasionally, if that's what you want to know. Not very often. She had her Hugh in London, and I have my girlfriend in Madrid. The weeks are very long, and the terms even longer.'

'And last night?'

'Yes, last night too.'

'Every time you met?'

'Yes, more or less, with the occasional exception. But, as I said, not very often. I didn't matter to her, and she didn't matter to me. She lived for that man Hugh. We just provided each other with a reciprocal, superficial way of passing the time. You'll have to look elsewhere.'

Morse ignored that last piece of advice.

'How long have you been a "reciprocal way of passing the time"?'

'Well, it started in my first year here.'

Morse raised his eyebrows in genuine surprise, and said:

'Something that happens repeatedly over a period of several years is an odd form of superficiality.'

Then Southworth decided to help his student out, feeling that there was more in that last remark than there actually was, a degree of distrust and incredulity, an insinuation, although, in fact, the policeman's words merely reflected his lack of familiarity with the customs of those ten or fifteen years his junior, or, at most, were an abstract expression of disapproval of sexual mores that he assumed to be loveless, indelicate and inconsequential.

'One can spend one's whole life going to bed with someone and never get beyond the superficial, wouldn't you agree? I'm sure many a marriage must follow this to the letter.' Mr Southworth was such a very precise man that he found it impossible, under any circumstances, to keep silent and not point out the finer details of a topic. He was greatly feared in the erudite seminars held in the Sub-faculty of Spanish.

Morse shrugged.

'I don't know,' he said. 'I'm not married, but I find that hard to believe.' This sounded faintly nostalgic, as if he were remembering a particular person whom he might have married. 'I wouldn't . . .'

He was about to say more, but did not go on. He opened his hand and looked at his palm, and he did this twice, perhaps feeling the lack of the wedding ring he wasn't wearing; it was a gesture that seemed to be saying: 'But what do you care about that? What does my opinion matter? Let's drop the subject.' He thanked them both, asked Tom not to leave town without first receiving authorisation, and warned him that he would probably be asked to give a signed statement in the next few days, at the police station, setting down exactly what he had just told Morse. His collaboration might also be needed for an artist to create an identikit picture based on his description of the man who had arrived at Miss Jefferys' door just after he had left.

'Quite a character, that Morse fellow,' Tomás said to Southworth when they could hear Morse's footsteps on the stairs.

But Southworth did not seem relieved, quite the opposite. He told Tom to sit down again and said very seriously:

'I'm not sure you realise how bad things look for you. I'm sure they won't be able to come up with any reason why you'd want to kill the girl, but they don't always need to find a motive and, for the moment, you'll be the prime suspect unless they can locate that other man and establish that he did go to Janet's flat and not to someone else's, because you have no idea where he might have gone. She couldn't be pregnant by you, could she? They'll perform an autopsy and if she is, they'll find out.' Southworth spoke very rapidly, albeit in a perfectly calm voice, which was precisely what betrayed his feelings of alarm.

'No, she was on the pill. And if for some reason it didn't work, it's far more likely that she'd be pregnant by that man Hugh. But please don't ask me to worry about that now, to worry about myself, I mean. What matters is that someone killed Janet, I still can't get over the horror of it. I was with her last night, Mr Southworth. I had sex with her, and that might be why she was killed.' Tomás Nevinson clasped his head in despair. This hadn't occurred to him until that moment, until he said it.

'Yes, I realise that, Tom. I understand,' said Southworth protectively. 'But you're wrong. You *are* the one you should be worrying about. I can understand your horror, your grief, your shock, but she's no longer important to you. To the living, that is. The person in danger now is you. Talk to a lawyer who can advise you, defend you. Defend you from what might happen next. The situation is so urgent, though, that it's probably too late to consult a lawyer anyway. You shouldn't have told that man Morse so much. So openly and unreservedly. He used his good manners to excellent effect, and took full advantage of your inexperience. I tried to warn you.'

'I've got nothing to hide.'

'Don't be so naïve, Tom. You can never know just how much you have to hide. What you deem to be true is irrelevant, as is what happened, unless it's corroborated by someone else. The important thing is what other people understand from what you tell them, or what they decide to understand. As well as the use they make of it, especially if they want to distort it and turn it in their favour. How did they know about your visit last night? Did someone see you go in?'

'Yes, I passed a neighbour when I arrived, not for the first time either. I seem to remember Janet introducing her to me on the stairs once, ages ago now, and they stopped to chat. She might have remembered my name, but I don't, of course, remember hers. Although I doubt if my surname was mentioned.'

'It doesn't matter. They'll have asked at Waterfield's and asked the young woman's friends too. You don't know how much she might have talked about you, nor in what terms or with whom. You may have been more important to her than you think. You might have been more than just a way of passing the time or she may have been hoping that you might, one day, step up and save her from Hugh.' He fell silent for a moment, then added, in French, something that sounded like a quotation: *'Elle avait eu, comme une autre, son histoire d'amour*... We don't always know about other people's love stories, not even when we're the object, the goal, the aim. Find yourself a lawyer quickly. You really have no idea.'

'But where do I get one, Mr Southworth? They're expensive, and I wouldn't want to ask my family for help. I wouldn't want to frighten them or involve them in any expense unless it's absolutely necessary.

After all, this may come to nothing. I mean, as far as I'm concerned. They may find that man and find evidence against him.'

Mr Southworth always wore his black gown for the tutorials in his rooms and at the classes held in the Taylorian. The skirts of the gown fell about him in a cascade, and he wore it with distinction, allowing the folds to drape about him in waves; he resembled a Singer Sargent portrait. He placed the fingertips of both hands together, thus increasing his clerical air, as if he were about to say a prayer right there and then, in that book-lined room full of some most ungodly books. He wasn't yet thirty, but he already had a few grey hairs, which gave him a greater air of dignity and respectability than corresponded to his youth. It was as if he couldn't wait to leave youth behind him.

'Hmm. Hmm,' he murmured pensively, almost theatrically. He crossed and uncrossed his legs a couple of times, showing considerable artistic flair in his management of the black gown enfolding him. 'Hmm. Speak to Peter.' Despite the difference in age and rank, Southworth called Wheeler by his first name. 'Speak to Professor Wheeler,' he said, correcting himself. He was, after all, addressing a student, however brilliant and however much admired by his teachers. 'He'll know someone, he'll know what to do. He can advise you better than I can. Better than your family and your godfather Starkie, better than anyone. He has endless contacts, and there'll be very few areas in which he hasn't. Tell him what has happened, although he'll almost certainly have heard about it already. By now,' he looked at his watch without registering what time it was, 'he'll know everything, possibly more than you do.'

'Really?' asked Tomás Nevinson in surprise. 'How can he know? How can he know more than I do, given that I was there?'

'Well, he won't know precisely what you got up to last night with the young woman, and he wouldn't be interested anyway. Unless you'd killed her, of course, which I don't believe and nor would he. It's likely, for example, that he'll have found out the identity of her long-term lover, Hugh. And about Morse's visit; he may even have known it would take place. And about what kind of man he is, whether he's helpful or not.' He shifted his glasses to halfway down his nose in order to peer at Tom over the top of the lenses with what Tom thought was a strange mixture of sarcasm and gravity. 'Very little of what happens in this town escapes Peter. And certainly not a murder.'

Wheeler, it turned out, was so well informed that he didn't even deem it necessary to meet Tom face to face. 'I was expecting your call,' he said over the phone, without a hint of alarm or drama. 'What's this mess you've got yourself into,' he added, more as a statement than a question, although Tomás took it as such and launched into a long explanation, a defect of youth. Wheeler pulled him up short: 'I know all that, and I don't have much time.' Tomás thought he must be offended or disappointed, or still vexed by his negative response a week or so earlier. Since then, he had only attended one of Wheeler's classes, and when they had passed in the corridors of the Taylorian, they had greeted each other perfectly normally, but hadn't stopped to talk, not that there was anything strange about that either. And yet the Professor was one of those men so convinced of the rightness of whatever he thinks or proposes that he cannot understand when someone resists or fails to see his ideas or proposals in the same clear light. He was probably more disconcerted than wounded. 'Now, listen, and pay attention. I'm afraid you've got yourself into a far more serious situation than you realise. There are certain factors of which you know nothing and that will make it very hard for you to extricate yourself; things really don't look good. An acquaintance of mine from London, Mr Tupra, is going to help you and see what he can do,' and he spelled the man's distinctly un-English surname. 'He'll

89

be in Oxford tomorrow. He'll meet you in Blackwell's at half past ten, on the top floor, in the second-hand section. Talk to him and listen, he'll find some way out of all this. It's your decision as to what you do, but I would advise taking serious note of what he says. He's a very resourceful fellow. He won't offer you any unfounded optimism or false hopes. But he'll give you some sound advice.' 'And how will we recognise each other?' asked Tomás. 'Ah yes. Pick up something by Eliot. He'll do the same.' 'T.S. Eliot or George Eliot?' 'The poet, Tomás, the poet, your namesake,' Wheeler replied with a touch of exasperation in his voice. '*Four Quartets*, *The Waste Land*, *Prufrock*, whatever you fancy.' 'Wouldn't it be better if you introduced us, Professor? So that you can hear what he has to say to me?' 'I'm not needed there at all, and I want nothing to do with it. This will be entirely between you and him. Between you and him,' he repeated. 'And what he tells you will be perfectly sensible, even if you don't like his advice. Although, in your circumstances, I don't know that you're going to like anyone's advice.' Wheeler paused. He had spoken very quickly, like someone eager to finish a conversation, an assignment. Now, though, he took a few seconds to make a minor digression: 'It would be far worse to be arrested on a charge of homicide, wouldn't it? You never know how a trial might end, however innocent you are or however well things seem to be going. The truth doesn't count, because that has to be decided upon, established by someone who can never know what the truth is, namely a judge. It's not a matter that should be placed in the hands of someone who is simply flailing about in the dark or tossing a coin and who can only guess or intuit the truth. When you think about it, it's absurd that anyone should be judged. The prestige and longevity of the custom, and the fact that it's spread throughout the world with greater and lesser degrees of success, and even in places where there's absolutely no guarantee of impartiality . . . that it exists, in short, even as farce . . .' He broke off and began the sentence again: 'That no one seems to realise the impossibility, the senselessness, of that age-old, universal task is something I've always found incomprehensible. I wouldn't recognise the authority of any court. If I could avoid it, I would never submit myself to a trial of any kind. Anything but that. Bear that in mind, Tomás. Think about it. You can be sent to prison on a mere whim. Simply because they don't like you.' In other circumstances, Tom would have asked him what he proposed to replace the courts with, and if no one was qualified to decide what was true and what was false, apart from the interested parties, who, precisely because they were the interested parties, could not be believed or have their views taken into account, then surely we would be left with a real paradox: the only people who knew what had happened, the accused, would be the least trustworthy, and yet would be authorised to lie and invent. He also wanted to ask if he believed him to be innocent of Janet Jefferys' death by strangulation. Given what he had said and given his clear desire to help, he presumably did, but Tom would have liked to hear him say so, just for his own peace of mind. None of this was possible, though, because Wheeler immediately hung up, without even wishing him luck or saying goodbye.

Tomás Nevinson arrived at Blackwell's at a quarter past ten, went straight up to the top floor and prepared to wait. There weren't many other customers, since most undergraduates and dons would be at lectures. He found the poetry section and saw that there were plenty of second-hand copies of Eliot, but he decided to wait until half past before actually choosing a book and starting to leaf through it. He wandered around the spacious area, browsed a few other shelves and looked about him. He had no idea what Mr Tupra looked like, nor how old he was. In the history section, he noticed a fat man who kept taking books off the shelf, holding the spine at arm's length as if he were very long-sighted, then putting them back without opening any of them, and he did this with extraordinary rapidity, as if he were checking they were in the right order, whatever that was, chronological or alphabetical by author. He saw a lecturer from Somerville College whom he knew by sight, as did the whole town, a woman as distinguished as she was curvaceous, with a full, sensual mouth that piqued the male imagination, and the kind of attractive figure not commonly found among women in her profession; all her heterosexual colleagues were mad for her, not that heterosexuals were necessarily the overwhelming majority in that university; she was looking at books on botany, which was perhaps her subject. He saw a skinny near-adolescent with a large nose, who was wearing a shabby raincoat that was too long for him, and whom he had seen before in other second-hand bookshops – Thornton's, Titles, Sanders, Swift's and even Waterfield's, where Janet used to work – searching the scant shelves of fantastic literature or books on the supernatural, about which he was clearly as enthusiastic as he was about his dog, his constant companion, polite, silent and meek. He saw, too, a man in his twenties, who arrived at exactly half past ten, wearing a pinstripe suit with a double-breasted jacket, a red silk tie on a pale blue shirt with a white collar, and, over his arm, a brand-new raincoat; he looked like a minor functionary at an embassy or a ministry, someone who has recently been promoted and wishes to appear elegant, but instead looks rather absurd, precisely because he's trying so hard to look elegant, when he lacks the necessary experience and poise, and is, besides, too young and too lacking in aplomb to have acquired either experience or poise, and would, at best, have to wait a few more years before he did. The pinstripe was too wide, the very loud variety one finds only in England, shouting from the rooftops his impatience to rise up the social ladder. None of those present – certainly not the lecturer from Somerville or the near-adolescent and his dog – looked as if they had been sent by Wheeler, nor as if they could help him in his hour of need; the fat man was too fat and too distracted, and the functionary too young and carnivalesque, to be considered resourceful types.

Finally, at two minutes after half past ten, Tom went over to the poetry section, picked up a slender volume entitled *Little Gidding*, opened it and immediately began reading the occasional line while he waited, one or two or three or four, even though he was in no mood to really take it in:

'And what the dead had no speech for, when living, they can tell you, being dead,' he read, and, not really understanding this, moved on:

'Ash on an old man's sleeve . . . Dust in the air suspended marks the place where a story ended.' Then he skipped a couple of pages:

'For last year's words belong to last year's language and next year's words await another voice.' He glanced to either side of him, but there was no one near; he did glimpse out of the corner of his eye the shapes of two new customers, but preferred not to look up and observe them openly.

'And the laceration of laughter at what ceases to amuse.' No, no one came. But it was still not too late.

'. . . indifference which resembles the others as death resembles life, being between two lives . . .' And there he paused to wonder: 'Does death resemble life? Yes, Janet dead will resemble Janet when alive and will still be recognisable, but for how many more hours? Time continues to pass for corpses, and takes its toll on them far more quickly too, and they can tell you nothing, whereas the night before last, Janet told me what might save me today. But who did they ask to identify her? Because they didn't make me go and see her.'

'What we call the beginning is often the end,' said another of those lines; he didn't want to read on, he found it all rather glib, not realising that it probably wasn't glib in 1942, when it was first published, and in time of war.

'And any action is a step to the block, to the fire, down the sea's throat or to an illegible stone.' He stopped again to check that his bilingualism wasn't leading him astray and also because of a sudden sense of foreboding: 'block' must be what in Spanish is called '*tajo*', that is, the block or piece of wood on which the condemned meekly place their head so that the executioner can chop it off; and perhaps that – the block, the fire, the sea's throat, the illegible or now indecipherable text – was what awaited him if that Mr Tupra didn't turn up and get him out of this mess. 'Things look really bad for you,' Mr Southworth had warned him, 'you're the one in danger now.' And still they came, the bad omens from that long poem of which he was reading only a few scattered ashes:

'We die with the dying: see, they depart, and we go with them. We are born with the dead: see, they return, and bring us with them.' And infected by those words written in 1942 or before, Tomás thought confusedly: 'It's true that we do go with them, at least initially. We want to accompany them, to follow them into their dimension and along their path, which is already the past; we feel they are abandoning us, that they have set off on another adventure, and we are the ones left alone to continue along the dark path that is no longer of any interest to them and which they have deserted; and since we cannot follow or do not dare, we are reborn as toddlers taking a few hesitant steps, we are born again each time we survive someone close to us, each time someone falls and tugs at us to follow, but without succeeding in dragging us into the sea's throat that has swallowed him or her. And I couldn't have been any closer than I was

94

the night before last, when I was inside a living being who is now dead, now irreversibly a ghost and a gradually fading memory for the rest of my short or long days, and to think I even wanted to go back inside her, imposing my will and my instinct. Perhaps that would have prevented her murder, and the man coming up the stairs wouldn't have found her alone.'

'History is a pattern of timeless moments,' he read three lines further on. There were only a few lines left to the end, he had made only a pretence of reading, merely skimming the pages, skipping over far more than he actually read, but then that is what happens when you leaf through a book.

'Quick now, here, now, always . . .'

That was one of the last lines, and then he emerged from his reverie, looked up and discovered that there was not one, but two men, each of them leafing through a book by Eliot: the pinstriped man was holding *To Criticize the Critic*; another, whose arrival he hadn't even noticed, was reading *Ash Wednesday*. Not wanting to turn and look at this new arrival directly, he moved away slightly in order to observe him more discreetly, albeit partially: he was a burly individual, wide and tall, much taller than either him or the vain young man, and wearing a duffel coat and, on his head, a beret identical to that worn by Field Marshal Montgomery, who was still alive at the time, and, like Montgomery, he wore it pulled slightly down on one side, although minus the military badges. He must have been an imitator or a fan to want to copy Montgomery's uniform so exactly. He also sported a fairish moustache similar to that of the war hero, but there the resemblance ended: Montgomery of Alamein, as he was called when he was made a viscount, was a gaunt, bony man with a lined face, while this fellow was a veritable tower, given his height and girth and solidity, and his plump, firm, rosy cheeks. He hadn't had the good manners to remove his beret despite being indoors and he seemed improbably absorbed in that other poem, *Ash Wednesday* ('Ash on an old man's sleeve,' that line had stayed with Tom, as had various others). He was standing to Tom's right, and the arrogant functionary to Tom's left (the latter might also have been a rather inept City gent trying to out-dapper other veteran City types), and they didn't appear to be together, and Tomás wondered which one could be Mr Tupra, because it would be most unfortunate if a third bibliophile should have chosen that precise moment to read some Eliot. He decided to wait until one of the two spoke, since the other man would have no need to, and Tom was the only one who was unmistakably an undergraduate. However, half a minute passed without either of them speaking or making any sign at all. Ever more convinced that what has happened is unimportant, only what one decides or infers to have happened, ever more aware of the abyss he was walking towards ('Any action is a step to the block, to the fire') and that this Mr Tupra was, right now, all he had to hold on to, he lost patience and chose to turn towards the military-looking gentleman; after all, the letters in the names of the most famous secret services, MI5 and MI6, did stand for 'Military Intelligence'. He closed his book and, in a whisper, shyly asked the massive Montgomery lookalike:

'Mr Tupra, I presume?'

With his left hand, the tower indicated the other man, the eternal aspirant to an elegance he would never achieve, and said coldly:

'He's there beside you, Nevinson, and has been for some time.'

Tomás may have been very young, but he rather resented that man omitting the 'Mr' before his surname, given that it was the first time they had spoken, so a little respect would not have been out of place. He was even less pleased when he held out his hand to greet Mr Tupra and the latter made a contemptuous gesture as if he were ordering him to wait or telling him off, saying: 'Not now, boy, can't you see I'm busy with something else?' He didn't even turn to face him, and the respective reactions of those two strangers only increased Tom's sense of dependency on them: they were treating him like a mere nuisance, like someone who has come looking for a job or to ask a big favour; that's how you address subalterns, pupils or apprentices, by their surname. Tupra, who hadn't even deigned to look at him and had left him with his hand in mid-air, was swaying gently back and forth on his heels, his hands behind his back, while he contemplated the lecturer from Somerville, who was still rummaging through the shelves, not in the botany section now, but among the art books: she was crouching down to inspect the lower shelves, and since skirts were much shorter than now, she revealed a large part of her voluptuous thighs encased in glittery tights, and this was what Tupra was so brazenly admiring, more like a foreigner – a Spaniard for example – than an Englishman. When Tom noticed this, he looked at the woman too, infected by Tupra's lascivious gaze, and it seemed to him that the lecturer was not only perfectly aware of this, but was joining in the game, picking up huge, unmanageable volumes that made her skirt ride up still higher when she rested them on her sturdy thighs; and she kept shooting rapid sideways glances at that shamelessly gawping man. This was rather surprising, for as far as Tomás knew, the unusually curvaceous teacher treated her legion of suitors with great contempt, and was famously unapproachable; and yet there she was happily submitting (submitting at a distance, that is; or perhaps hypothetically) to the salacious eyes of this vulgar individual who was, besides, much shorter than her.

Tomás looked at him while Tupra was looking at her. Tupra's bulbous cranium was mitigated by a thick, curly head of hair, so curly that, at the temples, the curls were almost ringlets. His eyes were either blue or grey and adorned by overly long, thick lashes, which were feminine to the point of seeming false or painted. His pale eyes had a mocking quality, even if this were not his intention, for they were also rather warm or should I say appreciative, eyes that were never indifferent to what was there before them and which made anyone on whom they fell feel deserving of curiosity, as if they had a history worthy of being unearthed. Tomás Nevinson thought that anyone capable of such a gaze must already have it made; anyone who can focus so clearly and at the right height, namely, a man's height; anyone who entraps or captures or, rather, absorbs the image before him, will probably prove irresistible to many women, regardless of class, profession, experience, beauty, age or degree of vanity. Even though this acquaintance of Wheeler's was not exactly handsome and possibly used his boldness as his main asset, Tom had to admit that the overall image was, nevertheless, attractive, and imposed itself on certain features that might otherwise prove displeasing or even repellent to the objective eye: his rather coarse nose which looked as if it had once been broken by a blow or by several more since, the nose of someone who has been involved in fights since he was a child and has perhaps even practised boxing or handed out a few beatings and occasionally been on the receiving end himself; his disturbingly lustrous skin, which was the lovely golden colour of beer, a rare sight in England and suggestive of origins in southern Europe; his eyebrows like black smudges and with a tendency to grow together, although he probably plucked them now and then; and especially his overly soft and fleshy mouth, as lacking in consistency as it was over-endowed in breadth – Slavic lips which, when kissed, would give and spread like pliable, well-kneaded plasticine, or at least that's how they would feel, with a touch like a sucker, a touch of always renewed and inextinguishable moistness. But nothing is so short-lived as the objective eye, and once it's gone, nothing seems repellent, and you don't even notice what, at first glance, seemed so displeasing. Besides, there would be no shortage of women whom that mouth would immediately please and inflame, for there are men who arouse primitive impulses and use this to seduce women effortlessly, without even having to try or work hard at it, as if all they had to do was exude a sexuality whose direct and elemental nature oozes insalubrity. Mr Tupra was young in years, but his insolent, resolute attitude indicated that he was, in fact, ageless or had spent centuries installed in one unchanging age, one of those individuals who must have had to grow up very early or who, having been born grown up, instantly understands the way of the world, or that darkly sinister part of the world he happened to be born into, and decided to skip childhood, considering it a waste of time and an education in weakness. He was not much older than Tomás, and yet it was as if he were his senior by a whole lifetime or two.

'So,' thought Tom, 'he's the kind of man capable of postponing or abandoning his tasks to spend a while ogling someone picked up by his antennae, or simply for the pleasure of looking.' He waited patiently – or was it submissively – for Tupra to conclude his visual flirtation, but that only happened when the gorgeous lecturer from Somerville (Tom felt that she seemed to grow more gorgeous by the minute; some people's lust can be transmitted like a disease) finally stood up, gracefully smoothed her skirt (when she was standing her skirt came to just above her knee, so it had ridden up an awful lot when she was crouching down, too much to have been purely accidental) and, clutching a book, began going down the stairs, because the cash tills were all on the ground floor. Tupra swiftly plucked from the poetry section the same slender volume Tomás had been leafing through, *Little Gidding*, and, still without greeting him or shaking his hand or even looking at him, he beckoned to him and Montgomery to follow, as if they were part of an entourage. 'It's just not going to happen,' Tom thought. 'This guy is going to do his own thing, and for who knows how long, and my presence and my problem won't affect or trouble him at all; he's going to buy that book just so that he reaches the till at the same time she does and then he'll doubtless chat her up; let's just hope they make a date for later on and he doesn't leave me stranded, otherwise my problem will remain unresolved for yet another day, and, with each hour that passes, things will only get worse for me, and that policeman Morse, with his honest, sympathetic eyes, will come and arrest me.' The Montgomery lookalike placed one iron hand on his shoulder and propelled him gently towards the stairs.

'Come on, Nevinson, we're off. Get moving.'

Again that use of his surname. The order issued by the intermediary. Again he felt diminished and did as he was told, what else could he do, since he had no one else, no one else to turn to. Once they reached the queue at the till, he saw Tupra place himself immediately behind the lecturer, without keeping the usual polite distance. He was standing so close to her that she must have felt his breath on the back of her neck, or even the edge of his jacket touching the seat of her skirt, for she, like him, was carrying her coat over her arm. Far from taking a step forward and thus avoiding such close proximity, the lecturer from Somerville remained where she was, waiting for the customers ahead of her to finish their business. Tom was astonished by the man's skill, for not only did Tupra not provoke the rejection or mistrust of his chosen prey, she even subtly and wordlessly encouraged him; presumably those grey or blue eyes gave off such warm, all-enveloping signals that they did not, at first, offend or even intimidate, but rather invited the woman to lower her shield and take off her helmet, the more easily to be captivated by his gaze. Then Tupra made some remark about the book she was about to buy (*Tomb Sculpture* by Erwin Panofsky, Tomás read on the cover of that hefty tome, and he wondered what on earth that man could possibly have to say about it, a man who had doubtless been educated in billiard halls, steamy, crowded basements, gambling dens, bowling alleys, dog tracks and other even worse places in unimaginable parts of town; the book's subtitle was *Its Changing Aspects from Ancient Egypt to Bernini*). Then he must have made a joke, because she laughed with rather less restraint than one might expect in such an erudite person (she really was very sensual, either that or the contagion was growing, the all-absorbing eyes infecting the eyes transfixed by that undisguised absorption). Tom could hear very little, for Tupra was addressing the woman in confidential tones, but he did hear them introducing themselves: 'Ted Reresby, at your service,' he said. 'Carolyn Beckwith,' she said. 'Reresby?' Tomás jumped mentally, then remembered that the tower had told him that this was, indeed,

Mr Tupra. He deduced, therefore, that Tupra preferred not always to give his name, if, that is, the name mentioned by Wheeler was the real one. Perhaps he didn't want to frighten off a possible cracker of a conquest with such a scandalously foreign surname, something that still provoked suspicion in England or condescension in certain snobbish circles. His accent and his diction, though, seemed to Tom irreproachable, with just a slight Oxbridge edge to it, which led him to suspect one of two things: Tupra had either passed through Oxford University, despite his pretentious garb, or else he, too, was an artist when it came to mimicry, a genius at adopting whatever accent he fancied.

He and the bulky General Montgomery waited behind them like two henchmen, as if they were also part of the queue, and Tomás could not resist trying to dispel his own disquiet, because at least Montgomery had addressed a few sullen words to him and thus acknowledged his existence, unlike the man who appeared to be his boss.

'Did he say his name was Reresby?' he asked in a quiet voice. 'I thought it was Tupra?'

The burly viscount still had his black beret firmly on his head and his duffel coat fastened, he needed only to pull up his hood to complete the effect. His moustache was a very skilful copy of his hero's moustache, it was just a shame that physically he was the exact opposite of the famous Spartan General, as Montgomery was also known. He shot Tom a scornful glance.

'Mr Tupra calls himself whatever he pleases depending on the occasion, and as best suits us,' he answered abruptly. 'It's not your turn to ask questions yet, Nevinson.' He had not abandoned his stern stance, and it was odd that he should treat someone so much younger than him like that, for this rival of the victor of El Alamein was thirty-five if he was a day. He treated Tomás like a schoolboy or like someone of an inferior rank; he was clearly a military man, dressed in semi-civvies. Tom increasingly had the impression that the fellow felt he was doing him a favour simply by staying by his side and allowing him to gaze on Tupra and the lecturer.

The imposing Ms Beckwith paid and Tupra followed, and she hung back so that they could emerge together into the light and breadth of Broad Street. Tupra, or Reresby, continued not to look at Tom or speak to him, still busy as he was with playing the gallant. Tom and Montgomery followed them like servants of old, keeping a respectful distance while the two flirts exchanged telephone numbers and cards, brief laughter and jokes, then said goodbye, presumably, Tom thought, until a few hours later. Then Tupra tossed his raincoat over his shoulders with an elegant, almost cocksure gesture, and strode off towards St Giles' without even turning round to urge them to follow him, his coat flapping behind him like a cloak in the wind. When he reached the pub, The Eagle and Child, he walked straight in, and his two followers hastened to do likewise, the student guided by the field marshal, who was steering him along with his great hand on his shoulder, a very firm hand that did not, however, go so far as to actually propel him onwards.

Once they were all seated at a table next to the large window and with three glasses of beer before them, Tupra finally addressed Tom, clearly feeling that no formal introductions were necessary. He obviously thought that, since they both knew who was who, why waste time on superfluities. Tomás Nevinson was, by then, feeling utterly cowed and diminished, a bundle of nerves or, rather, a bundle of fears; ever since he'd woken that morning, he had gone over and over in his stubborn imagination the worst things that could possibly happen to him, from his imminent arrest to his condemnation with no right of appeal, to life imprisonment in an English jail (where conditions were legendarily harsh), his whole life ruined almost before it had begun. Tupra's disdainful attitude and the unexpected presence of his bluff companion had only contributed to further intimidating and unnerving him. The tiny, minimal sense of calm that Wheeler had instilled in him over the phone had completely vanished. He clung to and superstitiously repeated Wheeler's more hopeful phrases ('He'll help you out', 'He'll find some way out of all this', 'I would advise taking serious note of what he says', 'He's a very resourceful fellow'), and the less welcome these two strangers made him feel, the more convinced he became that his fate depended on them, and the more inclined he felt, in his tormented inner self, to listen to and accept their instructions. They had succeeded in undermining his hopes with their postponements and indifference, and he had ended up clinging to them as if they were the last people on Earth.

Tupra had certainly taken his time, but he did finally look up and fix his gaze on Tom, meanwhile unhurriedly sipping his beer. Then, putting the glass down on the table, he intensified his scrutiny and regarded Tom with the same flattering attentiveness he bestowed on whatever happened to be there before his eyes; Tom immediately felt protected and, therefore, well disposed towards this person who, up until then, hadn't even acknowledged his existence, not even as an obstacle. With those lines from *Little Gidding* still in his head, Tom thought: 'For him, I was like a dead man who has departed, an outcast of the universe. Now perhaps I'm like a dead man who returns, bringing the universe with him.'

'Things look pretty bleak, Nevinson,' Tupra said, coming straight to the point; his voice was quite a lot deeper than it had been when he was chatting to the lecturer, perhaps he had been putting on that other voice, or perhaps he was doing so now. 'You've been most unlucky. Professor Wheeler told me what happened. I've also seen the report from that honest policeman, Morse. You made quite a good impression on him, but that won't be of much help. It certainly won't be enough. Anyway, I'm familiar with your version of events, so there's no need for you to repeat it. I'm going to show you a few portraits now to see if you recognise anyone. Blakeston.' He held out one hand to the general, who was still wearing his heroic beret even in the pub, perhaps he never took it off, perhaps he never washed his hair or perhaps he had no hair, it was impossible to tell. So the man's name was Blakeston, unless he assumed a different name depending on the situation or the context. He opened the slim, handleless bag he had been holding under one arm, the kind a female student might use; he produced an envelope and passed it to Tupra, who took out eight A5 photos. He placed them on the table in two rows, like a card player revealing his hand at poker. 'Take your time and study them carefully. See if one of them is the man you saw arriving at Janet Jefferys' apartment after you left. Or so you say. It may be, of course, that no such man exists.'

Tomás was not amused by this implied distrust, but then again, why should anyone believe him? Why should he be believed by a judge or jury who, as Wheeler had pointed out, would have no idea what really happened? He said nothing and studied the faces. They all looked rather distinguished or respectable, well-to-do. They certainly didn't resemble criminals, rough and tough and sinister, they were all well dressed and neatly coiffed. And the photos weren't mugshots taken in a police station. They were, to use Tupra's word, like portraits. Not studio portraits, but gleaned perhaps from newspapers. Some were wearing the obligatory pinstripe suit, de rigueur among the rich and powerful in England. Tom soon whittled them down to two; he'd never seen the other six before.

'It could have been one of them,' he said, pointing to the two men whose features most closely resembled those he had seen at a distance: a nose with slightly flared nostrils; one of the men had small, rather drowsy eyes, while the other man had large, somewhat vehement eyes, or perhaps he had merely been dazzled by the flash; both had a slightly cleft chin, although the cleft was longer in one than in the other (like the actor Christopher Lee, who, at the time, was known for playing Sherlock Holmes and Dracula), but, of course, in the photo, that dimple could be a shadow, a trick of the light; and dark hair, although not as wavy as he remembered seeing in the light from the street lamp, but that image, which he had never made any real effort to retain, was already growing blurred. It's infuriating that the harder you try to remember certain features and summon them

106

up, the faster they tend to fade, grow dim and slip away. The same thing happens with the faces of our lost loved ones too, those you saw on a daily basis when they were alive; it happens with those who are merely absent, their faces tending to freeze in one expression or look; it happened to Tomás with Berta's face whenever they were apart, her face appearing in his mind again and again, quite still, as if she were a painting, not someone full of breath and movement. 'Yes, I'd say it was him,' he added, choosing the one with the vehement eyes and the smaller chin. 'Who is he? What's his name?' And he hoped that, whoever he was, his name was Hugh.

Tupra picked up the six rejected photos and put them back in the envelope.

'Are you sure, Nevinson? Look again. Is that the bloke you saw?' That was the word he used, 'bloke', not exactly respectful. 'Because if he was, then I'm telling you, that's very bad news for you. You need to be absolutely certain.'

'Why bad news for me? What have I done wrong? I can't be one hundred per cent certain. Bear in mind that I saw him at night, for maybe a second. This is only a photo, and it may not even be a recent one. Perhaps if I saw the man in the flesh, then I'd be able to identify him more accurately, or maybe not: by his stature, his build, the way he walked. All I can say is that, if he's six foot two, then it's not him.'

'I think he's five foot seven at most.'

'Then it probably is him. I'm inclined to think it is. But why bad news for me?'

Marshal Blakeston smoothed his moustache as if he needed to make some mechanical, manual, nervous preparation before intervening in the presence of his boss and without being told to, and his intervention took the form of jabbing with his index finger at the photo, which would need to be thoroughly cleaned afterwards, of fingerprints and possibly sweat and the odd drop of beer.

'And you've never seen him before, Nevinson? I mean on the TV or in the press. Not that he appears very often, but from time to time. This man is Somebody.' And he said it like that, as if it were capitalised, just as Janet had on her last night, or, rather, last hour. She'd used exactly the same expression. 'Perhaps you recognise him because of that, rather than from seeing him standing in the doorway of your lover. Think carefully now.' The already rather antiquated word 'lover' grated on Tom, he had never thought of the assistant from Waterfield's in that grand manner. She was simply a young woman he occasionally had sex with, and with no intention of continuing that relationship or giving the matter any further thought or importance. That's how it was among people his age, among students and non-students. If anyone was a 'lover', it was that man Hugh in London: he and Janet had been together for years, and she was unhappy, fed up with nothing changing, and she'd just given him an ultimatum.

'No, I hardly ever watch television, and I just glance at the newspapers. I have no idea who he might be, and I certainly don't recognise him from the TV or the press, but from having seen him the night before last in St John Street, ringing the bell of an apartment that might or might not have been Janet's apartment, that's the truth. Nor could I swear it was him. He certainly looks like him, but what do you want me to say? I can't be certain. Who is he? What's his name?' he asked again, and now, having heard those doom-filled words 'bad news', he wasn't sure if he wanted him to be called Hugh or something else.

Tupra again took the floor, having first, with one imperative hand, brushed aside Blakeston's finger, although without actually touching it, rather like someone shooing away an insect. Blakeston had kept his finger pressed down on the photo rather too emphatically.

'He's an MP,' he said. Despite all the time he had spent in England, Tomás took a few seconds to remember that those initials stood for 'Member of Parliament'. 'His name's Hugh Saumarez-Hill, and it's highly likely that he was the man you saw, because, as we've known for some time, he's been in a sexual relationship with Janet Jefferys. It makes sense, then, that he should visit her.'

'You knew? Who? The two of you? Then it must have been him.'

'We two are more than two, indeed more than a hundred, I've really no idea how many.'

'Probably more than a thousand, Bertram,' said Viscount Blakeston proudly, again quickly smoothing his moustache. But Tupra took no notice of him and went on:

'And we, who are more than a hundred, know quite a lot. Not everything, but a lot. Some know some things and others other things, but when we put it all together, we know almost everything, at least about MPs and those in positions of responsibility. Given those facts, it would seem likely that it *was* him, but, then again, it can't be, because Mr Saumarez-Hill is beyond suspicion. Our diligent Inspector Morse has been talking to him, as well as to a few people who work with him. Morse went up to London yesterday. Mr Saumarez-Hill didn't deny his relationship with Janet Jefferys, that would have been foolish. The last time he saw her was last weekend, as usual, and he has no idea who could possibly have wanted to harm the young woman, whom he never visited here in Oxford, she always went to see him, they met in a small flat belonging to his family, and which he uses as an occasional office and for informal work meetings. Mr Saumarez-Hill says that he and his wife are estranged and have very few activities in common, not even on Saturdays and Sundays.

Politics takes up all his time, a handy excuse, but more or less credible, or one that you could at least pretend to believe.'

'I wouldn't believe him if I were his wife,' said Blakeston, and again Tupra continued speaking as if he hadn't heard him.

'So the bloke has no idea what Jefferys used to get up to during the rest of the week, or what friends she had. He'd never even heard of you, sir, but then that's understandable.' It was odd that he should suddenly address Tom respectfully as 'sir' when he had just referred to Saumarez-Hill dismissively as 'the bloke'; this seemed a deliberate ploy, not a slip of the tongue. 'According to Morse, he didn't seem at all curious about her life, but then some people are after one thing only and anything else is surplus to requirements. The fact is, though, that he spent the whole of Wednesday night in London and has witnesses to that effect. He couldn't have been in Oxford, unless, that is, his witnesses are mistaken or are lying. The former is unlikely, given that the night before last is still very recent; the latter is perfectly possible, it happens a lot everywhere. But since there's no proof of that, their testimonies are valid. That's why I said earlier that, if he was the bloke you saw, then that's bad news for you, because he's out of the picture and you are still the main suspect, pretty much the only one actually. Everything will point to you because there isn't anyone else, do you understand? Laying the blame on a thief or a maniac, well, the police only resort to that in the most perplexing of cases, or when a lot of time has passed and they're still completely in the dark. Right now, that would be premature.'

'Or inadmissible since there's already a fellow who had carnal relations with her around the time she was killed,' said Blakeston, having first adjusted his beret, which had been in no need of adjustment.

'As Blakeston put it so simply and graphically, Mr Saumarez-Hill is Somebody. He's influential and important and protected by his party. A Whig with a future, you see. The police aren't going to try to catch him out without some reason, without some clues. On the contrary, even if there were any such clues, they would still tend to hold back, to wait, and investigate other avenues, because of who he is. You on the other hand . . .' Tupra paused and looked Tomás up and down with his all-embracing eyes, as if what he saw in him were his fear and exhaustion, his imminent ensuing surrender. 'You, on the other hand, are nobody.'

'An outcast of the universe,' was Tom's immediate thought, echoing Wheeler's words, copying them mentally, 'although put more crudely and without the literary reference. Yet they say it as if this were not simply what awaits us all from birth onwards, to traverse the Earth without our presence changing it one iota, as if we were mere ornaments, bit-part players or eternally motionless figures in the background of some painting, an indistinguishable, dispensable, superfluous mass, all of us replaceable and invisible, all of us nobodies. The exceptions are so few that they hardly count, and, after only a short time, a century or ten years, no trace remains of them either: most end up the same as those who were never important anyway and then it's as if none of them had ever existed, or perhaps only as a blade of grass, a speck of dust, a life, a war, a handful of ashes, a thread, the kind of thing that matters to Wheeler, but that no one else remembers. Not even wars are remembered once the battle-field has been cleaned up.' He decided to go no further with these thoughts, since he urgently needed to consider his own situation, to think about himself. He allowed himself one final outburst, by way of puerile compensation: 'Even that Saumarez-Hill fellow will one day be forgotten, contrary to what they seem to believe; he, too, will be nobody, given that he shared his lover with me and was, therefore, the same as me, whether knowingly or not.'

'Would they hold back?' he asked, genuinely surprised, and with a touch of premature desolation in his voice. This would have been normal in a dictatorial country like Spain, with a police force that was, at the same time, arbitrary and servile, and basically corrupt. But he wouldn't have imagined such a thing possible in England. Perhaps there were sectors, spheres, in which all countries resemble each other and are all governed in the same way. 'Would that include Morse? He didn't strike me as being the kind to turn a blind eye and do nothing.'

'No, he might not,' said Tupra, and took another sip of his beer without, for an instant, taking his eyes off Tom. 'But he's of little account, a mere pawn. He'll never rise very far in the ranks unless he learns to adapt. He reports to his superiors and obeys orders, and the higher up the ladder those superiors are, the more sensitive they are. Sensitive to favours, I mean. Not so much receiving favours as handing them out. Doing favours is what people like best, Nevinson; you must have noticed that, despite your youth; even a child knows that, he picks it up from his dealings with adults. Receiving favours diminishes, doing favours enlarges.'

'Yes, it makes you feel really good doing someone a favour,' added Blakeston, who apparently never disagreed with his young boss. 'Even if those favours will never be repaid. Some people don't even say thank you or deign to notice, and they're the ones who remain undiminished, proud, ungrateful people who think the world owes them. There are quite a few like that. But it still makes you feel really good doing someone a favour, even when you get no thanks.' He must have been speaking from experience; perhaps he was one of those men with no initiative, someone who has to be directed and guided like a wind-up toy, the kind whose only talent is to serve and who expects nothing in exchange, only new orders and new tasks to keep them on the move. Without some external stimuli they would sleep out their life from cradle to grave.

'I see,' said Tomás. 'So what do you suggest I do, then? You're going to do me a favour, I assume, even though I'm nobody, and I certainly need a favour. I'm already diminished enough, and I don't mind being a little more diminished if I can get out of this mess. Professor Wheeler told me you would advise me, Mr Tupra, that I should listen to your suggestions, but you haven't yet made any. All you've done so far is paint a very bleak picture of the future, even bleaker than it was before I met you. I was hoping that this Hugh fellow would save me, that, if I was lucky, he'd become the main focus, and now you're telling me that, precisely because he is the man I saw, or so I believe, I'm even closer to being charged and, very likely, condemned. Is that right?' And he recalled Wheeler's warning words: 'You've got yourself into a far more serious situation than you realise. There are certain factors of which you know nothing and that will make it very hard for you to extricate yourself.' He must have been referring to the fact that Janet's boyfriend was an MP, something he must already have known, which meant that he was presumably in constant, fluid communication with Tupra; so what exactly *was* their relationship? Tupra and Blakeston fell silent, as if concurring, or as if, when something is self-evident, there is no point in wasting words on it. Tupra was regarding him almost wryly, as if he found the situation merely entertaining rather than downright comical. He must have been accustomed to spreading confusion and despair, to causing people to think there was no way out or that any possibility of escape depended entirely on him (perhaps that was his job, driving the people he interviewed into a corner and forcing them to beg him for a solution, a fix, to intercede on their behalf, to rescue them; and he did this very subtly, as if he were not imposing any decision on them at all, leaving scorn to do his work for him, because scorn disheartens and undermines). Blakeston was trying hard to imitate his superior, but failing miserably: his gaze, also fixed on Tom, was entirely neutral or, worse, impenetrable. He had barely touched his beer, limiting himself to blowing at the foam, even when the foam had gone. Tom rubbed his eyes with thumb and forefinger, unable to bear this continued scrutiny, as if both men were expecting him, not them, to propose some solution. He took out a cigarette, and, so immersed was he in the mental fog surrounding him, he didn't even offer one to Blakeston or to Tupra, causing Tupra to take out one of his own from a packet – the brand was Rameses II, decorated with colourful Egyptian figures and pharaohs – and each then lit his own, Tomás lighting the same kind of Marcovitch cigarette that Janet had knocked from his lips when she accidentally scratched him. 'How odd that those fingers can no longer caress or scratch or pick anything up,' he thought. 'The night before last, they could do whatever they chose and now they can do nothing, it makes no sense at all, and death is nothing like life, nor does it make any sense that one should succeed the other, let alone replace it.' The scratch and the cigarette spotted by Morse would both work against him, and Tom again touched the tiny scab. It made him angry being forced to see his life in such an absurdly gloomy light, his future snuffed out or dark and overcast. 'Anyway, who are you? Who do you represent?' He realised suddenly that he had no idea. He had his suspicions, but neither Tupra nor Blakeston, nor Reresby nor Montgomery, had actually introduced themselves, or told him on whose authority they were acting, nor what body they belonged to – if they belonged to any (they were probably free agents, mafia men authorised to do deals, to blackmail, since, according to Southworth, Wheeler knew people from all walks of life) – nor, of course, had they shown him a card or a badge, so he had no idea how much influence they had or whose side they were on either, nor if their power lay in the sheer breadth of their influence, greater than that of the police, the courts, even the Cabinet. He nursed the brief illusory hope that they might be omnipotent and capable of erasing the episode completely, even her death by strangulation, and bring Janet back with them; but this lasted only a second. They hadn't so much as offered to help him – yet. So far, all they had done was set out the problems facing him. The truth is, he had no idea who he was talking to, and yet he had placed himself in their hands, had surrendered himself to them.

Then Tupra gave a short laugh, a sympathetic laugh. He was, all in all, and despite his offhand manner, a pleasant man: he may have devoted himself to intimidating and dissuading, to spreading gloom and despondency, possibly terrifying all those he met, but he did so with grace and charm. He could doubtless turn coldly, methodically violent (the coarse, broken nose, the bulging cranium that his thick curls failed to attenuate), but what prevailed in him was a certain affability (the thick eyelashes, the permanently moist lips). Blakeston laughed too, lagging slightly behind his boss. He had been given permission or been set an example.

'Did you hear that, Bertram, the boy is asking us who we represent? I mean, what an absurd question!' he exclaimed jovially, and this caused him to laugh out loud again, and he began then to laugh stridently and unstoppably, his laugh infinitely more piercing than his voice, and which continued to grow still louder, a real attack of the giggles, ha ha ha, ha ha ha, each guffaw slightly longer and more outrageous, so much so that the denizens of The Eagle and Child craned their necks to look over at their table, for, up until then, their conversation had been conducted very quietly, none of them wishing to attract attention, and now here was Blakeston attracting it in spades, and since it was hardly normal to go around dressed as a war hero, moustache and all, everyone would retain that image of him as a hysterical viscount. 'We don't represent anyone, Nevinson, no one. That's the funny part, we never represent anyone,' he managed to blurt out in the midst of his extravagant hilarity. His laugh was at once infectious and embarrassing, a laugh Tom had only heard before from certain jolly, ingenuous homosexuals. The real Field Marshal Montgomery would definitely not have approved of that laugh, he would have been indignant even to be associated with it, even at one remove, in the form of a not very successful lookalike. The toggles on his duffel coat, all tightly fastened, prevented Blakeston from giving full rein to his guffaws. Tomás thought he might burst out of them, but instead, Blakeston, still laughing, succumbed to a coughing fit, intermingling coughing and laughing.

'That's enough, Blakeston,' Tupra said. 'Stop laughing and have something to drink. You'll choke if you don't stop.' But he, too, had been infected by his colleague's giggling fit, and he sounded singularly unauthoritative. Even Tom was affected, despite his anxious state.

Montgomery pulled his hood up over his beret, covered his mouth with a few paper napkins, and his laughter gradually subsided. He then drank his beer, downing half in one go.

'*Pardon, pardon,*' he said in French. 'It's just that I thought it was a question we might well ask ourselves.' And he very nearly began laughing again, this time in rather more difficult circumstances (hunkered down inside his hood), but fortunately he managed to get a grip on himself.

'Blakeston is quite right in what he says,' said Tupra, addressing Tomás. 'Although it hardly merits such hilarity. My friend Blakeston is sometimes overcome by these giggling fits, luckily not that

117

often. What he finds so funny is that we don't really belong any-where, neither officially nor officiously. We are simultaneously somebody and nobody. We both exist and don't exist. We both act and don't act, Nevinson; or rather, we don't carry out the actions we carry out, or the things we do are done by nobody. They simply hap-pen.' These last utterances sounded to Tom like something out of Beckett, who was very much in vogue at the time among the intelli-gentsia, and whose plays were staged in London with elitist veneration; he had, after all, been awarded the Nobel Prize only a short time before. To continue in that vein, Tom both understood and didn't understand. 'We can change things, but we leave no trace behind and so can't be held responsible for those changes. No one will call us to account for the things we do but don't do. And given that we don't exist, no one gives us orders or sends us anywhere.'

'I'm not sure I understand you, Mr Tupra.'

Blakeston had completely calmed down now, and so he took off his hood, but did so rather too abruptly, accidentally removing his beret as well and briefly uncovering his head to reveal a most unex-pected sight: a shock of reddish hair which he had kept carefully tucked under his beret, and this made him look still more intimidat-ing, like some kind of Hells Angel. He took on a rather savage appearance and entirely lost his martial air, although only for a few seconds, because he very skilfully scooped up his hair again with one hand, and, with the other, pulled on his (badgeless) Montgomery beret, although the real Montgomery would have loathed that hair even more than he had the man's shrill laughter. The result of this manoeuvre was that, unbeknown to Blakeston, the napkins with which he had muffled his cough ended up in the hood of his duffel coat. Tom couldn't take his eyes off them, they lay there all crumpled up, and rather resembled cauliflower florets in a basket.

'We're a bit like the third-person narrator of a novel, and I'm sure you've read a few novels, Nevinson,' Tupra went on didactically. 'He's the one who decides what will happen and the one who does the telling, but he can't be challenged or interrogated. Unlike a first-person narrator, he has no name and he's not a character, therefore we believe and trust him; we don't know why he knows what he knows and why he omits what he omits and keeps silent about what he keeps silent about and why it is that he can determine the fate of all his creatures, without once being called into question. It's clear that he both exists and doesn't exist, or that he exists but, at the same time, cannot be found. He's even undetectable. I'm speaking about the narrator, mind, not the author, who is stuck at home and is not responsible for anything his narrator says; even he can't explain why the narrator knows as much as he does. In other words, the omniscient third-person narrator is an accepted convention, and the average reader of novels doesn't usually stop to ask why that narrator takes the floor and doesn't relinquish it for hundreds of pages, droning on in that invisible man's voice, that autonomous, external voice that comes from nowhere.' He paused, twiddled one of the ringlets at his temple, then took a sip of his now flat beer. 'Well, we're something similar, an accepted convention, just as one accepts and doesn't object to chance, as one accepts and doesn't dispute accidents or coincidences, illnesses, catastrophes, events fortunate and unfortunate. We can stop a disaster from happening, but rather as a sudden change in the wind direction can save a boat, or a fog can conceal the pursued from their pursuers, or a snowfall can erase the footprints of the former, disorienting the latter and their dogs, or as black night can stop someone in their tracks and block their view. Or just as the sea parted to make way for the Israelites, then closed again on Pharaoh's army following behind them in order to destroy them. That's what we are, and we really don't represent anyone.'

'Here we go again,' thought Tomás. 'They're a blade of grass, a speck of dust, a life with no origin and a war with no cause, a handful of ashes, a puff of smoke, an insect, simultaneously something and nothing.' However, the main message he retained was this: 'We can stop a disaster from happening.' Perhaps that was true, perhaps they could bring to a halt the disaster hanging over him, but they still hadn't said how, or what they needed to do in order to become a change in the wind direction, a snowfall, a fog or a black night or a sea that parts. And yet he couldn't resist saying to Tupra:

'I assume you must have studied literature, Mr Tupra, to have had such thoughts.'

Tupra gave a rather condescending laugh, which seemed to say: 'What do you take me for? An unthinking man of action? Yes, I'm capable of taking action and jettisoning all scruples, but I do so knowingly and consciously.' Anyone would have thought he was not just a few years older than Tom, but about twenty-five years older.

'I've studied many things,' he said. 'Here in Oxford and in other places too. I've spent my whole life learning. My main subject was Medieval History, but you and I have shared some of the same teachers, and they might be the ones who will, indirectly, save you, Nevinson.' This explained the slightly Oxonian accent Tomás had noticed. He wondered how someone like Tupra could have gained admission to that snobbish university, someone who could well have come from a rundown area like Bethnal Green in East London, or even worse places like Streatham, Clapham or Brixton. He must have a lot of good qualities, or be very astute or, as Wheeler had said, resourceful. He must come across as extremely convincing, either that or rather frightening.

'Indirectly?'

'Yes, through us,' said Tupra, smiling. 'Through the encroaching fog. You know the person who acted as intermediary.'

Then Tomás decided to ask him straight out:

'Can you stop *my* disaster from happening?' Yes, that was the expression that had stuck in his mind.

'Possibly. It depends. We might be able to make you cease to be a nobody and become Somebody, isn't that right, Blakeston?' Blakeston nodded somewhat doubtfully. 'In that case, you could become as armour-plated as Saumarez-Hill. Not in the same way nor for the same reasons, but to a similar degree. It would, of course, be a problem getting rid of the two individuals who were in Janet Jefferys' flat on that worst of all possible nights to visit her, let alone have sex with her. Namely, you certainly and Mr Saumarez-Hill only possibly, or perhaps not at all. Be that as it may, those two people would have to be quietly airbrushed from the picture. Yes, that would be slightly problematic, but not impossible. That all depends on you, Mr Thomas Nevinson. On whether it would be worth our while starting the snowstorm or changing the direction of the wind.' And for the first time, he didn't just call him by his surname, but added 'Mr', as if he were trying it out, as if he were demonstrating the considerable difference that exists between being nobody and being Somebody.

'And if you did get rid of us, what then? Wouldn't that cause a terrific scandal? What would that man Morse say? How could it be explained away?'

'Oh, he'd get angry and protest, as, doubtless, would his immediate superior, assuming he's made of the same stern stuff, but their complaints wouldn't get very far. They would immediately be silenced, as happens in all hierarchical institutions. Janet Jefferys' death would, for the moment, remain an unsolved case: a lack of proof, a lack of sufficient evidence for charges to be brought; no one wants to bring a case they won't win. And there are a lot of such cases. Sometimes it takes years to discover the guilty party, and sometimes they're never found. Leaf through the files of fifty years ago, or twenty or ten. The people of this country love a good crime, but they soon forget all about it if there's no continuity, no conclusion, with the exception of the occasional nutter who keeps sending letters to the police until even he finally gets bored. If the number of unresolved cases was made public, there'd be a huge outcry and people would live in a permanent state of fear. But the number of cases that do get solved keeps them happy, and there are enough trials and sentences handed down to give an impression of efficiency. If you were to ask the general population, the majority of them would be convinced that our police and our legal system work far better than any other, and that a murderer is unlikely to go unpunished here. But people don't keep track of the cases that fade into oblivion, or that are left in a limbo no one ever peers into.' Tupra was obviously rather pleased with that last phrase, because he paused before saying it, as if it were the clinching line of a poem. 'In six months' time, no one will remember Janet, except those close to her. Not even the inhabitants of Oxford, who are currently all stirred up and agog for news, and will remain so for several weeks, but after a month or two with no news, well, no one can stay on tenterhooks for that long.'

'But news will get around that I was with her. The neighbour who saw me will already have spread the word. People will eye me suspiciously, they'll wonder why I haven't been arrested and will cut me dead. Or worse still, they'll turn nasty.'

'Possibly, for those first few weeks,' said Tupra calmly. 'Then they'll assume you had nothing to do with it, that you're innocent, precisely because you haven't been arrested or charged. Some may even think: "Poor boy, his girlfriend was killed on the night after he'd been with her, he must have been through hell. He made love to her and then someone strangled her." Besides, you've nearly finished your studies, haven't you? You won't stay here much longer. You'll go back to Spain or be posted somewhere else temporarily to perfect your languages. And when you visit Oxford at some later date, no one will remember you or make the connection.'

'That is, of course, if we do stop your disaster from happening, I mean, if it's stopped,' added Blakeston. Tomás's immediate thought was: 'If it's not, then I might be stuck here for years, behind bars, behind a wall, living with murderers.'

He noticed that a lock of Blakeston's reddish hair had escaped from his beret and hung down at the back on the left, giving him the absurd appearance of a Mongol or a Tartar, and there was something rather creepy about that long stray lock. He pointed this out to Blakeston, and the viscount quickly stowed it away again beneath his beret. Tomás also took the opportunity to slip his hand into the viscount's hood and remove the napkins, which, to the astonishment of the other two men, he then placed, rather queasily, on the table.

'You say it depends on me. How exactly? What would I have to do?' Tomás already knew, but he needed to hear it put into words. This was far too vital a decision to be made on the basis of conjectures, although they weren't really conjectures, but certainties.

'Not so long ago,' said Tupra, 'one of the teachers we share in common made you a very attractive proposition, which, I understand, you rejected. To be of use to the country and to place your exceptional abilities at its service. Ours is a grateful, trustworthy country, unlike yours, at least as far as I know, since I've only spent brief periods there. You wouldn't trust what a Spaniard promised you, would you, Nevinson, or not very much? Still less if it was someone with power and influence, I mean, someone who could bring on black night or part the waters so that you could pass . . . You could never be sure that he wouldn't close the waters over your head again, or make the fog lift just when you thought you were safe, but were, in fact, still visible to your pursuers. Here, on the other hand, we keep our word. If you agreed to collaborate with us, you would become Somebody, and poor Janet Jefferys would have to wait a while for justice to be done. We still have the superstitious belief that the dead care whether those who killed them are punished. They may have cared just before they breathed their last, while they were still trying to live and were struggling and fighting or resisting their murderers; but that moment immediately becomes consigned to the distant past as soon as they stop breathing. We superstitiously continue to attribute to them the qualities and responses of the living, that's all our imaginations can do, but the abyss is far too deep, and they care nothing about their earthly desires, not even their very last one. They are prepared to wait until the end of time if necessary, because they don't even know they're waiting and cannot even understand the concept of waiting. In short, they no longer know anything. They cannot feel impatient or have desires.'

'That isn't what the poet thinks,' thought Tom. 'And what the dead had no speech for, when living,' he recalled, 'they can tell you, being dead.' Those lines remained incomprehensible to him, and, besides, he was in a hurry to get something clear:

'Janet would have to wait for justice to be done even if I was arrested and charged, assuming I've understood correctly what it is you're offering me. Because I didn't kill her, I thought you were clear about that. At least our shared teacher is. And he must have told you so.'

Tupra shrugged and smiled, sympathetically, almost proudly. He was a man who was very pleased with himself, with his personality and his appearance, as often happens with those who are successful with women. He was doubtless convinced that his broad pinstripe suit was the height of good taste.

'It doesn't matter what he thinks. It doesn't matter what we think. It doesn't matter what you say. No one can be certain of anything, except the dead woman, if, that is, she saw her murderer, because she might not have seen him if he'd attacked her from behind; and she can no longer speak. You could have killed her, we don't know that and it can't be ruled out, it remains a possibility, and to a judge and jury it would seem probable or even proven. And that is all that counts: what is recorded and what the law decides. In cases where the law makes a decision and where records are kept, of course, because many things go unrecorded, as we ourselves well know. Our work partly consists in leaving no record of our work, but if you continue to be a nobody, Nevinson, you risk exposing yourself to the opinions of a judge and a jury, putting yourself in their hands and meeting a very bad end.' This was similar to what the protective Mr Southworth had said, and reminiscent of Wheeler's disdain for the justice system. In Oxford, no one seemed to consider it essential or to hold it in high esteem. Or perhaps that was just the world in which Tupra, Blakeston and Wheeler moved (and Wheeler had a lot of influence over South-worth); perhaps they evaded or passed over it, as if they really were the wind, the black night, the snow or the fog, and were never called to account, their activities deemed to be above the law and left unre-corded. 'That would be a shame in one so young,' added Tupra gravely. 'You've barely begun your life, you're only a beginner.'

'Who, then, would keep their word?' Tomás asked suddenly. 'Who? If you don't represent anyone? If you are but don't exist, or exist but aren't or whatever. What was it you said? If you act but don't act, if you're both somebody and nobody. According to you, this is a grateful, trustworthy country, but I don't know who in this country I'm speaking to, who it is making this promise to get me out of trouble. How can you expect me to give you an answer if no one is going to call you to account, if no one has sent you or given you orders? Who am I speaking to, then, a ghost?'

'What on earth are you going on about, Nevinson?' said Blakeston impatiently. 'You're speaking to Mr Bertram Tupra, and the only reason he agreed to this meeting was in order to help you.' And he pronounced the name of his boss in a tone bordering on idolatry, as if he were a kind of institution, a totem. It was very striking, that admiration for someone much younger than himself.

'Oh really?' answered Tomás rather irritably. 'I'm just as likely to be speaking to Mr Ted Reresby, as that Beckwith woman thought she was. Not even your name seems very stable.'

Tupra seemed amused or pleased by Tomás Nevinson's attentiveness to such details. It must have tickled him that Tom had been listening so carefully when he introduced himself to the pneumatic lecturer from Somerville. He ignored his remark, however, and went on:

'Do you still not know, Nevinson? Do you really still not know who you're talking to? Come on, our shared teacher was quite explicit, or so he said. As explicit as you were in your rejection. He was very disappointed, by the way. But to continue with the examples: if the fog does get you out of your predicament, you're not first going to demand guarantees or to know how long it will last. You'll just take full advantage of it, won't you, hoping that it will conceal you long enough for you to get away. More than that, you'll wrap yourself in it, blend in with it, and from then on, you, too, will be fog, English fog, which has, for centuries, been so famously dense. And you'll trust it absolutely, I'm sure of that, because now you'll be part of it and will go with it wherever it goes. You will become part of all the accidents or coincidences, all the illnesses, all the events fortunate and unfortunate. And in time, you'll be the same as us: you will simply happen. Something that is so utterly indistinguishable from you couldn't ever leave you in the lurch or abandon you, because you would never abandon yourself, would you? Are you following me?'

He was following and not following. He got the general drift, but became lost in those metaphorical disquisitions in which he sensed the influence of their shared teacher, Professor Wheeler; it was highly likely that Tupra had also once been a favourite student of his, and that, in his day, Wheeler had even recruited him to perform the vague, phantasmal tasks to which he now devoted himself. If so, it wouldn't have been hard for him to persuade Tupra or Reresby, because Tupra's life prior to Oxford would probably have been not just a life of action and improvisation and difficulties, but of delinquency too. The more Tomás talked to him, the more he noticed in his face – coarse in origin and gradually refined – and in his diction – perhaps common at first, now artificially impeccable – a past life of unscrupulousness and drastic, even violent solutions, which he would not have fully renounced despite the – still incomplete – process of civilisation and determined refinement he had undergone. He was probably a man who had struggled to improve himself not out of conviction, but out of convenience, in order to become more presentable to the world and to facilitate his rise; he would have realised that he needed to learn to walk the corridors of power to achieve his aims, but his utter scorn for them and for offices and salons would have remained unabated. He would have been forged in the street, and doubtless knew that the street is what lasts and what counts, the thing to which one always has to resort in order to get ahead and solve problems and overcome obstacles, especially when situations turn nasty. Tupra would not have had a cosy early life, a straightforward life that he could leave behind or discard. Getting involved in what he was involved in, blending in with the fog, to use his words, would have been a kind of salvation for him, a resolution, a clean slate or legitimation of his twisted impulses.

'My life is certainly straightforward and on track,' thought Tomás, 'and yet it seems that I've lost it, that it's suddenly slipped away from me and become irrecoverable, relegated to what's past. How stupid the days are, how stupid any day can turn out to be, without your ever knowing which day; instead you plunge blithely into a day you should have avoided, had there been any way of guessing which one would be the accursed day of block and fire, of the sea's throat, the day that destroys everything . . . And how stupid, how futile, will be the steps you take on the day when you should never have taken any steps at all or even left the house. You get up as you always do, you visit a bookshop, you enjoy a quick fumble with an intermittent lover of no importance and arrange to meet her later on that night, out of boredom or out of perfectly controllable and trivial desire, or so as not to feel alone or a pariah, it would have been far better to stay at home and save yourself the subsequent troubling thought: "Now that it's so joylessly and rather sadly over, it really wasn't worth it; if I could go back, I wouldn't bother." And that stupid date and that superfluous fuck ruin the planned and established trajectory of your life. What I had planned to do is now irrelevant, my future vanished or replaced, perhaps I'll have to give up Berta or any kind of normal life with her, a more or less harmonious life with no dark secrets; or perhaps secrets will be the foundation and the rule and what controls us. In its place they offer me two options, neither of which I want (but the ability to choose what I want is a thing of the past). In the worst case, prison and an uncertain trial, with a possible sentence and more years in prison; or a murky, unimaginable task of indefinite duration and for which I'm not prepared: passing myself off as someone else and dealing with unpleasant strangers, with enemies with whom I'll have to make friends so as to betray them later on, that's what Wheeler was suggesting, because he did mention the word "infiltrator", I didn't dream that. "You would make an excellent infiltrator"; "You could pass for a native in quite a few places," he said, then tried to sweeten the pill: "No mission would last very long"; "Your family or friends wouldn't find this odd or unusual. Everything would carry on as normal when you were in Spain. When you weren't, well, I won't lie to you, you would live fictitious lives, lives not your own, but only temporarily: sooner or later, you would always leave them and return to your own self, to thy former self." Yes, he had been quite clear and explicit, and I've tried to forget it, but a proposal made by him when everything was still fine, a proposal I could reject, is not the same as what these two, Blakeston and Tupra or Montgomery and Reresby or whatever they're called, are wanting to impose on me. But prison would be even worse, worse than anything, and besides, my life would still be ruined when I left prison, at what age, with what expectations, in what state of mind: who would want me, who would employ a man convicted of murder, an outcast? Berta would have gone her own way and married someone else and had his children and not mine, she might not even want to see me again or know anything about me or hear my name, but erase me from her life like someone shaking off an oppressive nightmare or a shameful mistake. If I accept, I won't lose her, although it will mean a dark, confusing life together, plagued with silences and deceptions and absences, and, in the best-case scenario, with half-truths and vast shadowy areas; if I reject their offer, I could be found not guilty or I might not even have to go on trial, and simply continue along my path as if that stupid day had never happened; after all, I didn't kill Janet or anyone else. But the risk is too great and who knows, who knows; I'm afraid, and fear clouds both eyes and reason, fear is unbearable and I want to be rid of it . . .'

'I'm thinking,' he said at last, and he could sense in the air the growing impatience of those two men. 'I just need to think a little.'

'About time too,' said Tupra, and he drummed on the table to emphasise his impatience and fluttered his feminine eyelashes. 'We haven't got all day. We're offering you a way out, Nevinson, you'd better grab it while you can. It's up to you, but be quick about it.'

'Quick now, here, now, always . . .' Tomás thought, remembering that quick line in the final part of *Little Gidding*. 'What is now will be always, and it's odd because whatever decision I take, I will probably become an outcast of the universe; the thing Wheeler urged me to avoid is precisely what awaits me. I will be who I am not, I will be a fiction, a spectre who comes and goes and departs and returns. And I will simply happen, as Tupra says, I will be sea and snow and wind.' He realised that he had already decided, but he preferred not to acknowledge it out loud, he preferred to keep it to himself for a few seconds, in his mind; you can always turn back as long as you keep silent. 'Dust in the air suspended marks the place where a story ended.' Those two lines rose up again. 'What's mine ends here. What awaits me, because I'm still here now, and now is always. This is the death of air.' He had caught that line too. 'But one survives. What good fortune and what ill luck.'

III

I married Tomás Nevinson in May 1974, in the church of San Fermín de los Navarros, very near the school we both attended, and where we first met when he arrived there, a latecomer, at the age of fourteen. We were not yet twenty-three when we emerged from the church, absurdly arm in arm (we had never gone arm in arm before, nor did we afterwards), with me dressed all in white, carrying a bouquet, my veil lifted and a triumphant smile on my lips. I suppose this was the fulfilment of a decision made years earlier, one of those ambitions you fix on in childhood and adolescence and which are so hard to eradicate – or even moderate – regardless of how circumstances may have changed. And regardless, too, of how feelings may have changed, but, in order for us to be able to observe and acknowledge this, a great deal more time has to pass, and, besides, it seems important to complete old projects before even considering abandoning them. You have to cross a line that cannot then be uncrossed in order to understand and repent, to be able to accept that you've made a blunder; no, you have to make that mistake very thoroughly before realising it was a mistake, and then, when you try to extricate yourself, it's already too late to do so without causing harm, without wreaking havoc. To me, separating from Tomás would have been unthinkable even before I bound myself to him so completely and in full knowledge of all the consequences, which, in a country where divorce did not yet exist, were seen as pretty much definitive, although there were already some couples living separate lives; sometimes you have to tie a knot very tightly before you dare untie it, if it comes to that. It's as if we had a weakness for the most enormous and impossible of tasks, indeed, some people spend their entire lives wrestling with such tasks, because they cannot conceive of any other way of living their lives except in agony, struggle, conflict and drama: they become entangled in order to disentangle themselves, and thus they fill their allotted time on Earth.

That isn't why I got married, of course, that would have been cynical. On the contrary, I thought marriage would put an end to the anomalies and oddities I'd begun to notice since he finished his studies at Oxford and returned to Madrid, or, rather, to which he did not entirely return, or not as I'd expected he would. Things were going really well for him, apparently; it was clear that an Oxford degree brought with it many advantages, because, despite his youth, he had immediately gained a position at the British embassy, working with the cultural attaché and earning a reasonable salary that allowed us to live very comfortably, especially when I, too, began to earn a modest but complementary amount as a teacher at our old school, which frequently took on responsible ex-pupils when there were still vacancies to fill at the beginning of term. They clearly thought highly of Tomás at the embassy and perhaps in still higher places too, which is why he was regularly sent to England for periods of a month or sometimes longer, so that he could undertake some kind of semi-diplomatic or semi-commercial training, teaching him protocols, crisis management, people skills, budgeting and so on, all of which I found tedious in the extreme and which, besides, didn't seem particularly relevant to his current post nor to any future post he might occupy. That, at least, is what he told me. If they were giving him all that training, it could only be because they thought he had a bright future and were intending to promote him and use his talents to the full; and, even though he had never actually done a degree in diplomacy and international relations, I was inclined to believe that perhaps, later on, some English ministry would claim him, the Foreign Office for example, where he would be an intelligent, efficient civil servant with an extraordinary gift for languages and for getting on with people. Us moving to the UK therefore remained a possibility, as did being posted to another country where he could be of most use, possibly in the Americas.

Oddly enough, I was the only one who speculated about this. Tomás merely did what he had to do when he was in Madrid, never wondering about his future or giving it any thought, almost as if he had no future or as if it had already been carved in stone and he had read what was written. He didn't seem interested in what life might hold in store, and appeared to have no goals or ambitions or anxieties, nor even any questions. I sometimes had a sense that I was living with someone whose fate had already been decided, who felt trapped, with no possible escape route, and who therefore viewed his days with indifference, knowing that they'd bring him no major surprises and no pleasant ones either. In a way, he was like a very elderly person who waits only for the days to pass and for night to fall, rather than for the nights to pass and day to break. And I say this quite literally: whenever I opened my eyes, whether in the middle of the night or in the morning, I would find him already awake, as if his continuous thoughts wouldn't allow him to sleep or only very lightly, so that I only had to move, however minimally, or brush against him, to wake him instantly. I would sometimes ask him very quietly if he was awake, but he didn't usually reply, and I never insisted, fearful that I might be mistaken and be interrupting his sleep, if sleep it was.

But his breathing was invariably that of someone awake, of someone pondering or silently cursing his fate, his mind always alert and always giving off a sad mixture of dissatisfaction and resignation. And on quite a few nights, I would see the tip of his lit cigarette glowing in the dark, as if it belonged to a soldier in the trenches, too exhausted and disillusioned now to care about giving away his position and being killed by one sure bullet guided by that persistent light. Then I would dare to raise my voice a little, certain that he was awake, and ask him:

'Can't you sleep? What are you thinking about?'

'Nothing. I'm not thinking about anything. I'm just smoking.'

I would place one hand on his shoulder or stroke his cheek, hoping this contact would calm him.

'Can I help? Do you want to talk?'

Sometimes he would say 'No, go back to sleep', and at others, he would stub out his cigarette in the ashtray, draw me to him, lift up my nightdress and immediately penetrate me in a way that was almost brutish, with no preamble, his penis suddenly erect, or perhaps his insomnia gave him an erection; he was, after all, still very young. I had the feeling that, more than anything else, he was trying to wear himself out or release tension, that any woman would have served his purpose, except, of course, that I happened to be that woman, and it happened to be my bed too, and he didn't have to sound me out or ask permission or else he took it for granted, as many men do once they are husbands. Perhaps this was one of the few ways in which Tomás could empty his mind a little, and find some rest from his strange nocturnal or diurnal afflictions, or at least merge them with a physical urge or tremor, perhaps he simply wanted his body temporarily to deceive or confuse his mind, or silence it by drowning it out with the body's own elemental nature (sex always does seem rudimentary, however many refinements one may add; which was not the case here). When he'd finished, I'd go to the bathroom, and, when I came back, I would find him dozing. If it was still not time to get up, I would slide very stealthily into bed and watch for a few moments, interpreting his face and his breathing. And if these were not those of someone soundly asleep, I would gently stroke the back of his neck and whisper:

'Lie very still, my love. Don't move or turn around, that way sleep will come upon you without you realising it and gradually you'll stop thinking. I wish you would tell me what it is you're thinking about. So many hours spent awake. Deny it if you will, but you're constantly thinking about something that keeps you from sleeping. Something is troubling you, and I don't know what it is.'

But those last words I said more to myself than to him.

During the day he would go about his work diligently and do his best to appear normal. He would smile his usual broad smile, make his usual amiable, pleasing jokes, and – at the numerous suppers and social events we were obliged to attend – he was always willing to entertain the other guests with one of his celebrated impressions. They were just as amusing as they had been at school, except now the audience was an adult one, noisier, more prone to exaggeration. Since then, he had perfected his impressions and become a real virtuoso, from whom no accent, voice, no public figure or private individual was safe, and more than one person had suggested he make a career of it as a professional on British or Spanish television. However, in the midst of our rather easy, cheerful daily life, I sensed an underlying indifference to his own existence, an enigmatic lack of curiosity about the future that prevented him from enjoying the present. And then again, his mood would change whenever one of those month-long absences in England was approaching: moments of anxiety and anger alternated with depression, along with the unease he had brought with him when he came back from Oxford. The young man who returned after completing his studies was not the same youth who had left – not that there was anything so very strange about that – but nor was he the same young man who, over the years, had continued to spend most of his long vacations here and whom I had continued to see on each of those visits and with whom I had continued to have sex, with growing desire and intensity after our first, belated and somewhat disappointing, attempts. Nor was he the same person he had been on the previous occasion, during the five weeks he had spent with me in Madrid between the end of Hilary term and the beginning of Trinity, carefree and unpreoccupied, giving off, more than anything, a feeling of serenity. He had become someone with a dark, evasive edge to him, often quite withdrawn, whereas during his stays between terms at Oxford, he had still been the same person, more or less. There was an increase in the restlessness that had always characterised his grey, almond-shaped eyes, and which was in such marked contrast to his usually affable manner: his eyes no longer seemed to rest, as if they reflected an unceasing torment, that of a single fixed idea that neither advances nor evolves nor reaches a conclusion. At first, I put this down to the unsettled state of someone who has just reached the end of a particular stage in life, to a temporary – albeit often long-drawn-out – process of adaptation, of someone returning to his setting-off point only to stay rooted to the spot, after a few years of not belonging anywhere, of coming and going between two different places, and never being entirely here nor entirely there. He immediately put me right, telling me that his itinerant lifestyle had not yet ended, that he would have to spend periods of time in London on various of those advanced training courses with a view to jobs already promised or agreed, probably starting in September or October. I, of course, asked him about his intermittent sadness:

'Has something happened to you in the last few months? You seem different, as if you'd suddenly aged ten years. As if you were carrying a weight on your shoulders that wasn't there before, or not until recently.'

He looked at me, puzzled, as if surprised I should notice a change he had done his best to disguise by being flippant, jokey, good-humoured. Perhaps in order to delay having to respond, he twice pushed back his hair, even though he wore his hair combed back anyway. Then his eyes grew opaque, and I had the impression that he was hesitating about whether to tell me something or not. If so, he finally opted for evasion:

'No,' he said, 'not at all, what could possibly have happened to me? I suppose it's finishing my degree. The end of the party and of a life of irresponsibility. The fact that whatever steps I take from now on will affect the rest of my life, that there are no more trial periods, no time to put things right. The feeling that what I do now will have consequences over the next twenty years, and yet I don't feel any more capable of choosing than I did when I was fifteen, no, eight years old. That this path does actually lead somewhere from which there is no return, and that it will be very difficult to turn back, I don't know. The same thing will happen to you next year.' In Spain, a degree course lasted five years, and when Tomás came back, I still had one more year to go; it's true that I'd put off deciding what to do when I graduated, apart from marrying him, of course – but that had been decided ages ago – it was something I still had to sort out and that was, at last, approaching. Not for nothing had I waited all those years, struggling hard with my yearning for him to come home, with that long separation; and if those separations were to recur period-ically, that was fine, even if they continued for the rest of our lives, but I would not allow myself to waver, absolutely not. Tomás may have come home a changed man, he may have somewhat abruptly entered adulthood, he may have acquired that opaque, sorrowful air, but I could live with that and grow up equally fast if he needed me to keep pace; I certainly wasn't going to back down. It wasn't just the time and emotion I'd invested, it was because I was resolutely in love with him, and I use that adverb deliberately: I hadn't just been in love with him since adolescence, I'd *resolved* to be in love and approved that resolution; and there is nothing more immovable than that conjunction of sentiment and will. I'd had the occasional sexual adventure in his absence, as was only natural for a woman my age and in such generally rousing times, but none had undermined, or even diminished, my determination and my certainty, my unconditional love. I'd picked him out with my tremulous finger (tremulous with emotion) when I was still very young, and nothing would make me step back from that defining moment. But what about him? I took it for granted that he, too, would have had some insignificant adventures, but I'd never noticed any change in his relationship with me, the slightest cooling or lessening of enthusiasm. Although troubled by his disquiet, I felt almost sure that I was not the cause. Our initial idea was to get married more or less a year later, once I had finished my degree. Then, as if to support his earlier denial, Tomás added: 'Besides, what could possibly happen to me in Oxford? As you know, nothing ever happens there. Nothing serious, I mean, or even anything unforeseen. It's a protected place, and entirely ruled by ceremony, in which everything is mummified or preserved in formaldehyde. With its good and bad qualities, its unreality, it's . . .' And here he paused, hesitated, as if it set his teeth on edge to say what he was about to say: 'It's like an outcast from the universe.'

'And are you including me among the things you fear you might not be able to put right? One of those things that might perhaps become a burden in twenty years' time, that you might wish did not exist, or had never happened? Is that how you see me, as an irreversible step, an obligatory path from which you'll never be able to diverge? I don't know, nothing is certain, and no one can tell what

143

the future might hold, and I'm not asking you that, I can't. But I wouldn't want you to feel that I'm just another threat. If you're no more capable of making a choice than you were at eight years old, it would be ingenuous on my part to think that didn't include me. But the last thing I would want is for you to see me already – and so soon – as a tie and a constraint. That you should view me with dread.'

He said only: 'No, Berta, no.' But such succinctness did little to ease my mind. And when I said nothing, but sat looking at him anxiously, he again smoothed back his hair with that nervous, superfluous gesture, and, after a few seconds, added: 'Of course not. Of course I don't include you in that. In fact, you're one of the few things that isn't obligatory, that I've been able to choose freely. In other respects, I have a sense that the die is cast, as if I hadn't so much chosen as been chosen. You're the one thing that is truly mine, the only thing I know I myself wanted.'

Those words seemed to me exaggerated and rather cryptic. I didn't know what he meant when he said that the die was cast and his freedom limited. Nothing obliged him to accept the job he'd been offered, indeed, it was a privilege to get such a good job so early on, as soon as he'd finished his degree; most of our contemporaries could expect a period of anxiety, of provisional jobs and difficulties, and even, for the more inept, a period of enforced unemployment. Nor did I understand the sense he had of being chosen, rather than having done the choosing himself. 'Something must have happened to him, something strange and disquieting that he prefers not to tell me about now,' I thought. 'He'll tell me eventually though. We have years ahead of us, and everyone ends up telling everything to the person who sleeps beside them night after night; it's difficult to keep anything secret from that person for all eternity.' As usually happens in moments of insecurity and fear, egotism prevailed, and I clung only to what concerned me, to what seemed to be a ratification, almost a declaration of love. I gave a sigh of relief and banished everything else, gave it little thought. Still less so when he drew me to him with one arm – a slightly awkward embrace – pressing my face gently to his chest, so that, for a moment, I could no longer see him and focused instead on the smell of fresh cologne, cigarettes and good English cloth. I felt comforted and safe, and stroked the back of his neck as if to calm him, and, later on, when I remembered that scene and that conversation, I wondered if my feelings derived in part from the fact that his troubled features had suddenly disappeared from view: my face pressed against his jacket, no longer able to see the full lips I always liked to touch and kiss, nor his fair aviator-ish hair, nor the turbulent eyes which I never again saw untroubled and at peace, or entirely at rest.

He took a long time to tell me, though, and never did tell me everything; I grew accustomed, however, to not asking for details, and he proved very skilled at concealment, greatly helped by the absolute prohibition he was under to reveal anything. Such a ban means that whenever you feel the temptation to confess, you think of the reprisals you might suffer, the risks to which you might expose others, and you realise, too, that you would be opening the door to endless questions. Better to remain hermetically silent and not utter a single word, better to invent lies, and, if you must, deny everything.

We'd been married for two years and our first child had already been born when Tomás had no alternative but to speak. Not that he said much, only what he was authorised to say, and he had to ask permission first, despite pressure from me, despite the apparent danger to which he had laid us open with his distant activities. At least I knew what those activities were. Or, rather, I imagined what they might be, and, as all we know, the imagination is often far wilder than reality, even if it lacks the latter's precision and terrible force, so you can always dismiss what it tells you and say to yourself: 'That might well not have happened, and since I have no idea what really happened, nor ever will, why torment myself with conjectures?' From that moment on, I began to live in a state of constant diffuse fear, especially for him, but also for our son and for myself, and, of course, later on, for our little girl. He swore to me that what had happened would never happen again, let alone anything bad, and I thought how easily some people swear oaths about things that are not in their power to avoid or fulfil. (Usually the brazen types or those who feel cornered.) And yet, foolishly, I believed him, or perhaps I needed to. I had no option but to believe him if I wanted to continue living a semi-normal life. Although, afterwards, nothing was ever very normal. He swore in vain in order to save the situation (so he must have felt cornered), and I believed him equally in vain so that my fear remained just that, diffuse, transitory and latent, rather than piercing and overwhelming.

Yes, the episode that obliged him to tell me what he was allowed to tell me of the truth occurred about three years after his return from Oxford. As expected, Tomás had taken up his post at the embassy and was alternating periods spent in Madrid with those spent in London or in other parts of that second country of his, which bore all the marks of having already become his first, since that was the country he was working for and the one that paid him a rapidly increasing salary, so that, in contrast, my contributions to the family economy soon became merely symbolic, and I tended to spend my earnings on myself or on the child, for children are a ceaseless, limitless drain on resources. His training courses grew so prolonged that the day finally dawned when Tomás had to come up with a more permanent excuse: given his bilingualism, his ability to get on with people and his other talents (people always took a liking to him and became fond of him), the Foreign Office wanted to keep him in London for longer periods, in a consultative, intermediary, persuasive capacity, as did the BBC World Service to help with their broadcasts in Spanish, and any English-language programmes about Spanish or Latin American matters; and so his sojourns in England would continue indefinitely, sometimes longer, sometimes shorter, their precise duration being hard to predict.

We became a couple who shared our lives only intermittently, but we were already used to that and didn't find it particularly hard to accept. More than that, loving each other as we did or thought we did (I'm speaking mainly for myself here), we were, in a way, pleased to be able to maintain the privilege of missing each other, or giving ourselves time for desire to condense (both physical desire and the desire to see each other), to avoid the agreeable routine of someone's constant presence, which, because it lacks any end-date, any inter-ruption, can become a burden or, if not that, something you take for granted and never struggle to achieve, because the person is there every day, including those days when you'd like to be alone with your thoughts and memories, or else simply get in the car and drive off somewhere, wandering aimlessly here and there and spending the night in a hotel in some unknown city where chance and nightfall have brought you: pretending that you're single again, with no responsibilities and no one to go home to. I welcomed the months he spent in Madrid with renewed enthusiasm and excitement, as if it were a gift, something that, at first, always seemed exceptional, the void filled and everything in its place, his body in bed at night giving off warmth or heat; when I knew he was awake or drifting off, I would reach out one hand and run a fingertip down his back just to make quite sure he was there and to experience the incredulous joy of knowing he really was there, so close, by my side, after I had spent months of finding only empty air on the pillow and the sheets and thinking, half in dreams: 'When will he come back? I know I didn't just imagine it, he did once occupy this space, he was once here.'

Knowing that this shared life would come to an end, that, after a while, he would go away again, and that another period of nostalgia and waiting would begin, made me celebrate – as if it were an important event – each morning that we got up together and the close of each day when we had supper at home or went out, because when you work at an embassy there are always social functions to attend. No, he wasn't the same young man, and I sensed in him an affliction of which he never spoke, or only to deny its existence, an affliction that, to me, was inexplicable; but the blithe, ironic young man had not entirely disappeared, had not been entirely cancelled out by that man who seemed ever more grown-up and even prematurely aged in his lack of interest in the future; if that young man had survived somewhere, he would be there inside him. And so when he was with me, it didn't matter that he had changed and seemed tormented or elusive and suffered from an insomnia I could rarely cure; what mattered was seeing his smile when he smiled, his alert grey eyes, hearing his jokes and providing an audience for his impressions when he felt in a jocular mood, kissing him, cautiously or not, on the lips, and having him with me day after day, however changed or, if I can put it like this, however disfigured a version he was of the first Tomás, the Tomás I'd known for so many years.

Once his absences in one place or another were established, though, he tended to return to Madrid in a very disturbed, exhausted state, as if he had just emerged from a nightmare or from a prolonged period spent under extreme tension, but after a few days, he seemed to calm down and recover his energy, as if he were gradually detaching himself from what he had experienced and was embracing the respite before his next excursion. As the weeks passed in my company, and despite his nebulous state, he grew quieter and his spirits lifted, and he allowed himself a breathing space, reacquainted himself with family and friends and the daily life of the city, which included attacks by ETA or by some other group, as well as occasional crimes committed by the far right, conflicts and arguments and threatened military coups, the state of permanent uncertainty that filled us all with both hope and disquiet after the death of Franco the interminable. None of this appeared to affect him very much, as if it were none of his business, or as though he were accustomed to far worse things, which didn't make much sense if all he had to do in England was rub shoulders with the powerful, deal with paperwork, attend receptions and act as interpreter or mediator. I can't say that I never suspected anything, that it never occurred to me that he was doing something else, especially when, after an absence of just over two months, he returned with a mark on his face: I mean, with a visible scar on one cheek left not by a razor blade, but by a knife or dagger. By the time I saw it, the wound had healed. It hadn't been a deep cut, but would probably leave a mark for quite some time or possibly for ever if someone knew where to look, unless, that is, he had plastic surgery, as he said he would and which he clearly did, because when he next returned, there was, incredibly enough, not a trace, as if no knife had ever slashed his cheek; some eminent surgeon, a consummate professional, had obviously intervened. But when I first saw the scar, I was alarmed.

'What happened? Who did that to you?'

He ran his thumbnail caressingly over his cheek, as if this had already become an habitual gesture.

'Oh, it happened some time ago now. Two muggers pounced on me one night when I'd left work late and had decided to walk home, and I was nearly there too. A couple of guys with knives. They were after my wallet, which I refused to give them. I kneed one of them in the chest and ran off, but not before the other guy had lashed out and cut my cheek. Fortunately, it was just the tip of the knife, not the blade. It was only a superficial wound, although it bled a lot initially. Anyway, as you can see, it's healed up nicely.'

'It might be superficial, but it's quite long.' The scar went from the top of one of his sideburns down almost to his jawline; the fashion then, of course, was for long sideburns. 'It'll leave a permanent mark. Why didn't you tell me about it when it happened?' And then it was my turn to stroke the scar tentatively, tenderly. We used to speak on the telephone when possible, and he had never even mentioned being mugged, either at the time or afterwards. 'It must have really hurt.' I noticed a texture similar to that of his lips, at once soft and faintly ridged.

'I didn't see the point in alarming you. You'd have wanted to come over. As for the scar, don't worry about that: as soon as it heals, they'll send me to a specialist who'll get rid of it. According to my bosses, a scarred face wouldn't go down well in certain circles, it would inspire distrust. I'd look like a hoodlum, a thug. They assure me that not a trace will be left, my face unmarked. Just as if the mugging had never happened.'

And so it was. Afterwards, I could never see any evidence of that incident on his face, even though, out of sheer amazement, I tried to find it, and really looked, looked hard, while he was sleeping or pretending to sleep, and when light was already coming into the bedroom. Strangely, though, what he did retain was that habit of running his thumbnail over his now smooth cheek, as if he rather liked the gesture: after all, in terms of duration, the scar barely existed. And yet, despite his perfectly credible explanation (at the time, London was full of muggers, partly as a consequence of that ghastly film *A Clockwork Orange*, which aroused such interest), I couldn't help thinking that he might sometimes be involved in rather riskier missions than might be expected. When you work for the State, they ask and go on asking, go on tugging at the string, and generally squeeze both employees and citizens ('Do this out of patriotism, this out of loyalty, this other thing out of solidarity with the weak or simply for the common good'), and there's no way of knowing what they will end up demanding or extracting, what aberrations or sacrifices they will require. I've always been discreet, though, and have always known it's best not to ask questions that won't be answered, at least not truthfully. That only brings frustration. Best to wait for the other person to tell you when he has no alternative, when his situation is desperate or has been uncovered, or when he can no longer bear to keep silent (and almost no one can keep silent until the grave, not even about something that stains and will prejudice his memory). And the reason I know this so well is from personal experience and practice: I've almost never given an honest answer about anything I would prefer others not to know.

And yet the day did come when I had to ask him, knowing that I would receive only a splinter of the truth, and when Tomás felt obliged to tell me that splinter of truth, to satisfy me with a wisp, a speck, a mote, a thread, or perhaps it wasn't such a small thing, for him it was doubtless much more than that, an excess, which he hated having to tell me about. As I said, two years had passed since our wedding and three years since his definitive return from Oxford, quite a long time to keep almost absolute silence, to conceal completely the true nature of his activities in his second or first country, and no doubt in others too; I realised that I would never know for sure where he was each night and in whose company, where he spent his days, weeks and months. When I did finally ask, contrary to my usual custom and my natural discretion, it was out of fright, alarm, fear, in order to take precautions and find out precisely what precautions I should take, and to ascertain just how worried I should be. If you feel threatened, you need to know what's going on, because ignorance is the greatest danger. Then, if you can and if you dare, you're free to disregard that information, although you'd do better not to.

The episode began in our local park, the Jardines de Sabatini, which I visited most mornings while I was on maternity leave, with my little boy in his pram, to get some fresh air and have a walk; we lived very near, in Calle Pavía, off Plaza de Oriente, opposite the Palacio Real, next to the Iglesia de la Encarnación. I would stroll through the little park, then sit for a while on a bench, almost always the same one, holding a book in one hand and, with the other, rocking Guillermo back and forth; Tomás had chosen the boy's name, and I'd heartily approved: a homage to the literary hero of his childhood, William Brown, or Guillermo el Travieso or Guillermo el Proscrito, as Richmal Crompton's character was known in Spain, and whose adventures Tomás – even though he was bilingual – had read in Spanish translation, so that he could discuss them with his school friends, who wouldn't have known who he meant if he'd started talking about Just William or William the Outlaw.

I never managed to read more than about ten lines of my book when I was there, for any mother – or for me as a mother – it's almost impossible not to keep checking that your child is still there, however often you pause to confirm that he is, whether emitting small sounds, or silent and asleep, or silent and awake. And in that small, unfrequented eighteenth-century-style park (mostly visited by tourists), with its modest labyrinths of box hedges and its small pond with a few ducks, whenever I heard footsteps or spotted someone out of the corner of my eye, I would immediately look up to monitor, if I can use that word, any change to the usually peaceable situation. And thus I saw the couple approaching some way off, a man and a woman, apparently married, she holding his arm, and they seemed inoffensive, even good-natured, but that is the foolish, stereotypical impression given by fat people, as if a fat person could not be just as dangerous as a slender Dracula or Fu Manchu. He was the fat one (a nimble fellow who walked briskly), she was not; but the plump do tend to infect those around them with their plumpness.

They sat down on a stone bench, immediately opposite the wooden one I was occupying in the shade of a tree; they, on the other hand, remained in the sun, on that very mild May morning. I noticed at once that both of them were studying me intently, while trying not to be too obvious, almost as if they recognised me or were trying to, as if my face rang a bell and they were struggling to remember where they had met me before. As far as I was concerned, they were total strangers. They smiled at me and I smiled politely back. The man was wearing a raincoat-coloured raincoat, doubtless surplus to requirements given the weather, and he must have been about forty, with short, brown, curly hair, and unnecessarily large plastic-framed glasses, too big for his rather beady eyes; he had very small features – or perhaps his abundant flesh made them seem small – a short nose and thin lips, but a broad, sympathetic, pleasant smile, his teeth as orderly and regular as typewriter keys, an affable figure. The most striking thing about the woman were her large, blue, slightly squinty eyes, which a malicious person might have described as cross-eyed; she was a similar age to her husband, and one sensed that her skin was not quite as firm as his beneath the possibly exaggerated or rather old-fashioned layer of make-up she was wearing, her lips painted very red and her blonde hair either fresh from the hairdresser's or from prolonged titivation in front of a mirror. She looked foreign, and he might or might not have been; if he'd let that curly hair grow longer (or grow fuller at the sides), he would have looked like a real party animal or a flamenco singer, but his skin was too white and soft, almost freckled only without the freckles, but in excellent condition: not a hint of a wrinkle, he would age far more slowly than his wife. She had a more elegant, immaculate air about her, that of a refined, well-dressed lady, with an equally cordial smile and a bust that was more maternal than provocative: she wasn't fat in the least, but not skinny either, and her tailored jacket did little to conceal her breasts, prominent and curved (albeit pointed at the ends), which might prove almost overwhelming to a grown man, but welcoming to a child or a youth or, perhaps, to another woman. That squint, though, was rather unsettling, you could never be sure at any one moment where she was looking, although all four eyes – hers and his – were observing me, the pram with its hood up (they were probably curious about the child, as is only natural), even the book I was holding, they were doubtless trying to decipher the title and the author's name. So insistent were their looks and smiles that I began to feel uncomfortable and was tempted to go home. Then the fat man spoke to me:

'It's Señora Nevinson, isn't it?' And he got up and came over to me, his smile growing wider, holding out a hand for me to shake.

I responded purely mechanically; it's almost impossible not to reciprocate that friendly gesture.

'Do we know each other?' I asked. 'I don't recall . . .'

'That's only natural. Why ever would you remember an old married couple like us? Not like your husband and yourself, so young and handsome. We met a few months ago, at a cocktail party at the embassy, I mean at Thomas's embassy.' It was unusual for someone in Spain to call him 'Thomas', he was always either Tomás or Tom. 'We chatted for a while, but, of course, one can't possibly remember all the people with whom one has exchanged a few words on such occasions. Besides, we don't really make much of an impression, ha ha,' and he guffawed modestly and falsely to support this statement: the two of them were, in fact, very memorable, he because of his sheer bulk and she because of her squinting blue eyes. 'Miguel Ruiz Kindelán at your service. And this is my wife, Mary Kate.'

The woman joined us then and kissed me on each cheek, as is the custom among women in Spain ('No, don't get up, my dear,' she said, placing one strong, heavy hand on my shoulder and addressing me with female familiarity), although from her name and accent I realised that she was, in fact, a foreigner, even though she spoke very correct and fluent Spanish, which suggested she must have been living here for some time. He, on the other hand, spoke just like Tomás or me, more Ruiz than the more foreign-sounding Kindelán. And when the two of them saw Guillermo's face, they could not conceal their admiration, which was, it must be said, somewhat over the top ('Oh, but he's just gorgeous, the little cherub!' exclaimed Mary Kate); people do tend to go overboard with babies, even the ugly ones, of which there are a few.

'Kindelán?' I'd heard that name before, it didn't sound Spanish, and yet it's not so very unusual in Spain, I'd doubtless heard or seen it written somewhere, and more than once too. 'Isn't there someone famous with that name? I can't quite remember who.'

'Well, there was a general who died some years ago, Alfredo Kindelán. He was the first Spaniard to get a pilot's licence, and he wrote a few books too. Perhaps that's who you mean, General Kindelán. I believe he took part in the uprising, and he may have been in charge of the Spanish Air Force during the Civil War. I think he has a street named after him. No, I'm wrong, that's General Kirkpatrick. As you know, there are quite a few Irish names in Spain, presumably because of the Catholic connection. O'Donnell was given a very nice central street, wasn't he? And General Lacy did rather well too, certainly better than O'Farrill, O'Ryan, Wall, and O'Donohue and others, and yet O'Donohue ended up being Viceroy of Mexico; but then, of course, he did help facilitate Mexican independence, which didn't go down too well. Did you know that he became O'Donojú, with a "j" and an accent on the "u"? It's funny, isn't it, Juan O'Donojú, that was his official name. He was from Seville, I believe. And he was a well-known freemason.' He pronounced all those names (apart from

O'Donojú) as a British speaker would, so perhaps he was bilingual, like Tomás.

I couldn't help noticing his use of the term 'uprising', which might indicate that he did not disapprove of the military rebellion against the Republic in 1936, although some people used the word unthinkingly, out of habit or contagion, or after all those decades of hearing the propaganda machine use it to refer to the initial failed coup d'état and the successful one three years later. (It was still being bandied about in 1976.) Thankfully, he didn't accompany it with the usual *franquista* adjective, 'glorious'.

'Is Kindelán an Irish name, then?'

'Apparently, yes. Although, as I understand it, there have been Kindeláns in Spain since the year dot, certainly since the eleventh or twelfth century. Originally, it would have been O'Kindelán, but who knows. Several of them became Knights of the Order of Santiago.'

'And you belong to that very ancient, illustrious family, do you?' I asked with a touch of irony, for he didn't look the part of the aristocrat or someone of noble birth, although he was impeccably dressed, apart from his shoes, which were dusty from the sandy paths in the park, and his shirt, which, because of his large belly, protruded slightly above his waistband. He must have had to buy shirts with very long tails, as voluminous as sheets, so that they remained firmly anchored. I found that nimble fat man and his conversation most amusing. He knew things, and certainly knew about those Irish Spaniards (I'd only ever heard of O'Donnell), and it was interesting to learn about names and facts, strange and unfamiliar, at least to me. Despite my family and friends, I spent a lot of time alone. When you have a small child, you do tend to be left very much alone with him.

'No, no.' And again he laughed. 'Well, I must be distantly related, I suppose, but the branch I belong to is quite unconnected to all those medieval knights and Santiago and so on. Perhaps one of my ancestors fell from grace or committed a dishonourable act and was rebuffed and repudiated, ostracised, exiled for ever from the Kindelán universe. That's where I must come from. I've certainly never known any of the nobility. I'm middle class at best.' Again that modest laugh. He laughed very heartily, despite being told off by Mary Kate.

'I don't know why you always have to talk such nonsense. You have no idea what happened. You must be related in some way to those knights and that aviator general. Miguel does like to joke, dear Berta. Your name is Berta, isn't it? If I remember rightly, that is.'

'Goodness, you do have a good memory!' I said in astonishment. They even remembered my first name, and yet I still had no memory of them at all, and the more I saw and heard them, the more I thought that, if I *had* talked with them at any length at a reception, I would definitely not have forgotten or erased their faces. The woman's eyes were almost frightening when fixed, squinting, on nothing at all, as if in a trance, although when glancing from side to side, they seemed oddly ingenuous and defenceless.

'All right, all right,' he said, defending himself. 'Let's just say that he, my noble ancestor, was the one who cast off the family. People do sometimes renounce things, even privileges, even happiness, even the very best of things, not to mention a quiet life. There are people who simply head off and never come back, who disappear, go missing, every family has its black sheep, individuals filled with some kind of deep unease, who don't want to be who they are or are destined to be. They decide to lead a life entirely unsuited to either their birth or upbringing. Sometimes they vanish completely and their relatives say "Good riddance!" Do you know that English expression?' Again, he pronounced the phrase like a native speaker, so he must have been bilingual. 'It's not quite the same as the Spanish saying: *A enemigo que*

159

huye, puente de plata – literally, "If your enemy flees, build him a silver bridge" – because, for a start, he's not the enemy, on the contrary, but that's the general drift. And of course, if, one day, he did become an enemy, there's no worse enemy than someone of your own blood or a spouse. But forgive me,' he said, 'I can be a bit of a chatterbox. Tell me, how is Thomas? I haven't seen him for a while.'

'He's in London. He spends quite long periods of time there because of his work.'

'What!' said Mary Kate, somewhat shocked. 'He leaves you all alone with this little treasure, this cherub?' And she coochie-cooed at Guillermo, waving her hands to attract his attention. Her various bracelets tinkled as if we were in a china shop after a visit from a bull. The baby enjoyed the noise, and Mary Kate again gesticulated like a mad thing, once or even twice.

'Well, it can't be helped. Work comes first. And Tomás is needed over there.' When I addressed them both, I did so formally as *ustedes*; after all, Ruiz Kindelán had only addressed me as *tú* once and had then immediately corrected himself. Since I was very much their junior, I didn't want to seem overly familiar. 'But I manage fine. I have a nanny for part of the day and on any nights when I have to go out, and I get help from other people too, my mother, my mother-in-law, my sister and a friend. Children spend the first years of their lives entirely among women, we're their universe, the one thing they have to hold on to and almost the only thing they feel and see. They depend on us for everything in order to survive. It's odd how slight a mark that leaves on them, don't you think? On men, I mean. Perhaps they're in rebellion against their beginnings, against a world that was so much gentler than the one they discover later on. Perhaps it enrages them to have been at our mercy. I do hope Guillermo won't turn out like that.'

'Don't you believe it, dear Berta,' said Mary Kate in her strong, possibly Irish accent. 'According to the psychologists, the first months and years are the building blocks of the personality, and we women are totally responsible for that. Be in no doubt, we are the civilising force,' and there she made a grammatical error in Spanish, omitting the irregular subjunctive, which some foreigners never do master, 'and it doesn't bear thinking what the coarser boys would be like if they hadn't been cared for by us initially. They would be little better than animals. You can't imagine some of the children you meet in Ireland, they're worse even than in Spain and Italy, and that's certainly saying something.'

'Filthy little beasts,' commented Ruiz Kindelán. He quickly realised, though, that his comment was both excessive and uncharitable, and tried to rectify this impression – rather difficult to do in the presence of a new young mother. 'I mean, you do encounter some very wild, very feral children, especially in small towns. Spanish and Italian children are terribly spoiled and badly brought up, but Irish children are even fiercer. They're very backward.' It occurred to me that, in his childhood, assuming he'd spent it in Ireland – or even when he visited as an adult – he had probably been bullied and had stones thrown at him because he was so fat. The obese are always a favourite target of cruel people everywhere. 'The priests do what they can, but it's not enough,' he added to my surprise, since I would have thought that the priests contributed in no small measure to the general backwardness.

'More backward than in the villages here?'

He thought about this for a second.

'No, you're right. You get some terrible bullies in Spanish villages too, and they'll doubtless grow up to be complete oafs.'

'Are you Irish?' I asked. 'Do you have children?' Up until then, they had only told me their names, and no surname in the case of Mary Kate. I didn't know what work they did nor why we'd met at that cocktail party at the embassy. The embassy wasn't particularly choosy who they invited, but nor did it open its doors to just anyone. By then, they had sat down beside me on my bench, and I'd had to shift up to make room for them; it was distinctly cramped. They were invasive people, albeit pleasant and friendly.

Mary Kate *was* Irish, and before she married, her name had been Mary Kate O'Riada ('Like the composer, may he rest in peace,' she said. 'Some people pronounce it O'Reidy, others don't.' I had no idea who this composer was). Ruiz Kindelán was Spanish, but had lived part of his life in Dublin and travelled all over Ireland, which he knew like the back of his hand. They both worked at the Irish embassy, which is how they knew Tomás, and the reason why they were occasionally invited to parties and diplomatic suppers. No, they had no children. And now it was getting rather late for that.

'Not that we've really tried. We've always been too busy.' And Mary Kate squinted across at a pair of young ducks swimming in the lake, as if they reminded her of the children she hadn't had, or perhaps as though children were no different from a few foolish creatures demanding to be fed. 'We devote ourselves to each other,' she added blandly. 'Miguel looks after me, and I look after Miguel. We're not just a married couple, we're a team and almost always together. Until death do us part, and, with luck, death will take us both at the same time, isn't that so, Miguel?'

'Oh yes, absolutely.'

In the four or five weeks that followed – which is how long that whole episode lasted, if I can continue to call it an episode, when it was probably more like fear and panic – I had the sense that they really did form a team and were always together. I never saw one without the other. Their appearances in the park became more frequent (they may have been there before, but I'd never noticed them), or they would find me in other parts of the neighbourhood, for they claimed to live close by, without ever specifying where, sometimes pointing vaguely in the direction of Paseo del Pintor Rosales. As befits a certain type of childless couple, they 'adopted' me very easily, even with alacrity. They seemed cheerful and amiable, protective and concerned, offering to help me in any way they could, even babysitting were that necessary (it wasn't, and I would never have entrusted Guillermo to such recent acquaintances, ones who had introduced themselves, however affectionate they were, however unconditional they declared themselves to be). Up to a point, I allowed myself to be courted. I did sometimes feel very alone when Guillermo was still too small to let him out of my sight for a moment; initially, it's terribly difficult to be away from a child for an instant, not to have him permanently in your arms, smelling his skin and wanting the world to stop right there, wanting him never to grow up and for everything else to be placed permanently on pause and for that situation to continue for ever, me and him, him and me, and for everything else to disappear. Nevertheless, it can be very isolating, and it was pleasant to have that gift of company and conversation, to feel protected by those parentally inclined neighbours to whom I could turn in case of difficulty. They gave me their telephone number, and I gave them mine, and, from then on, they began to call me often, as if we were old friends, to find out how everything was going or if I needed anything, if they could run an errand for me or do me some other favour or service, if they could bring me something I'd forgotten or been unable to buy. I sometimes found it odd that they weren't at the embassy in the morning, precisely when people are usually at their busiest; that was why, during the day, I couldn't count on my mother, my mother-in-law, my sister or any of my friends, all of whom were busy women with things to do. One day, I asked them about this, and when they explained that they had a very flexible timetable, I gave the matter no further thought.

During one of Tomás's infrequent and always hurried phone calls, I mentioned them to him and told him how we'd met, and asked if he remembered them, given the familiar way in which the fat man had referred to him as Thomas, as had Mary Kate, although she was perhaps merely imitating her husband.

'No, the name doesn't ring a bell, not that I remember,' he said. 'Maybe if I saw their faces . . . But there's nothing very odd about not remembering them. In my line of work, I go to so many cocktail parties and meetings and get-togethers of all kinds that, by the time the year is out, I'll probably have spoken to hundreds of people. You talk to a person for a few minutes and instantly forget them, unless, of course, they happen to be particularly important or dazzling or make a big impression on you.'

'Well, I wouldn't say they were dazzling exactly, but once seen, never forgotten; that's why I find it so odd that I have no recollection of them. He's enormously fat and she has a squint. She's a very attractive woman, but that squint can be rather troubling.'

'I don't know, I've no idea, perhaps I met them at some event organised by the AHGBI. Anyway, I've got to go now. I don't have much time.'

'The AHGBI?' He had said those initials in English. 'You never have much time, do you? What is it they make you do over there?'

'The Association of Hispanists of Great Britain and Ireland. We organise events with them, and when any of their members visit Spain, they usually take the opportunity to drop in at the British Council or the embassy, especially if there's a drinks do on. There have always been a lot of Irish visitors ever since Starkie was in charge, because, of course, he himself is Irish and very proud of having been the first professor of Spanish at Trinity College Dublin, and of having Samuel Beckett as a pupil. If you're curious, ask him. He's sure to know them.'

Walter Starkie had been the founder and director of the British Institute, where Tomás had studied before transferring to my school. He was a good friend of my father-in-law, Jack, and had been a huge help to Tomás, and was, I imagine, partly responsible for his swift appointment to his current post. Now, after a long spell teaching in California, Starkie was coming back to live in Madrid, although he would die only a few months later, following a fatal asthma attack.

'No, I don't want to bother him, he's very old now. And I'm not that curious. The fact is, they're very kind to me. They make a huge fuss over Guillermo. The other day they dropped in and brought him all sorts of little presents. They're really very pleasant and considerate.'

I should have been more curious, that might have saved me from that whole episode, from the fear and the panic. Although it did also allow me to find out something more about Tomás.

Miguel and Mary Kate often asked about him (we were soon on first-name terms and addressing each other as *tú*, because, already in the Spain of 1976, it was becoming difficult to maintain the more formal *usted*), and they did so with a somewhat insistent interest, which I took for deference, an attempt to console me, to show their solidarity with and concern for me.

'What news of Thomas? Have you heard from him at all? What's he up to in London? Or is he somewhere else now? Depending on what his job is, he'll probably have to travel. What does he do exactly at the Foreign Office? Which department does he work for? And who's his boss? We know various people there. He probably works with Reggie, a good friend of ours. Ask him if he knows Reggie Gathorne. He spends far too much time away from you, don't you think? If he's working with them on a temporary basis, it's not really temporary enough, I'd say. They should bear in mind his family circumstances, because there's really no justification for him being away so much when his son is still so young. Not that I wish to criticise him, you understand, and work is work, but he really should spend more time at home, because the first year in a child's life is the most difficult, the one that requires most trouble and effort. I can see how exhausted you are, even though you have help. Besides, he's missing out, young children change so quickly, from one day to the next. May I ask why he's in such demand there? When does he think he'll be back? What's keeping him? It must be a very complicated job or mission or whatever. And he must miss you both enormously. He'll be longing to see the two of you, especially you.'

I couldn't really answer their questions either precisely or imprecisely. The truth was that I knew almost nothing, not even the date of his return. I'd never heard him mention Reggie Gathorne and I'd never got a complete picture of his day-to-day life in London. Telling me about it seemed to bore him when he did come home, and it would have bored me to hear about it. I've never been the inquisitive sort, and even from when he was very young – from the time we first met as adolescents – there had always been an element of opacity about him, which had only grown over the years. The one sphere we truly shared – which was the largest and most essential, the one that really counted and on which every couple should count – was home, bed and the baby, the sphere of laughter and kisses and conversations containing no information or tedious details about work, the sphere of sheer pleasure in each other's company, in going out together and being at each other's side, face to face, or on top, or aware of each other's breathing from behind. I suppose someone less modest would say 'the sphere of our love'. And yes, I did miss him enormously and imagined that he missed me too. But what someone else feels always belongs to the world of the imagination. You never know for certain, you cannot even know if the most passionate declarations are true or mere interpretation or convention, if they are deeply felt or merely what the other person feels he or she should feel and is prepared to put into words. I really did long to see him, but whether he longed to see me, I have no idea. As I said, a silent weight kept him at a distance, whatever the weight was that he'd placed on his shoulders when he completed his studies at Oxford, the weight that had chosen him. Desires wane and fall asleep when the die is cast and one can no longer choose freely. In a way, there's no room for them any more, or they seem mere chimeras, mere daydreams, and are fated to be discarded after a few moments of weakness.

When the couple came to our apartment one day, in the middle of the morning, about a month had passed since my first meeting with them. Guillermo had been feverish all night, and I preferred to keep him in, not to expose him to anything. So they came to us instead, to see how Guillermo was doing. His temperature had gone down in the early hours, but he still seemed sleepy and tired, because he had cried a lot and not slept enough. I had barely slept a wink myself.

For the first few minutes, Miguel, who was usually a jokey, animated, talkative fellow, seemed rather silent and irritated. They sat down on the sofa, and I sat in an armchair to their left, having brought in Guillermo's cradle so that I could keep an eye on him; he lay at our feet between us. In those days, people smoked even in the presence of babies, and they were both smoking. Not heavily, but they were smoking nonetheless, just as Tomás and I did, for I had resumed the habit after having stopped for nine or ten months. Ruiz Kindelán took a cigarette from his leather cigarette case, but did not yet light it, passing it instead from hand to hand, or even placing it behind his ear like a mechanic or an old-fashioned shopkeeper.

'Berta, there's something we need to talk about,' he said suddenly, putting an end to the earlier small talk. He also set aside his rather irritated expression and attempted a smile, showing his small, square teeth, like miniature piano keys, trying to be his usual cordial, pleasant self, and speaking in a light tone so as not to worry me, even though those preliminary words never bode well, promising only misfortunes and abandonings and conflicts and bad news.

'About what?'

'Well, there are two things really. One is that, with profound regret, we've come to say goodbye. Can you imagine, we're being transferred. After all this time here in Madrid. It's most unfair. You gradually build a life in one place, become fond of it, and suddenly you have to leave and start another life somewhere completely different. In our profession, as you know, it can happen at any moment;

we've been dreading it for a while now, but the years have passed and we've managed to avoid it. Our luck has run out, though, and who knows when we'll be able to come back or if we'll be able to come back. At least they'll be sending us to wherever it is together. We couldn't possibly be separated. And that was always a danger. Remote perhaps, but a danger nonetheless.'

'Miguel looks after me, and I look after Miguel,' Mary Kate said, repeating the same words she'd spoken on that first day.

'Well, I'm really sorry, for you and for me. It's most unfortunate.' I really did feel sorry, we so quickly get used to people who take our side, who are protective and helpful. 'So you don't know where they're sending you yet?'

'There are a couple of possibilities,' said Ruiz Kindelán. 'Sometimes they don't tell you until the very last minute and then organise the transfer in great haste. It could be Italy, where we've been before, but it could also be Turkey, and we wouldn't like that at all. They're not Catholics, or even Christians, or only a handful of them are. The language is fiendishly difficult, appropriately enough, and not like any other. They say it's vaguely like Hungarian, but that's hardly a consolation. At least in Hungary we would be among Christians, although, apparently, there are quite a lot of Jews there too, if, that is, they managed to come back.' They had never spoken openly about religion, but I had already gleaned, from passing remarks, that it was of great importance to them. They went to mass on Sundays, which they mentioned openly, and perhaps not only on Sundays. 'We won't be of much use in Ankara, but they're short of personnel there, and we have to do what our bosses tell us, which isn't to say that they're right, of course. Anyway, the transfer is definitely imminent.'

'How imminent?' I felt superficially upset.

'Within the week, we think. Ten days at most. But, apart from that, dear Berta, we have to say goodbye because you wouldn't want to see us again anyway. Not after the other matter we've come about.' He didn't say this gravely, but continued to smile. He took out the black Zippo lighter he usually used. He didn't even open it, but simply played with it. These lighters were still very fashionable at the time. American soldiers had used them during the Vietnam War, which had ended a year ago. It was said that they had used them to set fire to villages and settlements, that they were far more efficient than torches.

Then I did begin to feel worried.

'What other matter? Why wouldn't I want to see you again?'

Then he asked again about Tomás.

'Tell me, are you quite sure that his work in London is what he tells you it is? Are you even sure that he's in London? That he's there right now?'

'Well, I only know what he tells me. As I said, that isn't very much, and he doesn't go into details that are no concern of mine, and, to be honest, I don't pay much attention.' I paused for a second. 'Besides, you can never necessarily trust what people tell you, can you? And although he's the one who usually phones me, I have two numbers for him in London should an emergency arise. Why wouldn't he be where he says he is?'

'Is he always the one to answer the phone?' asked Mary Kate, joining in the interrogation. 'Are those numbers his home phone, his apartment, where he works, an office somewhere, or at the Foreign Office?'

I found this insistence very odd on both their parts, but I still saw nothing very strange about their questions. They were always very curious, wanting to know all kinds of things.

'Look,' I said, 'I've only used either of those numbers once at most, and on neither of those occasions did he pick up the phone himself, which is perfectly logical really, since one is his work number, where he spends more time than he does at home, and the other is an apartment block with a switchboard, near Gloucester Road. That's where he lives, or rather sleeps. The two individuals who answered said they'd pass on my message, and he did phone me back shortly afterwards. I don't know if he works at the Foreign Office itself or somewhere else. Why do you ask? What is all this about?'

'We've received information that he doesn't work for the Foreign Office at all, but for MI6.' Seeing my look of puzzlement, Ruiz Kindelán thought it best to explain just in case, although my puzzlement had nothing to do with ignorance, I knew what MI6 and MI5 were, as anyone does who's read spy novels or seen any of the James Bond films. 'It's the secret service for overseas operations.' And when I said nothing (a silence provoked by the kind of amused astonishment you feel when you suspect someone of pulling your leg or not being entirely serious), he went on to explain, as if I were stupid or younger than I was: 'In a word: spies.'

I did laugh then, briefly, incredulously, in response to that unnecessary explanation, which seemed almost ingenuous.

'He's never said anything to me about that, but then if someone is a spy, working for the Secret Service, he's hardly going to shout it from the rooftops,' I joked. The couple were still smiling, still addressing me in the same friendly tone, although there was now a slightly harder edge to their questions. 'And what if it's true? I don't much like the idea, but I suppose it's not that difficult to move from the Foreign Office to MI6, occasionally anyway. Perhaps they call him in sometimes to interrogate some foreign agent, or to act as interpreter. He has a great gift for languages, he knows quite a few, most of which he speaks perfectly. If he could be of use to MI6, they're hardly going to waste his talents.'

'It's not that easy. MI stands for "military intelligence", in case you didn't know. It's a military organisation, not diplomatic or part of the civil service. It's part of the army, it's above the police and almost any other authority. Its agents are given ranks, part of a hierarchy, and are subject to army discipline. They belong, in short . . .' He pulled a face and corrected himself. 'They're officers in an invading army.'

'Invading? Invading what?'

'Ireland, of course. Our country,' Mary Kate was quick to say in her accented Spanish, and when she said this, her eyes fixed angrily on me, or so I thought. Her squint became even more marked, and again it provoked in me a faint, momentary flicker of fear, an irrational fear while it lasted, which was usually only for a matter of seconds. This time it lasted slightly longer. It took a while for those eyes to return to their more benign selves, and it was as if that simultaneously fixed and divergent gaze were bitterly reproaching me: 'Do you know nothing, you stupid girl? Are you entirely ignorant of the world, entirely indifferent? An army intent on invading our country.'

I looked away and down at Guillermo, doubtless seeking refuge in him. His gaze was gentle and inconstant, he didn't yet fix it fully on people or objects, it zigzagged erratically, unable to focus properly on any one thing, unlike Mary Kate's eyes. For some time, he had been quite calm, his eyes open, with not a trace of fever. He lay at our feet, gurgling distractedly.

I bent down and stroked his cheek with one finger; there was my brand-new little boy, so soft and round, so fresh. Absurd though it may seem, the sight of him calmed me, as if, as long as I was by his side, nothing could happen to me and everything else vanished; as if we protected each other, and yet how could he, poor thing, protect me? The sound of the Zippo lighter made me look up. Ruiz Kindelán had finally raised the cigarette to his lips, flicked open the lighter cover with his thumb and tried to light it, but no flame appeared. He shook the lighter hard and tried again, but still no flame. I glanced down at his shoes, which were always slightly grubby or, rather, never exactly gleaming; he probably neglected them, feeling, as many men do, an invincible distaste for the brush, cloth and polish, and it occurred to me that this must explain the existence of shoeshines; his shoes were in marked contrast with his rather good-quality, well-kept suits, even though some were slightly shiny with wear. The raincoat that he usually carried draped over one arm even in June lay beside him on the sofa in an untidy heap.

'Look, my dear Berta,' he said, and as soon as he said this, he gave a rather inopportune laugh, as if wanting to lend a festive tone to the conversation. 'We have received information that an individual working for MI6 is causing a lot of damage in Belfast or is about to be let loose either there or in some other place, whether he's on his way or already in situ we don't yet know.' He pronounced the name of the city with the stress on the second syllable, as almost no Spaniard would, or not at least a Spaniard of unmixed race, and he had used the same form of words as before: 'We have received information', but who from? And who was that 'we'? Just him and Mary Kate, or someone else? An organisation, a government, a country? 'We're not sure who he is or who he's pretending to be, we don't know what he looks like because he may have changed his appearance once already or even twice. He may have had fair hair before and now be dark, having been a redhead in between. He may once have had a thick thatch of hair, and now wear it almost shaved. He may be sporting a beard, whereas before he was clean-shaven and, in between times, might have grown long sideburns and a moustache, a moustache like Crosby's and sideburns like Stills or Neil Young.' At the time, the music of that supergroup Crosby, Stills, Nash & Young still echoed in the air. And yet I was surprised that someone like Ruiz Kindelán should know who they were. 'He didn't wear glasses before, but now he wears some as big as mine.' He touched the bridge of his glasses, pushing them further up his nose with his middle finger, and taking the opportunity to smooth his curly hair. 'It's only natural that he should hide his real face, or try to present various faces so as to seem to be different people and put others off the track, to sow confusion.' He laughed again, apparently spontaneously, as if this were all a game or a riddle. 'We suspect he may be a fairly new agent, recently trained, not burned out, not spent, probably deployed to act as a mole, an infiltrator, well, you know what I mean. And we suspect that he might be Thomas. How is Thomas's Irish accent? Do you think he could pass for one of us? Apparently, he's a real prodigy when it comes to imitating accents and voices and ways of speaking. Apparently, people almost split their sides laughing when they hear him.

We haven't yet had the opportunity ourselves to hear him in action, but people say he's amazing.' And he laughed for a third time, as if he were actually witnessing that prodigious display, then he picked up his raincoat and started carefully rummaging around in one of its many pockets, as he continued talking in an almost jocular tone, with not a trace of drama. 'Not that we're saying it is him, we don't know, it's very difficult to find out, of course; that's the job of his superiors, to make finding out as difficult as possible. We're not even sure he is employed by MI6. We hope not, we really do. We'd love this to be all a mistake. It would be very painful to learn that someone we're so fond of is working to the detriment of Ireland; that would upset us greatly. The husband of someone we adore, imagine.'

'And the father of this angel too, this little cherub,' added Mary Kate, using her favourite word for the baby, and leaning forward to jingle her bracelets over him, a sound he always responded to, as if it were a substitute rattle.

'But there are some ugly rumours going around,' Ruiz Kindelán went on. 'And rumours do sometimes turn out to be true, but let's hope that's not the case this time.' He still had his cigarette between his lips, his lighter with the lid down in one hand, while with the other, he continued calmly, unhurriedly, casually feeling about in his raincoat, barely paying any heed to the task, as if he were sure that what he was looking for would turn up sooner or later. 'It would be good to know, and rule out the possibility. The sooner the better, for us and for you. For everyone. I think you could do that, Berta, I think it's up to you to find out and to talk to him about it. And if that ugly rumour proves true, to convince him to stop, he wouldn't lie to you, would he, not about a grave matter that would affect you and the child, all three of you. At least as regards Ireland, I mean. He must keep out of Ireland, or we'll all end up the losers, and then we'll be in a real mess. Do you understand?' And he finally removed from an inside pocket the object he'd been searching for: a small can of lighter fuel, also bearing the brand name Zippo, and black like the lighter but with a red plastic lid, on top of which was a kind of spout that you turned one way to close and the other way to open, allowing the fuel out through a tiny orifice when your lighter needed refilling. It wasn't that the flint was worn out, for on the two occasions when he'd tried to light it, it had sounded perfectly normal and had produced a spark, but no flame, that rather showy and, initially, lively Zippo flame, apparently less controllable than others, which is perhaps why it wasn't easily extinguished, not even by a slight breeze, which is also perhaps why the lighters are more efficient than torches when it comes to starting fires, to burning things down. It had run out of fuel and he had come prepared; in those days, everyone – well, certainly all smokers – knew how they worked: you extracted the lighter from its metal casing and injected the fuel through a small hole into the cotton or foam packing or whatever it was, until it was saturated and the lighter ready for use. 'We'll be in a fine pickle if he can't be persuaded,' he added, smiling his usual pleasant, attractive smile, and then I noticed that the spout on the can was open and not closed as it should have been, and when Ruiz Kindelán shook the can before using it, as if it were a carton of fruit juice, a few drops (or perhaps a dribble) of that inflammable liquid fell onto Guillermo's cradle, onto his tiny sheets and tiny pyjamas. It all seemed entirely unintentional, a mistake, the can must already have been open when he took it out of his pocket, and it happened so quickly, from its first appearance to those few fallen drops onto the very worst of places (all it took was one slight movement of the arm), that I could do nothing to avoid this absurd accident. My first impulse was to snatch my child up in my arms and carry him off to the bathroom, where I could

176

undress him, clean, wash and bathe him, and remove him from the presence of that couple who, in the briefest of times, had gone from inspiring me with confidence and offering me protection to provoking sheer terror. And it was terror that kept me from moving, because, before I could pick up the child, Ruiz Kindelán again flicked open the lighter with his thumb, as if wanting to try again to light his cigarette, even though he hadn't yet injected any fuel into the foam packing; nor did he close the spout on the can, as anyone else would have done after making such a blunder. He still had the cigarette between his lips, the can of lighter fluid in one hand and, in the other, the open lighter. I froze, suddenly understanding what I had preferred not to understand, I froze and sat quite still in my armchair, afraid I might make matters worse, counterproductive and worse, irremediable and worse. 'The flint obviously works,' I thought rapidly, and, in my anxiety, I began to breathe very hard, what would nowadays be called hyperventilating, 'and, if he tries again, it's possible that this time it will light. And if it does, he could throw the lighter into the wicker cradle, onto the sheets and pyjamas, then it would take only a moment for the whole thing to go up in flames. Or he might accidentally drop the lighter and its inextinguishable flame.' Difficult though this was, I remained quite still, when what I most wanted was to run away, to escape with my child, but I didn't dare, I forced myself to remain in that paralysed state. I addressed him as if I had still understood nothing and as if the situation were perfectly normal. I pretended, I spoke with complete aplomb, almost casually, although my breathing and the panicky tremor in my voice must have given me away. I pretended I wasn't begging, but I was:

'Please, Miguel, put the thing away, you're surely not going to light it now. You've spilled lighter fluid on the cradle. How could you even think of refilling your lighter with the baby right there in front of you. And close the spout on the can too. What on earth are you doing with it open anyway? It'll have leaked into your raincoat pocket. You'll stink of the stuff.'

I could smell the fuel from where I was sitting, and Guillermo would be even more aware of it, breathing in those vapours would be bad for his little lungs, and he could do nothing about it. It occurred to me that with one swift, energetic gesture I might be able to rescue Guillermo from one of the two weapons or indeed both; anything can become a weapon, the inventive human mind is horribly quick in that respect. I noticed, however, that Ruiz Kindelán had both things firmly in his grasp, and, if I failed, the risk was still greater. 'He can't do anything,' I thought, trying to convince myself and drive away my fear. 'If he were to set fire to a child, he'd be put in prison, there'd be no escape, unless he set fire to me too. But what use would it be to me if they did send him to prison, because once the deed is done, it can't be undone.' Miguel raised his eyebrows as if nothing had happened, as if there were no danger at all and he was surprised at my fears. He laughed.

'Don't be ridiculous. Nothing bad is going to happen,' he said, adding his usual supposedly reassuring laugh. He closed the spout on the can of lighter fluid, but not his lighter. 'At least that's one less threat,' I thought, mentally thanking him, then I realised that this wasn't true at all, the fuel had already fallen on the sheets, there was no need for any more to be spilled. 'I wonder how long it takes to evaporate,' I thought, because I had no idea. Fortunately, Guillermo still wasn't crying or complaining, but lying with his little fists clenched and raised as he stared waveringly up at the ceiling, uttering a few guttural sounds and the occasional gurgle, despite the pungent smell, which might make him feel nauseous.

I glanced at Mary Kate in search of help or support, perhaps some female solidarity, but she provided no consolation at all. She was looking fixedly, expectantly, at her husband seated to her left, as if she were waiting for him to do what he had to do or what they had agreed he would do. And it seemed to me now that her squint-eyed gaze had taken on a fanatical, visionary gleam, as if her spectacularly blue eyes had been stripped not only of the ingenuousness or vulnerability they sometimes revealed when in movement, but also of all compassion, as if they were waiting for precisely what I did not want, the irremediable and the worst. I recalled that, for her, the children they hadn't had were a couple of silly ducks swimming on a pond. And I remembered, too, that for him, they were filthy little beasts.

'Nothing bad, dear Berta,' echoed Mary Kate, barely averting her gaze from her husband, or only enough to take in my almost undisguised look of supplication. 'No, nothing bad, given that it all depends on you, the very best of mothers. You betcha,' she added, slipping suddenly into unusually colloquial Spanish (unusual for a foreigner): *Si lo sabré yo.* For some reason, I found myself staring at her massive, prominent bust, either simply so as to not to have to see her terrifying squint or to persuade myself that any woman with such a welcoming bosom could not possibly harm anyone, still less a baby. Or as if this were a way of appealing to the maternal instinct she had doubtless never felt. I was feeling increasingly bewildered and could find no comfort in optimistic thoughts: deep down, I was sure she was capable of harming absolutely anyone, if her cause demanded it, and I could guess what that cause, or country, was. Far too many people appoint themselves as sole interpreters of the needs of their country, whatever that country is, and tend to infect it with their own contagious fervour.

'Of course,' I said, and I felt as if I were agreeing with a couple of mad people in order to placate them, something that the mad always notice and dislike intensely, it often irritates them and makes them still angrier, but I didn't know what else to say, what other tone of voice to use. 'Of course,' I said again, 'I'll talk to Tomás as soon as I can, I'll ask him about it and try to convince him, don't worry. If there's any truth in the rumour, which there probably isn't, it's doubtless just another false rumour, a case of mistaken identity, and he isn't him at all.' This last statement made no sense, but I assumed they would understand what I meant. Prolonged fear makes us think and speak as if we were in a fog.

'Yes, but what if he denies it?' said Mary Kate.

'If he denies it, that's because it's not true.'

'How would you know? He could deny it even if it were true. If he's working for MI6, they will have trained him to deny even the undeniable, that's just how it is. He could be standing in one place and yet swear blind that he isn't.'

My mind was incapable of following this exchange, however brief. I was entirely occupied with my defenceless child and that open lighter, for if Ruiz Kindelán flicked the wheel with his thumb and, this time, a flame did emerge, just one, the next step could be catastrophic, whether by accident or intention. The anxiety of knowing that I was incapable of protecting or saving Guillermo was becoming unbearable. My eyes were fixed on that thumb, my treacherous breathing ever louder and faster, and the fact is I was prepared to do anything, they could have ordered me to commit the most humiliating, indecent or abject act and I would have obeyed. I would certainly have betrayed my country – which, after four decades of dictatorship, I didn't hold in very high esteem – or my parents, or Tomás; I wouldn't have hesitated for an instant if it meant removing the threat of fire from my child. I wouldn't allow myself even to imagine him burning, because if I had, I would have fainted and not even have been able to keep watch.

Ruiz Kindelán continued smiling his usual sunny smile, he even giggled as if amused by Mary Kate's last words.

'Why ever did Thomas get involved in the first place,' he said, not so much as a question, but taking for granted that it was true and as if he found it interesting or diverting to speculate. 'Having spent most of his life here in Spain, he can hardly be such a great English patriot. And no one ever emerges from that business well, dear Berta, if, that is, they do emerge. I've known a couple of men like him, and studied a few more, and they usually come out either mad or dead. And those who aren't brought to justice and don't go entirely mad, end up not knowing who they are. They lose their life or it splits in two, and those two parts are irreconcilable, mutually repellent. They lose their identity and even their earlier memories. Some try to return to normality years later and just can't do it, they don't know how to reintegrate themselves into civilian life, if we can call it that, into ordinary passive life, with no sudden shocks or tensions, into enforced retirement. It makes no difference what age they are. If they're no good any more or are burned out, they're withdrawn from service, just like that, sent home or left to vegetate in an office, and some individuals don't even reach thirty before feeling that their time has passed – like football players. They miss their days of action, of villainy, deceit and falsehood. They remain attached to their murky past, and are sometimes overwhelmed by remorse: when they stop, they realise that what they did was utterly vile and achieved little or nothing; that they were, at best, dispensable; that anyone could have done what they did and with the same result; that all their hard work and the risks they ran were pointless, almost futile, because no one individual ever plays a truly decisive role or makes a truly radical difference. They also discover that no one will thank them for their efforts or their talent, their astuteness or their patience, that they will receive no gratitude, no admiration. What was important, no, crucial, for them is of no importance to anyone else. How could Thomas have been so stupid as to get involved in that? And so imprudent. As I said, no one comes out of that world in a good state. No one.' I wasn't paying much attention, but I did think: 'As long as he goes on speechifying, it will be all right. He'll be distracted and forget about his cigarette, and won't try to light it.' And then I thought: 'But who is he? Who are they? Perhaps he's referring to himself when he says all this, because he knows that one day the same fate will await him, the tasks he's charged with must be similar to those he attributes to Tomás, otherwise he wouldn't be warning me, he wouldn't be urging me to distance him from those tasks. Not that I believe that this is what Tomás does, there must be some mistake, and they're confusing him with someone else. But how little I actually know.' – 'And he's putting you and yours in danger too. Don't you realise that, dear Berta? The people he's trying to harm will do their best to deflect that harm. They'll try to neutralise him by any means possible. They'll take their revenge.' – 'He's talking about himself now,' I thought, 'about him and Mary Kate, who are a team, not just a married couple, but he speaks as if those taxed with dissuading or taking their revenge were other people, not them. He has the cheek to talk like that when he's just spilled lighter fuel into Guillermo's cradle and is holding an open Zippo lighter in his hand; true, it's nearly out of fuel, but it might yet have a drop left that could ignite at any moment, because something can appear to be empty and yet not be, I've seen it happen in films when someone gives an apparently empty water canteen a good shake, and, finally, a drop, like a drop of sweat, slips slowly out . . .'

Guillermo began to cough then, and I could stand it no longer.

'Look, I'll do anything you want, Miguel. But please put the cover back on your lighter and let me pick up my baby, let me clean him and wash him, he's probably choking on that strong smell, see how he's coughing. If I can smell it, imagine how much worse it must be for him. And he's so tiny, everything about him is so tiny. Please, let me.'

'Best just to mention the smell, rather than a fire, best not give him ideas,' I thought foolishly, since it was clear what his idea had been from the start of that fake accident; he was trying to frighten me so that I would give in to any demands, would promise what I wasn't even in a position to promise. I leaned down and held out my arms, determined to lift Guillermo out of the cradle, whether Miguel gave me permission or not. He didn't give me permission, because it was then, when he saw my determined, but incomplete gesture, that he flicked the thumbwheel of the lighter to light the cigarette that was still between his lips. No flame emerged then either, but I didn't have time to breathe a sigh of relief – I'd held my breath for a fraction of a second, or my heart had skipped a beat – because he closed the lighter for a moment only to open it again and repeat the threat. I had stopped so abruptly that I remained with my arms outstretched, frozen halfway, as if unable to reach my baby, as though I were separated from him by some invisible barrier, by railings, a glass screen, by the greatest force that exists: fear. Kindelán looked at me, smiling his usual smile and giggling, amused by himself.

'How easily frightened you are,' he said benevolently. 'I've already told you that nothing bad is going to happen. See?'

And he again flicked the thumbwheel of his lighter and now, perhaps to his own surprise, a brief, minuscule, fluctuating flame emerged, just as I had foreseen.

I did what any mother would have done, I suppose. I instinctively blew out the flame and snatched up my baby. It was enough to have

183

seen that feeble flame. I was sure that both Ruiz Kindelán and Mary Kate had finished their business. I was sure that the danger of the day had passed, but it could also return, and this was only an inaugural danger. He snapped the lighter shut – an unmistakable sound –and put it away in his jacket pocket. 'Yes, I can rest for today,' I thought, 'but from now on, I'll never be able to rest easy again, because these two people might come back. Or perhaps it's all just a bad joke, which is how I'll see it tomorrow.' It's amazing how easily we drive from our mind the things that preoccupy and worry us, that prevent us from living normally; just as in between bombardments, in time of war, people make the most of that parenthesis and pretend the bombardments don't exist and go out into the street and meet in cafés, I would need to believe that what was still happening hadn't happened at all; for they were still there, the Kindeláns, and I wondered who they really were; it suddenly seemed to me impossible that two embassy employees could behave like that, despite their efforts to ensure that everything appeared entirely fortuitous, I knew there was nothing fortuitous about it, but how could I prove that, I couldn't denounce them or write a letter of protest to their superiors, I could only talk to Tomás, tell him what had happened and ask how much of it was true, if any of what they had said was true. And even though I felt safe now, I was still breathing hard, you can't just stop that agitated breathing, or simply detach yourself from a horror.

Then he did the same with the little can of lighter fuel, returning it, safely sealed, to a pocket in his raincoat, the two weapons gone. He picked up his crumpled coat, threw it over his arm as it had been when he arrived, and almost sprang to his feet – he was always disconcertingly agile for such a very fat man – and his wife followed suit. Her lipstick had smudged a little, spilled over the edges of her lips. She noticed this, opened her bag, took out a small mirror and a

Kleenex and carefully wiped away the lipstick (she also examined her teeth, in case they had become smeared with lipstick too) as if nothing at all had happened. At most, her eyes swivelled restlessly away from the mirror, flickered here and there about the room, but avoided resting on Guillermo, as if the little cherub had ceased to exist. I was clutching him to me as hard as I could, covering his head with one hand to protect him, keeping him as far away as possible from those two people. Holding him close, I was even more aware of the smell of lighter fuel; poor thing, I feared for his lungs, although he had stopped coughing as soon as I picked him up and took him out of the cradle, and I would, anyway, summon a paediatrician for advice, Dr Castilla or Dr Arranz.

The Kindeláns were clearly taking their leave, I just hoped they really were being dispatched to Turkey or to Outer Mongolia, once their mission, their repugnant mission, was completed. They walked calmly to the door, but I did not accompany them, the further away they were the better. I waited until they were on the other side of the door, then rushed over and bolted it, a purely superstitious move. Before he pulled the door shut, though, the fat man smiled again and gave that same little giggle:

'You see, dear Berta, we were right, weren't we? As I said before, you won't want to see us again after today.'

IV

That same afternoon, as soon as Dr Castilla had left (he very kindly came as soon as I called, and gave me his usual mumbled assurances), I phoned Tomás's two telephone numbers, but without success. The switchboard at his apartment building merely put me through to his flat, where no one answered. I dialled again and asked the telephonist to give Mr Nevinson the message that his wife in Madrid needed to speak to him urgently. When I called his work number, I was told to wait, then put through to an extension, where the phone rang and rang to no avail, until it cut out. I realised then how completely isolated I was from him. I didn't even know who his colleagues were or his closest friends. I racked my brains, and remembered that, on a couple of occasions, he'd mentioned a certain Mr Reresby, and another time a Mr Dundas (he had, in fact, said 'Dundás', with the stress on the final syllable) and another time a Mr Ure, a surname whose spelling I couldn't even imagine (he'd pronounced it 'Iuah' or something like that, and then, to my amazement, had spelled it out. 'Scottish in origin,' he'd said, referring to the name, not the man, and he'd said exactly the same thing about Dundas when he first mentioned that name too). And so I dialled again and asked to speak to Mr Reresby, but no one of that name worked there; I then asked to speak to Mr Dundas and received the same answer. 'Can I speak to Mr Ure, then?' And I tried to pronounce it just as Tomás had done (my English was quite good, but nothing like his, of course). I felt ridiculous saying 'Iuah' and then spelling it out just to make sure they would understand what, to me, sounded more like an ejaculation, not that it did me any good, because no one called Ure worked there either. Desperation can bring inspiration, and I suddenly recalled hearing Tomás mention the name 'Montgomery', so I asked to speak to Mr Montgomery, although Montgomery could also be a first name, at least in America, except, of course, we weren't in America. The person on the other end became politely impatient: 'No, madam, there's no Mr Montgomery here. Are you sure you're calling the right number?' 'This is the Foreign Office, isn't it?' I replied. 'Mr Nevinson does work there, doesn't he?' There was a surprising silence after my first question, as if answering it was neither reasonable nor desirable; and it's true that whenever anyone answered the phone there, they never gave the name of the institution, but merely a curt 'Hello', as if it were a private number. 'Yes, Mr Nevinson does work here, I'll put you through to his extension –' 'No, you did that before and no one answered,' I said, interrupting. Then it occurred to me to try another name, that of the Kindeláns' supposed great friend, Reggie Gathorne, and I had more luck with him, but still not enough. 'I'm sorry, but Mr Gathorne has been away for a week now, and we don't know when he'll be rejoining us.' So at least the couple had been telling the truth about something, and if a Reggie Gathorne did work there, then it must be the Foreign Office or part of that same ministry. I begged the person to give Mr Nevinson the message that I needed to speak to him as soon as possible. 'Something very serious has happened. I'm Mrs Nevinson, his wife,' I added, to give myself a vague air of authority (not that being a wife carries much authority). 'I should warn you that he, too, has been away for some days, madam,' said the person on the other end. 'And we don't know when he'll be rejoining us either; I doubt I'll be able to pass on your message very soon.' 'And you don't know where you can find him, where he is?' 'No, madam, I'm sorry, but I don't have that kind of information.'

I stood for a long time staring impotently at the telephone. Now and again, I tried the other number, but always without success. The telephonist had said Tomás was away, which suggested that he wasn't in London. And if he wasn't in London, then I had no means of locating him, and I really needed to speak to him, to tell him what had happened, and ask him what the hell he was up to and what kind of mess he'd got us into, as well as what his work actually involved, if, that is, they were right, the Kindeláns, whom I did indeed hope never to see again, either in the Jardines de Sabatini or anywhere else. I needed to ask him to arrange matters so that it couldn't happen again.

I was still staring at the phone when it rang, half an hour after that whole frustrating experience. I pounced on the receiver. 'They must have given him the message, it must be Tomás.' But an English voice asked in English for Mrs Nevinson, that is, for me.

'I'm Ted Reresby,' the voice said. Right from the start, his tone was relaxed and confiding, nothing like the stiff tones of the person I'd spoken to before. 'I'm sorry to bother you, but it seems you phoned your husband a while ago and then asked for me and for a few other people, and the person you spoke to was quite wrong as regards myself, telling you that I don't exist. Well, while he was obviously unaware of my existence until a few moments ago, he won't forget it now. Don't blame him, though, he's rather new and doesn't know everyone here.' 'Here', he said. I would have liked to ask him if 'here' was the Foreign Office, so that I could at least be clear about that, but those first words came out in such a torrent that I couldn't ask anything, and I had to concentrate very hard on trying to understand him, for he spoke in a drawling yet mellifluous voice, not easy for someone only accustomed to listening to diplomats at formal or social events, and the telephone – when you can't see the mouth of the person speaking – only makes understanding even more difficult. 'Tom isn't in London,' he went on, still not allowing me to get a word in edgeways, 'he's with a delegation somewhere near Berlin and won't be back for several days. I hope it will only be a few days, and that no complications arise that will delay his return, but one never knows with these things. They told me you needed to speak to him urgently, which is why I'm returning your call, Mrs Nevinson, in case I can be of any help, since there is currently no way of communicating with Tom.'

'No way of communicating with him?' I asked at last. 'How can that be? Can't you pass a message on to him?'

'No, madam, I'm afraid that's not possible. The delegation isn't allowed any contact with the outside world while the negotiations or talks last. That's how it is sometimes. It's all slightly absurd, rather extreme. In our defence, I should say that such conditions are usually laid down by the other party. We're less susceptible to that kind of thing.'

'Are you telling me that the delegation is completely cut off and you can't contact them for days and days?'

'Not exactly. We can contact the leader of the delegation and he can contact us, but none of its other members are authorised to have any communication with the outside world. We could pass on your problem, your message, to the leader of the delegation, and he might pass that on to Tom, but I'm afraid that could prove counterproduct-ive and possibly troubling, since he could do little or nothing about it while he's there. But, please, tell me what the problem is, and if it's a grave or urgent matter, we can see what we could do from here. Have you spoken with the embassy in Madrid?'

It made no sense to tell a complete stranger what had happened, over the phone and in my limited English. Plus I didn't know who this Ted Reresby fellow was. Tomás had mentioned him a couple of times, but I don't recall him explaining who he was or else I wasn't paying attention. I didn't know if they were friends or merely colleagues, nor who was under orders from whom. Or his name may simply have cropped up in conversation with another person.

'No,' I said. 'Not yet. It's something I need to speak to Tom about first.'

'I do advise you, though, to talk to the embassy, Mrs Nevinson. It would be easier to help you from Madrid, if you need help, that is. Would you like me to get in touch with them? I can call them from here.' I remained silent for a few seconds, somewhat bemused by such solicitude. 'Please, tell me, are you all right? You have a little boy, don't you? Is he all right?'

The truth is that I *was* all right and so was Guillermo. We didn't need immediate help, that wasn't the problem; I had needed help that morning, but not now. That morning I'd needed a lot of help, I'd come within an inch of seeing my son set alight. 'And any action is a step to the block, to the fire.' I'd heard Tomás repeat that line sometimes, from a poem he knew by heart and which he murmured to himself in English. Perhaps it could wait, it would have to. There was no point now in speaking to that man Reresby about the Kindeláns and the way they'd wormed their way into my life, about the Zippo lighter and the lighter fuel, about their accusations, their suspicions about Tomás. If he was somewhere near Berlin, that meant he wasn't in Ireland or in Northern Ireland, and so couldn't be inflicting damage on that country. Always assuming this man was telling me the truth.

'Yes, we're both fine now, that's not the problem.'

'Now? But you weren't before?' I said nothing, it bothered me that he should be so alert to every word I uttered, and then he changed tack: 'Will you allow me one question, or rather two? If, that is, I'm not being indiscreet. Is this a personal matter or to do with Tom's work? The reason why you want to speak to him so urgently, I mean.'

I found this question odd coming from a complete stranger, an Englishman to boot, because in those days, the English still tended to be rather reserved. My urgent need could have been a mere whim, I might simply have been missing Tomás, or suffered a long-distance attack of jealousy or uncertainty or felt an urgent desire to hear his voice.

'I really don't think that's relevant, Mr Reresby,' I answered, a polite way of telling him it was none of his business. 'If I can't speak to him, I can't speak to him. I'll do so when he returns. When he's not incommunicado. When he's not forbidden from knowing anything about his wife and child. It's strange that he didn't warn me he'd be out of contact, and for several days too.'

'Of course,' he said, excusing himself and ignoring my last remarks, my near-reproaches. 'I was only asking because, in the latter case, I might have been able to be of assistance.'

I didn't insist.

'And your other question?' I was tired of straining my ears to understand him. I was beginning to grow impatient and to think that the Kindeláns were perhaps right, that Tomás didn't work for the Foreign Office and I wasn't speaking to anyone from that ministry, but someone from MI6.

'Oh, nothing. Mere curiosity. According to the telephonist, you asked for me first, then for Mr Dundas, Mr Ure, Mr Montgomery and Mr Gathorne. May I ask where you got those names from? As I say, it's mere curiosity. Mr Gathorne and I do exist, but the others don't. Not here, that is. Although I imagine they do in some other part of the United Kingdom.' He intended this last remark as a joke, but I was in no mood to laugh at his jokes, even out of politeness.

'I don't really know,' I said. 'They're names my husband has mentioned occasionally. The telephonist didn't know or didn't want to tell me where he was, and so I thought one of you might be able to inform me, as has proved to be the case. Mr Reresby, tell me, I am speaking to the Foreign Office, aren't I?'

'Naturally,' said Reresby. 'Forgive me for not having made that clear when I introduced myself. I assumed you knew. Who did you think you were phoning?'

'Why, the Foreign Office, of course. Anyway, many thanks for returning my call, Mr Reresby, you've been most kind. At least I know now where Tom is and that I'll have to wait for a few more days.'

'It might be longer than that, Mrs Nevinson, it might be longer.'

'Fine. But do tell him that I need to speak with him as soon as possible. Tell him, please, if you have the chance.'

And with that, I brought the conversation to a close. Yes, I would have to wait. I would have to wait for him to come back from those secret negotiations in Berlin. And then I realised that Reresby had said 'near Berlin', not 'in Berlin'. Maybe I was ill-informed, but it occurred to me that near Berlin – that is, outside West Berlin – there was only Communist Germany, East Germany, the DDR. That is why, or so I thought, you could only reach West Berlin by air, or perhaps there was some kind of cross-border corridor, where cars couldn't stop or leave. How then was it possible for Tomás to be 'near Berlin'? Like the other so-called Iron Curtain countries, the German Democratic Republic was pretty much hermetically sealed, with barely any dealings with the West. But for all I knew there was contact at a diplomatic or governmental level. 'Or some other kind of contact,' I thought. 'Some still more under-the-counter, secret contact.' It seemed very strange to me that Tomás hadn't warned me that he was going there, and that I wouldn't be allowed to contact him.

The following morning, I phoned the Irish embassy in Madrid and asked to speak to Don Miguel Ruiz Kindelán. I risked being put through to him, and the last thing I wanted was to hear his jokey and now odious voice, but I could always put the phone down without saying a word. Or give them a false name if they asked: 'Who's speaking?' In the end, I didn't need to, because a woman with an excellent Spanish accent told me that no one of that name worked there. I asked if he had perhaps worked there before, because I was under the impression that he was about to be transferred, which might be why he didn't appear on the current list of personnel.

'No, there's never been anyone of that name here, *señorita*. Nor anyone with a name remotely like that.' My voice and my tone must have sounded rather youthful to her, hence the *'señorita'*. Then I asked about Mary Kate O'Riada, and I pronounced the surname in both Spanish and Irish fashion, just in case. 'No,' came the response. 'Who told you these people worked at the embassy?'

'*They* did,' I said, with a candour born of my bewilderment.

'Well, I'm afraid they were having you on, *señorita*. We've never had anyone at the embassy called O'Riada or Ruiz Kindelán. Like General Kindelán, I suppose. They were obviously trying to impress you.'

Then I phoned Jack Nevinson, my father-in-law. I didn't usually tell him or his wife, Mercedes, about my friendships or what I got up to: a hangover from adolescence, for like other members of my generation, I preferred to keep quiet, keen to protect my own little world.

196

I'd told them nothing about the Kindeláns, but now I asked if he'd heard of them, if he had any idea who they were.

'No, I've never heard of them,' he said. 'Why?'

'Oh, nothing. I just happened to meet them and was curious.' The first person to know what had happened had to be Tomás, I didn't want to alarm anyone unnecessarily or put my foot in it: as far as they were concerned, I imagined, Tomás did what he did, and that was that.

I even dared to approach Walter Starkie, despite his advanced age. He knew everyone in the diplomatic world and in various other worlds too; over the decades, he had met everyone, and, besides, had an extraordinary memory. His answer was the same though:

'No, dear Berta, I've never heard those names before.' And he didn't even ask me why I wanted to know.

'How easy it is to be in the dark, or perhaps that's our natural state,' I thought in the days and weeks that followed, while I waited patiently for Tomás to give some sign of life, or to turn up in Madrid without warning. Whenever I heard footsteps on the stairs or the lift coming up, I was filled by the unjustified hope that it was him, that he had decided not to phone, but to come home straight away to see me, to see our son and me, once he'd returned from his mission, perhaps, who knows, alerted to my anxieties by Reresby and coming direct from Berlin. 'We know nothing of what we're not told, nor of what we're told either. We have a tendency to accept the latter, to assume that people tell the truth, and we give it very little thought and don't bother to doubt it; life would be unliveable if we did, if we questioned even the most trivial statements, why should anyone lie about their name, their job, their profession, where they come from, their tastes and habits, about the vast amount of information we all blithely exchange, often without being asked to, without anyone showing the slightest inclination to find out who we are or what we do or how we are, we nearly all tell more than we need to, or, worse, impose on others facts and stories they don't care about in the least, and we assume a curiosity that doesn't exist, why should anyone be curious about me, about you, about him, very few people would miss us were we to disappear, still less wonder about us. "No, I don't know what happened to that woman," they'll say. "She had a little boy, she lived here for a while, and although her husband was only at home intermittently, but more often than not away, she was always around. She must have moved, on her own or the two of them together, I don't know, I wouldn't be surprised if they'd separated, she always seemed rather solitary in a way, but always much happier when he came back. But the child is sure to have gone with her, that's what usually happens." Yes, we believe what we're told, that's the norm, and yet Tomás might not be what he told me he is and might not be where he tells me he is, and those names I remembered hearing him mention – although quite when, I don't recall – don't exist, Dundas, Ure and Montgomery don't exist at the Foreign Office, whereas Reresby does, although who knows if what he told me is true, I have no idea if Tomás is in West Germany or East Germany or neither, if he's in Belfast or some other place; the Kindeláns have never been seen at the Irish embassy and so they won't be about to be transferred to Ankara or Rome or Turin, that's all a fiction, and it's more than likely that they're not even called O'Riada or O'Reidy or Ruiz Kindelán, or Miguel or Mary Kate, they would have chosen those surnames because they were famous and sounded good, after that musician I'd never heard of and after that Francoist general and aviator.' She probably was Irish or Northern Irish, possibly a member of the IRA; it's odd, though, that she should speak Spanish so well, although that organisation must have collaborators and supporters in many places, certainly in fanatical Catholic countries, as mine still was at the time. But him? Perhaps he belonged to ETA or had close links to it, for, as we now know, the two groups were in contact and helped each other; a member of ETA who, at the same time, had perfect English, there can't be many of those, if any; perhaps he really was bilingual, half-Basque and half-Irish. He was an educated, knowledgeable man, so perhaps he was a priest, the Church had a lot to do with the creation, protection, rise and impunity of those terrorist groups. Or perhaps he was half-American, because the States used to send a lot of money to the IRA.

'How easy it is to know nothing, how easy simply to grope one's way forward, how easy to be deceived, let alone to lie, an action entirely devoid of merit and available to any fool, it's odd how liars believe themselves to be intelligent and skilful, when lying takes no skill at all. Anything we're told could as easily prove to be utterly decisive or a matter of complete indifference, either innocuous or crucial, either something that affects our whole existence or barely impinges on it. We can live in continual error, believing that we have a comprehensible, stable, graspable life only to find that everything is uncertain, murky, unmanageable, with no firm foundations; or a complete façade, as if we found ourselves in the theatre convinced we were in the real world, not realising that the lights have gone down, the curtain has gone up and that we're on stage, not in the audience, or on a cinema screen, unable to escape, trapped in a film and forced to repeat ourselves with each new showing, transformed into cellu-loid and incapable of changing the facts, the plot, the shots, the angle or the light, or the story that someone else has decided will always be the same. You realise in your own life that some things are as irre-versible as a story already seen or read, already told; things that lead us down a path from which we cannot stray or on which we can, at best, allow ourselves to improvise, perhaps a gesture or a wink that goes unnoticed; a path we must follow even if we intend to escape, because although we may not have chosen it, we are on that path and it conditions our every move, our every poisoned step, regardless of whether we follow it faithfully or run away from it. The truth is, we walk that path against our beliefs and against our will, someone has placed us there and, in my case, that someone is my husband, the man

I've loved for years and to whom I've bound my existence for ever –
or so I thought – and that someone is Tomás.'

During those days and weeks of waiting, I felt as if I were in the
middle of a dense mist, constantly conjecturing, alternating between
optimism and the deepest pessimism, thinking, in effect, that anything
was possible: that Tomás was himself, whatever that meant, and the
Kindeláns were wrong; or that Tomás had lied to me from the start and
led a life that was so different and so secret that he even had to hide it
from me. I felt so oppressed by this constant back and forth that I
would repeat to myself another of those lines that Tomás would sometimes recite distractedly, for example when he was shaving, or else he
would sing or murmur one of those lines he had by heart, and which
were many and long, I wasn't sure if they were all from the same poem
or the same poet, but I knew that some were by Eliot, whom he often
read, out loud sometimes and at top speed, I would have to ask him
about this when I saw him again, although who knows when that
would be. That line resonated in me now: 'This is the death of air'. And
it wasn't as if I myself lacked air, it was something far worse; it was as
if there were no air anywhere, as if there were no more air left in the
universe and it had ceased to exist. And after a few more lines which I
didn't understand and so didn't remember, Tomás would add: 'This is
the death of earth'. Then, a few lines later came the condemnation of
the other two elements: 'This is the death of water and fire'. If only the
fire had been dead on the morning of the Zippo lighter and the lighter
fuel. But the one line that kept going round and round in my head was
that first one, 'This is the death of air'.

And yet I knew, despite all these speculations and uncertainties,
despite the hope that I was wrong, despite the necessary doubts that
allowed me to pass from one day to another and to live, what the Kindeláns had suggested and suspected explained far too many things for

it not to be true. It explained the change in Tomás's character and his volatile moods, ever since he'd finished his studies. And his difficulty in sleeping and his nervousness or the depression that only increased when it came nearer to the time for one of his sojourns in London. It explained why, in such a short time, he had become so much older than me, even though he was the same age, explained how he had aged mentally, explained his occasional silences; the way he made love to me during the night or in the small hours when he couldn't sleep, as if I were a receptacle for his accumulated mental tensions or the wretched fate that had already been drawn up and deciphered and read, and which he hoped to slough off momentarily, agitating and emptying his body, thus for a few minutes – or seconds for a man – allowing body to prevail over mind, as usually only happens with illness and pain, and, of course – as in this case – with pleasure. It explained his lack of curiosity about the future, his indifference regarding tomorrow or the day after tomorrow or a year from now, his scepticism about the unexpected, as if the unexpected could no longer happen, not to him. It also explained in part what he had said to me once, shortly before we married: 'You're one of the few things that isn't obligatory, that I've been able to choose freely. In other respects, I have a sense that the die is cast, as if I hadn't so much chosen as been chosen. You're the one thing that is truly mine, the only thing I know I myself wanted.' The years have passed and I still treasure those words, perhaps because there have been so few that were so explicit, so treasurable. I had stored away only their flattering aspect, as if they were exclusively a declaration of conviction, reaffirmation, exception and love. Now I realise that there was much more to them, there was, above all, a comparison. I had seen this at the time, it's true, but had brushed it aside, we tend to preserve the meanings that favour us and to dismiss or tone down others, especially in our memory and in echo and repetition.

If Tomás was subject to military discipline, he might, even then, have had the feeling that the die was cast, that in his future life there would be scant room for surprises, that he would always be obliged to obey orders and carry out whatever missions they charged him with, and that he wouldn't have the freedom to choose. Whenever he returned to England he would be at the disposal of his superiors on the ground, with no possible postponement, no mediation, and that could easily make him depressed or get on his nerves, and keep him from sleeping. The worst imaginable thing is never being able to say no, or even to discuss or reason or argue, having to obey whatever someone of a higher rank orders you to do, even things you disapprove of or find repugnant, having to swallow down the disgusting wine another person gives you to drink. This, to a greater or lesser extent, is what happens to us all, whatever our role in life, from cradle to grave: there is almost always someone over us telling us what we have to do, someone we cannot contradict, but in a military organisation everything is more marked, the hierarchies are more visible and are the basis of everything. That diabolical couple were right, MI5 and MI6 weren't dependent on the Foreign Office or the Home Office, but on the army, although its members probably – or, rather, certainly – never donned a uniform. But if the Kindeláns were right and Tomás *was* working for the Secret Service, there must have been agreement and acceptance on his part, and, I imagined, he could also withdraw, step aside. Of course, according to Kindelán: 'They usually come out either mad or dead. And those who aren't brought to justice and don't go entirely mad, end up not knowing who they are.' How had Tomás got involved in all that, assuming he was involved? And what was the meaning of the enigmatic phrase among those other words spoken long ago now and of which I was so fond: 'I have a sense that I haven't so much chosen as been chosen'?

After a couple of weeks of absolute silence and no sign of Tomás,

I decided to call Ted Reresby, supposedly of the Foreign Office, again. I asked for him directly, and not for Tomás. He didn't answer and could not be found, but he returned my call half an hour later, more or less as he had before. His voice had become my one link with my husband.

'Mr Reresby,' I said, 'I've had no news of Tom since you and I last spoke. Is he still away? Is he still in Germany? Did you manage to get my message to him? Does he know that I need to talk to him or does he still not have the faintest idea that I've been expecting him and hoping to hear from him for two weeks now?' And I added, perhaps unwisely: 'There's one thing I'm not quite clear about. Is he in West Germany or East Germany? If you can tell me, that is.'

Reresby was far less considerate and attentive this time, as if my questions bothered him and as if he found this second phone call entirely unacceptable. It seemed to me that he had lost all respect for me, or perhaps he had lost all respect for Tomás for not being able to keep his wife meekly silent and waiting. Or was it perhaps that Tomás had let him down and was no longer so important to him. Reresby sounded vaguely disappointed.

'Mrs Nevinson,' he said, without answering any of my questions, 'you are being far too impatient and that is of no help to your husband. As I said before, the matter could drag on for much longer. If Tom hasn't been in contact, that's because he hasn't yet been able to. So why insist? Let him finish the job in hand. He will come back.'

This time, I decided to tell him everything, so that he could gauge the importance of what had happened, but also to alarm him a little and provoke his curiosity.

'Mr Reresby, our son's life was put at risk. Please understand, this is not a trivial matter. Please understand, too, that I need to speak to Tom urgently. He has to do something, he has to make sure this doesn't happen again. I don't know what's going on or what Tom's job actually involves. I only know that his job is the reason why our son could have been burned alive. Someone told me that Tom works for MI6. You must know. Is that true?'

But Reresby was not a man to speak out of turn nor to give in to a sudden angry impulse, and he may have noticed that my own apparent impulse was calculated, artificial, for it would have been far more natural to have given in to it during our first conversation, when the events had just taken place, not two weeks later. Nor was he the kind to take the bait and, in doing so, allow himself to be drawn out, nor to respond to a question he didn't wish to respond to. He didn't ask me what had happened, nor who had threatened the life of my child, nor what I meant about him being burned to death, nor who had spoken to me about MI6. Entirely unperturbed, he merely said:

'I'm sorry to hear that, Mrs Nevinson, but perhaps Tom shouldn't have allowed himself to have a child at this stage in his life, when his career is just beginning. I can't say any more. As far as I know, Tom works for the Foreign Office and in our embassy in Madrid, and he does so most efficiently too; believe me, he has a very promising future. And if he had been recruited by the Secret Service, I can assure you that I wouldn't know. As is only normal, and as I'm sure you must be aware, no one knows who works for the Secret Service. Otherwise, what sense would there be in the word "secret"? When he returns to Madrid, talk to him, ask him what you're asking me. I can't give you an answer to something I have no way of knowing.'

'How easy it is to believe that you know something and yet know nothing at all,' I thought. 'How easy it is to be in the dark, or perhaps that's our natural state. Tomás will also be in the dark, not just me, no, not just me. He, too, must be in the dark in that murky, anxious world, and in the dark, too, as regards me.'

Tomás took four weeks to reappear after that episode or incident, after the terrible fright from which I've never quite recovered, I still dream about it sometimes and wake up panting and bathed in sweat as if I were still there on that same morning, and that the years hadn't passed. He phoned the day before, but put off having a proper conversation until his arrival in Madrid.

'There's no point telling me anything now, in haste, I mean. There's no point arguing either. And now is not the time for reproaches. We'll have supper together tomorrow night when I'm back.'

'But I can't wait any longer,' I said. 'What happened is really serious, you can't imagine. I don't know what you're up to, but things can't go on like this. Why haven't you been more open with me? Why haven't you told me the truth? What are you playing at, Tomás? You put our baby's life at risk, don't you realise that? They threatened him.'

'Someone did mention something about that here in London when I got back. I'm sorry. I only arrived yesterday, so at least give me a day's breathing space.'

'Arrived back from where? You knew you were going to be away all that time and you didn't even warn me. How could you do that?'

'Oh, here and there,' he said in answer to my first question, as if he were an adolescent responding to his parents' demands to know where's he's been until that late hour, which suggested to me that he was in no mood to be told off or to issue a *mea culpa*. He did, however, add, less as an excuse than as a simple explanation: 'It was all very rushed and unplanned. That's what the job's like. I couldn't have warned you.'

'Where have you just arrived back from?' I asked again. 'Germany, as your friend Reresby told me, or have you been in Belfast?' And I pronounced that name as Miguel had pronounced it, when he was still 'Miguel'.

'Like I said, here and there,' he repeated, and it sounded exactly as if he'd just said: 'That's none of your business, Berta, and however hard you try, you're never going to find out.' 'We'll talk tomorrow, tomorrow I'll explain as much as I'm allowed to explain. I don't yet know how much that will be, I've asked, and the people here are looking into it, they'll let me know today. And of course you can wait. It's only one more day. Anyway, don't worry, whatever may have happened won't happen again, I promise.' People always promise things they're in no position to promise.

Luckily for me, during all that endless waiting, the Kindeláns didn't make another appearance. And some days after the incident, I plucked up the courage to go out alone with Guillermo again, even taking a stroll in the Jardines de Sabatini, although I did keep a sharp eye out for the couple and jumped whenever I spotted another human being, and even, absurdly enough, when a statue loomed into view, but I didn't see the couple again either there or in the neighbourhood. I tried to steer well clear of the Paseo del Pintor Rosales, where they lived, although who knows if that was true, that or anything else they told me during the month I knew them. No, much to my relief, I didn't see them, but one afternoon, to my horror, a few days before

Tomás resurfaced, Mary Kate phoned me. As soon as I heard her voice, I could see those troubling blue squinting eyes, those painted lips, like a smear of blood on her face.

'Don't hang up, dear Berta,' she said in a pleading and, at the same time, authoritative tone of voice. 'I'm calling you from Rome, where we've more or less settled in, insofar as one ever can in Italy, of course. You've no idea how badly organised the Italians are. Anyway, in the end they sent us here, which is the lesser of various evils.' I was astonished that she should still try to maintain these fictions, when she could not possibly presume to be my friend and had probably never worked at an embassy in her life. Of course, those who gave them their orders and sent them to terrorise me may well have posted them there, to be near the Pope and the papal Curia. She, doubtless out of necessity, wanted me to believe that she really was making a long-distance call, that she was far away and I was safely out of reach.

'How dare you, Mary Kate, always assuming that is your real name, because no one at the Irish embassy has ever heard of you.'

She ignored this remark and went on:

'I couldn't bear to spend another day without knowing how you both were, the little cherub and you. I often think of you and really miss you. Are you all right?'

I was tempted to hang up. Perhaps I should arrange to have our number changed and make sure the new one was registered in the name of Isla, not Nevinson; that way, undesirable people wouldn't be able to find us so easily, there are quite a few Islas in the phone book. However, I didn't immediately give in to that temptation, I thought it best to find out what she wanted, because she certainly wasn't interested in our health.

'We're fine. Infinitely better now that the two of you are far away.'

'So you're still blaming us for that inconsequential little accident.

208

It was just Miguel being clumsy, he gets more and more distracted and clumsy as time goes on, you've no idea the number of blunders he's made here already,' she replied, unperturbed. 'But as you saw, Berta, nothing happened. Guillermo is still his beautiful, bouncing self, isn't he? Tell me, have you spoken to Thomas yet? Has he come back? According to our calculations, he should have come back or be about to. You know how much we disapprove of him leaving you so alone.'

'Calculations? What calculations? Do you know something about him, where he is?' Tomás's prolonged silence and his inaccessibility, as well as my own desperation, made me take the bait.

'Oh, so he's not back?' Mary Kate said. 'Interesting.'

'No, he hasn't come back, and he hasn't phoned me either since the two of you were here, Mary Kate. I've had no news from him at all.' I was prudent enough not to mention my conversations with Mr Reresby. 'I wish I could have spoken to him and told him what you did to his child, what you were about to do. I don't think he's as easily frightened as me.'

She barely reacted to this either, or only with her first words, once again dismissing the incident as unimportant:

'You do exaggerate, Berta. Like all mothers.' And then, what had merely been a hint in her voice rose shamelessly to the surface, and her tone became one of authority, warning, recommendation or instruction: 'When he does come back, be sure to talk to him. Just because we're far away doesn't mean the matter is resolved. And it has to be resolved satisfactorily. Give my love to the little one, please. And Miguel sends his own clumsy kisses to you both as well. Can you believe it, he's got even fatter.'

I didn't go to meet Tomás at the airport. His plane came in rather late, and I didn't want to inconvenience anyone in our respective families by asking them to stay with Guillermo. I could have hired a babysitter, but I thought it best for Tomás not to be confronted by my anxious face as soon as he got off the plane, nor to see how I bit my tongue when I couldn't ask him any questions in the presence of witnesses, instead, I would allow him a little more time alone, without being interrogated, once he'd landed in Madrid and taken the taxi from Barajas to our house in Calle Pavía, right next to the Teatro Real, with all those tall trees to look at; we were so lucky in that respect, I sometimes spent hours watching them, fascinated, listening to them rustling in the breeze. To allow him time to get used to the idea of being home, to familiarise himself with the landscape again, to see the Torres Blancas building on Avenida de América announcing that he was finally entering Madrid, heading along the Castellana via the curved slope of Hermanos Bécquer, then straight into the very heart of the capital; to allow him to realise that what must have seemed to him so far away, perhaps a dream from a remote past impossible to recover, was once again there before his eyes, regardless of where he had been and what he had been involved in. I decided to wait for him at home, with a cold supper ready, to listen for his key or the bell if he had lost his key, it's so easy to lose or forget a key that you don't use regularly or that you don't need to use for a couple of months or more, I couldn't now remember the exact date when he had left, his absence had seemed endless, given the circumstances, given my fear, given my increasingly well-founded suspicions, because now I was almost sure that the Kindeláns had been telling the truth, or part of the truth. I decided to give him extra time to firm up and put in order, even rehearse mentally, what he was going to confess to me, because he would have to confess something. He'd consulted his superiors, whoever they were, and they were considering the matter; he'd said 'They'll let me know today', which meant yesterday, so he would be telling me whatever he could tell me with their consent, or perhaps he wouldn't, perhaps he'd tell me nothing and say only: 'Don't ask, Berta, don't ever ask me again. If you still want to stay by my side, you'll have to remain in the dark as regards the Tomás who leaves and isn't here. Now, if you can't accept the one who comes back and is here, then that's your choice and I wouldn't blame you. It will break my heart, and I'll have nowhere then I can call my own, and my whole life will be in jeopardy, but that won't be your fault and I'll understand completely, and I won't protest either.'

However, as the evening wore on, I couldn't simply sit and wait. Already, before the time I'd calculated for his arrival (my own optimistic calculation, assuming there had been no delays), I began going out onto the balcony and looking down into the street, it was likely that the taxi would drop him next to the church, and so, whenever I stepped out, I would look to the right, but also over towards Plaza de Oriente and Lepanto and Bailén, taking full advantage of our ample view. I don't know how often I did this, I only know that not even the storm that broke when there was still just a sliver of light (it was one of those interminable days in June, July or August in Spain) dissuaded me from going out onto one of our three balconies and leaning out of first one, then the other and the other. These were only brief sorties (I came in as soon as the rain became too heavy), but my hair and face were drenched, as were my blouse and skirt, and my high-heeled shoes, which would be ruined, not that I cared. I didn't bother getting changed, because, if I did, my dry clothes would only get soaked when I was seized by another attack of impatience; I just couldn't sit still, and I couldn't phone him, I couldn't try to lure him in by my irrational presence out there on the balcony, after all, how would he know? After so much time apart, I wanted to be wearing a short skirt and heels when he first saw me: that's how he liked me to dress, although not only like that, and I realised that, as well as my disquiet and my fear and my general bewilderment after gaining those brief insights into his life, as well as the panic that had returned in spades since Mary Kate's recent phone call, I still needed him to desire me, to see in his appreciative eyes an immediate renewal of that most elemental of feelings. After his long absence and what I imagined to be his many vicissitudes, of which I knew nothing, that gaze would have been lost, or become vitrified or grown indifferent or lethargic, he might not be capable of or even interested in recovering it, and so it had to be revived at once, without delay; after a long period without seeing one another, so much depends on that first encounter. The face we initially take such pains to remember is very clear and omnipresent, but as time passes – probably precisely because of that effort of memory, which wears away that person's face, distorts and deforms – it begins to fade, and it becomes almost impossible for the mind's eye to summon it up and show it to us in faithful form. We suddenly find ourselves studying a photograph in order to recall their face, and even then, the still photograph gradually supplants the real face with its gestures and movements, the features freeze, and only those in the snapshot remain, and we spend so much time looking at the photo that, eventually, it replaces the person and erases or exiles or drives them out, which is why it's so hard truly to remember the dead as they move away from us in time. And if that had been my experience, what would it be like for Tomás with regard to me, for he had been busy in far-off places, possibly on missions that would have demanded all his attention and required him systematically to forget his former self.

I had no delusions about this: it was also perfectly possible that he would have been with other women, out of desire or weariness or a need to rest or out of obligation. Perhaps he would have had to gain the confidence of a woman by going to bed with her or making phoney declarations of love; or he might have had no alternative but to give in to the whims of some other woman, possibly ugly or horribly fat or a spinster getting on in years or an easily seduced old maid, in order to achieve his goals or glean a little information, one fact or two. But, as we all know, what we begin with reluctance or even with a sense of repulsion, can end up drawing us in by sheer force of habit or an unexpected taste for repetition. Contrary to all predictions and to your own initial feelings, you can find yourself being captivated by a person who didn't attract you at all to begin with. Just as when we dream of having sex with someone unimaginable, the next time we meet, we can't help looking at them with a vague, reticent, even guilty lasciviousness, as if we'd been infected with a virus while we were innocently sleeping; however much we might reject that person when awake, in our consciousness they have taken on a dimension they previously lacked and which, with our waking senses, they were doomed never to have. A dimension that is so much more easily acquired by someone who has tested and seduced us, who has been able to arouse us despite our own lack of desire, our resistance and passivity, who has made us feel shame and regret for our consensual

213

pleasure, against all the odds and *à contrecoeur*. Who hasn't experienced this at some point in their lives?

And so I wasn't just angry with Tomás for concealing the truth from me and for having placed Guillermo and myself at risk, for having disappeared when I most needed him and for being absent long enough for his features to become blurred, I was also fearful of his reaction when he saw me again – on the coarsest, most lascivious level, I admit – as if I had to win him back, as if I had immediately to drive away the scent or stench, the smooth touch or the grime, the memory of soft or rough skin, firm or flaccid flesh, the attractiveness or ugliness of the other woman or women who might have been with him and those he might have become more or less accustomed to; that, as far as I was concerned, was the best-case scenario. By then, I was completely drenched, and my shoes were ruined, they would survive the night, but I'd have to throw them out in the morning, after all the downpours and all that frenzied opening and closing of windows and repeated leaning out from balconies, calling to him, thinking: 'Why don't you come? Where are you? They can't have refused you permission at the last moment, you can't have missed the plane, you can't have decided to delay your return, you can't spend another day absent from my life, I mean, as it is, I can hardly remember you.' At one point, I went into the bedroom and looked at myself in the full-length mirror. In a moment of insecurity or vanity (they're so often the same thing or else coexist, or, rather, struggle with each other), I thought that I looked rather good drenched to the skin, it suited me, given my predominant feelings at that moment – my coarsest, most lascivious feelings. My blouse was transparent, my skirt was wrinkled and had ridden up a little and clung to my thighs, and there was something vaguely obscene about my buttocks when viewed from the side as a man would. My hair had suffered most, but that didn't matter, it lent me a wild, rumpled look, which might give me an advantage over my rivals. Now I was afraid I might dry off too soon, that it would stop raining, and then I felt cheap and ridiculous, and what bothered me most was that word (or idea) 'rival'. Why did I feel like that, why did I feel threatened in that particular sphere, when the real threat was quite different and infinitely more serious, and didn't include just me, but the three of us? And yet, despite everything, that was the most urgent issue preoccupying me, my main concern.

At that moment, I heard the key in the door and I jumped, I had failed to see him arrive and get out of the taxi, I had failed to reach a decision about whether to change my clothes or not. It was too late now, and I rushed out of the bedroom just as I was and saw him putting his suitcase down in the hallway with a resigned, weary gesture, and he looked so different that, for a second, I didn't recognise him: he had grown a short, fair beard and his hair was longer, although not that long, and it seemed fairer too; he had lost a few pounds, and it was as if, in his absence, he had also lost any vestige of his youth, as if he'd taken the irreversible step that leads us into a maturity from which there can be no going back. Yes, he was a proper man, an attractive man who now seemed definitively, utterly foreign, as if he had also lost his half of our country, my country which, unlike Tomás, is the only country I have.

He looked at me in surprise, as if he didn't quite recognise me either, or had forgotten what I was like in the flesh, and, during those months of who knows what adventures and missions, or what servitudes, the image that had prevailed in his memory was a static one, frozen, bereft of sight, speech, intensity and pulse, a dim, dull image, perhaps of me as a mother, men do sometimes develop a pernicious respect for their wives once they've given birth or even before, once they've seen her change, aware that she is no longer alone, but carries within her an invasive creature that never ceases to grow and make demands. That had all been some time ago, but perhaps Tomás had taken away with him the image of my pregnant self, then of me as a nursing mother, that of someone who suddenly has another priority and pays little attention to anyone else. I had completely regained my figure, and no one seeing me for the first time would have thought I had a young child, not with any certainty. Tomás seemed to belong to the category of someone seeing or discovering me for the first time, and I felt foolishly flattered that his look was one of appreciative surprise, that is, of unmistakable sexual admiration, almost as if he were saying to himself coarsely: 'Well, aren't I a lucky bastard. I'd almost forgotten.' Many women complain about being eyed up, about what today we call being seen as a 'sex object', and almost none will admit how annoying it can be, how humiliating, depressing and discouraging, never to be looked at like that, at least not by those we feel have that obligation. Or we presume to choose, to select: he can look at me, and so can he, but not him. But I had chosen Tomás Nevinson many years ago and had waited for him, had waited, when we were young, for his eye to fall on me, and later had waited just for him, and, at last, he had returned.

'Why are you so wet?' he asked. I must have looked a very odd sight indoors in my sodden clothes.

I didn't answer, I may even have blushed. I raised my right hand to touch my blouse and skirt, as if I hadn't noticed they were wet and needed to confirm what he could see, and with my left hand I pointed vaguely over at the balcony, at one of the balconies.

He came closer, took four steps – one, two, three; and four – and embraced me. That embrace was short-lived, though, because he then did as I had suggested, whether intentionally or not I'm not sure, he felt my blouse and my skirt, or the flesh beneath the blouse and skirt. Then he turned me around and embraced me from behind, his hands on my breasts, his lower body pressed against my buttocks, perhaps he'd had time to observe them from the side in a vaguely obscene manner. (It didn't even occur to him to ask about Guillermo, who had been asleep for a while now; that would have been incongruous, and I actually preferred it that way.) He abruptly lifted up my skirt and pulled down my knickers, and I recognised this almost brutish approach from his many sleepless nights, with no preamble, no foreplay, when I had a sense that, in his anxiety-ridden state, any woman would have served his purpose, except that, fortunately, I happened to be the woman who was there, who had always been there until tonight. And tonight I was there again, and I was that 'any woman'.

He did his best to make that night one of release and respite, of physical reunion and languor; he did his best to avoid talking and to avoid me telling him this or that or asking questions, which is why, after a while, he wanted to do it again, once I'd dried off after having a shower, without my wet clothes on now and in the bedroom, in the bed that was more and more mine and less and less his, for it had been far too long since he'd visited it, and it was becoming what another classic writer, not Eliot this time, described as a 'woeful bed'. I'd been reading Eliot in English, as best I could and with a dictionary beside me, out of curiosity, and to understand why he was so important to Tomás and to try to understand Tomás better. 'The day was breaking. In the disfigured street he left me, with a kind of valediction, and faded on the blowing of the horn.' I, too, was beginning to know a few lines by heart, although without entirely understanding them, not that I needed to; I repeated them like the fragments of a prayer, which is perhaps how it was for him too, nothing more. 'Repeat a prayer also on behalf of women who have seen their sons or husbands setting forth and not returning.' But you have come back, at least this time. 'So I find words I never thought to speak in streets I never thought I should revisit when I left my body on a distant shore.' And what about the next time? Will you come back? Or will you leave your body on a distant shore? Isolated phrases and random lines, although probably not entirely random.

After my shower, I'd put on a bathrobe, but hadn't lain down next to him, not even on the bedspread, instead – feeling angry again rather than indignant – I'd perched, very erect, on the edge of the bed, as far away as possible while still sharing the same space; if I'd sat down on a chair, that would have signalled my regret or displeasure at what had just happened, and that isn't how I felt at all; he would have dug in his heels then or found some instant justification for saying nothing and keeping any account of what had happened to him until the following day, until the next morning or evening or night or dawn.

'In the disfigured street he left me,' I said, then paused. 'With a kind of valediction,' I added, then paused again.

He couldn't resist finishing the line:

'And faded on the blowing of the horn.'

'How many times is it now that you've left me, Tomás, and how many more times will you leave me? It's always going to be like this, isn't it? And each time it will be longer and more uncertain.'

He'd pushed aside the bedspread and drawn the sheet up over him – just one sheet because of the heat – briefly covering his face, as if realising or acknowledging that he could postpone it no longer, that I wouldn't agree to have sex again, just like that, free now of my earlier impatience, nervousness or insecurity, my superficial vanity satisfied. (When he saw me come into the room in my bathrobe, he had untied the belt and opened my robe, and I had immediately closed it again.) The moment he'd been dreading had arrived, the moment when he would have to explain what he had been authorised to explain.

'Yes, Berta, that's true. That's true,' he said, and he got out of bed and buttoned up his shirt, and put on the trousers he'd taken off, and put on his shoes and socks, as if he had to be fully clothed and protected before we had that conversation. 'And yes, it will always be like that, although "always" is always a vague term, a manner of speaking.' And once protected by his clothes, he lay back down again, his head on the pillow and his shoes on the sheet, not that it mattered, I wasn't going to tell him off. 'That is, of course, if you want to stay with me. If not, that's how it will always be for me, but not for you. Anyway, tell me exactly what happened.'

I then began to tell him about the Kindeláns, the sly way they'd befriended me, gained my trust, the questions they'd asked about what he did, as well as what they'd told me about him, the information they'd received and the ugly rumours. The incident with the cigarette lighter and, perhaps the worst thing of all, the things they'd said: 'He's putting you and yours in danger too. Don't you realise that, dear Berta? The people he's trying to harm will do their best to deflect that harm. They'll try to neutralise him by any means possible. They'll take their revenge.' To which I'd responded with words of unconditional surrender: 'I'll do anything you want, Miguel.' What Miguel wanted was for me to find out the facts – although he already knew quite a lot – and then, depending on the circumstances, to convince and dissuade Tomás. It was up to me to dissuade him and, if I succeeded, it would doubtless be best for everyone. Including his enemies, including the Kindeláns.

'How could you? Where have you been all this time? Do you realise what you've done?' I concluded my story with those three calmly worded reproaches (I wanted at all costs to remain calm, not to succumb to despair or anger before he'd had a chance to confirm anything).

He answered insofar as he could, I suppose; he told me what he was permitted to tell me, what wouldn't land him in deep trouble. I asked the occasional question, but I can't remember now what those questions were, I only remember what he said, almost as if I'd memorised his answers or he'd dictated them to me; sometimes it seemed to me that it wasn't Tomás speaking, but someone above or behind him. It also occurred to me that he'd got dressed again not to protect himself, but in order to dominate and command: someone who is clothed and shod has more authority than someone who is naked beneath a bathrobe.

'Given the situation,' he said, 'you need to know something for your own good. Something. As little as possible, only the bare essentials. I can't tell you much. And you'll have to get used to the fact that I'll never be able to tell you everything. That's just not possible, and, besides, what would be the point? You'll have to make do with this, that I don't only work for the Foreign Office, and that I do sometimes work for the Secret Service. I've been doing so for some time, it's nothing new, although it's new to you. It's been like that for a while, and so it hasn't really impinged on the life we've led together, the life you've accepted up until now, the life we lead. I do get sent to places, and sometimes they have no idea how long I'll have to stay there; they can only make a rough guess, which usually turns out to be wrong. The truth is that when I leave here, I have no idea when I'll be back, I don't even know where I'll have to go, it all depends on what they ask me to do, on what urgent need may arise, on where I could be most useful. But it's not always like that, sometimes I don't go anywhere and I stay quietly in London. You mustn't ask me what I'm going to do, because I'll never know. You mustn't ask me what I've done either, because I won't have done anything, what I've done won't have happened, there'll be no record of it anywhere, not a trace, nor should there be. Whatever happens will have nothing to do with me, because those of us who do this work both exist and don't exist. We both act and don't act, or, rather, we don't carry out the actions we carry out, the things we do are done by nobody. They simply happen, like some atmospheric phenomenon. No one will ever call us to account. And no one gives us orders or sends us anywhere. That's why, if you decide to stay with me, you mustn't ask me, you must never ask me, because there's a part of my life that has nothing to do with you, and although it takes up time, it doesn't exist, not even for you. Not even for me. But you mustn't worry. As for the Kindeláns . . . Nothing like that will ever happen again. There must have been a mistake, they must have mixed me up with someone else or with someone who doesn't even exist. People like them believe in the existence of things that don't exist. They'll know that now. They won't bother you again.'

I do remember saying rather irritably:

'Really? So how come Mary Kate called me a few days ago from Rome or wherever it was? Why did she ask me about you again? And how did she know you were about to come back? What do you mean by "people like them"? Do they belong to the IRA? Who are they? Have you been in Belfast?' I didn't like that idea at all, but for other reasons entirely. Only four years before, in 1972, so-called Bloody Sunday had taken place in Londonderry, in Northern Ireland. I couldn't bear the idea that Tomás had been there helping the English, whose army had opened fire on the unarmed participants of a peaceful demonstration and killed thirteen people and wounded several more, without those responsible ever being punished or even admonished. In fact, some time later, they were decorated by the Queen. If the IRA were already committing violence before that, the slaughter on Bloody Sunday only helped to justify this in the eyes of the people and strengthened their support.

But Tomás only answered my first question, keeping strictly to what he had just told me: 'You must never ask me.'

'They obviously hadn't been told they'd made a mistake. I can assure you that they will have by now. Something like that can never happen again. You mustn't be afraid for Guillermo or for yourself. None of this has anything to do with you, it doesn't concern you, and no one will know about me. This was pure chance, so much so that it can't happen a second time. It was an excess of zeal, if I can put it like that. People who live under siege, and in a state of permanent suspicion, suspect everyone, and sometimes, by chance, they're right, or partly so. It's like the policeman who doesn't rule out anyone as the perpetrator of a crime. If you don't rule out anyone, then the criminal is sure to be among your suspects, but that doesn't mean you know who he is. They probably suspect the whole Foreign Office, and that would include me. But rest assured, I promise you it won't happen again.'

'Oh, right,' I said, and my irritation grew. I stood up, lit a cigarette and walked around the room. As I walked, I revealed my legs beneath the bathrobe, and I knew this because I again caught Tomás's appreciative look; it's incredible how some men notice these things even in the middle of a really important discussion or argument. Perhaps he hadn't been with a woman for a long time, I thought, and was ashamed to find myself thinking this, hoping childishly that it was true. Of course, I wouldn't know about that either, I wouldn't know about anything, nor where he'd been or what he'd done, and I began to accustom myself to the idea that it would always be like this if I stayed with him. I had no other plan in life but to remain by his side, and now, suddenly, I had to reconsider this. 'Right, so you're just one in a thousand and yet they took the trouble to waste a whole month of their time on me. Do you mean there will be others like the Kindeláns doing the same with the families of everyone who works for the Foreign Office? No organisation would have enough staff for that. Come on, please, don't make me laugh.'

223

He was the one who laughed, rather inopportunely, as if he were amused by my response, my way of thinking.

'No, that isn't how it is, Berta, I was exaggerating. They would probably have suspected certain relatively new people, who are still fresh, who have particular qualities, and I happened to fit the bill. Given what you've told me, they were clearly up to speed on my talent for mimicry, but there's nothing so very odd about that, half of Madrid or half of Oxford and even a few groups in London know about that. We have infiltrators, and so do they – when they can.' I couldn't help noticing that 'we', it was the first time I'd felt that it had a strangely patriotic ring to it, if 'patriotic' is the word. Shortly before, he'd used the expression 'those of us who do this work', which was similar, but somehow not the same ('Thus, love of a country begins . . .' another line from Eliot, although I couldn't remember how it continued). 'Look, I shouldn't tell you what I'm about to tell you, but I'll make an exception this time, because you do need to know something. Today, tomorrow or the day after it will be different. I can confidently tell you that they'll have realised their mistake, will know that I'm no longer a suspect and will never bother you again, and that's because this very week the person they thought could be me has gone down. The one who, according to what you were told, was doing a lot of damage in Belfast or was about to. Fortunately, before he went down, his job was pretty much done. They can be quite sure it wasn't me.'

'"Gone down"? What do you mean? Killed?'

'No, they simply saw through his disguise or else he let his mask slip, I don't know. Whatever happened, he's no longer useful there, he's finished. They would kill him if they could, I suppose, but he'll be miles away by now, with another name and another identity, possibly with another face.'

'The same way they erased that scar of yours.' This wasn't a question, but a statement. He raised his thumbnail to his cheek, but didn't answer. 'If that man has "gone down",' I added, 'that means there *are* things that don't exist.' He looked at me uncomprehendingly. 'You said that people like the Kindeláns believe in the existence of things that don't exist. But they do exist. They always do, isn't that right? And that's what you're involved in, what you do. You work with what does exist.' I wasn't so much afraid for myself and for Guillermo now, as for him: perhaps others, if not the I R A, would want to kill him if they could, for the damage he had done.

He stood up and came over to me, I'd continued my pacing up and down the room while we were talking. He again took hold of the end of the belt on my bathrobe, this time as if asking permission to give it a tug. How could he possibly be thinking of that again? But if someone thinks a thing and reveals his intentions, it makes the other person think it too. I again felt foolishly flattered, I couldn't help it. However, I brushed aside his hand.

'No, it's the other way round, Berta,' he said, drawing back and raising his hands like someone accepting defeat (I didn't want him to accept defeat, but simply to postpone things): 'Even what exists doesn't exist.'

There was a pause, a truce, I hadn't looked in on Guillermo for a while, I hadn't heard him moan or cry; he now had his own room, with the door open day and night, and Tomás, who hadn't seen him for months, wanted to see him. 'Goodness, he's changed,' he said, even though the cradle was lit only by the light from the corridor and Guillermo's eyes were closed; best not to wake him unnecessarily. For a couple of minutes we stood watching him together, as we would have done every night before going to bed, leaning slightly over the cradle, had I not been alone for most of those nights and Tomás far away somewhere, with who knows who and pretending to be who knows what, but not himself. He put his arm around my shoulders to complete the image that had been absent for so long, as if with that gesture he were saying: 'Look, he's yours and mine, we made him together.' He reached out to stroke Guillermo's cheek, very gently so as not to wake him; not, I think, with the nail he reserved for his scar, but with the tip of his thumb. 'He's starting to look more like you, don't you think?' he said. He hadn't yet had any supper, he was tired from the journey and was hungry, and would be tired from other things too, from all kinds of experiences that were now opaque and impenetrable to me, as all future experiences would continue to be, if one part of his life did not include me. Yes, he did look tired, he'd just returned from Germany or wherever, with only a brief stopover in London, perhaps he'd spent months doing what he'd been sent to do, like that man in Belfast; perhaps he'd been unmasked or had somehow given himself away, and so couldn't go on. He'd grown a beard, and his hair was longer, but his face was still his face. Perhaps he really had just come from Germany, perhaps, if Mr Reresby had been telling the truth, it really was just some diplomatic mission. But what if one day he changed his face, what then?

'That Reresby fellow I spoke to, he must have told you I wanted to talk to you urgently. Is he your boss? Is he involved in what doesn't exist as well?' Tomás had said I must never ask him anything, but I found that instruction, at least at first, impossible to obey. And I realised that this night was an exception, and I should make the most of it. There was no harm in trying; he could always stop me, or only answer questions he was prepared to answer.

We sat down at the table, which I'd set with melon and ham, asparagus tips, some razor clams, cheese, pâté, tortillas, quince jelly, and a few nuts; he would say if he wanted anything else. He was still fully dressed, and I was still in my bathrobe.

Inevitably, he didn't want to answer that question.

'I can't tell you about something that doesn't exist,' he said. 'How can I tell you about nothing?'

'At least tell me why.'

'Why what?'

'Why you got involved in the first place. When and for how long. Was it in Oxford, or later? Don't tell me it was before we got married. Was it afterwards? No one forced you to, did they? I mean, you're not even wholly English, and your life was here.' I realised that I was repeating or adopting the arguments of Ruiz Kindelán, but what did that matter when, basically, the fat man was right: Tomás's steadfast, dangerous commitment made no sense. 'Kindelán, or whoever he really was, told me that he'd known a few people in that world, and that they never came out of it well. They either lost their minds or died, he said, they either went crazy or were murdered. They lose their life and their identity, and they end up not knowing who they are. No one admires them or thanks them, not even for the sacrifices they've made. And when they're no longer useful, they're withdrawn from service just like that, like clapped-out machines. He seemed to know what he was talking about, as if he were one of them. I suppose the dangers are the same for anyone belonging to an organisation, be it legal or illegal, clandestine or official. Why did you get involved? I can't understand it.'

Tomás looked up from his plate, he was eating very slowly, picking at different things. He looked at me with a kind of moral superiority, almost commiseration, the way one looks at a complete ignoramus or someone terribly superficial.

'Have you never heard of the defence of the Realm?'

'What defence? What Realm? What are you talking about?'

'The Realm is different in different situations, depending on the time and the place, but Realms have always needed to be defended. How else do you think we got where we are? Why do you think people can live in peace, can get on with their lives, focus on their personal sufferings and hardships, can look after themselves and their loved ones, who are never very many, can curse their bad luck without a thought for anything else? Why do you think people are able to live quietly and devote themselves to their own particular disquiets? None of that would be possible without that defence. Why is it, do you think, that each morning everything is still more or less in order, and people can run their various errands, why do letters and other deliveries arrive punctually, why are the markets full, why do the buses and the metro work, the trains and the airports, why can the bankers open their banks and the citizens go there to do their business and put their money in a safe place? Why is there bread in the baker's shops and cakes in the cake shops, why do the street lamps turn on and turn off, why does the stock market go up and down and everyone receive his or her high or low salary at the end of the month? This seems perfectly normal to us and yet it's really quite extraordinary, it's amazing that each day begins and ends. And the reason why all this happens is because of that permanent, silent defence of the Realm, about which almost no one knows, nor should they. Unlike the defence provided by the army, which is only noisily visible in time of war, ours is always active and unspoken, both in time of war and in time of peace. It's likely that without it, there would be no peace – or apparent peace. There is no Realm in history that hasn't been attacked, sacked, invaded, undermined, destabilised from within or without, and this goes on ceaselessly; even when it seems there are no threats, there are. Europe is full of castles, walls, towers and fortresses, or their remains and ruins. The fact that we don't build them any more doesn't mean they don't exist and aren't necessary. We are the watchtowers, the moats and the firebreaks; we are the lookouts, the watchmen, the sentinels who are always on guard, whether on duty or not. Someone has to remain alert so that everyone else can rest, someone has to detect those threats, someone has to anticipate them before it's too late. Someone has to defend the Realm so that you can go for a walk with Guillermo. And you ask me why?'

I hadn't expected such a committed, self-righteous speech, which wasn't like him at all, for he had always been so distracted, so uninterested in finding out about himself, indeed had always been almost indecipherable both to himself and others. That was a large part of his attraction, that he was both of the world and unconcerned about the world, still less a presence in it. Then he had fallen victim to those glum, unsettled moods, and I now understood why, but he'd never before shown such commitment to a cause. 'They've probably trained him and persuaded him of the importance of his task,' I thought. 'Most of us like to believe we're irreplaceable, that we contribute something by our existence, that our existence is neither entirely useless nor insignificant. Since I became a mother, I myself consider that this makes me a kind of heroine, and I walk the streets feeling that I deserve the world's respect and gratitude, as I've seen other mothers do. I believe I've contributed to the whole, having brought into the world someone who might prove fundamental. Poor child, poor children, if they knew how much abstract faith we place in them. We almost all like to believe something similar, but most of us know it's not true. Everything Tomás listed, all those things would carry on without us, because we're interchangeable and replaceable, indeed, there's a long endless line waiting for the space we occupy to become vacant, however modest that space might be. If we were to disappear, our absence would go unnoticed, and our space would instantly be filled, like a piece of bodily tissue that rapidly regenerates, like the tail of a lizard that grows back again, and no one remembers who cut it off. He, on the other hand, has been given permission to think he's important, he's just said as much, the sentinel always on guard, the one who wards off danger and defends the Realm, who allows others to sleep easy in their beds. How can he be so ingenuous and so malleable, how has he let himself be seduced by mere verbiage? Because it is pure patriotic claptrap, although that kind of claptrap is probably never entirely without some basis in reason, built as it is on half-truths: of course there are snares, enemies, dangers. That's why the masses are so easily led, eager for simplifications and apparent truths. But Tomás isn't the masses, or he wasn't, so perhaps he's had to come up with an alibi for his decision and to justify this to himself; no one can submerge himself in that kind of fictitious life, that renunciation of his own life, the life he had wanted and had lived, without believing that he's providing an essential service to others, to what he has started calling the Realm, his country. And since when has England been his country?'

He stopped eating or paused to smoke a cigarette. He got up from the table and went over to one of the windows to watch the storm and the trees being buffeted by the wind. The rain had stopped while we were in the bedroom, but had since started up again. I followed him and stood by his side and said:

'And how come you agreed to be part of all that, given that you were born here? And don't give me that nonsense about not being as Spanish as I am. You are and always have been. When did you become the great English patriot? Since when is Spain not your home? It's where I and your son both live.'

'No, I'm not as Spanish as you are, Berta,' he answered. 'You're a *madrileña* to the core, but I'm not. That's where they caught me. That's where they saw my potential, and asked me to join them. They could see I could be valuable to them, and we do, in large measure, belong to the place that values us, especially the place that actively wants us and draws us in. No one has ever wanted me here, but then that's typical of this country, which always fails to take advantage of those who could be most useful to it, and instead drives them out or persecutes them. Besides, what did you expect me to do? Here, we have no idea what's going to happen next. Even assuming that the dictatorship needed me, I certainly wouldn't want to work for them. You wouldn't like that. You would have found that even stranger, and would probably never have forgiven me. Up until only a few days ago, the prime minister was still Arias Navarro. And we know nothing about this Suárez fellow. We're told that he wants to bring about real change, but we'll soon find out whether that's true or not, or if he'll even be allowed to change things, however much support he gets from the King.'

He said this not as if it were a rumour, but as if he had reliable information ('we're told', he said; again that 'we'). And if he was working for the British Secret Service, then why wouldn't he have, I thought. In fact, on 1 July, not many days before, King Juan Carlos had forced the resignation of Arias Navarro, who had been one of Franco's men and his appointee, the man who, his voice breaking with emotion, eyes filling with mawkish tears, had announced Franco's death on television, only six or seven months ago, although it felt as if years had passed, despite the continued presence of Franco's henchman as prime minister. I believe he was nicknamed 'The Butcher of Málaga', because of the harsh, repressive measures he took in that province, where he was public prosecutor at the end of the Civil War: hundreds were executed without trial or only after a mockery of a trial; he was a bloodthirsty, sentimental fellow like so many others throughout history – that odd mixture is strangely frequent – and the overly sentimental are always to be feared, with their private emotions so close to the surface and their ruthless treatment of others. On 3 July, Adolfo Suárez had been appointed, and he really did change things, but, at the time, he was an unknown quantity and could hardly inspire much confidence. England was not in a good state then, either. Prime Minister Harold Wilson had resigned a few months before and been replaced by James Callaghan. Callaghan was partly responsible for the rise and, three years later, the ultimate victory of his rival Margaret Thatcher, but we knew nothing about her then, in 1976, the year that marked my life for ever, when I found out the true nature of my life. That night, I realised I was faced with a dilemma and had to make a decision, whether or not to stay with Tomás, whether to follow his life even more intermittently than before, knowing about half or perhaps slightly more of his existence, knowing about half or perhaps slightly more of how he spent his time, to what extent he sullied hands and mind, to what extent he had to deceive and betray those who would consider him a colleague or friend, how many he sent to prison or to their deaths, and all without being allowed to ask him anything. Putting myself and my child at risk – although Tomás had sworn there would be no more risks – and with enormous risks for him. I began thinking all this as I stood looking out from the balcony window at the rain in the Plaza de Oriente, standing so close to him that I had only to move my hand to touch his, to tilt my head to rest it on his shoulder, to turn round to embrace him and be embraced: 'Perhaps one day he won't come back, perhaps one of his absences will grow longer and longer and the months and then the years will pass with no news of him. Perhaps I'll have to wait indefinitely, not even knowing if he's alive or dead, if he's been unmasked and executed, as Kindelán said could happen. Or perhaps he might be the one to decide to disappear and not come back, to remake his life elsewhere, become someone he is not. What is the point of that, having him and not having him, spending my time waiting for him, always wondering if he'll come back or will vanish in a mist, in a snowstorm or a cloud of smoke, disappear into the black night or into a storm, if he'll be one of those husbands who leaves no letter, no body, no trace, but has vanished down the sea's throat. The alternative is to give him up, for us to separate and for me slowly to forget him or make him fade away as I slowly look for another man, another love, and it would have to be very slow. (I'm young, there's plenty of time; they say you can forget even the unforgettable, or so older people say.) To detach myself from worrying about what he's up to and where he is, always waiting for him to reappear or wondering how things are going for him in his chosen, secret portion of the world, which is not mine and can never be; to know nothing, given the impossibility of ever knowing enough, and closing down anything that will now never be taut or smooth or flung wide open, but will always be crumpled and nebulous or, worse, pure darkness. Then again, for a long time now, nothing has been diaphanously clear and everything has been like a chink in a door, partly because of my own lack of interest. For some time now, the periods he spends in London – or, rather, the periods I thought he was spending there – didn't exist for me, but were merely tedious parentheses to which I'd become accustomed since his university days; the truth is that, for years now, we've lived our life in fragments, so what difference is there? Ah, but there's a huge difference: it's one thing for him to be engaged in diplomatic business at the Foreign Office and quite another for him to be a mole, an infiltrator, an impostor, changing his appearance and using his languages and his brilliant gift for mimicry and accents to pass himself off as an enemy of the Realm, and to fraternise with those enemies and pretend to be one of them, to think like them and even, perhaps, to conspire, in danger of being unmasked or betrayed and becoming the victim of a subsequent settling of accounts, for a spy is a spy even in times of peace, or apparent peace, and will probably be executed anyway, and, of course, in the Northern Ireland of the Kindeláns there is no peace . . .'

'But, Tomás,' I said, 'that isn't what I mean. What I'm saying is that nothing obliged you to make that choice, either in Spain or in England, I don't know how else to put it. You could simply not have done it, and then nothing would have happened, that couple wouldn't have appeared in my life or threatened to set fire to Guillermo, I mean, do you realise how dreadful that was? Do you realise what

I went through?' He said nothing, as if admitting he'd been indirectly guilty, guilty at a distance. 'Nor would we have to be thinking now about whether we should stay together or not. Or rather, as you put it, I wouldn't have to ask myself that question. I understand that you want us to stay together, despite everything, despite what you tell me, despite the anomalous situation you're proposing, with me unable to ask you any questions, with you imposing your rules in the peculiar way that I find so unsatisfactory. I don't understand why you didn't consider or weigh up the consequences.'

He turned to look at me. I was still staring straight ahead, at the trees and the storm outside; but I caught the expression on his face out of the corner of my eye. This time it wasn't a look of moral superiority; on the contrary, it was one of inferiority. The look of someone caught out or someone who has broken something valuable. That of someone regretting certain actions that are now impossible to undo.

'I wouldn't be authorised to answer your questions, Berta. That could land me in prison. And, yes, of course I want to stay with you. You have no idea. You're the only thing that allows me sometimes to remember properly who I am. But you don't know the obligations I'm under, you don't know what those obligations are,' he said.

'Well, tell me, then.'

He remained silent for some moments, as if considering the advisability or even the possibility of telling me what those obligations were, as if he were tempted to do so, but knew he shouldn't, that he would regret it for the rest of his life if he succumbed to that temptation. Then his anguished expression softened and he said:

'The obligation to avert a tragedy, Berta, does that seem so very trivial? That's what we do. We avert tragedies. Again and again and again. Endless tragedies.'

I was certain that this wasn't the obligation he'd meant, but I felt that was enough for one night, it sounded good. The rain had stopped again. I was tired now, and he must have been exhausted, and who knows what troubles and sorrows he was carrying with him, from where and for how long. He had, after all, come home, he would sleep beside me, I would see his body next to mine in the bed, his face or head on the pillow, his now bearded face. Unlikely though it might seem, this calmed me. Tomorrow I would think about what I should do. I rested my head on his shoulder, a gesture he doubtless misunderstood.

V

That night I genuinely didn't know what to do, but I did, of course, stay with Tomás; you would need to have lost an awful lot before you'd be willing to renounce what you have, especially if what you have is part of a long-term plan, part of a decision that contained a large dose of obstinacy. You curb your impetuous urges, your expectations, you accept the somewhat tarnished version of what you were hoping to achieve or thought you had achieved, and besides, there are disappointments and imperfections at all stages of life, and you become less demanding: 'Never mind, it wasn't meant to be,' you say. 'All is not lost, it's still worth my while, I can still make do, it would be far worse if there were nothing at all and the whole thing had fallen apart.' When a woman first finds out about an infidelity (as people rather unimaginatively call it), she allows herself to fly into a fury, to heap abuse on the unfaithful partner, to throw him out of the house and shut the door on him. There are some very proud people, or perhaps they're simply more puritanical or more virtuous, who take this attitude to its logical conclusion, but most people, after that first access of rage, begin to hope that it was merely a minor misdemeanour, a whim, a caprice, the product of boredom, vanity, a temporary moment of blindness, and not something serious that looks set to end in a complete separation from the so-called injured party, replacing her and usurping her position. That reaction can't be put down solely to natural conservatism, the desire to keep hold of what you've earned and still possess – a fear of the void and an infinite reluctance to go back to square one – there's also the advantage that the other person is then in your debt. If you stay by his side, if you ignore that transgression, you'll always be able to point to your scar and reproach him, even if only with a look, the way you walk or even breathe. Or by falling silent, especially when falling silent is inappropriate, because then your other half will ask himself: 'Why doesn't she answer, why doesn't she say something, why doesn't she look at me? She must be thinking about what happened.'

This wasn't so in my case, or, rather, any likely infidelities would have occurred out of necessity, as part of his job, or possibly in order to survive; perhaps it was something more akin to the kisses and sex scenes that actors and actresses have to perform. One assumes they *are* acting, and that when the director says 'Cut' those actors and actresses stop, draw apart and treat each other as if there hadn't been the slightest hint of intimacy between them. Or only with their bodies, but not with their souls, which is perhaps one of the few areas in which such a separation can exist. Tomás, of course, would have to perform with no director, no cameras, no team, there would be no witnesses of any kind, no one saying 'Cut'. On the contrary, he would have to appear totally sincere and real, certainly to the other person, who would perhaps have fallen so stupidly in love that she would have revealed more than she should have to the one person to whom she should have said nothing, the person seeking her ruin, a hidden enemy, an impostor, a traitor, and she would tell him these things as evidence that she was in the know and had information that could prove useful, or – just to be kind – to offer him a date or a name and thus unwittingly betray someone else, purely to show off her knowledge, to boast. In the arena of love, a certain amount of boasting is inevitable, before or afterwards, out of a longing to feel more loved, and in that arena you do talk a lot, and you end up talking endlessly, as if that were the greatest possible gift you could give, to satisfy the other person's curiosity and provide them with sometimes unnecessary facts. These are, however, wasted gifts, because most people instantly forget how they found out such-and-such a thing and therefore feel no gratitude or admiration for the person who told them. Once they possess a piece of information or data, they quickly come to believe that they acquired it independently, rapidly forgetting how they did actually acquired it or where, and the messenger soon fades into nothing.

One day, I tried to get Tomás to give me just such a modest gift. Since such gifts were forbidden, I tried to make my question as general as possible, not wishing to compromise him in the least, and so dared to ask him directly:

'If you have to pass yourself off as someone else when you're wherever it is they happen to send you, I imagine that sometimes you must have to go to bed with a woman, even if only to get information out of her or gain her confidence and to create the kind of bond that will encourage her to confide in you. Is that right? You can tell me, I'll understand. I won't hold it against you.'

This wasn't entirely unbelievable – that I would understand, I mean; after all, the 1970s were more permissive, more forgiving in that sphere: nobody was anyone else's property. Contracts and bonds were things to be despised: if I'm with you and abstain from being with others, that isn't out of obligation, but a matter of desire and will, we're free and each day we start anew; that was common currency among numerous couples at the time, even if people still got married believing it was for life. Besides, Tomás and I had spent a lot of time apart since very early on, when we were both still very young, which is when you're most likely to succumb to temptation. He hadn't even been the first man in my life nor had I been the first woman in his, that was clear when he and I finally got together; I mean fully, deeply, when, as they say in the law, we consummated our relationship. We hadn't told each other any details or mentioned specific encounters or names, but we both assumed their existence and took it for granted that they were our own personal business. They had happened in the past, and, therefore, had also become a fiction, up to a point. And we assumed, too, that they had taken place before our wedding. While getting married didn't change anything for us – or perhaps it did in my case, for I naïvely experienced it as a kind of achievement, the fulfilment of a goal – there is a kind of strange, inherited mysticism about marriage to which almost no one can remain immune or indifferent, like the mysticism surrounding motherhood. These are doubtless atavistic feelings, but the married woman and the married man will never be quite the same as those who have never married. Even if you don't believe in ceremonies, however simple or businesslike, they do have an impact, which is why they were invented, I suppose: to draw a line, to establish a before and an after, to make something that wasn't serious serious, to underline and solemnise. To make an announcement and for that to be embraced and sanctioned by the community. No one needs to be told who the new king is (unless there's no heir and there are dynastic disputes), and yet no monarch has ever renounced or chosen to skip the coronation ceremony. Perhaps the question I'd asked was weightier than I thought. We were sitting outside a café in Rosales, underneath the trees; it was the tail end of summer, late September, and we were alone, having left Guillermo with Tomás's parents. Tomás looked at me, surprised and rather embarrassed, which partly answered my question, or so I thought.

'Why ask that now?' he said. 'I thought we'd agreed that you wouldn't ask me any questions.'

'Yes, and I'm not asking you anything specific, where you've been or why, nor who you've been working with or against, nor what you've done or not done. I'm just asking if that happens. In general. It's natural curiosity. Wouldn't you be curious if it was the other way round and I were in your shoes, pretending to be another person and mixing with strangers as if I wasn't married and didn't have a child? You would, wouldn't you? You'd be really curious. I'd be very offended if not.' I tried to make light of the question, and smiled when I made this last remark, but the joke fell flat.

He looked away and appeared to be thinking. He took a sip of his beer, then put his glass down on the table only to pick it up again.

'What good will it do you to know? You'll be worrying about it every time I go away, worrying about whether I'll be going to bed with some woman for the sake of the mission. Nothing that happens on those missions has anything to do with you, I thought that was clear, that you accepted it. It simply doesn't exist as far as you're concerned. It shouldn't even exist for me. And it doesn't exist, I don't know how I can put it more clearly. It doesn't happen, it doesn't take place. Haven't you heard about soldiers who, when they return home, never talk about what they experienced in the war or what they had to do? They never mention what they saw and, fifty or more years later, they die without ever having spoken about it. As if they'd never been in combat in their lives. Well, it's the same with us, the only difference is that they choose to remain silent and we have no choice. We're under a strict obligation to say nothing. If we did, we'd be accused of giving away State secrets, and that's no joke, I can assure you.' Again and again that word 'we'; he clearly felt himself to be a member of a body, or perhaps a club, and that comforted him.

243

'Yes, but I still don't understand why you got involved in the first place,' I said. 'You and your colleagues may be defending the Realm, to use your word, but no one will ever know that, so you can't even boast about it. Isn't that too high a price to pay? I can understand that absolutely all your activities are what the English call "classified", secret, confidential, and will remain so until you die and even beyond the grave, but I can't see what you gain by it, apart from being well paid, because I imagine we're largely living off your salary. But no one will ever see you as heroes, or even as patriots. What you do will be relegated to oblivion or obscurity. However important it may have been, however great the tragedies you may have averted, no one will know. A threat aborted, a tragedy prevented, becomes down-graded to a fear, and, *a posteriori*, people tend to see any fears that come to nothing as unjustified, as exaggeration and paranoia, almost a joke. All those people who built nuclear bunkers in the 1950s and 1960s, especially in the United States, must feel rather foolish now. It's as if what doesn't happen somehow lacks prestige. And it's the same or worse with what we don't know. The chasm between what happens and what doesn't happen is so vast that the latter fades into insignificance, becomes unimportant and barely worth thinking about. We respond to the sheer force of facts and are guided by that. Look what happened to me. If Kindelán had set fire to Guillermo, and I'd watched my child being burned alive, well, if he'd died, our lives would have been destroyed for ever and I would never have been able to forgive you. I would probably have gone mad right there and then, or perhaps run into the kitchen, grabbed a knife and stabbed them both, Miguel and Mary Kate. I would probably have been sent to prison or, best-case scenario, locked up in an insane asylum. But since it was only a threat, a nasty scare, since it didn't happen, I could tell you about it in retrospect with relative calm, because nothing fundamental changed, Guillermo emerged unscathed, he continues to grow and thrive and will have a normal life, or so I hope, and who knows, perhaps one day I'll tell him, as a striking anecdote and even with a touch of humour, about the terrible danger he was in when he was still in his cradle. The distance between what can occur and what does occur is so huge that we forget about the former, even if it came within an inch of happening. All the more so if we didn't know that it could have happened, because then it can't even be forgotten. Imagine if Franco's coup d'état had failed after just a few days. It would have been a mere footnote in the history books, another incident that occurred during the days of the Republic. Or as if it had just been something that was greatly feared or rumoured, but never actually happened. No one would know the names of those who stopped it, would they, those who would have averted a civil war and nearly a million deaths. Since those deaths would not have occurred, the crushing of the uprising would have had no dramatic consequences and would, therefore, be of no interest, no significance.' I fell silent for a few moments, while Tomás stared at me, surprised at my verbosity, and I added: 'According to what you tell me, you belong to that group of people and always will, to those whose names will be forever forgotten or forever unknown. And you seem quite happy with that.'

Tomás was sitting with one elbow resting on the table, and he raised one hesitant hand as if he were holding in it a heavy globe or perhaps Yorick's light skull. I don't know why, but I interpreted that gesture as condescending.

'You don't understand because you can't understand, Berta. But then you're not involved. The proof that it's beyond your grasp is that you got your tenses wrong, you're thinking in terms that simply don't apply. You said that what we do will be relegated to oblivion and never even acknowledged. It would be more accurate to say that what we do has already been relegated to oblivion the very moment we do it. Of course it's unacknowledged, like the actions carried out by someone who never was. Something like that. Even before we do it, it's already non-existent. There's really no difference between before and after. Before something has happened it hasn't happened, and afterwards it hasn't happened either, so everything is always as it was and remains exactly the same. It hasn't happened, or, rather, it doesn't happen even while it's happening. I admit it's not that easy to understand.'

'It's not that difficult either,' I thought. 'This is something he's been taught. They've drummed this into him, and he's taken it fully on board. Now he's boasting to me, now that he's been given permission to tell me something, although only what he needs to, and so, finally, he can boast. Although only to me, to his wife, I'm now more than nobody, I'm somebody. Everyone boasts a little, it's inevitable, even if you've happily resigned yourself to not boasting, even if it's forbidden and you're happy to obey.'

'It's not that difficult either,' I said, and returned to the subject that had begun our conversation beneath the trees: the more he refused to answer me, the more curious I became. 'As for those unknown and doubtless foreign women, at least tell me if we're in the before or the after of what hasn't happened or isn't happening and, needless to say, won't happen. I assume we're not in the "while it's happening" phase.'

This time my joke worked a little better. He smiled at me, still holding that imaginary globe in his hand, and agreed to answer. Inevitably, there was no reason why his answer should be true, and it probably wasn't. He finished his beer and said, slightly smugly:

'It hasn't happened yet. But it might.'

'And, according to you, if it does happen, it won't have happened.'

He realised that he'd said too much and, in a moment of inattention, had contradicted himself. Yes, with those two brief, spontaneous – or perhaps boastful – utterances, he'd contradicted himself and left the door open to the future, a chink through which I could ask more questions, something to hold on to. It was as if he'd inadvertently slipped up, lit a fleeting match in the darkness. It was as if someone who never was had started to be born. He'd admitted that something, that 'it', could happen. He tried to put things right, to rectify matters, but too late. Even so he tried, and said:

'That is, it won't have happened, because, as you say, it won't happen even if it happens.'

And so one year, and then two, three, four, five and six years passed. Once Tomás had been able to tell me, at least partially, what he actually did, he seemed less preoccupied, more light-hearted and in a better mood when he was in Madrid; the bouts of despondency and insomnia were no longer permanent, only appearing or getting worse just before he had to leave for London, although he also brought them with him on his return, as if he needed time to let go of his other life, his other lives – which, however transient, were doubtless lived with greater intensity – so as to get used to the idea that his other life, whichever one it was, had been left behind him for good, and that the only recurring life, the only one that could be repeated and recovered, was the life I offered him in our city. Little by little at first, then ever more quickly, he would become calmer and seemed able to detach himself from whatever it was that he'd done during one of his long absences, from what he'd experienced and from the people he'd had dealings with, although who knew where, and on whom he had doubtless practised a deception, pretending to be one of them for weeks or possibly months, pretending to share their religion or region or country with his amazing talent for imitation and pretence, as impostor and actor, because that was what it came down to. I tended to assume he would be going back to London and, from there – although not always – to some other place. I learned to know or rather guess when he was somewhere else, because while he remained in London, presumably at the Foreign Office or the offices of MI5 or MI6, assuming these were different entities, he would call me with a certain regularity, especially after the birth of Elisa, our little girl, for whom he always felt a particular paternal weakness, as most men do with their daughters, seeing them as both more amusing and more vulnerable, and never as future rivals, as individuals who will one day believe themselves to be superior to them and despise or displace them, as fathers often view their sons even from birth.

That contact became less frequent when he was elsewhere in Great Britain, undergoing, as I deduced or as he implied, some specific training. In that strange profession it seemed they never ceased learning, studying, polishing and perfecting, probably because each mission required its own bespoke coaching and preparation, an impeccable command of a language or an accent, absolute fluency and naturalness in a particular dialect, a thorough knowledge of history, a familiarity with dates, place names, geography, customs and traditions. In my imagination, it seemed possible to me that Tomás, or whoever, could successfully pass himself off as someone else, but not as various different people in different places and circumstances, however radically he changed his appearance or disguised himself, because a person's memory is so chock-full of different factors, which all have to be taken into account when you bring that person to life or interpret them or invent or supplant them. Whatever the truth, I assumed that when he stopped phoning, he had set off on another mission, or 'field trip' as I'd heard him refer to it. When those calls stopped, they stopped completely, and the silences would last for a minimum of a month, but usually two or three and sometimes longer, and I couldn't help but find those silences troubling, disturbing, alarming. They would pass without a word from him, without my knowing if he was still alive, always wondering if he'd been unmasked and, if so, what, if any, measures would be taken against him, if he would manage to get out of wherever he'd been sent and return once more to my side, if he had the necessary support or an escape plan when things turned ugly or he was caught, if that man Reresby or someone else would lend him a hand or abandon him to his fate and give him up as one of the disappeared, the lost.

I not only feared for what might happen to him, I was also concerned about the kind of thing he was involved in. In theory, I wholeheartedly wanted the best for him, and, naturally, I took his side: he was, after all, my husband, the father of my children, and he was still the same Tomás I'd always known, even though he'd changed and chosen a strange, dark life that was beyond my comprehension, and for which I saw no need. Sometimes I couldn't help thinking that he must inevitably be causing harm by his actions: that he must be duping men and women into trusting him, into greeting him like a brother, a lover, or even their one true love, and then he would betray them, inform on them, revealing their names and descriptions and any surreptitious photos he might have managed to take, he would report on their plans and activities and perhaps lead them to their deaths ('And any action is a step to the block, to the fire, down the sea's throat or to an illegible stone . . .'), and how could you cause or make possible the death of someone who has been your affectionate friend or faithful colleague, someone who has held you in their arms in bed, skin against skin, someone who would have given their own life to save you? All those things were possible, for Tomás was the kind of person people took to easily, and even the hardest, most ruthless of individuals can, despite themselves, grow fond of others or have moments of weakness or sympathy, and even mere sexual desire isn't something you can necessarily control, still less who you fall in love with. What a feeble thing our will is. Tomás would facilitate the detention or failure of those ingenuous folk who had put their faith in him, and some countries and organisations cannot forgive failure, not to mention being tricked by an infiltrator, by an enemy agent to whom you have given too much information about what has been done or remains to be done.

I understood that while this was precisely what his job entailed, he also averted tragedies, but then when it comes to enmities and conflicts, it all depends on one's point of view, because what is a tragedy for one side is a blessing for the other. He had dedicated himself to the cause of England, his chosen country, whether its causes were just or not, something which, I imagined, was not for him to judge, his job was merely to accept and obey. But I was in no position to share his patriotism – if I can call it that – how could I? And at the time, most Spaniards (well, those of us who hadn't been Franco supporters) felt an unwavering distaste for the secret police and infinite scorn for all infiltrators. They had belonged to only one side, that of the dictatorship, the far right, and had been the detested members of the Brigada Político-Social, the so-called *sociales*, who had passed themselves off as workers in factories, as miners in mines and as dockers in dockyards, as trades unionists in the illegal trades unions, as militants or leaders of political parties (all of them clandestine), as political prisoners in prisons and as students in universities. With their feigned radicalism they had even encouraged many people to commit crimes they would never have committed without their pressure or their urging, their aggressive speeches, their persuasive powers and their flamboyant extremism. Many people had ended up in prison because of those impostors, who had not only acted as traitors but also as instigators, in the hope of increasing the sentences that would be handed down to those 'subversives': distributing pamphlets was quite a different matter from throwing stones at the windows of a bank or a big shop; running away from the *grises* at a demonstration was not the same as turning on a policeman and knocking him off his horse with an iron bar; being a member of a political party was not the same as shooting an army colonel. The *sociales* wanted peaceful people to stop being peaceful, for free spirits to form organisations or associations, and they didn't restrict themselves to finding out facts and names, for they spurred on whoever fell under their influence, so that they could then be accused of the gravest of crimes. There were also those who administered torture and threw detainees down stairs or out of windows, as happened, in my day, with that student, Enrique Ruano, and with others who, according to the *sociales*, were always trying to escape when there was no escape route and either fell or 'jumped', despite being handcuffed with their hands behind their backs and under permanent guard. That sinister body had still not been entirely dissolved or dismantled, and none of its members had been punished or suspended, still less brought to justice: in the end, they had been found jobs and tasks that were more covert and more in accord with the new democratic era.

I still clung to the idea that England was different, that it had never had a dictatorship and that its Secret Service would be sure to comply with strict laws and be controlled by elected politicians and by honest, independent judges, given that, as a nation, it enjoyed separation of powers and a free press, things that we were only just beginning to enjoy; that they would never commit abuses or crimes comparable to those of the *sociales*, and, if they did, they would not go unpunished, as had so many of those who served under Franco for nearly forty years, some in anodyne posts, others in more sinister roles. But I couldn't be absolutely sure. I took a few books out of the British Institute library in Calle Almagro, and read about the Second

World War; and the cruel operations of the SOE, the SIS, and the PWE (I soon came to know all the acronyms) made my hair stand on end. I did my best to convince myself that, in wartime, everything is different and more exaggerated, that anything is permissible, and that you have to do whatever is necessary to defeat the enemy, and, above all, to survive and not be crushed; that those excesses were a thing of the past, the product of that truly terrible conflict. However, it also occurred to me that when you do perpetrate some cruel act, even when obliged to by extraordinary circumstances – and it makes no difference if it's a country or an individual doing the perpetrating, although a country will often turn a blind eye and choose not to know – there's always a trace left of that cruelty, and then it's much easier than we imagine to resort to it again. All it takes is for us successfully to sidestep the rules just once for us to see that it's really not such a dreadful thing to do and then to do it again, even if it's not strictly necessary. It's simply the easiest, shortest route, and there's no need to explain yourself or make excuses to anyone. That's what people usually say about murderers: once a murderer has taken the first step, once he's injected the poison or dealt the fatal blow and discovered that he can still live with that weight on his conscience, or, indeed, finds that the weight grows lighter by the day, that it's actually not so very hard and that he can half-forget about the life he took because he's actually better off without that burden, obstacle or threat, that presence – that he can breathe more easily without the other person's presence in the world and that his own life is far easier to bear – once he's gone through that phase, once he's crossed that line and found that the consequences are not so very burdensome, then he's much more likely to reoffend and commit a second and a third and even a fourth murder. It's almost a cliché to say this, but there's a lot of truth in it, as there is in all clichés.

No, I wasn't at all sure, and in one of those books that I skim-read or half-read with my now much-improved English, perhaps a book entitled *Trail Sinister*, the autobiography of Sefton Delmer, the main organiser and brains behind the PWE or Political Warfare Executive, a secret body devoted to waging a dirty war and spreading what they called 'black propaganda' during the war with Nazi Germany, I came across certain paragraphs that echoed what Tomás had said about doing something and yet not doing it, about what happened without happening, about the non-existence of what existed and – the impossible thing we all want – the ability to erase our actions. (It was probably the other way round, and the words Tomás had learned were an echo of those used by the PWE.) Delmer would give this speech, or something similar, to the Germans who joined his team (former members of the International Brigade, émigrés, refugees, some prisoners of war prepared to collaborate, deserters): 'We are waging against Hitler a kind of total war of wits. Anything goes, so long as it serves to bring nearer the end of the war and the complete defeat of the Reich. If you are at all squeamish about what you may be called upon to do against your own countrymen you must say so now. I shall understand it. In that case, however, you will be no good to us and no doubt some other job will be found for you. But if you feel like joining me, I must warn you that in my unit we are up to all the dirty tricks we can devise. The dirtier the better. No holds barred. Lies, phone-tapping, embezzlement, treachery, forgery, defamation, disinformation, spreading dissension, making false statements and accusations, you name it. Even, don't forget, sheer murder.' I still remember that English expression: 'sheer murder'.

At the time, I happened to read an article about the Watergate affair, a scandal that rocked the English-speaking world, a world to which, for obvious reasons, I was paying ever closer attention, and the author of the article, a certain Richard Crossman – a minister under Harold Wilson in the 1960s and, in his day, almost as important a figure in the PWE as Delmer – acknowledged that, between 1941, when that implacable, unstoppable organisation had been created, and the end of the war, England basically had an 'inner government' with rules and codes of conduct completely at odds with those of the visible, public government, adding that, during total warfare, this was a necessary mechanism. Since he had been very high up in the PWE, it wasn't easy to contradict or disprove what he said, for he also admitted that black propaganda, like the 'strategic' bombing of German cities and the civilian population – Dresden, Hamburg, Cologne, Mannheim and others – was 'nihilistic in its aims and purely destructive in its effects'.

I also read, either in *Trail Sinister* or its sequel, *Black Boomerang*, or somewhere else, that Sefton Delmer's unit didn't officially exist and that its members were told to deny its existence to everyone, including other almost equally hermetic organisations, with whom the PWE did, in practice, collaborate (not in theory, of course, since there was no record of its existence), such as the SOE – in charge of commando units and surprise attacks – and MI6, in charge of espionage. Neither its name nor its acronym became public knowledge until long afterwards. Many of the people who worked there didn't even know they were working for it and thought they were just part of the Foreign Office's PID, Political Intelligence Department, supposedly a small, non-secret section of the ministry. The people who wrote the white propaganda (the BBC broadcasts intended for Germany and occupied Europe, for example) tended to know absolutely nothing about the existence of the black propaganda being created by their colleagues, who were working in separate divisions and in utmost secrecy. The great advantage of black propaganda, and the terrible, limitless damage it caused, was that no one ever acknowledged that it was British in origin, and the government, of course, when they had to, always denied having anything to do with any acts of excessive barbarism. As a consequence, the people involved had a completely free hand, unhampered by scruples or restraints.

The PWE was considered to be such an anomaly, even while it was in operation (and there can be no doubt that it was crucial in winning the war), that not only was it dismantled as soon as the Germans had signed the unconditional surrender on 7 May 1945, its members were given more or less the following instructions: 'For years we have abstained from talking about our work to anyone not in our unit, including husbands, wives, fathers and children. And to keep it that way, we want you to continue as you have up until now. Don't allow anything or anyone to provoke you into boasting about the work we've done. If we start to show off to people about the ingenious things we got up to, and which proved far superior to the most evil of minds, who knows where it will end. So, mum's the word.' Reading all these things, sometimes skipping over whole sections, it was hard to determine if that unit had been dismantled so quickly for reasons of prudence or of shame, so as not to give away information to future enemies or to hide what it had been obliged, or not even obliged, to do. Perhaps being superior to the most evil of minds implied, in a sense, being even more evil. Whatever the truth of the matter, the PWE was buried alive – once it was dead. In other words, it didn't exist while it existed and when it ceased to exist, it hadn't existed, until, I imagine, someone spoke about it many years later. Until someone, whether evil or not, could not resist boasting.

Tomás did pretty well, and hardly ever succumbed to the temptation to boast. I mean that he obeyed the order not to reveal to anyone the nature of his travels or the places they took him to, nor the real reason for his absences or for some of them, nor the names of the people he had been involved with, doubtless in order to bring about their destruction or ruin. I assume he didn't reveal anything to anyone, because he didn't even confide in me, and I was really the only one who needed to be informed of his activities, at least in Madrid; the only one who, given my position and to assuage my suspicions and other evils – perhaps even my own acts of espionage, my rummaging around in his belongings at home – the only one who had a right to be kept up to date on his double life. We had agreed that I wouldn't ask him any questions about the part of his life that took place far away, out of sight and hearing, and that had nothing to do with me, but there were moments when curiosity got the better of me, and I couldn't resist asking him something openly or obliquely. (The desire to know is a curse and the greatest source of misfortune; even if you're already in the know or can guess what's happening, it's impossible to repress that desire.) He would then stop me in my tracks with a few predictable words: 'Look, it's best you don't know', or 'You know you're not allowed to know that', or 'Just be grateful I'm not authorised to tell you, that I'm bound by the Official Secrets Act' (which meant that what he'd experienced or done was very grim indeed and nothing to be proud of), or simply 'Don't ask. Remember what we agreed'. Or sometimes he would frighten me, which is always the easiest and most effective way to dissuade any individual, as well as the masses: 'If I were to tell you anything, I'd be putting you at risk, you and the children, and we don't want that, do we? We don't want any more Kindeláns or someone even worse, someone capable of throwing the lighter into the cradle instead of putting it away. Because they did put it away, didn't they? And our children are safe and sound.'

There are many roundabout ways of showing off, even if reason tells you not to. Tomás had integrity, he was discreet, but he did sometimes make leading comments, as if drawing attention to himself or perhaps looking for a little compassion or appreciation – after all, he was the one who did all the work, who suffered, the one who brought most money into the household, a lot of money, I realised, for they were paying him more and more, and we were living very comfortably. His return from some particularly difficult or dangerous mission, or one that had required a high degree of ingenuity, or that had worked out perfectly, would sometimes provoke one or two comments that were impossible not to respond to. 'You can't imagine the hell I've been through this time', for example. Or: 'I'm absolutely shattered. I need to sleep for about three whole days, more than anything to recover from the things I've seen, and to stop seeing them even when I'm awake.' Or: 'You have no idea how hard it is having to bring down the people you have to bring down, even if it's vital for us and they really deserve it. And the bastards certainly deserved it this time.' And I would always fall into that initial trap, how could I not? 'What hell have you been through? What have you seen? Who did you have to bring down? Which bastards are you talking about?

If you don't tell me, how can I console you? How can I even understand what you mean?' But Tomás would immediately clam up, and the most he would allow himself were long disquisitions on the nature of his work, which was the least he should be allowed to do with his wife, perhaps the only person in the world he could talk to, colleagues apart; but they would never admire him or feel intrigued or astonished. 'Sorry to go on about it, Berta, but it's best this way, better that you know nothing about the life you're not a part of. It's often really unpleasant, full of sad stories, none of which end happily, for one side or the other,' he said, then again talked for a while in general terms.

No, Tomás was very disciplined and barely said a word about his work, although I could see he wanted to; he doubtless had to remind himself of the oath he'd sworn and had to bite his tongue each time he came home, and then again every few days while he remained at my side. (How sad not to be able to tell anyone about what's happened or what you've been through, the dangers survived, the plots hatched, the dilemmas faced and the decisions taken, for many vicissitudes are bearable only if you can tell someone about them later, and I imagine his work was full of such hazards.) And I certainly showed no signs of indifference or resignation. I would try to draw him out, in fact, talking to him about what I'd been reading and about the past exploits of his remote antecedents. I told him about the PWE during the Second World War and about MI6 and the SOE and their audacious raids, about the SIS and the SAS and the NID and the much smaller PID, about all the different acronyms I'd been learning (even about novels written by Ian Fleming and John le Carré, which were fictional and contemporary). There was nothing wrong with investigating the past, still less one of the most exciting periods in history, which was there for anyone to discover. My interest in that whole world had clearly arisen from my discovery of what he did, from his succinct, authorised confession; if I wasn't allowed to know what he got up to, I could at least get some idea by studying what his predecessors had done during that more glorious, active period, three or four decades before. I also had an alibi that allowed me to pretend that my motives had nothing to do with him and the life he'd chosen and in which I played no part: during those years of resignation and impatience, I finished my doctorate, and immersed myself in the special subject I'd studied during my last three years at university, which also happened to coincide with the situation closest to home, biographically, I mean. I was appointed part-time lecturer in the English department at the Complutense University, and, as such, I found myself being used as a kind of jill of all trades: sometimes I would have to teach English literature, some-times phonetics, sometimes English history, depending on the availability or not of the professors or senior lecturers, who were often lazy or passive or else on official sick leave – the lax behaviour of the Franco era continued unabated. I was able to fit in my studies and classes around bringing up the children, as so many women did in my pioneering generation. It's true that, thanks to Tomás's gener-ous salary (it all came from the Foreign Office in theory, and was paid in pounds), I could manage far more easily than most people. My English came on in leaps and bounds, but could never compare with my husband's innate bilingualism, or with his extraordinary gift for learning languages. And so I had to refresh and deepen my know-ledge, and England's long history certainly kept me busy.

'Why do you focus so much on the Second World War?' Tomás once asked me somewhat suspiciously, after hearing me going on about Vivian, Menzies, Cowgill, Crossman and Delmer, thus dem-onstrating that I knew my stuff; I even knew that Menzies was pronounced 'Minguiss', at least that's how the name of that particular head of the Secret Service was pronounced. 'Presumably you also need to tell your students about Alfred the Great and William the Conqueror, the Wars of the Roses and Cromwell. You won't have time to cover everything in a year.'

'Well, since no one cares what I do and no one checks up on me, I choose my favourite subjects,' I said. 'And it seems to me more important that they should know about relatively recent history, which has got us where we are now, and which is, in large measure, still relevant. After all, MI6, or whatever it was that replaced the Political Warfare Executive, is still active, isn't it? Because I'm sure something must have replaced it. Indeed, it would surprise me if its black, super-secret practices hadn't spread to other democratic countries. The non-democratic countries have them already.' I meant what I was saying, but I was also trying to get him to talk, if not about concrete facts, then about more abstract things. And this was one area he was willing to discuss with me.

'Why do you say that? What do you base your opinion on?' He was clearly bothered by my remarks. 'If you've done your research, you'll know that the PWE was dismantled as soon as the war ended. It lasted for as long as was necessary, not a minute more, and it was something that was very much of its time, when it truly was a matter of life and death. If Germany wasn't defeated, then England would have had to surrender. Sometimes you simply can't act within the law or go around asking permission for everything you do. If the enemy has no scruples, then the side with scruples is doomed to defeat. That's how it's always been in time of war, for centuries. The modern concept of "war crimes" is ridiculous, stupid, because war consists of crimes being committed on all fronts from the first day to the last. It comes down to this: either you don't embark on wars or, if you do, you have to be prepared from the outset to commit whatever crimes are necessary, whatever you need to do to achieve victory.'

'Would that include "sheer murder", which is what Delmer apparently demanded of his assistants and acolytes?' I took every opportunity to show him how well informed I was about these things of the past; my readings in the British Institute library were haphazard and partial and erratic, but I just had to drop in a few names and the odd fact to seem positively erudite: I *was* boasting. And I didn't know how much he knew; he would have been on courses, but he might have neither the necessary curiosity nor the time. 'I mean in the rearguard and against civilians, just to demoralise them and sow panic and create a general atmosphere of insecurity, not carrying out combat missions or raids. You're not telling me that kind of thing doesn't still go on.'

'Of course it doesn't.' And that emphatic 'of course' made me think he was lying. 'We're not at war now, not openly at war. Where did you get that idea?'

'From a simple belief that one of mankind's characteristics is that he never renounces something he's already tried – if he's done so with impunity or success, that's all that matters. What has been done once will be done again, either by an individual or by a collective. Whatever has been invented is sure to be put into practice sooner or later, even if it's not necessary, simply because it's feasible and has been invented. What can be done will be done, science has no qualms about its discoveries and advances being put into practice; on the contrary, it can't wait for that to happen. Everything accumulates and nothing is wasted. For all our obligatory horror at and rhetoric about the Nazis, their lessons have been learned and assimilated by their enemies too; it's the same with the Soviets. And why wouldn't you hang on to or make use of something that contributed to overcoming and beating the Nazis, no less? Not necessarily continuously, as then, but occasionally, sporadically, to eliminate someone quickly and efficiently or to ward off a major threat. Nothing is ever totally abandoned, everything is kept in reserve. Everything that has been tried and dismissed as excessive, criminal or unjust hasn't really been dismissed, it's there waiting, latent, dormant, call it what you will, and begging to come back, to be woken from its sleep, hoping for less considerate, more vicious times to return, as they always will. And I'm sure that, when necessary, those things will be taken up again. You yourself have told me that what you and your friends do hasn't been done, hasn't happened. The only way for someone like me to understand this is to think of it as something that goes unrecorded, unacknowledged, that must always remain hidden away, which is precisely the doctrine applied by the PWE to their existence and their activities.'

He didn't like me referring to him and his friends and immediately made a face. Nor did he like such a direct comparison to the unit run by Delmer and Crossman or whoever. He seemed really upset, and made as if to bring his fist down hard on the coffee table, for we were in the living room, on the very sofa occupied by the Kindeláns on that day I will never forget and have never forgotten. However, he managed to contain himself, although he was visibly growing ever more agitated and eager for me to stop.

'Look, just drop the subject, will you,' and this sounded like an order, and Tomás was never one to give orders, he rarely did. 'I've already told you, that kind of thing doesn't happen now. It stopped happening in 1945. And I'm not having you telling me what my job involves. I mean, really, what do *you* know about it? I think I would have a slightly better idea, don't you think?'

He spoke in an irritated, sarcastic tone, again unusual in him, and that should have acted as a warning, but I was on a roll and wasn't going to stop just because he said so.

'You're right when you say that it was a matter of life and death then. It really was, and the world would have been an inferno if England had failed. I suppose we lived through a slightly less ferocious version of that here, less ferocious for us than for our parents. But every age exaggerates and needs to brag, and all ages feel that their conflicts are equally serious, a matter of life and death. They all consider that their circumstances justify extreme measures and they're incapable of thinking they're not important. Every age believes itself to be exposed to great dangers, and every age is prepared to break its own established rules and regulations, to feel constrained by its own restrictions and to find ways of ignoring them or getting round them. People like you live in fear, as you yourself said: "We avert tragedies", you said, and anyone who spends his life doing that will see tragedies looming everywhere, every day, and will probably overstep the mark in his eagerness to prevent them. Every molehill will become a mountain, any strange activity will set alarm bells ringing, will put him on his guard, ready for action, to observe that activity and then crush it. It's like that line from your beloved Eliot: "And in short, I was afraid".'

He repeated it after me, as if it were a reflex reaction. How many lines by Eliot must he have memorised? And although that was all he said, his voice sounded hoarse and alien, as if it were not his voice and emerged from inside a helmet and not from his own chest:

'And in short, I was afraid.'

I ignored him and went on:

'If you continue in that job, if you don't leave, that line will sum up your entire life. And fear doesn't care about anything, it doesn't stop to consider what's good or bad, what's proportionate and disproportionate, what constitutes a crime and what might be the consequences, and, needless to say, it doesn't care about justice. I'm afraid of what you do out of fear, Tomás, afraid of all those things I know nothing about and will presumably never know. I can only imagine it, and from what I imagine, it seems to me that, apart from some evident differences, it's not that different from what the *sociales* did here. They, too, lived in fear and saw enemies everywhere. They, too, devoted themselves to preventing what, for the Franco regime, would have been tragedies. They, too, passed themselves off as other people. They, too, infiltrated and betrayed. And actions can't be erased.'

This time he did bring his fist down hard on the table, making the ashtrays and the other objects tremble – a magnifying glass, a small clock, a compass; a small lead figurine representing two duellists actually toppled over; while the ice in our whisky glasses clinked so loudly I was afraid it might wake the children, who had only just gone to bed as darkness fell. His usually amiable face – even when he was full of angst – became one of utter rage, his eyes darting wildly about. Again, though, the most unrecognisable thing was his voice, which sounded like that of an old man, a furious old man:

'Don't ever, ever compare me with the *sociales*. What the hell does a dictatorial regime that emerged from a horrific civil war and repressed its compatriots for decades have to do with what I do? What does that have to do with one of the oldest democracies in the world and its fight against the worst evil ever known in history, against Franco's allies and protectors, in fact. The England we know comes out of that, out of that war against those people on the other side. Don't you ever dare compare me to them. What do you know. What do you know about what we avoid or avert, about the good we do and how many people we help. What do you know about what's being cooked up in some basement or tavern or farmhouse. What do you know about anything.'

I felt as if he were only a step away from turning violent, physically

266

violent, which was something unknown in him. The idea leapt into my mind: 'So he's capable of violence, then. He must have learned that during one of his training sessions too.' Now it was my turn to feel slightly afraid, but it was a different kind of fear, instantaneous, sudden, the fear of a shout or a blow or a harsh, angry tone; not his kind of fear: silent, constant, vigilant, ruthless, vengeful, the kind that's always on guard, scanning the horizon for some threat to be crushed, a fear which he'd inhabited for years now and from which he would be unable to extricate himself. And it was, as I've said, the improbable voice that frightened me most, far more than his fist coming down on the thick glass tabletop and the proud look on his face: the voice of an old man, yet still vigorous, as befitted his actual age. However, now that he had advanced, I wasn't going to fall meekly silent at the first assault. For years now, I had respected the conditions he'd laid down and had remained at his side, and that was my choice and because I still loved him, it's not easy to stop loving someone you decided to love very early on, our most deep-seated feelings are all forged when we're young; but perhaps also because it suited me, for it was, after all, a fairly comfortable life, even privileged; you can get used to anything, and we'd been accustomed to living apart right from the beginning, and impatience does gradually tend to wane rather than increase, so surely I could curb it now that I'd turned thirty. Besides, I wasn't asking him concrete questions about his travels or his missions or his possible, officially approved crimes, the ones he wasn't authorised to tell me about. I suppose I was just vaguely admonishing and dissuading him, which, admittedly, most people would find irritating. I did my best to continue gently and deliberately:

'You're right, Tomás, I don't know, and I don't pretend or aspire to know.' This was a lie, because sometimes I really burned to know and to find out what he did, in detail: who he pretended to befriend only to betray them later, why his plans sometimes fell apart and who was responsible, and what were these terrible tragedies he averted; which women – widows, girls or spinsters – he cajoled into giving him information that would condemn their fathers or brothers, and whether any of them left an impression on him or left him with so much as a twinge of regret. 'But one thing I do know, because it happens everywhere: you think you're working for a democratic and supposedly irreproachable government and defending its security and its values – its debatable values. Fine, but you only ever see or hear the leaders of that government on television or in the press, never in private, and in that respect you're no different from the most insignificant citizen. You deal with the lieutenants and sergeants, if you like, but never with the generals. And lieutenants and sergeants make whatever decisions they want, at least vis-à-vis their inferiors. And this suits the generals and government ministers too. It suits them not to have to give orders, but to let others interpret their wishes, so as not to be compromised and to be able to say one day, if necessary: "I knew nothing about that, it was done without my knowledge and, of course, without my consent." You think you're working for Mrs Thatcher, who is, by the way, a pretty nasty piece of work to have as your boss: she didn't stage a coup d'état, start a civil war or impose a dictatorship, which is all to the good, but for the rest I'm not sure she's so very different from Franco.' I was exaggerating just to annoy him and to see how far his patriotism went. He didn't react, though. 'Just as, before, you would have thought you were working for Callaghan, Wilson or whoever. You know, you've never even told me when you actually started doing this work; it wasn't when you were still a student, I hope.'

'Heath,' he said.

'What?'

'Edward Heath preceded Wilson as prime minister.' He said this in English (however bilingual he was and however much my English had improved, we never talked to each other in that language), and I thought I heard a trace of an American accent, as if he were imitating someone. His voice was still that of an old man.

'Well, whoever it was, it doesn't matter,' I went on. 'One thing is certain, though, none of those prime ministers would have known what you know, you and your friends, the troops, although you may already have been made a sergeant or a lieutenant. And they certainly won't have issued any orders. And as for what you call the Crown, well, the Queen will have no idea and won't want to, poor woman – very wise. And nothing will have changed in that respect since the Second World War, Tomás, not in England or anywhere else. The people who worked for the PWE believed they were working for Churchill, for the nation that he embodied at the time, but they would only have been doing so very obliquely, if at all. They were working for Lockhart or Crossman or Delmer.' I continued to throw names at him, as well as acronyms, to impress him with my pseudo-knowledge. 'Or for someone beneath them. And the MI6 people would be working for Menzies or Vivian and for their close or distant subordinates; whether Menzies met with Churchill every day, I've no idea – he may have done – but it would make no difference: the troops were leagues away from Churchill, as far as you are from Thatcher and from whoever's in charge of you at the moment, and that's how everything is everywhere. The people ultimately responsible for any decision-making always delegate and wash their hands of things, and cover themselves with a veil. The veil has the advantage of letting you see and not see, or to see only vaguely if that's what you want; you just have to fold the veil in two to make it thicker, or into four and then you can't see a thing. So almost no one knows who they're working for, nor who actually gave the orders they're carrying out. It's absurd, everyone thinks they know who or what they're serving when really they're just groping in the dark, flying blind. But then even if they did know . . .'

I paused just to test his mood, to find out if he was still furious or was at least listening to some of what I said. It seemed to me that his fit of rage had abated and he was more or less paying attention.

'Dick Franks, I believe.' I assumed he meant that this was the man in charge of them now. 'Go on. What do you mean by "even if they did know"?' He was still speaking in English and in that vaguely American drawl, which I found discomfiting and unsettling. However, he said so little that I didn't pause for long and went on:

'Do you remember that scene in Shakespeare's *Henry V*?' My English literature classes at the university had required me to do a very close reading of the play, in case I was asked to teach it.

'Which scene?'

'The one where, on the eve of battle, the King wraps himself in a cloak and joins three soldiers who, unable to sleep, their weapons at the ready, are anxiously waiting for what the next day will bring. He presents himself to them as a friend, he passes himself off as one of them, sits down by their fire and they talk. The soldiers speak very freely, as among equals, and two even get a bit stroppy with him at one point, because, for them, he isn't the King or anything, just as they are not, at that moment, his subjects, they can argue with him and say whatever they like, for the King is in disguise, has hidden his face.'

'Yes, that's a very famous scene, very famous indeed. And it's followed by the speech about ceremony, I think. Anyway, what about it?'

Tomás appeared to have calmed down, but I found that decrepit voice and that entirely inappropriate accent far more frightening than his angry shouts or him thumping the table. I didn't know what he was playing at or why, it was nothing like the playful mimicry he had always indulged in, nor was this the right moment for such things. It was suddenly as if I were speaking to a stranger, someone remote, another person. I could see him and he was him, despite his changed appearance, for he always returned from one of his prolonged absences looking quite different: with long or short hair or almost shaven-headed, with his hair fairer or darker, with a beard or a moustache or mutton-chop side whiskers, a few pounds heavier or lighter, his face and body thinner or fatter, almost puffy, his nose broader and with shadows under his eyes; a new scar on his back, the product of a car accident, nothing serious, he told me. But it was his accent I found troubling; more than that, it filled me with the beginnings of panic, as if he were possessed by the spirit of an old actor in Westerns: Walter Brennan, for example, who had appeared in a hundred films and won Oscars for Best Supporting Actor; Brennan always spoke as if he were chewing tobacco or had forgotten his false teeth, and I often found him incomprehensible, I'd seen him play that role in classics like *My Darling Clementine*, *Red River* and *Rio Bravo*, which both of us loved. The disconnect between Tomás and his voice and his accent made me feel insecure, or, for some reason, in danger, as if I were treading on unstable ground: if he could transform himself like that, then he would be capable of anything, I thought, of not being himself even in his actions. But he urged me on with an energetic, impatient gesture, like the young man he was, and I hastened to answer:

'Those soldiers know that they serve the King, even though they've never seen him in person and are happy to serve him, as you have been now that you're serving your unexpectedly beloved England. But even those simple men wonder about the battle they will fight the next day and in which they might lose their lives. And one of them says: "But if the cause is not good, the King himself has a heavy reckoning to make when all those legs and arms and heads, chopped off in a battle, shall join together on the last day and cry all, 'We died at such a place.'" And the truth is that no one can ever know if other people's causes are good or bad, even those of your own country when that country isn't a source of shame, as, until only recently, was ours; or should I say, my country. Causes belong only to their representatives, remember, and they are always temporary and lose authority as one succeeds another. Think of the current fashion for apologising for what was done by compatriots who have been pushing up the daisies for centuries now. It's ridiculous. So, tell me, how can you say that your causes are just causes, if they're given to you by intermediaries and lieutenants and sergeants, causes that are doubtless disfigured, distorted or fake, perhaps not even explained; I doubt very much that they take the trouble to justify to you what they're ordering you to do. They'll send you off here or there, saying "Do this" or "Get rid of him", nothing more, I bet. If we find it hard to know whether our own causes are good and can blithely deceive ourselves about them, imagine how hard it is to know about other people's causes. We don't even know what they are.'

I was about to go on, because that wasn't my main point, only a preamble, but he took advantage of my pause to interrupt me and this time he spoke for longer, still – infuriatingly – in that Walter Brennan voice, which grew more sinister with each second that passed. It was really unnerving to hear it issuing from his throat and his lips.

'If memory serves me right, someone else says in that famous scene: "If his cause be wrong, our obedience to the King wipes the crime from us." We study Shakespeare in our work too, you know. Of course, what Shakespeare says isn't the current doctrine, which even accuses and lays the blame on the poor cabin boy of some ship whose captain committed a felony. Perhaps that modest soldier in *Henry V* had more sense than our world, which, with its pretensions to virtue, is more hypocritical than any other. But I don't know where you're going with all this or what you're trying to say, girlie.' He called me 'girlie' as if he really were an old cowboy and I was a little kid, or, who knows, a horse. 'That's how it's been for as long as there have been bosses and hierarchies: there's a chain of command and each person receives instructions from the person immediately above and passes them on to the person beneath. If each link in that chain questioned those instructions and made deep moral speeches about them, nothing would work and nothing would be possible, chaos would ensue. That's how it is in armies and in businesses, even in grocery shops. And no one could operate efficiently, no wars would be won, not even the odd skirmish. I know there's a long trad-ition of that in Spain: undisciplined troops full of harebrained schemes, *ideas de bombero*' – he shifted back into Spanish at that point, for every language has a yearning for other languages – 'who argue about everything, hoping to impose their ideas, and if they don't, then they go it alone. Obviously, we haven't been helped by the string of incompetent, disastrous leaders we've had since time immemorial. England does things differently, and it's not so very strange that I should have chosen it. Historically, it, too, has had its fair share of fools in charge . . .'

Our little girl had been crying and calling out for some time, when Tomás was only about halfway through his spiel, but he hadn't stopped speaking, pretending that he hadn't heard her, or perhaps thinking it wasn't urgent enough to keep him from finishing his speech. And he clearly hadn't finished, just as I hadn't finished mine, but, at that point, I could bear it no longer and I got up and went to fetch her, but before I did, I said:

'Will you stop doing that? Why are you talking to me like some old cowpoke from the Wild West? What are you playing at? You're making me nervous, you're frightening me. You sound as if you were someone else, I don't know, Walter Brennan or someone. I can't even understand you properly and I just don't recognise you. So stop it now, stop arsing around.'

I went into the bedroom and picked my daughter up in my arms. She was thirsty, and so I gave her something to drink, then took her into the living room to be with us, cradling her head against my shoulder and rocking her back and forth, to calm her, and hoping she would fall asleep to the murmur of our voices and my gentle pacing. This wouldn't be easy unless Tomás reverted to his normal self. His relationship with Guillermo and Elisa was a contradictory one. I'm sure he loved them and was deeply fond of them, and he just adored Elisa, but he always tried to maintain a certain distance from them when he was in Madrid. He reined in his affection and reined in their instinctive affection for him, as if he didn't want to become overly accustomed to such fond displays, so that he wouldn't miss them too painfully during his inevitable future absences. Even though he was often at home for several months at a time, he knew he would be summoned to London again and would again have to leave, that he was only at home with us temporarily, and he could never discount the possibility that he might not come back. This thought so saddened me that my feelings of disapproval diminished somewhat. Thomas knew that, one day, he might become an outcast from our universe, and, as a consequence, he tried hard not to become too attached to it, to be, up to a point, a visitor, insofar as that was possible. He held out his arms to take the child, and I handed her to him and he laid her on his chest, patting her gently on the back and rather inexpertly rocking her back and forth. She stopped crying, and her tears were replaced by little groans, heralding a return to sleep, and he took advantage of that moment to answer me, still in English, but in a completely different voice and accent this time: now he sounded like a rather uneducated Englishman, the kind who pronounces nearly all his vowels as 'o's, and instead of 'like' or 'mind' says 'loik' or 'moind', just to give a couple of examples. To be honest, I couldn't always tell the difference. It was a harsh voice, that of a coarse young man, not a decrepit old fellow.

'More like Charley Grapewin,' he said. I had no idea who that was, although I presumed it was some other supporting actor. During their training sessions, they were probably shown films, new and old, to help them learn to imitate all kinds of voices, ways of speaking and accents. As well as listening to tapes of different languages and dialects, I suppose. 'If you find that so upsetting, see what you think of this one.'

I found this other voice equally disturbing, because what was so unnerving and frightening was seeing him and yet hearing not his voice, but that of some complete stranger who had slipped into my house and taken possession of Tomás or supplanted him: if he'd done that kind of thing in a different age, someone would have called for an exorcist. His mimicry was now of such a disquieting, not to say terrifying, perfection that he could pretend to be whomever he wanted. They had certainly taught him well, and, during those years, had really honed his skills, transforming him into a chameleon-like actor or a professional mimic of the sort who appears on the radio and makes listeners believe that it really is the prime minister or the King or the Pope speaking. Once, those verbal incarnations had been intended to divert or amuse, but now they were deadly serious, and their very seriousness made them horribly sinister; they were a brilliant forgery, like a fake painting that is presented and sold as authentic, or like a seducer in one of those classical comedies, who slips into the bed of a woman under cover of a moonless night, pretending to be her beloved, and has his way with her: that was the stuff of deceit. Someone capable of such shams could fool anyone and was, therefore, highly dangerous, and I found this idea utterly repugnant, that my husband, my old love, should be so gifted at pretence, and deployed that gift and used those skills when he was far away in that part of his life to which I had no access. All the more reason, despite my unease, to return to what I was saying, to what I most wanted to tell him and which I had left half-said. Elisa didn't seem bothered by her father's phoney, albeit sonorous, voice, and was slowly falling asleep in his arms, doubtless breathing in the smell of his skin; perhaps children find any voice soothing and only need to know they're not alone and that someone is watching over them.

'Listen, Tomás, tell me what you think of this. One of the soldiers in that scene, called Bates if I remember rightly – no, Williams – gets embroiled in an argument with the King, who is partly muffled up or entirely covered by his cloak, I'm not sure, but his face is certainly obscured, plus they're in the dark. Williams says something disrespectful about his monarch, and the King defends him (that is, he defends himself as if he were someone else), the two quarrel and promise to settle accounts after the battle, if they survive. And they exchange gloves, by way of what they call a 'gage' or 'guarantee', so that they'll recognise each other when they meet again, if they meet again: one will wear it pinned to his helmet and the other to his cap. And a few scenes later, they do meet. Henry V has survived, of course, and as he's waiting to receive a full count of the numbers of deaths on the French and English sides, he sees Williams pass by. The King is now clearly the King, surrounded by aides-de-camp, and he's the one who addresses the soldier when he spots him with the glove pinned to his cap. He asks why he's wearing it, and Williams describes what happened the previous night with an unknown Englishman or Welshman. Henry comments mischievously that perhaps his enemy was "a gentleman of great sort", to which Williams replies, with the agreement of a captain who is also present that, however great the gentleman with whom he quarrelled, he is honour-bound to keep his oath and strike him if he sees him alive and in one piece. There are various other bits of business that I won't go into now, but, at last, the King shows him the other glove, the fellow of the one he gave to Williams in the dark when he was in disguise. And then the King dares to censure him for abusing his King: "It was indeed I you vowed to strike, and you spoke in most bitter terms," he says. The last time I read it for my classes, I noticed that he even resorts to using the royal "we" to intimidate him: "It was ourself thou didst abuse." And the captain, who is also there as witness to this dialogue, quickly changes his mind and urges Henry to punish Williams, declaring "let his neck answer for it".'

'Yes, I remember the first really famous scene, but have no recollection of that part, none at all,' said Tomás, and he said this in Spanish and in his normal or true voice, as if he'd suddenly returned to his old self, perhaps because he was interested or intrigued by what I was telling him. 'And what does the King do? Does he order his execution? That would be most unfair, an abuse of power. How could the soldier know who he was actually talking to that night? For him, he was just another soldier, an equal, someone with whom he was perfectly at liberty to get into an argument.'

'This is what Williams says in response: "Your Majesty came not as yourself: you came to me as a common man, and what your Highness suffered in that guise was your fault, not mine; for had you been what I took you for, then I caused no offence; I ask your Highness, therefore, pardon me." I'm quoting from memory, of course,' I added, 'but that's essentially what he said.'

'I don't even know why that man Williams should ask to be forgiven,' Tomás said rather vehemently (the vehemence felt by more innocent readers and spectators, by children and the very young). 'He had clearly done nothing wrong. If the King doesn't behave like the King, if he supplants himself and appears in disguise, then he isn't the King for as long as he keeps up that pretence. What anyone says to him while he's in that disguise doesn't count, even if it's offensive, subversive, even treasonous; it's as if anything said hadn't been said, and should be ignored or wiped from the record. So what does Henry do then? Does he have him executed or pardoned?' Tomás was anxious to know what happened next, whether Henry V took advantage of his deceitful mode of inquiry, of having learned that one of his soldiers despised him (which was the cause of the quarrel, the argument, the summons), or if he absolved Williams of all blame, whatever his opinions and regardless of who he had challenged, because, at the time, he didn't know who he was taking on or who he was talking to.

I stood looking at Tomás for a moment, with a mixture of perplexity, tenderness, pity, even unwitting mockery, I'm not sure which, and the latter might have been unavoidable. He was still somewhat ineptly jiggling Elisa about, even though she was already sound asleep, her light breathing regular and peaceful. I was tempted to take her from him and return her to her cot, but I waited, I held back.

'You're quite right, I think, and so was the soldier, as we will see. On the eve of battle, the King has infiltrated his own troops, those who serve him and are prepared to die for him and for their country, which, in those days were two indistinguishable entities, and, for the troops, were one and the same. There are even politicians today who try to make out that there's no difference between the country and them, and, despite the way the world has changed, quite a lot of people are persuaded by their arrogance, so just imagine what it would have been like in 1415. The soldiers may have questioned whether the cause of the war was good or bad, but they had no intention of running away or disobeying their leader. For that very reason, because he was an infiltrator, the King would have no right to make use of what he heard, of what the soldiers had told him, frankly and in good faith. If he took advantage of that, if he punished that particular soldier, he would be abusing the trust placed in him by one of his subjects, who was unaware that, by speaking so freely, he risked losing his head at the hands of his friendly interlocutor, when they were not on equal terms and he could not defend himself. That's how we would see it now, isn't it, and presumably that's how it was seen in Shakespeare's day, two centuries after that battle. Henry's behaviour would seem sly and aberrant. The King, though, was all-powerful and his will always prevailed, which is probably why the fickle captain urges him to punish the soldier immediately, and take the life that had not been taken by the enemy in the recent victorious struggle. According to him, what did it matter how the King learned of Williams's disrespectful remarks, what did it matter who Williams thought he was threatening with a slap across the face and a subsequent duel? He was still threatening the King, and the King is always the King even if he dresses as a beggar, as happens in fairy tales. That, at least, was the captain's reasoning, or, rather, his belief. His name was Fluellen . . .'

I paused, realising that Tomás had become suddenly more alert, slightly on guard, as soon as he heard me pronounce that word which I might, perhaps, have kept back for a little longer. 'He's obviously taken the word "infiltrator",' I thought, 'as a reference to him. He may know or sense where I'm going with this, why I mentioned that particular scene and what I'm trying to say, to make him reconsider what he's just said, namely, that the soldier is blameless and the King unjust if he chooses to condemn him; that the consequences of what is said and done, even their gravity, also depend on what fair or unfair means are used to find them out, what good or bad offices are deployed.' He didn't respond, not immediately, but asked again about how the dilemma was resolved:

'Don't make me go and look it up, Berta, Act so-and-so, Scene so-and-so. Just tell me what the King does. Like I say, I don't remember this episode at all, it's as if I've never read the play. I imagine he has him hanged. No, he probably lets him go, because he fought so bravely in the battle. The King can't be seen to be meting out harsh punishments to those who fought for him and gave him a victory so unexpected that it will go down in the annals of history.'

I determined to make him wait a little longer, so that he would once again lower his guard. I went over and took Elisa from him: 'Give her to me, she'll be better off in her cot,' and carried her to her room, where I also made sure that Guillermo hadn't woken up, and that Elisa hadn't been disturbed by the move from her father's arms to bed; then I returned to the living room, sat down, took a sip of my drink and put him out of his misery:

'Yes, you're right, Henry ignores Captain Fluellen. He orders the Duke of Exeter, his uncle, to fill with crowns the glove that Williams has held on to all through one very long night and day. "Keep it, fellow," he says, "and wear it like an honour in your cap till I do challenge it." Which is a bit odd, but that's what he says. Your English is infinitely better than mine, as you've just proved. You can look it up later, if you like.' I was sure that now, with his curiosity aroused, he was bound to consult the play when he was alone.

'And how does the captain react to that? After all, Henry has discredited his opinion before witnesses.'

'Oh, he turns like a weathercock. He acknowledges the soldier's valour and adds another twelve pence from his own pocket, advising him in fatherly fashion to serve God and, in future, avoid quarrels and dissensions, since that way he'll get on much better in life. But Williams rejects the money. "I will none of your money," he says.'

'A proud man, that Williams fellow – honourable.'

'Yes, but Shakespeare, with his usual skill, doesn't allow him to have the final word, that would have been too easy. The captain insists, assuring him that he acted out of goodwill, but yet again manages to offend him: "It will serve you to mend your shoes. Your shoes are not so good." Looking at someone's shoes and then making some rude comment about them, well, it's just not on. There are no stage directions to help us, but one imagines that Williams does finally take the shilling: alms from someone who, only a minute before, had wanted to send him to the gallows. Williams's shoes were presumably in a very sorry state indeed.'

Tomás stroked my chin and gazed into my eyes, for thirty or possibly sixty seconds, without saying a word, but with a smile in his eyes whose meaning escaped me, assuming it had a meaning. Perhaps he was amused by my last remark, I don't know. Or perhaps he knew what was coming next, what I would say. Then he looked away and over at the balcony window and beyond, at the tops of the tall trees in the Plaza de Oriente; we often sat like that, together or separately, by night or by day, I more than he, because I was almost always in Madrid and he wasn't, he went far away, never knowing when he would come back, or if he would come back. He became lost in thought for a moment ('In the disfigured street he left me, with a kind of valediction') and murmured as if to himself:

'Imagine what shoes in 1415 would have been like. And the troops had marched all the way to France as well. A fair old way. I don't know how armies survived over the centuries, given how burdened down they were. For most centuries, really. And people nowadays have the nerve to complain about their lot, for God's sake.'

He certainly didn't complain about his lot, or perhaps he wasn't authorised to do that either, because he might let slip some vital fact or detail. And he doubtless belonged to a kind of army too, 'Military Intelligence' it was called, although he would never have fought in open combat like Williams and Fluellen or other soldiers from six centuries or so before. I wondered what rank he was now, since he was sure to have been promoted over time; he was probably an officer. Since telling me what he was allowed to tell me, several years ago, even his silent complaints or unexpressed anxieties had diminished. (Not that he'd ever put his complaints into words.) You can get used to anything, people say, and however banal the cliché, it's very true. He must have agreed to carry out his missions, and may even have embraced them with something resembling intermittent excitement or enthusiasm. When you choose a path, full of doubts or unwillingly, it's likely that, in the end, that path will seem to you to be the correct one; more than that, you may discover that you can't diverge from that path and don't even want to, and if you were relieved of your duties or asked to retire, that would be like taking away the very air you breathe ('If this is my life, then I must make it, and must believe it to be, fruitful and good, and even irreplaceable'). After all those years, five or six or however long it had been, Tomás must have felt committed to his tasks, perhaps convinced of his cause. If he hadn't felt like that from the start – for he'd never really explained, and I'd never managed to understand it myself, why he'd become involved when he was so young and why he hadn't declined the offer, when he wasn't subject to military discipline or any other kind of discipline – why had he chosen that life of duplicity and secrecy, at best troublesome and at worst mortifying? I certainly found it mortifying. The otherness, the lurking in the shadows, the murk, the mist. The moral ambiguity of it, to put it politely. Betrayal as principle, guide and method.

'You disapprove of Henry acting as infiltrator, passing himself off as someone else and making use of that deceit,' I said. 'Or, rather, you would disapprove of him taking advantage of that trick and punishing his unwary prey. How does that fit with what you do, Tomás? How do you justify it?'

He stood up and strode angrily over to the balcony, as if, after what I'd just said, he found it repugnant to remain sitting so close by my side. He opened the window and stepped outside, lit a cigarette and, before speaking, took two long drags.

'You're making odious, unfair comparisons again, Berta. It's wrong that the King should become an infiltrator among his own men precisely because they are his own men. You shouldn't mistrust those who are risking their lives for you, and you don't lay traps for the faithful. The King knows this, which is why he doesn't punish Williams for those scornful remarks. How could he not know that? I mean, in the same play, he gives his famous speech before the battle, addressing his troops, so few in number as "We few, we happy few, we band of brothers".'

'Yes,' I broke in. 'On St Crispin's Day. And he adds: "For he today that sheds his blood with me shall be my brother." How many people have thought of you as their brother only to find out, that same night, or the following day or a month later, that they've been with a Judas. From their point of view, of course.'

His voice rose in volume, but he didn't sound so much angry now as desperate, the desperation of someone who feels himself to be misunderstood and obliged to explain the obvious:

'What has that got to do with what it is you imagine I do? Because it is just pure imagination on your part, speculation.'

'No, of course I don't know for certain. You've always made it quite clear that you couldn't tell me and I couldn't ask, and we've both followed that instruction to the letter. But left in the dark, what else can I do but make suppositions? Or would you prefer me not even to ask *myself* questions? Not to wonder where you are and what you're doing, what risks you're running and what harm you'll be doing and to whom, when you spend half your life away from me? I don't like it, I don't like what I imagine, not one bit, but if you won't tell me anything, then I have only my imaginings to turn to. I don't choose them, I assure you. The thoughts that come simply come. As do my fears and apprehensions. My feelings of jealousy too, although I do know that, in theory, jealousy shouldn't enter into it and it doesn't, it's what the job requires and so on . . .' I wasn't actually sure how to continue and didn't finish my sentence, but abandoned or postponed it for another occasion, another day. 'My imaginings are what they are, what more can I say. Tell me they should be different, give me something else to fill them with, and then, who knows, I might succeed in changing them, but I can't do that if all I have to look forward to are more years of mysteries and the void.'

'Always supposing that I do work as an infiltrator, as you put it,' he said, with deliberate slowness now, trying to appear patient, almost didactic. 'Always supposing that I do infiltrate groups in the spy-story way you imagine, that wouldn't conflict with my views on the King and Williams, because it would involve infiltrating the enemy camp, not our own side, our brothers. That would be like reprimanding a soldier who, in combat, kills an adversary who's doing his best to kill him.'

'No, it isn't the same thing at all. A spy, an infiltrator, establishes a relationship with that enemy, gains his confidence and pretends to be his friend, and then, if he can, stabs him in the back. That isn't what a soldier does, he meets the enemy face to face and doesn't conceal his intentions. He doesn't coax or seduce or betray. He isn't underhand.'

Tomás gave a defensively sarcastic and very unspontaneous laugh.

'But what is it you're criticising, Berta? Espionage? What is it that you don't like about that? That we try to anticipate the movements of those who want to harm or destroy us? That we uncover and foil their plots and their attacks, their premeditated murders? That we stop them committing murder? That's all part of the defence . . .'

'What defence? The defence of the Realm?' He may have forgotten having used that expression with me before. The Realms that never attack, but only defend themselves.

'Yes, the defence.' He didn't repeat the whole phrase, perhaps because it suddenly sounded too pompous. 'Just as happens in land battles and naval battles and bombardments that no one foresees or expects. Do you really imagine that they involve no deceit, no treachery? There's something called "strategy" and another thing called "tactics", and what's fundamental to both is the surprise factor, the ambush, the diversionary manoeuvre, camouflage, pretence, concealment, the perfidy you find so reprehensible. Why do you think there are submarines, for heaven's sake? They're invisible, right? And there must be some reason for that, don't you think? Even at Thermopylae there was an infiltrator, or a traitor, if you prefer. And how do you

286

think the Trojan War was won? What else was that horse but a stratagem, a poisoned chalice, a deceit? The people who left it on the beach were not to blame, but those who dragged it into the city. The tricked are to blame, not the tricksters, because the latter are just doing their duty. Both sides know this and both sides are to blame. You have to be duplicitous in war, that's how wars are fought.'

For a moment, I felt very naïve. He was quite right, but I still didn't like it, and found what he did or what I imagined he did utterly despicable. More despicable than war.

'I still say it's not the same. The crew of a submarine don't establish a *personal* relationship,' and I emphasised the word 'personal', 'with the crew of the ship they sink, and that hasn't even detected them. They don't speak, they don't see each other's faces, they don't become deeply attached, they don't think they're colleagues or brothers. Perhaps in a proper war everything is more justifiable, I don't know, but then for those who come afterwards, it's not, those who didn't live through it, but benefitted from it and from the fact that victory was achieved using any means necessary . . . And there aren't any land battles now or naval attacks or bombardments, not in the wars England's involved in. You're talking as if the Second World War was still going on. It ended nearly forty years ago. Before, you said that what the disguised King heard his soldiers say, or the rude remarks they made to his face when his face was not his (if you see what I mean), shouldn't count or be punished, however offensive or subversive. Or even treasonous, you said.'

'I stand by what I said,' he replied, and yet it seemed to me that he wished he'd been less categorical. 'Those poor, frightened soldiers, caught off guard, on the eve of a battle, the possible eve of their deaths, aren't remotely like the individuals we spy on, who are spied on nowadays. War may not have been declared, but we still have enemies.

Bitter enemies. And, besides, there's always some kind of war going on, even though people don't see it or know about it and so can carry on with their lives in peace. It's our job to keep war out of sight. You don't realise how much good we do.' He stubbed out his cigarette and lit another one. He no longer smoked his old favourites, Marcovitch, I don't think they're even made any more. He stood looking out from the balcony and added: 'They're complete and utter bastards.'

I was surprised by this trenchant language, which was, again, unlike Tomás. He had suddenly introduced a personal, subjective note. He did, after all, know them. He knew them well, however often he took refuge in various absurd hypotheses, as if he still thought there could be any doubt about his activities.

'They'll think exactly the same about you and your colleagues. The *sociales* would have thought the same about the people they detained and tortured or threw out of windows. In short, you're all bastards.'

'Wrong again. I can promise you that I've never threatened to set fire to a baby in front of its mother. There are always lines you don't cross, there are degrees.'

A shudder ran through me whenever I remembered that sinister couple, the Kindeláns. Fortunately, they hadn't reappeared for years, not since that phone call from Mary Kate, supposedly from Rome. After that long-distance call (assuming it was), I still never picked up the phone without a feeling of trepidation, holding my breath for a second until I heard the caller's voice.

'Did you ever find out who they were? Were they from the IRA?'

'I don't know. Possibly. I've never been told. It's better like that, it's easier for someone to forget you if you forget them and don't seek them out or pester them. I can promise you that they will have completely forgotten about us.'

288

This wasn't the first time he'd spoken so emphatically. On one occasion, he'd told me: 'Nothing like that will ever happen again.' It hadn't occurred to me at the time, but I wondered now if perhaps Miguel and Mary Kate had been killed, had been identified, tracked down and eliminated. Not by Tomás himself, I hoped, of course (although, who knows, during one of those long absences about which he never told me anything, he could easily have nipped over to Rome), but by one of those people he included in that 'we', a fellow averter of tragedies. It was inexplicable really that the Kindeláns or someone similar had never reappeared, given how she had ended that conversation, which, to me, still felt like it had happened only days ago: 'When he does come back, be sure to talk to him,' Mary Kate had ordered in a semi-frivolous, but imperative tone. 'Just because we're far away doesn't mean the matter is resolved. And it has to be resolved satisfactorily.' Satisfactorily for them, needless to say. And she'd then had the nerve to send her love to Guillermo, as an unpleasant memento. And since I didn't believe that Tomás or his superiors had taken fright and stopped whatever it was they were doing in Northern Ireland (if they were doing anything), it occurred to me that Miguel and Mary Kate had dropped out of the game because they were dead, 'sheer murder', just like in the good old days. That's why Tomás was so sure they would 'have completely forgotten about us'.

I was surprised not so much by this idea, which had never once occurred to me in all those years, as by my own reaction to it. I discovered that I didn't care if that couple had been wiped from the face of the Earth, violently and before their time. I actually rather approved, it was a relief. They had gained my trust, they had deceived me and used me and cold-bloodedly placed the life of my defenceless son in danger, the very worst thing you could do to a mother and the one thing guaranteed to make her equally heartless. And the possibility that Tomás himself might have done the deed didn't arouse the feelings of horror or nausea I would have felt had I found out that he'd killed anyone else in cold blood, even if it was one of those anonymous enemy bastards. If it was the Kindeláns, that was acceptable and possibly fair; perhaps even praiseworthy. They had deserved it, they had earned it on that one eternal morning in my house; yes, there really are lines that cannot be crossed, and they had crossed them, and, to add insult to injury, they had done so with a hypocritical smile on their faces. Besides, any action is a step to the block, to the fire, and simply being in the world puts us at risk of stepping towards both, so there can be no complaints. How many steps would Miguel and Mary Kate – or whatever their real names were – have taken in their life of crime? 'Perhaps Tomás is contaminating me with his vision of things, just as others have contaminated him. You only have to listen to be exposed to that contamination,' I thought. However, I didn't want to mention my idea, or not yet. I still had something more to say about *Henry V*:

'Tell me, what should the King have done if the soldiers *had* said something treasonous? If, that night, he'd discovered a plot to murder him before dawn, a plot that would thus put paid to the battle in which they would lose heads and legs and arms. Should he still not have taken measures, handed out punishments, made use of what he'd found out from beneath his cloak? Given his disguise, he should ignore, erase, everything he hears, that's what you said. What, according to you, should he do in the case of a conspiracy? Allow himself to be murdered in his tent, go to sleep and not wake up, await the arrival of the soldiers and their daggers?'

Tomás smiled, this time approvingly, as if he were amused by my ruminations, or as if they made him think. He still liked my company, as he had since the very beginning. We enjoyed being together, despite the mists and smokescreens surrounding us. Despite my restricted view of his life, despite everything. It was as if I could see his life with only one eye, and the other eye was blind. I found it hard to bear sometimes, but I did bear it. And, yes, I still loved him, imperfectly and confusedly, as one does. No, like those who love best. I preferred to have a part of him rather than to say goodbye, to lose sight of him for ever and for him to become a mere memory.

'No, that would radically change the situation. In that case, Williams and the others would no longer be his men, they would have ceased to be friends and become enemies. And if, that night, the King already suspected a plot to kill him, which would mean that the battle would end in surrender, he would have every right to disguise himself and spy on his soldiers and officers and nobles, from the highest to the lowest. They would then be utter bastards and unworthy of respect. And that weathercock captain would be quite right to appeal to martial law and demand their heads. Executing them wouldn't be an abuse, it would be advisable and appropriate, so that they couldn't do any further harm to the Realm.'

I was reminded again of Franco's *sociales*. Everything is justifiable depending on one's point of view, and since everyone has his or her own point of view, being right is very easy. I let it pass, though, because now was the perfect moment to mention my idea:

'Is that what you did with the Kindeláns? Execute them, I mean. Is that why you're so sure they will have completely forgotten about us?' And I added lightly, so as to let him know that I didn't entirely condemn him (if the couple were dead meat, my children would be safer, and that was the most important thing, especially when they were still so young). 'They won't just have forgotten about us, they'll have forgotten everything, if, that is, you and yours bumped them off. Even their own faces. Even their names.'

291

My question caught him off guard (a lot of time had passed, and I'd never asked him before), or else he tried to make it look as if it had. Inevitably, he answered without entirely answering:

'What an idea, Berta. Of course not, we don't do that kind of thing, how absurd. Who do you take us for? For the KGB, the Stasi, Mossad, or DINA? For James Bond or the CIA?' An idea flashed through my mind: If all those other secret service organisations executed their enemies without trial, why wouldn't his lot do the same with theirs? 'Or worse still, the Mafia? I've told you before that, fortunately, I know nothing about them.' He broke off, stroked his now vanished, invisible scar, as if he were alone in his memory. Then he said: 'Anyway, why are you asking me questions when you're not supposed to, and when I'm not supposed to answer them?'

Tomás soon had an opportunity to prove the accuracy of what he'd told me that night, for, barely a month later, the Argentinian dictatorship took the ridiculous, and supposedly patriotic, decision to invade the Malvinas, or the Falklands – the name depended on which side you belonged to and which language you spoke – a British possession since 1833. As was only natural, and regardless of whether they were in the right or not, Great Britain certainly wasn't going to sit by and do nothing in the face of such an appropriation by force, a fait accompli, certainly not Margaret Thatcher the Ruthless, who was prime minister at the time, and even though the above-mentioned islands were in the middle of nowhere, or as we say in Spanish, *donde Cristo perdió el mechero*, where Christ lost his cigarette lighter: to the east of the Magellan Strait and to the north-east of Tierra del Fuego; that is, not very far from the Antarctic.

The fact that the invading country was also a dictatorship provided, at least formally, further justification for Britain's predictably bellicose reaction, despite the neighbouring dictator, Pinochet, in Chile, being on excellent terms with the lady, both at the time and until the end of their respective lives – I can't quite remember which of them died first – but then most politicians blithely ignore such contradictory sentiments. We watched the approach of that absurd war, which had seemed completely unimaginable right up until the day before the Argentinian invasion of the Falklands and occupation of the capital, Stanley, a war between two countries that were extremely remote from each other geographically, although rather less so ideologically; after all, the Argentinian military had been in power for six years, committing all kinds of atrocities, without the so-called free world reacting or expressing their hostility. Still, an act of aggression is an act of aggression, indeed, an act of war, and could not go unanswered if, as was the case, any diplomatic threats swiftly ran their course.

'Look at this,' Tomás said, brandishing the front page of a particularly belligerent English newspaper. 'Weren't you saying just the other day that we no longer see naval battles or land battles or bombardments? Well, I'm afraid you're going to see them very soon, especially naval battles, because there's nothing but ocean between us and the Falklands, which are three hundred miles from land. The main attacking force will have to be ships: frigates, destroyers, submarines, aircraft carriers, cruisers, troop ships and landing craft. With England involved, you'll have no option but to see naval battles being fought on the open sea. As I said, there's always a war going on somewhere, even if it only occasionally becomes visible. This war will be visible to the whole world, so everyone will know about it, although only for a short time, because it won't last long, I can assure you. Those military braggarts in Argentina have dug their own grave with this desperate action.' 'The sea's throat': the line came into my head unbidden, but with good reason this time.

He sounded almost pleased, boastful. He wasn't just pleased to be able to make the point that he had been absolutely right, he also seemed glad that there was about to be an imminent armed conflict that would incur deaths on both sides; perhaps not in enormous numbers if the matter was resolved quickly, but that would make it no less regrettable. Nor was there anything odd about that burst of enthusiasm, for it was there in the air, fanned by both Thatcher and Galtieri – the Argentinian general and usurper of the presidency – and, however remotely, Tomás served Thatcher, for she gave all the orders, apart from any it would be best for her not to know about; people in power, armour-plated as they are, let others interpret what they might want and avoid actually having to give an order themselves. Incomprehensibly, despite centuries of experience, especially on the English side, both the Argentinian population and the British were now all aflame and demanding that the other side be taught a lesson, because among the things people like best – unscrupulous people, and there are always millions who would never regard themselves as such – is the prospect of a nice big war, only the prospect, mind, before it has begun.

Then another idea occurred to me: if there was going to be a war against a Spanish-speaking country, then it would be only a matter of days before Tomás was summoned to London to act as interceptor, translator and perhaps interrogator. I didn't think he would be called on to infiltrate anywhere, for it seemed unlikely that any espionage would be necessary, given that the cards had been placed firmly on the table ever since the invasion; there wouldn't be much to find out or, I imagined, to anticipate, and the British military forces were vastly superior to the Argentinian forces, so much so that there was general astonishment at the latter's reckless, suicidal irresponsibility. In any case, I was sure that, if necessary, Tomás would be capable of doing an impeccable imitation of an Argentinian; if he could imitate those different ways of speaking in English, changing and transforming his voice in that alarming way, he would find it easy enough to pass himself off as an Argentinian, since the Buenos Aires accent, at least to Spanish ears, does always tend to sound like a caricature of itself, and someone with his abilities could carry it off without arousing any suspicions. And I, of course, in my state of absolute blindness, could never rule out anything; as I said, I had long since realised that I was condemned to being a slave to my conjectures and speculations. In my imagination, they could as easily post him to Buenos Aires as to Río Gallegos or even Tierra del Fuego.

When I say that Tomás still had time to enjoy what he saw as his triumph over me, that's because everything happened exactly as I had foreseen. On 3 April 1982, when the UN Security Council demanded the immediate cessation of hostilities and the withdrawal of all the Argentinian troops from the Falklands (that was what Tomás called them and so I followed suit), and urged the two governments to seek a diplomatic solution to the dispute, Tomás told me that he had to leave for England the next day. And only one day later, on 5 April, the British Task Force left Portsmouth, cheered and waved off by a pugnacious and surprisingly bloodthirsty crowd, clamouring for a fight to restore their cheapened honour, a bit of a comedown in comparison with past epic deeds and struggles. After all, in the last long century and a half, this was a nation that had stood up against Napoleon, the Tsar, the Kaiser and Hitler, among others – far too many others.

On 4 April, I went with him to the airport to say goodbye, something I rarely did. I had grown accustomed now to his departures, and although I could never be sure when he would be back, I tried to treat them as if they were the routine business trips of some restless or perhaps neurotic executive, of the kind who is always unexpectedly prolonging his travels around the world, as if he only really felt comfortable in a constant state of absence and movement. On this occasion, though, there was a real war in the offing, a visible war, as he would put it, and although I didn't initially fear that he might be sent to the front, on board some ship, acting as linguistic support or whatever, the fact is, he was of an age to be called up and, to me, anything was possible. Unlike those other occasions swathed in mist and mystery, I could now easily visualise the kind of danger he could be exposed to, for we've all seen films of horrendous naval battles, with ships in flames or sinking, crews dying in the water or else horribly dismembered. I accompanied him quite calmly and normally, barely speaking and, needless to say, not asking him what his mission involved, but then he might not even have known – yet. He seemed excited, in the good sense of the word (for the person feeling the excitement, you understand), not so much about what he might have to do personally, as about the warlike atmosphere, as if he had been infected by the awful swaggering bravado gripping England. I must confess I found that atmosphere both disturbing and repellent, and had felt exactly the same about the mass demonstration held on 2 April in Plaza de Mayo in Buenos Aires, in support of aggressively retaking the Malvinas, with Argentinians cheering on the very generals who had spent years committing crimes and were now prepared to sacrifice their young soldiers for no reason and with no likelihood of victory: in short, for a very bad cause indeed. Mrs Thatcher's cause was no better, unlike Henry V's at Agincourt, at least according to history and to Shakespeare, but then she had not shot the first arrow and, while that counts for something initially, it's soon forgotten if the response is disproportionate, involving shellings and sending in the Gurkhas, who were ferocious when it came to hand-to-hand combat with their horrible curved kukri knives.

'I assume you've no idea when you'll be back,' was almost all I said in the taxi to Barajas airport. 'Even less than at other times, I imagine. No one can ever know how long a war will last, can they, even the ones that seem easy to win.'

'Who said I was going to war?' he said slightly coquettishly, as if he enjoyed making me feel even more anxious than usual. 'I certainly didn't. It may be that, this time, I won't even move from London.' He didn't say whether he actually knew this or not. He avoided giving any facts.

'No, you didn't say anything about that, but you don't exactly have to be Sherlock Holmes to deduce that, if they summon you urgently when a fleet is being prepared to take back those islands from a Spanish-speaking country, it's probably going to be something to do with that. I'm not saying they'll put you straight on a destroyer heading for the Falklands (at least I hope not), but you're sure to be useful in such a conflict, don't you think?'

'I'm always useful, Berta,' he said with a rather arrogant smile; sometimes, he just couldn't resist. 'How he's changed,' I thought, 'how different from the man he was some years ago, now that he leads this absurd, clandestine life, which he can probably only boast about to me, and then only a little. The poor man must feel so frustrated sometimes, when a little domestic, conjugal showing off is all he can hope for. But how can he be so convinced, how has he turned into this staunch English patriot with no views of his own, or if he does have views, he keeps them to himself and firmly under lock and key, because showing that he disagreed with the Crown would be to cast doubt on his activities and his trajectory, his straight path, his very existence. The only thing that hasn't changed is his lack of interest in knowing or questioning himself, his utter lack of introspection: he does what he has to do, or perhaps what he decides to do, and that's that, he's always thought navel-gazing was a complete waste of time. He'll know by now what kind of man he is and what he's capable of, and he accepts that and is happy with who he is, perhaps even proud sometimes, or perhaps not proud, but pleased that he's proved useful. I doubt if he goes any further than that; what matters to him is being able to serve and use his talents. Of course I miss the person he was before, that goes without saying, but I still love him and the last thing I would want is to lose him, even if now I only have fragments of him. After all, the person he is now – the one who is and isn't, the one who comes and goes – still contains the person he was, and it couldn't be otherwise. He's still in there, half-asleep, like the victim of some very long enchantment. Let's hope he comes back soon. Let's hope nothing happens to him on those islands. Let's hope that stupid war doesn't last very long.' Then he added: 'Make no mistake, there are other conflicts going on as well, and, unfortunately, none of that stops just because some more striking event, some act of aggression, apparently obscures everything else. Our enemies never grow tired, never. While you're sleeping, they're still busy. And when they're asleep, they're dreaming about what other fruitful machinations they can bring into play later on. In fact, they make the most of another front opening up, so that, while we're distracted and our energies dispersed, they can ramp up their hostilities and deal us still lower blows. Or do you think that the Irish problem, for example, went quiet and offered us a respite during the Second World War? Not at all. Ireland declared itself neutral. Neutral. The cheek of it. And in 1944, in 1944 (when we'd already been at war, under attack, for five years, mind), Ireland refused to expel Axis diplomats stationed there, despite requests not only from us, but from the United States too.' It was incredible: that 'we' extended back into the past, to a time before he'd even been born; I imagined it stretching back, at the very least, as far as the Battle of Agincourt in 1415. 'Quite a few Irish people actually collaborated with the Germans as spies and saboteurs, because the Germans, of course, wanted to destroy us, and to the Irish this seemed a marvellous opportunity. What they didn't appear to have given much thought to was what would become of Ireland if the Nazis won. In comparison, our jackboot, our subjugation, as they thought of it, would have seemed a mild and benevolent dominion. So, you see, everything carries on even when it seems to have stopped. The Iron Curtain countries and international terrorists and Ulster, and other enemies that the press don't know much about, they all carry on regardless. There's a lot happening in the world, so don't assume you know where I'll be going just because of current circumstances. As I said, I may not even leave the Foreign Office.'

'All right, I won't make any assumptions. Let's just hope you're right.'

The mere mention of Ulster made me feel even worse, I would almost have preferred it if they assigned him to HMS *Conqueror*, a nuclear submarine which, according to what I'd read, was possibly going to be sent to the Falklands. I had learned to fear the Irish conflict ever since that business with those wretches, the Kindeláns, whose memory I could never quite shake off. I had got into the habit of following the news from Northern Ireland, not obsessively, but if any reports appeared in a Spanish newspaper, I would make a point of reading them. Absurdly, I was far less concerned about Eastern Europe or about terrorists, and yet, who knows, Tomás might well have been actively engaged in the pursuit of that hyperactive terrorist 'Carlos', who was, apparently, a Spanish speaker, possibly from Venezuela. I fell silent, then took his hand, which he squeezed hard for a moment before releasing it so as to take out a cigarette and light it. My impression was, however, that he let go of my hand so quickly because he was excited more than anything, as if that contact distracted him from his thoughts. He was clearly absorbed in his own affairs, and it occurred to me that he knew exactly what his role was to be, what awaited him the following day or that very night, what he would have to do and where he would go; and, in his mind, he was already there, focused on what his next steps would be. Perhaps 'excitement' isn't the word, but something close to that. He shared the British impatience to begin operations, for the British fleet to reach that far-flung corner of the globe and teach those insolent, dictatorial Argentinians a lesson; what were they thinking, that they could get away scot-free with defying the old Empire? Yes, England had suddenly, childishly, recovered its past and thought it was back in those distant centuries, a ghost of its lost Empire.

'Bye, then, take care. As usual, stay in touch while you can, or when you get back, if they send you somewhere far away. I hope it won't be for too long.' Those were my last words before he set off. I ran my finger over his lips, I stroked his smooth chin, we embraced as we usually did – that is, with the immense affection we had always felt for each other – despite my discontent.

'Of course I will,' he said. 'As usual, if I don't get in touch that will be because I can't, you know that. Don't get impatient if it takes a while, however long that might be. Anyway, this war won't last, you'll see. It may not even affect me, it may pass me by.'

I followed that war of two and a half months on a daily basis, in detail, from 5 April, when the Task Force set off from Portsmouth, to 14 June, when the appointed governor of the Malvinas, General Menéndez, surrendered to Major General Moore, the commander of the British forces, an act that was greeted with protests and riots by one segment of the Buenos Aires population.

I used to buy two or three English newspapers and devour them all. I sometimes thought this a pointless task, since the conflict might well have passed Tomás by, as he had suggested, but, needless to say, with so much misleading information, secrecy and silence, I couldn't be sure. My instinct told me that his sudden departure on 4 April was, in some way, related to the invasion, because he didn't once phone me from the Foreign Office or from MI6 or wherever, as he surely would have done if he'd been waiting there to be told where he was to go next, even if he'd only been there for a few days. I assumed that they would have transferred him somewhere else as soon as he landed in London, and those far-flung islands were the newest and most urgent matter at hand, and were, presumably, the main preoccupation of Thatcher the Intransigent and her Cabinet, as well as the Army, the RAF, the Navy, the diplomatic service and the Secret Service. But it was also true that other things don't just stop – there's no reason why our enemies should slacken their efforts (they're more likely to increase them) when their adversary is faced by an emergency, and I imagine that one shouldn't neglect any front, however secondary or minor it might appear to be. Basically, I was, as usual, completely in the dark. I decided to follow the war step by step, as the whole world was doing; it was a strange enough situation to keep everyone watching and to attract all eyes, beginning with those of Reagan and that globetrotting Pope Wojtyla.

On 2 May, I experienced a mixture of great sorrow and great relief. The nuclear submarine *Conqueror* torpedoed and sank the Argentine cruiser *General Belgrano*, causing the deaths of more than three hundred crew members. I found this enormous number of casualties deeply distressing, but then I thought how much worse it would have been had the casualties been British, for I couldn't rule out the possibility that Tomás might be on board some kind of ship.

On 4 May, I felt no relief at all: Argentinian Navy planes, equipped with Exocet missiles, sank the destroyer *Sheffield*, and, this time, twenty English marines perished. Who knows, perhaps on board with them was a mediator, an interpreter, a spy posted to the area.

On 10 May, relief definitely outstripped sorrow when the frigate *Alacrity* sank the *Isla de los Estados*, causing the deaths of the captain and twenty-one sailors. More than that, I was beginning to hope that England would soon crush that sinister Argentina currently in the hands of the military, however many poor soldiers lost their lives, so that more lives were not lost and peace was restored. I paid more attention to the setbacks than to the advances, to any situations unfavourable to 'our men' rather than to any triumphs, because it was the former that alarmed me most.

I had some terrible frights on 20, 24 and 25 May, because, on the first of those days, the British saw their frigate *Ardent* sunk and three Harriers and two helicopters shot down, at which point, it occurred to me that they might be ferrying Tomás back and forth by helicopter; on the second day, the frigate *Antelope* went down somewhere or other, and, on the third day, Argentine planes sank the destroyer *Coventry* and the heavy merchant navy ship *Atlantic Conveyor*. The number of dead remained unclear, or perhaps Thatcher, who, as I read recently, disliked hearing 'sad stories'– and didn't like telling them either, I imagine – preferred to leave things vague for the moment.

The British were winning the war and would win it in the end, it was only a matter of time, but victory came at a high price. I became a fan of the Navy, from a distance, from what I saw on the television and read in the papers, but alongside this were my paradoxically growing feelings of antipathy for Thatcher and for that England, so gleefully combative and bullying, changed out of all recognition, all restraint gone. Every demonstration or celebration in the streets of Britain made me cringe on their behalf, and almost my own, perhaps because I'm a European (Americans tend to be more theatrical and excitable, and over-the-top behaviour is less surprising in them). This didn't mean that, on 8 June, I didn't curse the destruction of the troop ship *Sir Galahad*, or that, on 12 June, my heart wasn't in my boots when I found out that a land-based Exocet missile had put the *Glamorgan* out of action, killing thirteen of its crew.

All these losses would, ultimately, be seen as occupational hazards, forgotten by everyone except the families of the dead, and although they were minor problems in the conflict as a whole, for as long as that conflict continued, I found any delay in its conclusion deeply disheartening, and anything that wasn't a complete walkover made me despair. Pope John Paul II appeared in Buenos Aires on 11 June, to pray for peace before a crowd of the fervent faithful who had been belligerent and vengeful the day before and would be equally so after. On 28 May, he turned up in London, where people took rather less notice of him (although, in Argentina, any notice they'd taken was purely superficial). That day-to-day monitoring of the situation proved exhausting: two and a half months spent in a continuous state of alertness and alarm can seem interminable. The only relief came when I clung to Tomás's deliberately ambiguous words, and I would think – poor consolation – that he was probably elsewhere, in one of the Baltic countries, or somewhere in the Arab world, in East Germany or the dreaded Northern Ireland. I drove that last possibility from my mind as quickly as I could, though, and not just for the usual reasons. Some time ago, I'm not sure when (perhaps it was after 1982, although I would place it earlier), one of the most horrific pictures I've ever seen appeared on the front page of various newspapers. So horrific that I only glanced at it, then quickly turned the paper over, and later, threw it out unread; and yet, even though I only glimpsed that blurred image, the memory of it still haunted me, and often came back to me and still does. In Belfast or Derry or some village, I'm not sure, a mob had attacked an English soldier and flayed him, not while he was alive, I hope. I tried not to know too much about the circumstances, preferring not to read about it (or only the caption, I suppose), not to know the details. I have a vague idea that the soldier's dead body was face down, with legs and arms splayed, like St Andrew on an X-shaped cross, presumably naked or almost so and propped against something, a wall, a pile of tyres, perhaps some beer barrels, I don't know, and I certainly don't want to search for the photo on the Internet, where everything comes back and nothing is erased. And there were people around him, he wasn't alone, his body hadn't been abandoned. Normal-looking people, such as you might find in Madrid or any other European city or in one of our villages, people who had gathered to look at him and

305

had not perhaps taken part in the atrocity, or perhaps they had, had carried it out and were now contemplating their work with no feelings of regret – perhaps that came later, or perhaps never – perhaps with the astonishment that follows certain actions, once they're over and done and cannot be undone. They were looking, looking at that body, which was darker than usual in a white man – a flayed body would, I suppose, be reddish in colour, no, best not think about it, besides, the image was in black and white – almost as you might contemplate an Ecce Homo painting in a museum, except that Christ is depicted as he would have been two thousand years ago and in a remote part of the world, and, besides, he's permanently there, painted and two-dimensional, never real and recent like that young soldier.

We have all felt real or abstract hatred at some time in our lives; we feel it, but almost never see it, or only rarely; and any representation of its results is difficult to take in, to admit, to accept, it's unbearable, even though in Europe we are, inevitably, accustomed to it, the inevitability of too many centuries past. It wasn't unknown for British soldiers to occasionally behave like brutes, but that young man might have done nothing more than don a hated uniform, he might have only just arrived. Whatever the truth of the matter, what is most shocking (I'm speaking for myself, of course) is the furious, uncontrolled mob and discovering what it's capable of. Years later, I saw another sequence (they showed it partially on television), which brought to mind that photo from Northern Ireland, although the scene from my own country was less grave and gruesome: some Basque nationalists were gleefully kicking a policeman in the head, while he lay, defenceless, on the ground, in the middle of the street, watched by a group of impassive spectators; no, not impassive, for they were actually egging the attackers on. He wasn't even a policeman from outside the Basque country, but a local man, as Basque as his aggressors. The man didn't die, fortunately, but I think he was in hospital for a long time, possibly having suffered irreparable harm. He will doubtless never forget that day, unlike the proud 'patriots', imitators of the Irish, but without the iota of reason the latter had. Something or someone interrupted them, otherwise they would simply have murdered the policeman, several of them gaily kicking him to death.

I drove that thought from my mind: it would be better if Tomás was in the South Atlantic, in a frigate, in a helicopter, in a hideout in Buenos Aires, rather than in Northern Ireland. Who knows what they would do to him if he was there and they found him out, an English infiltrator, a traitor, a spy. On him would fall all that real and abstract hatred, and the worst hatred of all, that of the deceived.

Yes, the War of the Malvinas, or the Falklands War, ended officially on 20 June with the return of the islands, and then everyone rapidly forgot about it. What has just occurred but is no longer occurring is of no interest, people's attention is immediately drawn to what comes afterwards, to anything that is about to happen or might happen, anything that is still an unknown or has not yet reached a conclusion; basically, it comes down to a desire to live vicariously in a state of perpetual instability and under constant threat, or at least to know that, somewhere on the globe, there are others having a far worse time of it than we are, and who remind us just how much danger is out there watching and waiting. That's how it was then, and as it continues to be now, only raised to the nth degree; we have become accustomed to the idea that some catastrophe is always looming, and that it's sure to affect us directly or indirectly, the days are long gone (and they lasted for centuries and centuries, for almost all of history and even for part of my own life, so I myself have seen this change) when we really didn't care about the problems of Afghanistan or Iraq or Ukraine, of Syria, Libya or Ethiopia or Somalia, or even of Mexico or the Philippines, which, after all, did once belong to us, to the Spanish, I mean.

Even the English newspapers gradually began to lose interest, after having milked to the full what they described as an heroic feat and praised, in toadying fashion, the national pride of those who had stayed safe at home, watching the BBC, without getting so much as a whiff of gunpowder or scorched or fragmented flesh, nor putting themselves at risk for a second. I, on the other hand, couldn't lose interest. Day by day, I followed the slow repatriation of troops, their staggered returns that were met with increasingly lukewarm enthusiasm, the steps taken for the future defence of the Falklands, so that the same thing didn't happen again, as well as the disgrace of the Argentinian military and the immediate resignation of Galtieri; the war did have benefits for the defeated country, namely the beginning of the end of the dictatorship. I even followed Galtieri's subsequent trial in 1985 or 1986, when he was accused, among other things, of mishandling the war. Found guilty of having led so many men to their deaths and his country to disaster, he was sentenced to several years in prison. He was never forgiven for a war that many of his compatriots had cheered on and encouraged; in defeat, we always look for a scapegoat – and here was one ready-made for the role, who deserved to be the scapegoat – and no one else takes responsibility, and the people always emerge as entirely innocent. Politicians never dare to criticise the people, who are often base and cowardly and stupid, they never tell them off or condemn their behaviour, they invariably praise them to the skies, when there is usually very little reason to praise any people anywhere. They have become untouchable and have taken the place of once despotic, absolutist monarchs. Like them, they have the prerogative to be as fickle as they please and to go eternally unpunished, and they don't have to answer for how they vote or who they elect or who they support, or what they remain silent about or consent to or impose or acclaim. Were they to blame for Francoism in Spain, for Fascism in Italy or Nazism in Germany and Austria, in Hungary and Croatia? Were they to blame for

Stalinism in Russia or Maoism in China? No, never: they are always the victims and never called to account (well, they can hardly call themselves to account; indeed, they always feel sorry for and take pity on themselves). The people really are the true successors of those arbitrary, capricious kings, a hydra-headed variety, but essentially headless. Each of them looks smugly in the mirror and says with a shrug: 'Oh, I had no idea. They manipulated me, forced me, deceived me and misled me. How was I to know, me, a poor woman of good faith, me, a poor innocent man.' Their crimes are so scattered that they fade and grow blurred, and the anonymous authors of those crimes are then poised to commit their next crimes – after a few years have passed and once everyone has forgotten about the earlier ones.

August came, and I left for San Sebastián with my family, and with my children, of course, for where I went, they went too. My parents tactfully took me in whenever they noticed I had been too alone for too long. They were used to Tomás's absences and barely asked me about them. At the time, moreover, there was an easy explanation for his delayed return: after a war that no one had foreseen, the Foreign Office needed to reorganise itself, there was much delicate work still to be done; heads would roll, and Tomás might find himself obliged to take the place of one of those fallen heads; I added this off my own bat, thus suggesting that he was doing well, and that his long absences were justified by our present comfortable standard of living and by an even better future.

With them, with friends and acquaintances, with my university colleagues, I pretended to have more contact with Tomás than I actually did during his periods abroad. When he was away from London (or when I assumed he was), I usually had no contact at all, not at least since, years before, he'd told me his fragment of truth, the authorised fragment. That fragment – the essence of what he did, and which was, by definition, small – had been enough to make me an accomplice to his secret and to his double life, and now I, too, would lie in order not to arouse suspicions or betray him involuntarily, so that no one in Madrid found his absences odd or saw our anomalous situation as too anomalous. I wasn't even sure the British embassy knew what he really did, with the possible exception of the ambassador, as the man in charge, or maybe he didn't know either: if London asked him to send them one of his staff, he would simply obey orders and wouldn't object or ask questions.

And so it was this time – again: on my return, in September, I still hadn't received a phone call, a letter or a postcard or a telegram, nor any indirect news from Mr Reresby or from any other of Tom's bosses or colleagues. 'He really must be somewhere else,' I thought, 'and to think I wasted all that time worrying about the Falklands, two and a half months spent watching that conflict and its consequences. He did warn me the war might pass him by. So where the hell is he, then, where can they have sent him? The world is a big place and there could be war fronts everywhere, in countries I've never even heard of.' This is what I told myself, but I couldn't be sure, and the fact that there had been a visible war with visible casualties changed everything; I needed to make sure nothing had happened to him, that he wasn't among the shameful losses, those that aren't reported officially or made public, that don't appear in the files and are never garlanded with honours because of the base, clandestine nature of their missions, whose existence would have to be denied until the end of time by all who had participated in them, known about them or ordered them (I thought Margaret Thatcher would be perfectly capable of denying any glaring fact, or omitting or ignoring any 'sad story'), as in the time of the PWE, which probably still continued under a different acronym, and nothing has really changed since; those casualties whose names will never appear on the endless lists on those war memorials so popular in England – or at most with some mysterious initials – because of the treacherous deaths they caused and the contemptible nature of their work.

I was tempted to call the old number at the Foreign Office or whatever it was, to ask Reresby (if he was still there and hadn't been transferred or defenestrated), or whoever happened to answer the phone, if I could speak to Reggie Gathorne, who undoubtedly did exist, unlike Dundas, Ure and Montgomery. Yet Tomás had told me not to get impatient however much time passed, those had been his final words at the airport. I should do as I was told, I would have to put up with it as I had so often before, even though this time was different, and the waiting was harder and my unease unbearable when night came and I got into bed alone and reached out for his absent body, for the empty space that seemed still emptier because I feared that, this time, it might be permanent. To resist the temptation, I would remember and repeat to myself every time I went to pick up the phone, which happened every day (I would say it out loud to make it more real): 'As usual, if I don't get in touch that will be because I can't, you know that.' And I had agreed: 'As usual, stay in touch while you can, or when you get back, if they send you somewhere far away.' I had to respect that agreement.

But on this occasion, things weren't as usual. September, October and November passed in silence. December seemed to me a propitious month for him to come home, and, filled with superstitious hope, I counted down the days: at Christmas, I thought, everyone takes a break, even moles and terrorists don't have much to do, any actions are postponed, there's a kind of atmospheric truce, and everyone has to spend those days somewhere; the executioners and their victims also have families who require their presence, or, rather, the former don't want to arouse suspicions or attract too much attention, while the latter carry on with their normal lives, almost never imagining that they're going to be victims. Of course, there are always some complete loners, people no one is expecting, who aren't invited anywhere and who never receive guests, for whom those days are just like any other, individuals who hide away in some small isolated country hotel, pretending that they've been to visit family and then returned. I hoped that Tomás hadn't become one of them and wasn't doing something similar, wherever he was, in Ireland, in Scotland, in Israel, in Palestine, in Syria, in Russia or in Czechoslovakia, perhaps even in Argentina, which, for security reasons, he hadn't yet dared to leave. These were, of course, conjectures – or, rather, fantasies.

I thought he might at least have phoned to say hello, to reassure me, to ask how the children were and if Guillermo still remembered him.

Elisa was too young to have any memory of him. However, as the month went on, and he still gave no sign of life, I grew desperate. If he didn't resurface then, when would he? Would the whole winter and spring pass with no news of him, then summer and autumn too, after all, why not? I no longer limited myself to staring at the phone, itching to call the Foreign Office number, instead, I dialled it on numerous occasions. And yet, after the first two or three rings – even after hearing the word 'Hello' several times – I would hang up without saying a word or asking to speak to anyone, overwhelmed by fear and regret at having made the call. The same old litany would echo around inside my head, or was it perhaps a spell intended to banish my worst fears: 'If I don't get in touch that will be because I can't. Don't get impatient if it takes a while, however long that might be.' How much more time had to pass? Sometimes the spell had an adverse effect: perhaps he couldn't send any news because he was no longer among the living, perhaps that was what he'd meant to say as well.

Walter Starkie, who knew everything, had died several years before, but Jack Nevinson, Tomás's father, my father-in-law, was still alive, although he'd now retired both from the embassy and from the British Council; he was about seventy by then, and Tomás was his youngest child. Eager to fend off inactivity, he'd leapt at the chance to teach English phonetics in my department at the university while the usual lecturer was on temporary leave or on sabbatical – I'm not sure which – another Spanish Englishman, the excellent Jack Cressey White, who had been my teacher too. And so, that year, I met up with my father-in-law more often in the university corridors than I did in my apartment or his, where I often left the children, never staying very long myself, precisely so that I wouldn't have to talk about Tomás, who was always our main point of interest. Now, though, I did want to talk to him about Tomás, before I gave in to temptation, before I butted in again and pestered that man Reresby, who would probably not even remember me. One day, I asked Jack if we could talk, without the children there and without his wife, Mercedes, Tomás's *madrileña* mother. He led me into Mr White's office, which was at his disposal while he was standing in for him, and he offered me a chair as if I were a mere colleague or a student and not his daughter-in-law; that is, he did so discreetly or shyly. He had slightly prominent blue eyes, very rosy skin, receding white hair and a very dimpled face – with a particularly deep dimple on his chin – a face that inspired confidence, that spoke of a natural innocence and kindness undiminished by age. He seemed incapable of deceiving anyone, even of lying. He had studied at Oxford (Pembroke College), and there, despite the difference in age with the first two, he'd been on friendly terms with Tolkien and C. S. Lewis and with Isaiah Berlin, but he didn't tend to tell stories about them or to boast.

'How can I help, Berta, my dear?' he said in Spanish, a language he'd never entirely mastered, despite his many years in Madrid, and which he spoke with a strong English accent that he never managed to shake off.

'Jack, will you be totally honest with me? What do you know about Tomás?' I asked.

He seemed genuinely surprised and replied in English, using my continued improvement in that language as an excuse to take a rest from the one that so stubbornly resisted his efforts.

'What do you mean, what do I know? I know what you tell us, Berta. In London he must be so busy, I imagine, that he only has time to phone you. He never calls us when he's away. And we understand completely, we don't take it amiss. You're his wife, and parents have to take second place. As far as I know, he doesn't get in touch with his sisters or with his brother either. He did warn us, a long time ago,

315

that when he was in England he would communicate entirely through you.'

'So he never talks to you? He never confides or asks advice?'

'Advice?' He laughed. 'No, I think he's always rather looked down on me as being a rather useless father as fathers go. He's a very different man from me. More confident and more determined. He hasn't consulted me about any doubts, if he has any, not since he was a boy, although he might tell me about them once he's resolved them.'

'So what has he told you, Jack? I haven't heard a word from him, nothing, not since the last time he set off, at the beginning of the Falklands War. Everything I've told you during that time, about vague bits of news or brief phone calls, has all been a lie, pure invention. I didn't want to worry you, and I didn't want it to look as if he'd abandoned us, the kids and me. He left on 4 April, eight months ago. He's never before gone for so long without contacting me. Two or three months, yes, perhaps a bit longer, I don't know, it's best not to count the days too exactly, and I'm used to that, I've learned not to worry overmuch and to wait. But, of course, this time, he left when a war was just beginning, and no one has told me anything since the war ended, no one from the Foreign Office or the embassy or anywhere has been in touch. If something grave had happened, they would have told me, wouldn't they? They'd have told you as well. Or perhaps not. Do you know anything more than that? Do you know what he actually does?'

Jack Nevinson opened his eyes very wide; he was one of those innocent men who opens his eyes wide in order to look more intensely. I understood what that intensity meant: he was trying to work out how much I knew. He obviously didn't want to lie to me, nor did he want to compromise his son, or go against his instructions.

'Oh, that,' he said.

'Yes, Jack, that. I think we both know something. Tell me, please, what do you know?'

My father-in-law sat perfectly still, momentarily lost for words. He was looking for a way of saying something without really saying anything. He asked if I'd like a cup of tea, but I shook my head; he stammered out a few unintelligible words, then, finally, managed to say:

'I probably know no more than you, Berta. He's probably told you a lot more. But I'm not as innocent as I may seem, and I've seen the look on my son's face when he returns from those absences or journeys, and it's not the look of someone who's just been on some diplomatic mission, however arduous and complicated it might be. It's the look I've seen on other men's faces; during the war, the Second World War, I saw it quite often. It's a look that's simultaneously a look of pride and horror, the two things mingled to form one indistinguishable whole. Horror at what they've seen, and pride at having been able to cope with it, for not having completely lost their minds or run away. A combination of horror and pride at the barbarous things they've done or were capable of doing. It's the look someone wears when he comes back from the front, but also from other covert activities. And since there's been no open warfare since then, I think I know what he's been involved with all these years.'

'But has he ever actually told you?'

'That's a very big question, Berta, but it really doesn't seem likely to me that he's been in the Falklands; sending him there would have been a waste of his talents.'

'He has told me, Jack,' I said cautiously, hesitantly. 'And I don't think I'm speaking out of turn by telling you that.' He didn't even blink, and I assumed that he knew everything, even if he wouldn't admit it. 'I know he works for the Secret Service, MI5 or MI6, or whatever. But I've never known exactly where he goes or what he

317

does or has done, or what risks he runs. He doesn't tell me, and I don't ask. That's what we've agreed.'

'It's more likely to be MI6, I think. He'd be more useful there,' said Jack, like someone picking me up on a minor error. 'Although they often swap personnel, depending on the mission.'

He spoke with a serenity that I increasingly lacked. Indeed, right there and then, I gave in to my despair. I clutched my head in my hands, my elbows resting on Mr White's desk, and was on the verge of tears.

'I don't know what to do, Jack. I've been patient, as Tomás advised me to be, but I need to know whether or not he's alive.'

'There's no reason why he wouldn't be. These matters sometimes take a long time, sometimes years, not months. You've been lucky so far, three or four months isn't bad at all. And the last thing he can do is make a false move, like phoning home, because someone might be listening in. Or sending a telegram. That would be even worse. Someone could read it.'

That isn't what I wanted to hear, I didn't want to imagine actual scenes, Tomás going to the post office or looking for a public phone box hidden away somewhere, fearing for his life if he were to be discovered doing something that would be perfectly normal for the rest of humanity. I wanted to be spared the sordid details.

'Eight months is a long time. For me, I mean. I can't take it any more, Jack, I need to know something. Once, years ago, I spoke to someone called Ted Reresby in London. Something really alarming had happened here, something I never told you about, and I couldn't get in touch with Tomás. If you don't know where he is now, I'll phone that man Reresby again, or at least try to.'

'Ted Reresby?' Jack said, repeating the name. 'I've never heard Tomás mention him. For me, the key name would be Tupra, Bertram

Tupra. That's who I'd turn to as a last resort, the person I'd try to track down. Tom introduced me to him when I was on a trip to London, when Tom was working there. I just happened to bump into them in the Strand one day. Tom gave me the impression that Tupra was his boss, that he was under his direct orders, whatever it was they did, and I'm not at all sure what that was. "We work together," Tom said. A charming chap, but a bit daunting; he was wearing a pinstripe suit, with rather too wide a stripe, complete with waistcoat, far too smartly turned out to be a real diplomat or a minor functionary at a ministry. When I say "daunting", I mean decisive, capable,' he added, thinking that the adjective might have alarmed me. 'Confident, self-assured. Look, Berta, I'm really not sure about anything. I have my own theories, but whether they're right or not, I have no idea. I am pretty sure, though, that I know what Tom does, even though I couldn't prove it. Whatever it is, he's involved in it body and soul, that I do see, that much is clear. At least when he's not here. When he's not here, he forgets all about here, we don't exist. You, me, his mother, even the kids, we all cease to exist. He becomes part of another life, he becomes another person and will sometimes believe he *is* that person. And that's how it has to be if things are to work out well. Then he comes home, and, insofar as he can, he becomes his usual self, he becomes himself again.'

Jack Nevinson was clearly well informed, or his suspicions were enough for him to take the facts for granted. He took it all remarkably calmly, as if he knew that, when someone has chosen a path, all you can do is watch them through binoculars, wish them luck and hope they make it back.

'Do you know how I could get in touch with that man Tupra? What a strange name, by the way.'

'It's certainly not English, of course, but he was an Englishman to his fingertips, and his spoken English was impeccable. I don't honestly know how you could get in touch. You could try ringing the Foreign Office or MI6, but phoning there will be like entering a labyrinth, and they'll end up asking *you* questions. I think you should wait a bit longer, just a little. As I said, it's not unusual for operations to last two to three years. At least wait until a whole year has elapsed.'

'Until April? How can I possibly wait that long, Jack?'

'Until April or May or even June. Don't imagine I don't worry about him, that I'm not filled with fear and anxiety whenever he goes off who knows where; he is, after all, my youngest son. But I put up with it, what else can I do? Nor could I criticise him for having decided to put his knowledge and talents at the service of my country. I wouldn't try to dissuade him either; in fact, I feel very proud of him. What I do know is that, in these matters, a pestering wife trying to find things out is a real menace. That could make Tom's work more difficult, or even make things more dangerous for him. The same would apply to a father or mother or a husband trying to track down his wife.'

When he mentioned the word 'mother', the penny suddenly dropped.

'What about Mercedes? Doesn't she wonder about him? Doesn't she get impatient or worried? Does she know anything about what he does?'

Jack placed one finger on his lips, as if bidding me to be silent. It was a courteous gesture, accompanied by a look from his clear eyes. It was a request not an order.

'She prefers not to think about it. She makes do with the lies you tell us. And if you don't mind, it would be best if you could carry on lying, and keep inventing those phone calls, without ever going into too much detail. Just as you have done up until now. You may not know it, but you're very good at pretending.'

I did as he suggested and waited a little more and then a lot more. I waited until April and May and June, and continued to wait without lifting a finger – literally: without dialling the Foreign Office number or any other English number – during the whole of July and August and September of 1983, and when you wait for a long time, you become filled with an ambivalent, contradictory feeling: you discover that you've become used to waiting and may not want to do anything else. You don't want it to be interrupted or to come to an end with the long-awaited phone call, with the long-awaited arrival, with the longed-for reappearance, but still less do you want the opposite, the news that this won't happen, that your husband will never be seen alive again, will never return. That second possibility is, of course, the graver and more dramatic of the two, but both come to the same thing, the end of the waiting and the uncertainty to which you've become so accustomed that you'd rather they didn't end and thus take away your reason for getting up in the morning or the thought with which you go to bed at night, you'd simply prefer that nothing changed. 'If Tomás comes back, he'll already have arrived in a way,' I told myself, although not in so many words, for it was more a sensation than a thought, 'and everything will be as it used to be, unchanged, exactly the same; yes, more time will have passed, and I'll have worried myself sick, but, basically, it will be just another

321

chapter in this absurd life of comings and goings and opacity on his part; it will become superimposed on the previous absences and a moment will arrive when I won't be able to tell that disappearance from all the others, especially if future disappearances go on for an equally long time, not just for two or three months but a year and a half like this one, who knows how long they could go on for. A year and a half about which he'll tell me nothing and about which I won't even ask, just as it's always been and always is. Then we'll enjoy another period of apparent normality until he gets the call and goes away again. Perhaps what I have now is better. It's the illusion of the future, to which I can give any shape I like, because the future is so malleable. I can imagine that the day he comes back, he'll tell me he's retiring, that this mission only dragged on for so long because he wanted to go out on a high, with one final crucial job, and that it's the last one he'll take on; that he's wasted the best years of his life and that nothing lasts for ever, that he wants to stop now and stay here; that he's had enough of the dark side of the world, the one we ordinary citizens are never obliged to see and that we don't even dare to set foot in or peer into. I can imagine him admitting to me that he's weary and has had enough, that what he's done and seen others do is so sickening that he doesn't want to be left alone with that vision of ugliness, unpleasantness, distrust, disappointment and cruelty, and to live indefinitely on the treacherous margins of the universe. I can treasure that idea for as long as Tomás doesn't return, because I know that, when he does, the idea will vanish and succumb to the inertia of events, that is, to habit. "Whatever it is, he's involved in it body and soul, that I do see, that much is clear," Jack said to me, and Jack is his father and knows him well, and has known him far longer than I have. Tomás won't be able to leave his chosen path, the path he's set off along; he's caught. By this stage, he probably needs not to be here, not to be him, but to be someone else or various other people, he won't be able to bear being ceaselessly, unequivocally one person. Jack had also said: "When he's not here, he forgets all about here, we don't exist. You, me, his mother, even the kids, we all cease to exist." And I have no illusions in that respect, I'm sure he's right: for long periods, Tomás will need us to be erased, to evaporate, to remove ourselves from his field of vision; no, more than that, from the field of his imagination and the field of his memory, just as Hyde doesn't remember Jekyll and Jekyll doesn't remember Hyde, or only as they leave each other, at the moment of transformation. He'll only retire if they make him, if someone else dismisses him as redundant and burned out, after having squeezed every last drop out of him, if Tupra or Reresby give him permission or whoever it is who issues the orders, perhaps the actual head of the Secret Intelligence Service, the SIS; before he left, he told me that there was or was going to be a new man with a strange surname, Figures, apparently the SIS heads are replaced every few years, perhaps so that they don't go mad, only their subordinates. That will happen sooner or later, they'll get rid of him, and then what?'

I hated to think about Ruiz Kindelán, but he had drawn a vivid picture of what lay ahead for retired agents, a fate perhaps not so very different from that of retired terrorists, which is why he knew about it first-hand, as if he assumed that this would also be his fate and that of Mary Kate. He'd said that most leave the service 'either mad or dead'. 'And those who survive end up not knowing who they are. It makes no difference what age they are. If they're no good any more or are burned out, they're sent home or left to vegetate in an office, and some individuals don't even reach thirty before feeling that their time has passed. They remain attached to their murky past, and are sometimes overwhelmed by remorse. The cruelty of the acts they

323

committed sullies their present, and what was important for them is of no importance to anyone else.' This didn't sound like a very attractive or consoling prospect either, welcoming home a thirty-two-year-old man longing for what was, a man who feels more like a seventy-year-old, someone aware that the best years of his life are over, someone perhaps unhappy and permanently embittered, aggrieved because he's no longer useful. No, there was no good solution, nothing could restore to me the Tomás I'd fallen in love with when I was very young (I'd always wanted to be Berta Isla de Nevinson, when it was the custom for women to add their husband's surname to theirs with that proprietorial 'de'), the Tomás who never went in for soul-searching and never had any interest in understanding himself. If they retired him, though, he would be continually looking back at himself, and everything he experienced with me would seem monotonous and insipid, insipid and disappointing, a perpetual decline and motive for dissatisfaction. 'So it's better to keep waiting,' I told myself, although not in so many words, 'it will be bad if he comes back, or if one day I find a letter from him in the postbox; and it will be bad if I learn that he's not coming back, that he can't, that he died in some remote place and all that remains for me is the process of loss and forgetting. It's better for things to continue as they are: unresolved and indefinite and utterly vague.'

That's why I responded with such dread to that ring on the doorbell in November 1983, the damp, rainy month that finds uneasy, melancholy souls such easy prey, snatching them up in its claws and plunging them into folly so as to avoid them committing the greatest and most tempting folly of all; and thus it urges them to find a 'substitute for pistol and ball', as Melville and his narrator say at the beginning of *Moby-Dick*, which I'd also had to teach on more than one occasion. By then, I could no longer keep my agitation at bay, or not always, and my eyes all too often filled with tears. I still preferred nothing to happen, for nothing to change my waiting state and for every day to be the same as the previous day, but that feeling alternated with moments of unbalance, even of lurking exasperation, when I longed to close the long chapter of my thirty-two years and bid him farewell, saying enough is enough; when I wished something would shake me out of my inertia and oblige me to leave without a backward glance, to move, to get in the car and drive off who knows where or lose myself in some unknown provincial city, to disappear like Tomás, so that, if he did come back, he would be as bewildered and alarmed as I was, and would go about asking everyone: 'Where's Berta? How is it no one knows where she's gone, how is it no one has reported her missing to the police, how is it that we don't even know whether she's alive and in hiding at her own choosing or hidden and

325

dead at the choosing of others, how could she have left no clue, no farewell note, no words of warning, no strange remarks even hinting at her decision?'

Most women, however, are prevented from doing so by their children, which is why we say nothing to them about it, but we often wish that they didn't exist and would leave us free and in peace, that they'd never been born or were self-sufficient from the start, that they weren't constantly wanting or asking things, that they didn't depend on us for everything, even getting dressed in the morning, let alone going anywhere or being fed, always having to dispel their fears and make them happy, which is their natural inclination. (What we never wish is for them to die, never.) I was bound to Guillermo and Elisa and that was that, and sometimes I rebelled against that commitment. They were as much mine as Tomás's (no, in practice, they were more mine, only mine), but he contributed more money to the household and was providing a vital service to his country, and that was alibi enough, neglect justified by duty. At least we didn't lack for money: during those nineteen months, his variable salary (he must have been paid bonuses depending on the merit, length, difficulty and danger of his missions) had been paid punctually into our joint account, as it had for years, whether he was in Madrid, London or some secret location unknown to me. I knew that this wasn't the whole of his salary, that part of it – perhaps certain extras not subject to tax, back-pocket payments – never left England and was transferred directly into an account over there, an account to which I had no access and about which I knew nothing except that it existed, but with no idea how much was in there, I mean, how much he had stashed away. 'It's always best to have some savings abroad,' Tomás assured me, 'and best to have it in sterling too, because you never know when you might have to leave Spain or how quickly. You might just get fed up or else be kicked out, because Spain is a country with suicidal tendencies, and, for centuries, has forced some of its best people into exile, the people who could have improved or saved it; the ones it didn't murder, of course; in that respect, there's no other country quite like it.'

It was a fairly loud ring, at eleven o'clock in the morning, on a day when I didn't have classes and the children weren't at home: Guillermo was at the school I'd attended from when I was a toddler and Tomás from when he was an adolescent; and Elisa was at nursery school. As it happened, I was in the middle of preparing a lesson on *Moby-Dick* for the American Literature course I'd been given to teach that year (I'd just come across Melville's strange way of describing the ocean: 'the watery part of the world'), and I looked up like a startled animal, because I wasn't expecting anyone. I tiptoed over to the door so that my high heels wouldn't betray my presence at home (I was always wary of visitors, ever since the Kindeláns), and peered through the spyhole where I saw a man with a bulbous cranium which he did his best to mitigate with a thick, curly head of hair, a man I'd never seen before. The tiny convex glass of the spyhole distorted the image, and so his head might not have been quite as bulbous as it seemed. At first glance, he looked English to me, not so much because of his features, but because I could see that he was wearing a dark grey suit with a double-breasted jacket, which was unmistakably English; and he wore his overcoat draped over his shoulders as if he were a gangster from Soho or the East End or wherever, or a posh denizen of Madrid. His appearance was mildly offensive, but, if he was an Englishman, then he might be able to give me news of Tomás, I thought. Still without opening the door, I asked:

'Who is it?'

'Mrs Nevinson? Mrs Berta Nevinson?' He was definitely English.

'My name is Bertram Tupra and I'd like to talk to you, if I may. I'm a colleague of your husband's and I just happened to be in Madrid. If you wouldn't mind opening the door . . .' He said all this in his language, of course; he obviously didn't know a word of Spanish.

When I heard that name, the name Jack Nevinson had mentioned, I hesitated no longer and opened the door, gripped by a mixture of panic – or was it horror – and curiosity. I just had time for this fleeting thought: 'If Tomás's boss has come in person, it must be to give me the worst possible news,' and I tried to accustom myself to the improbable idea that my husband had died. 'Tomás is dead,' I thought, and, at the same time, I didn't believe it. 'And now what? Now what?' And still I didn't believe it, as if it must be a lie or a mistake.

The man smiled when he saw me, which made me briefly correct my assumption: you don't smile when you've come to report some terrible misfortune, when you're about to tell a married woman that she's now a widow and her children are orphans, and so young too. Behind that slightly mocking smile and the blue or pale grey eyes, I caught a kind of appreciative male gaze, quite out of place if this *was* a sad occasion and he was about to present me with his condolences. But I know that some men simply can't help it, even if they're looking at the victim of a road accident lying in the street and they've hurried to help her; if, for example, her skirt has ridden up or the buttons of her blouse have been wrenched off in the impact. Bertram Tupra might be one of those men. There aren't many in England, it's true, but he did have unusually dark, lustrous skin, a broad nose that looked as if it had been broken by one blow or by several, a Russian mouth, and the long eyelashes of a southerner. Yes, he was definitely that kind of man: some women, myself included, can spot them a mile off, and we're not immune to that swift appraising glance, and such men, in turn, immediately pick up on that. I reckoned he was in his late thirties, possibly about five years older than me, but his physical appearance was so disquieting and so elusive that he could have been or claimed to be almost any age.

'Please, Mr Tupra, come in. I think I know who you are. Do you have any news of Tom? Is he all right? He is alive, isn't he?'

He raised one hand to stop my questions, as if saying: 'Patience, patience. It's not the moment to talk about that just yet. All in good time.' There was nothing else I wanted to talk about, but his gesture was so imperative that I immediately recomposed myself, postponed my eagerness to know, and did as he ordered. I suppose his air of calm provisionally calmed me down too, but the effect didn't last.

'Really?' he said, as if he hadn't even heard what I'd said. 'Has Tom spoken to you about me?'

'No, absolutely not. My father-in-law, Jack Nevinson, mentioned that he'd met you once.'

'Yes, indeed he did. Tom's father,' he said, as he slipped off his overcoat with almost bullfighterly grace and held it out to me as if I were the cloakroom attendant at a discotheque. He seemed very sure of himself and not in the least inclined to beating about the bush. 'Where shall we sit?'

I showed him into the living room, and he sat where Miguel Kindelán had sat on that nightmare morning, while I sat in the armchair to his left, as I had on that other occasion too, but now there was no cradle between us. I asked if he wanted anything, a drink or a coffee. He shook his head and wagged one finger in an almost dismissive fashion, as if he were telling me off and saying: 'Please, this isn't a social visit.'

My anxiety immediately returned, at least partially, but I managed to keep it under control. 'Yes, let's cut to the chase,' I thought. I still felt slightly calmer, like someone who has assumed that all is lost and expects the worst. Expecting the worse and hearing the worst are two very different things, and I hadn't heard it yet.

'Is there any news of Tom? I haven't had any news from him since 4 April last year. You can imagine how worried I've been. Tell me the truth, please. Is he alive?'

He looked straight at me with his warm or, rather, all-absorbing eyes. It was not the serious gaze of someone about to announce a death, but nor was it reassuring. There was a certain insolence in that gaze, possibly unintentional, possibly unwitting, as much a part of him as the colour of his eyes. He took out a strange, ornate cigarette case, and asked if he could smoke, I said he could, and he offered me a cigarette, which I accepted and then he took one too, and while he was lighting mine (while I was intent on watching the flame from his lighter), he began to speak:

'I very much hope he's alive, but I don't know.' That was how long the flame lasted; when he spoke again (and he didn't even pause), I'd already moved away from him and was conscious of the piquant taste of that tobacco (I had leaned a little closer to light my cigarette, and Tupra smelled good, of mint and a fresh herbal-scented cologne). 'That's what I've come to tell you, we've done everything we could before deciding, finally, to get in touch with you, and we're very grateful for your discretion and patience. Some wives would have moved heaven and earth in the face of such a long silence, they would have been ringing up every day, obstructing our work. Anyway, what I want to tell you is that we've had no news from him either. Not for quite as long as you, of course, but for a few months now we've heard nothing. Absolutely nothing. He's vanished without trace. He didn't come back when he was supposed to, insofar as we can ever know when anyone's supposed to come back; that varies a lot and is never very clear, subject as it is to unforeseen events, delays, complications and setbacks. He hasn't been in touch with the people he should have been in touch with. He hasn't asked for help or to be relieved, he hasn't advised us of any difficulties or warned of any imminent danger. That's why I think he's still alive, an agent usually knows in advance when it would be best to get out and abandon the field. And, obviously, he hasn't turned up dead anywhere, which is another fundamental reason for not getting too alarmed or assuming the worst, because dead bodies are much easier to find than living ones. After all, they don't run away or move, they stay put, which means that sooner or later, with a few exceptions, we do find them. But anything is possible. I don't want to ruin your hopes or get your hopes up either. Anything is still possible. He may have deserted, to use a military term; he may have grown tired of us and decided to disappear from a life that certainly wears a man down, he may feel he doesn't want to collaborate any more. It wouldn't be the first time. The easiest way of detaching yourself from something is to leave without saying goodbye, telling no one and simply not answering any calls. When it happens, that's what we call "playing dead". There are people who vanish completely and then reappear years later, and we discover that they've spent all that time hiding away somewhere, living under a false identity and working in a completely unexpected profession that has nothing to do with their aptitudes or their training – you'll learn to do anything if it will help you escape: herding sheep, milking cows, whatever is least likely to get you noticed. After all, we make use of that ability sometimes too, when we have to remove an agent from circulation and keep him safe from reprisals, so there's no reason why an agent shouldn't plan and organise his own exile. He may also have been captured. If that were the case, it would perhaps take us a while to find out, and we might not know anything until the other side wants to negotiate a prisoner swap. It's not uncommon, years later, for them suddenly to produce a name out of nowhere and put it on the table, a name we'd given up as having disappeared for good, as lost or even dead. Lastly, he might, for some reason, be trapped, hidden and submerged, waiting to resurface. He may have had no option but to become a sleeper, with no prospect in the short term of waking up. So it's still possible that he might yet reappear. Here or in London, or anywhere that will give him some guarantee of safety. Anyway, Mrs Nevinson, my advice to you is not to wait for Tom, not for the moment, not in the long term. I'm not saying you should lose all hope either, of course not, but you need to get used to the idea,' he paused for a moment to allow me to get used to the idea of what idea it was I should get used to; it was that rather than a hesitation, 'that he might not come back at all.'

Then into my head came one of the lines Tomás had been reciting for years and had, all unwittingly, transmitted to me; and suddenly I understood it fully: 'as death resembles life', for example, described the situation Tupra had just laid out before me. There was not much difference now between Tomás's possible death and his possible life. He might never return anyway, even if he was still alive and breathing in some far-distant place. I could choose to stop waiting for him or to continue waiting, I could 'declare' him to all intents and purposes dead or 'decide' that he still trod the Earth and traversed the world; I thought all this in a very inward way, to myself, for my own governance, so to speak. And what about externally?

'Where was he the last time you heard from him? Where did he go? Where was he sent?'

Tupra spread his hands wide in that universal gesture denoting impotence in the face of the inevitable.

'I'm sorry, but I can't tell you that, not until more time has passed and all this is ancient history. Until we know for sure what has happened.'

'You mean you can't even tell me that?' I asked, half-surprised and half-indignant. As tends to happen, my indignation helped me keep my composure. I hadn't yet assimilated the news, nor could I believe it (I was still in the land of unreality), but, at the same time, I realised

333

that my eyes were filling with tears and my chin was quivering and that, if I wasn't careful, I would break down in heart-rending sobs that would prevent me from speaking, from holding a conversation, and understanding what this man had to tell me. If I cried, he would feel obliged to put his arms around me, and the English don't do that kind of thing; at most, he might pat me on the back; then again, he wasn't a very typical Englishman, his gaze not veiled, but all-absorbing. I was determined not to give in to uncontrollable sobbing, not until I was alone; I bit my lower lip. Tupra seemed a considerate man, albeit cold and efficient. He could not have been clearer: he didn't want to ruin my hopes or feed them either. He was neither softening the blow nor hardening it. He was telling me the truth, telling me what he knew, what he was authorised to tell me, and I didn't intend to collapse in a heap in his presence. I imagined he still had things to say, possibly even on practical matters. 'I think I should have the right to know where he died, if he has died. Or, if he is a prisoner, where he's being held. Are you going to leave me to speculate on that for the rest of my life? At least tell me if he was sent to the Falklands. He left here just as the war was beginning.'

He ignored my last question, as if it hadn't existed.

'Believe me, Mrs Nevinson, I do understand, but Tom wasn't the only person to be sent where he was sent and where he may still be, against his will or as a precaution, or perhaps simply keeping out of our way. Others are still there, and any leak could put them at risk. It's not that I don't trust you, but our general rule is not to trust anyone and not to tell anyone anything. But you won't be left to speculate about it for the rest of your life, I promise. Sooner or later, we'll hear one way or another. We won't find out everything, but enough. And Tom could walk through that door tomorrow, I wouldn't exclude that as a possibility either. Or, as I said, you might never see him again.'

On the one hand, he wouldn't allow me to fall into absolute pessimism, and, on the other, he was careful to curtail my optimism. 'If that is the case, and I very much hope it isn't, we'll tell you as much as we can about his disappearance, but we can, alas, say nothing until we're certain.'

'So what should I do meanwhile? Should I go into mourning or continue to wait? Should I consider myself a widow or still a married woman? Do my children have a father or are they fatherless? How long will it take? Even you don't know that. I'm not sure you realise just how difficult this is, Mr Tupra. Just how . . .' I couldn't think of the word. 'Just how unmanageable. How impossible.'

'You can call me Bertram if you like. May I call you Berta?' Spoken one after another like that, our names sounded absurdly similar. 'Listen, Bertram.' 'Yes, Berta.' It would almost be better if we didn't bother.

'Call me what you like,' I said. At that point, I really didn't care, and besides, in Spain, everyone addresses everyone else as *tú* at the first opportunity.

'Everything is manageable, Berta, everything, at least in the long run. Think of the wives of sailors in past centuries, whose husbands were away for years at a time or never came back, their fate forever unknown. Or the wives of soldiers whose bodies were never recovered from the scene of an ambush or from a battlefield, or who might have been deserters relieved to be taken for dead. Or the wives of captives for whom no ransom was paid. Or the wives of kidnap victims. Or of explorers who never returned, whose bodies were never found and whose deaths went unrecorded. It was highly likely, but not certain. Something must have told those women whether they should cling on to hope or abandon it. When and for how long. Something must tell the wives of today, although such cases are far

less common. Need, for example, or a lack of need, or a feeling that they've had enough, or perhaps a growing sense of detachment from or resentment towards the disappeared husband for having gone off, thus exposing himself to all kinds of dangers, like Ulysses. Even if the man who left was obliged to do so, those feelings of resentment could still arise. So you forget when you want to forget, when you're ready or when remembering brings no pleasure or consolation and is just a weight that stops you moving forwards or even breathing. You can't imagine that now, Berta, but you'll find out. Obviously, it's a long process, it's not like an arrow heading straight for the bullseye, there are advances and retreats and times when it wanders off down side streets. Until, that is, you do find out what happened, if you ever do. Then the arrow hits the target and shatters in the air, I suppose.'
'This is the death of air,' I thought. English, of course, makes no distinction between formal and informal modes of address, but I imagined that, had Tupra been speaking to me in Spanish, he would still be addressing me as *usted* not *tú*, despite now calling me Berta. 'As for being a widow,' he went on, adopting a more administrative tone. 'The English law varies according to the circumstances and the probabilities, but when a person disappears with no irrefutable, definitive proof of his demise, the usual rule is that before he can be declared officially dead, seven years and a day have to pass since the last known sighting or communication. Only then can his heirs inherit or the widower or widow remarry. Unless there's been a divorce *in absentia*, that's something I haven't as yet looked into as a possibility, but it might be of interest to you later on. Anyway, after that period, the person is declared legally and to all intents and purposes dead. Yes, death *in absentia* it's called. Needless to say, if the disappeared person turns up alive later on, that declaration is, in most cases, deemed invalid.'

I found this absurd statement unexpectedly interesting. There's nothing like curiosity and comedy to distract us – if only for an instant – from our sorrows and anxieties.

'In most cases? Does that mean there are cases when someone undeniably alive is still considered to be dead? Even if he's speaking and breathing, walking and protesting, the law says: "Shut up, you can neither allege nor demand anything because you're officially dead and it says so on this piece of paper"?'

Tupra gave a broad, sympathetic smile, and understood at once why I was amused, insofar as I could be in that state of stunned desolation, which overwhelmed everything, apart from that brief exchange.

'You probably haven't read Balzac's *Colonel Chabert*, in which everyone tells the poor wretched colonel that he doesn't exist, that he's an impostor, because, according to army records, he fell and perished at the Battle of Eylau, during the Napoleonic Wars. That's a work of fiction, of course, but bureaucracy can be like that, or, you won't be surprised to know, even worse. People don't realise this and think they have inviolable rights and guarantees, but the power of the State must be and is absolute: that's the only way we can function, in democracies too, whatever claims we make for the separation of powers. There only has to be a change in the law or for new laws to be passed for people to be left without money or work or a home, or to be told they don't exist; you can be stripped of your nationality and citizenship and be declared an outsider, made stateless, thrown in jail or expelled; you can be declared mad, unfit or dead. People are very rash when they defy us, and very naïve too.' I picked up on that 'us', which had a different meaning from when he had used it before. Then he was referring to MI6 or the all-inclusive SIS, and now he was referring to the omnipotent State that he served and to which he

337

belonged, as Tomás had too, for some time now; I could clearly see Tupra's influence on him. 'But what I said earlier really means that if the heirs have divided up the inheritance, they won't be obliged to return it, especially if they've already spent it, as they probably will have. Or if the widower or widow has remarried, that second marriage is not automatically invalidated, because everyone acted in good faith and legally, according to a decision made by a judge. Such cases are extremely rare anyway. *The Count of Monte Cristo* is not the norm – certainly not in England.' 'So he reads novels, this fellow Tupra,' I thought fleetingly. As he spoke, his voice and his tone of voice began to seem familiar, as if this were not the first time I'd heard it. I was watching his soft, fleshy lips, which were moving quickly now, and I was sure that I'd never seen them before, they weren't the kind of lips you would easily forget. In the midst of my confusion, I became aware that while there was something slightly unpleasant about him, he was also strangely attractive (even when we're in a state of anguish and distress, we can't help but notice such things, although without really paying much attention). His unusual face was a magnet, as were his long eyelashes and grey eyes. I think he was taking advantage of my interest to continue distracting me from the main business, or so that I could gradually come to terms with the news, without being overwhelmed by it, that no one had heard anything from my husband for months, not even the people who told him what to do and where to go, and that I might have seen him for the last time on 4 April 1982. 'The average citizen is convinced that the State protects him, and, normally, that is the case, our key priority, I can vouch for that. What he doesn't know, though, is that if that same protection demands it or if he puts up any resistance to it (if he strays radically from the straight and narrow), then the State will remove or destroy him. How? It will strip him of everything, and if someone has nothing, then he can do nothing. His goods will be confiscated, any land or property will be expropriated, any money will be seized by the imposition of unexpected taxes or fines, there's always plenty of room for manoeuvre, all governments and parliaments make sure of that. Whatever they may preach beforehand, they soon change their tune when it's their turn to be in power and to pass legislation. But let's not go down that path, I can see I'm alarming you, and yet this all happens for the greater good; in difficult situations, there's no other choice. Imagine the uproar, the chaos that would ensue if the people were consulted on every vital decision? Everything would grind to a halt, because vital decisions are taken on a daily basis, not just every now and then.' 'For the greater good', that's what he said. There were moments when he spoke so fast that my English, more passive than active, struggled to keep up. 'I've had a quick look at Spanish law too, the law that would affect you – as regards those presumed dead, I mean – and, if what I've seen is correct, then there are some advantages. You don't have to wait quite so long when it seems clear that the disappeared person has perished. Only two years,' and he raised two fingers as if giving a V-for-victory sign, entirely inappropriate given the situation, 'when there's been a shipwreck or a plane crash in some deserted or uninhabited place, things like that. Or perhaps it was three years.' This time he raised three fingers. 'Whichever it is, there's a clear stipulation that could well apply to us, here it is, in Spanish and translated into English.' He took two typewritten pages from his jacket pocket, and held out the Spanish version for me to read. 'This, more or less, is what it says, is that right? "Anyone belonging to an armed contingent, or anyone bound to it in an auxiliary volunteer capacity, or who has participated in a purely informative role, and who has taken part in a campaign and disappeared during said campaign, may be legally declared dead

339

after two years have elapsed' – he couldn't resist doing an imitation of Churchill at this point –'"calculated from the date of the signing of a peace treaty, or, if no such treaty has been signed, from the date of the official declaration of the end of the war." Good grief,' he said, 'bureaucratic prose is the same old gobbledegook the world over. You're grateful if you can at least understand it.'

I *had* understood it, despite the convoluted language, which is why I said:

'The only recent war is the Falklands War, and you haven't told me yet if Tomás was sent there or not.'

'That doesn't matter,' he replied, still without answering my question. 'In order to have you legally declared a widow as soon as possible, we will state that he was in the Falklands and disappeared while on duty there. On the other hand,' he went on, 'under Spanish law, you have to wait longer to inherit.' He took a third piece of paper from his pocket. 'Yes, here it is: "Only once five years have elapsed following the official declaration of death,"' and this time he held up five fingers, ' "no legacies will be handed over nor can the heirs dispose freely (in the form of gifts, donations, etc.) of any goods or chattels thus bequeathed to them." Well, the cessation of hostilities in the Falklands War took place on 20 June 1982, so, according to that statement, on 20 June next year, in about eight months' time, Tom could be declared legally dead in Spain. And I don't think our country would raise any objections; in fact, we'd make sure they didn't. The only problem, Berta, is that you wouldn't inherit until 1989, five years on. But don't worry, we've thought of that too. You can't be expected to live on the little you earn from the university, that wouldn't be fair, not even if Tom has deserted, and until we find out one way or another, we'll assume he hasn't.'

Everything he said seemed to me to show an extraordinary lack of tact. Or perhaps not: perhaps it was a delicate way – delicate because it was so aseptic, measured and pragmatic – of telling me to abandon all hope and stop waiting; to give Tom up as dead and never buried. My eyes again filled with tears, but I didn't want Tupra to see this. I got to my feet, turned and went over to the balcony, where I rested one hand on my forehead and cheekbone, the better to control my tears (three fingers on my forehead and one thumb on one cheekbone), and looked down at the ugly statue in the square beyond the trees; I knew the inscription by heart: 'On the initiative of Spanish women this monument was erected to the glory of the soldier Luis Noval. Spain – never forget those who died for you.' It was dated 1912, and I'd never bothered to find out anything more about that soldier, whose effigy had enjoyed the support of, among others, Queen Victoria Eugenia and the writer, Emilia Pardo Bazán, whose name appeared on the inscription as the 'Condesa de Pardo Bazán'. Nor did I know in which war he had died, possibly in the Cuban War of Independence, fourteen years earlier, on the other side of the Atlantic, where Tomás had also perhaps died: 'down the sea's throat or to an illegible stone'. I'd never really taken any interest, and our country is very good at forgetting and allowing its inscriptions and stones to fade and quickly become illegible, something it does tirelessly, not caring in the least who dies for it and having no concept of gratitude, perhaps finding such a concept merely irritating. Luis Noval is a shadow, an empty name, a spectre; he may have a monument erected to him, but no one recognises his name and no one notices him. And Tomás would be even more of a shadow, a ghost, neither living nor dead, who wouldn't even be remembered by his children – and who, then, would remember him, if they did not? A blade of grass, a speck of dust, a lifting mist, a snow that falls but doesn't settle, a handful of ashes, an insect, a cloud of smoke that finally disperses.

'I wonder where his body is?' I thought, and struggled to hold back my tears. 'No one will have mourned him and no one will have closed his eyes, perhaps no one will have buried him either, or per- haps only hastily and on the run, making sure it didn't look like a grave, leaving the earth carefully flattened and with no gravestone, of course, hiding him away so that no one will find him, if anyone should ever want to.' I stopped thinking for a moment, because Tupra was speaking to me again, respecting neither my silence nor my back turned to him, he probably didn't want me to think too deeply or to abandon myself to grief, he wanted my mind to be occupied with practical matters, with legalisms and curiosities.

'Look, Berta,' he said, 'here, in Spanish law, it specifies what would happen if the dead man were to return later on. Listen to this: "If, after being declared legally dead, the disappeared person should appear and his existence be proven, he can recover all his property and goods, but only in the state in which he finds them at the time of his appearance." I assume they mean "reappear" and "reappearance". "He will also have the right," it goes on, "to be given the amount obtained from the sale of his goods or to be given the goods that accrued with said money. How- ever, he may only reclaim the fruits or profits earned from his goods from the time of his appearance." Again, it should say "reappearance", I think;

that would be more exact,' he added punctiliously, giving the piece of paper a disapproving flick. 'In short, if his heirs have spent everything, he won't see a penny of his former fortune, there'll be nothing for him to recover. What will he live on, the poor reappeared man (or woman of course)? He'll not only be dead, he'll be dispossessed as well. Will he live on the charity of friends? I'm not sure friendship lasts that long; beyond death, I mean. Or on the charity of his offspring? They, of course, might feel horrified, even threatened, to see him resuscitated, and, deep in their hearts, might wish him back in his grave. It would seem that the State has no intention of compensating him in any way, or of giving him a pension. I would say that someone who returns after having been deemed to be dead for years, should, at the very least, be treated like a retiree, or, indeed, better.'

I was barely listening to him. 'While leaving open the possibility that Tomás might still be alive, this Tupra fellow is basically telling me that I should get used to the idea that Tomás is dead: he may only talk about the legal aspects and what I'm going to live on in the future, but he's actually talking to me as if I were already a widow. A rather unusual widow, who needs to be recognised as such as quickly as possible, because I could find myself in difficulties if we don't do things properly. So that I can remake my life and even remarry if I want, for he doubtless assumes I won't lack for suitors at my age and with my looks, I've seen how he almost ogles me, trying hard to suppress any feelings of sexual attraction, but he doesn't fool me; Tupra clearly likes women a lot and is accustomed to making conquests easily, you can sense it in his attitude, and he must be cursing the fact that he's met me in such gloomy or pessimistic circumstances, as the bringer of news that strikes grief and despair into the heart, that overwhelms both mind and intellect, and precludes any advances he might make, which would be doomed to

343

failure as inappropriate, disrespectful and completely out of order. That's what constrains and impedes him, not the fact that I'm the wife of a close collaborator of his: such men are immune to scruples, they depend upon concealment and silence whenever things need to be concealed and silenced, that's their natural medium, their natural element. Yes, he imagines I could get married again whenever I choose, and doesn't even see as an impediment the burden I carry and will always carry, namely, two small children, so he's being very generous in his assessment of my chances. Anyway, he's prepared to help me even if Tomás is a deserter or has passed over to the enemy, become a defector, because that's also a possibility. He must be pretty sure that Tomás has done neither of those things, which is why he's given him up for dead, another outcast from the universe, although officially he's obliged to leave me with a slender thread of hope, a chink of light. Nothing is definitive without a corpse, without some clear evidence, and Tomás has vanished with no witness to the how or when of his disappearance.'

I hadn't moved away from the balcony, I was still standing with my back to him, still trying hard to contain the tears filling my eyes, and which I kept swallowing, so to speak, again and again. I finally managed to swallow them all, or so I thought. I heard Tupra light another cigarette taken from that ornate, Egyptian case. Several seconds later, and still without turning around, I said:

'I can assure you that if Tomás does return one day, his money will have remained intact. I won't touch it as long as there's the slightest chance that he might be alive, even if he's in the farthest-flung corner of the world,' I said

'I don't doubt your intentions, Berta, but don't be too naïve, intentions can only take you so far. You'll still need to earn a living, 1989 is a long way off, and 1990 even further, which is when, according to

English law, Tom could officially be declared dead, and when you could be eligible for a widow's pension from the Foreign Office. It would be most unfair, however, if the possible widow of one of our men should suffer any hardship. We usually try our best not to let that happen, we don't just abandon the family of someone who has fallen, we always provide them with the means to live.'

I interrupted him. That word 'fallen' fell like lead upon my soul, like a confirmation of a fact. But that isn't what I asked him about.

'1990?' I repeated. 'Does that mean that you still had contact with Tom this year, in 1983? So he didn't disappear in 1982, and he didn't take part in the Falklands War. Where did he go, then? At least tell me that, please.'

I had turned round now and moved a few steps closer to Tupra. He smiled as if amused by my rapid calculations, or perhaps by his own carelessness, something he realised he must avoid in future. Not that he was particularly bothered, he was an old hand and knew better than to answer my questions.

'Later, Berta. When, as I explained earlier, we've reconstructed what happened.' And he went on as if I hadn't asked anything. 'We've come up with the following plan for you: you will appear on the payroll as a translator, as is perfectly feasible, for one of the various international organisations that have their headquarters in Madrid, the COI or the OMT. People who work for them, as for the UN and the FAO and so on, are exempt from paying tax, so the salary they receive is paid gross, and it's really not bad at all. A privilege, a reward if you like, extended to those functionaries who often have to live away from their country of origin. That won't be the case with you, but you'll still enjoy that privilege. Your name will appear on the payroll, but you won't ever have to visit the organisation's offices. You can carry on teaching, continue your normal life, and, according to our calculations, you won't be any

345

worse off, and will receive more or less the same as Tom brought in. Slightly less, of course, but you'll hardly notice it. You see, if he carried out a particularly long, complex, difficult mission, one requiring special skills, he was sometimes paid bonuses in cash, which, to all intents and purposes, don't exist, and, obviously, that won't happen any more.'

'I don't know what the COI or the OMT are.'

'In Spanish, they're the Consejo Oleícola Internacional and the Organización Mundial del Turismo, respectively.' He pronounced the two names in halting Spanish, especially the word 'Oleícola', putting the stress in the wrong place. 'Both organisations have their headquarters in Madrid, as I say, and they don't object at all; they've already given their consent. Lots of places are happy to help us, you see, which is a great advantage. They're eager to oblige when we ask a favour.'

That vague 'we', again and again and again. Tomás had belonged to it, and still would after his death or disappearance, after his desertion or betrayal. They gave him the benefit of the doubt, or benefit of their genuine ignorance, and I suppose that was something to be grateful for. They could have washed their hands of him, left him to his fate, because an agent who has fallen can never be used again, he becomes useless or, worse, a nuisance. But perhaps, if he hadn't fallen, he would be of enormous value when he returned.

'You mean you'll be paying me for a job I won't do?'

'That's rather an unnecessary question, Berta. Don't tell me you'd object to that. If you knew the number of people in the world who get paid for doing nothing, for being on a board of directors or a member of a trust, for attending a couple of meetings a year, for being an advisor who never advises. They're really being paid for sitting still and keeping quiet. The State happily employs such parasites. Doing so frees it from all kinds of problems, calms any discontent, and can be considered an investment. Besides, in your case, it's more than justified. It's a question of fairness. It's the least we can do when you've lost your husband, who served his country. Believe me, this is the simplest and best way to go about things.'

I once more turned my back on him and went over to the balcony. This time, I opened the balcony doors and looked out. A ghost with a statue erected to him, the soldier Luis Noval. 'You've lost your husband,' he'd said. And I had, even if he was still alive or long since dead. I would have to assume that he wouldn't come back. I'd spent more than a year and a half without him, nineteen months, I thought. I'd long been used to his absences, or to his intermittent presence, but this was different. 'I'll probably, almost certainly, never see him again,' I thought. 'Never again.' And then, unable to stop myself now, I began to weep silently, with no sobs or moans. My eyes brimmed with tears, and I immediately became aware of them wetting my cheeks, my chin and even my blouse. I couldn't hold them back. (Yes, in the disfigured street he left me, with a kind of valediction.) Tupra noticed at once, he was the kind of man who noticed everything, and instead of staying where he was, waiting for me to compose myself, as any other Englishman would have done, I heard him stand up and approach slowly, quietly, doubtless counting the steps – one, two, three, four; and five. They were warning shots, as if allowing me the opportunity to stop him with a word or a gesture, the gesture meaning 'Wait' or 'Leave me alone' or 'Stay where you are'. But I felt too helpless at that moment to reject any human companionship, regardless of who it was. I heard his light breathing on the back of my neck, then his hand on my shoulder, his right hand on my left shoulder, his arm around my neck like a false embrace from behind. I buried my face in that arm, seeking refuge or somewhere to rest, and his sleeve immediately became drenched with tears. I don't think I ruined his suit though.

VI

The years passed and then more years passed. And the years continued to pass and pass, and, first, I grew less young, and then, slightly older, I may even have begun to age, although not that much it seems, for I've always looked younger than I am, I'm fortunate in that respect and have no complaints, people tend to think I'm at least ten years younger. Perhaps I resisted moving away from the age I was when Tomás disappeared, as if any change would be akin to abandoning or betraying him.

Accepting his probable and ever more certain death did not happen instantly. It never does, not even when you've seen someone die with your own eyes and have contemplated their still, silent corpse, watched over it and buried it with all due ceremony, step by step, and when there can be no room for doubt. You have a sense – a sometimes morbidly enduring sense – that the death of a loved one, who is as much a part of your life as the air you breathe, is a kind of false alarm, a joke or a fiction, a conjecture or a product of your most fearful imaginings, which is why dreams can often confuse us: we dream of the dead person, we see him move and perhaps touch us and penetrate us, we hear him speak and laugh, and, when we wake, we think he must be hiding and will soon reappear, that he can't have disappeared for ever and that it's our waking hours that are deceiving us. It might take a while, but he's sure to come back. Our reason is not good at accepting the idea of extinction or the concept of 'for ever', a term we so blithely bandy about in ordinary conversation. We understand 'for ever' to refer to the future, but it also includes the past, and that never dies, is never entirely erased. What was will be and what existed will still exist. What happened will happen and be repeated. And if our reason has difficulty in admitting and coping with those concepts, imagine how hard it is for our emotions. Your hand instinctively slides over to the side of the bed your husband used to occupy when he was at home, and you think you can feel the body that's no longer there, feel his leg brush against yours and hear on the pillow the restless breathing of someone who is no longer breathing anywhere now. It's very hard for our emotions and our reason to understand that a being so close to us can, inexplicably, become an outcast from the universe.

But everything comes to those who wait, and insistence does finally bear fruit, and one day, absence finally loses its lingering feeling of provisionality and imposes itself as definitive and irreversible, and even dreams lose their ability to confuse us: they're confined to their sphere of mirage and unreality, and when we wake they're immediately placed between parentheses, as being an irrelevance that we can and do skip over; and the years pass for the image of the dead person too, distancing and dimming it; he grows simultaneously older and younger, older because his death grows older and is no longer a novelty or such a calamity, younger, because as we, the living, continue to mature, the dead person seems to us more ingenuous and more childish, even if that's only because of the age at which he stopped or froze, an age that we left behind with unexpected speed; and also because he doesn't know what happened afterwards. A day arrives when we start to wonder if he ever did exist, if he ever was present rather than merely past, if there was a time when we didn't need to remember him because he was there within reach, he was here. ('This is the death of air', and then he truly is dead.)

I never knew for sure. Tupra never kept his promise. 'You won't be left to speculate about it for the rest of your life,' he'd told me. 'Sooner or later, we'll hear one way or another. We won't find out everything, but enough. Then we'll tell you as much as we can about his disappearance, but not, alas, before. Not until we know for certain,' and that didn't happen.

He came to visit me once again before returning to London, having first phoned to check that I'd be alone, and on the phone he sounded exactly like that Reresby fellow I'd spoken to years before, but again I didn't ponder the similarity; perhaps the Foreign Office or MI6 gave them all courses on how to deal with anxious family members. On that second visit, two days later, 'I succumbed', as they used to say of women in novels a couple of centuries ago, but never of men. This wasn't so very strange, or unusual: I'd been alone for a year and a half, from the morning of 4 April 1982, and it was now November 1983, far too long a time to be without any human warmth, something that some of us really miss, while others don't need it and can happily live without. I'd found him attractive right from the start, despite the pretentious suit he was wearing and that slightly repellent quality, but what at first repels can end up attracting, after a swift moment of adjustment or approval, once you've made up your mind. I had felt unconsciously tempted (that is, I'd postponed the temptation) even in the midst of my grief and my imprisoned, then liberated, tears, my shock; and the greater your grief or shock, the greater your state of desolation and numbness and abandonment, the lower your defences and the fewer your qualms; professional seducers know this well and are always on the lookout for misfortunes. Tomás's absences had, over the years, had a cumulative effect, and each absence weighed more heavily on me and fed my resentment, and perhaps there was no need now to keep Tupra at bay. Tomás's current absence bore all the signs of being definitive or, at least, *sine die*. And besides, he would never know. Tupra had put his arm about my neck the previous day, had placed his hand on my shoulder in a gesture of affection for which I was grateful, and I'd buried my face in his sleeve and smelled his smell, there had been physical contact, which is always the first step, even if it appears to be unimportant and asexual, merely a gesture of consolation and solace, somewhere to bury our face or simply keep us on our feet.

That one morning of intimacy gave me licence, if you like, not to wait passively and eternally, but to call him in London now and then and ask if there was any news of Tomás, if they'd found out anything, even if it wasn't yet 'enough' for him to phone and tell me. When he could or when he was there (I wasn't always put straight through to him, he was often away and I only had his work number), he would speak to me with a courtesy tinged with impatience, which I could sense in the ever wearier, ever more circumspect way he answered my questions. He treated me as you might treat someone with whom you happen to have incurred a moral debt, to whom you're bound perhaps only by conscience: deferentially and solicitously, but warily, and, needless to say, showing no sign of wanting to see me again or to repeat that carnal experience. Had he suggested it, I might have travelled to London – might. He must be one of those men for whom once is enough (perhaps the kind who likes to mentally tick off each new conquest, and once that's done, there's no incentive to do it again), and although such men don't regret or attempt to erase the experience, they do their best not to let it become a kind of safe-conduct pass to gain access to them or to any preferential treatment. In Madrid, I'd asked him if he was married, and he'd left the question hanging in the air without answering it, and I'd innocently taken this to mean 'Yes'. Some men pretend to be married so as to avoid being hassled by any occasional lovers.

'No, Berta, there's no news, absolutely nothing. If there had been, I'd have phoned you. It's as if the earth had swallowed him up, an earth that remains exasperatingly silent. We still don't know what's become of him.'

Then, invariably, I would ask further:

'And what does that indicate? How would you interpret that? Does it increase the likelihood that he's dead or that he's still alive somewhere? And if he is dead, he would have been killed, wouldn't he? Would his death have been a violent one? Can't you tell me where he was? Time has passed, and I'd like at least to know which piece of earth has swallowed him up. And if he suffered a lot or not at all.'

And he would answer, with variations:

'I won't lie to you, the more time passes, the more likely it is that he's dead. But, given that we know nothing, he might have had an accident or a heart attack, anything is possible. And, no, I still can't tell you where he was last seen, where he disappeared. Besides, we can't be absolutely sure. Tomás moved around a lot, but we didn't always know exactly when he did so, not beforehand. That depended on a number of factors. If many more months go by with no news, we'll publish an official version with a view to having him declared officially dead. The internal version, ours, the one we're using here, is that he disappeared in Buenos Aires in May 1982. Just for convenience's sake. As I said, it's easier to get the powers that be to issue a death certificate *in absentia* if someone disappeared during a war, in a shipwreck, a plane crash or some other disaster. On a spy mission in his case. When that version is made official, though, when his parents and so on have accepted it, you yourself mustn't believe it.

355

I'll tell you the true version, if we ever find out.' And the next time we spoke, that is, when I phoned him again at the risk of being a pest, he would patiently tell me the same thing, because there was never any news. But he added: 'I'm more pessimistic now. I'm beginning to think that we're always going to be left in the dark as to what happened. That's why, contrary to what I've recommended before, it might help you to believe the official version too, if you want. At least then you'd have a story, however incomplete or vacuous, but a story you could tell other people and tell yourself. You'll need to have some explanation to offer your children when they're older.' He paused. 'Eventually, I mean. A story they can remember. There may never be another one, we may never know anything more.'

And there was no other story, there was nothing, absolutely nothing, and, after a certain point, I stopped bothering Tupra, it was no use, and he, too, disappeared from my life, in his case very easily. The bureaucratic wheels moved at their usual leisurely pace, and, after the necessary time had passed, Tomás Nevinson was declared officially dead, in Spain and in England and, I assumed, in any other country too; and I became a widow and my children became fatherless, I mean our children, but he'd been so little present in their brief existences that I often forgot they were also his children. The children were always with me and belonged to me, just me.

I immediately began to receive the monthly, tax-free salary from the OMT that Tupra had proposed and arranged for me, so that I wouldn't have to go without while I waited for the declaration of death *in absentia* and for the slow arrival of 1989 and 1990, along with the inheritance due to my children and myself. In England, I didn't even have to wait for the obligatory seven years to pass, they allowed for exceptions – that is, a reduction in the term – depending on the circumstances and the probability of death, which, in Tomás's case, was very high: officially, he'd disappeared in a war scenario, even though, over time, the Falklands conflict had come to be seen as only a miniature war; but wars large and small produce corpses, although those who die in the smaller wars are granted less importance and are less likely to be remembered. And so once he'd been declared legally dead, the British government assigned me a widow's pension, as the widow of an employee of the embassy in Madrid, what they call a civil servant. Since I was already being paid that other undeserved salary plus what I earned at the university, where I was now a permanent member of staff, that additional sum helped me keep my resolution not to touch Tomás's money, at least not the money he'd kept in his English account, which was doubtless from some unofficial or obscure source, perhaps given to him in person by Tupra himself once he'd completed a mission, a deception, an infiltration, an abomination.

There is, almost everywhere, an element of superstition about bodies: until they turn up, no one dares consider them to be cadavers, not entirely. Especially if there's no oral or written evidence from whoever saw them die, and no one had seen Tomás die. I'd now read *Colonel Chabert*, after Tupra had mentioned it, and if Tomás did one day rise from the dead, I didn't want the same thing to happen to him as happened to that poor colonel, whose survival was denied even by his own wife, who was horrified at his resurrection, having since married a count and had children by that second husband who was richer, higher up the social scale and promised her a far better future; that colonel with the huge scar on his head from a sword blow to the skull, who could make her a bigamist and her children bastards; whom she had stripped of his fortune, and now, necessarily and logically, of his identity too; whom she accused of being an impostor, and who would end up utterly disillusioned and mad in an asylum, or else having forgotten everything, the state that best befits the living (or the uninterrupted living), his stubborn persistence abandoned at last. As I say, that was pure superstition. The truth is that I didn't really believe Tomás would come back, and, after all, Balzac's novella was a fiction.

This was not the case with the subject matter of a French film I saw shortly afterwards and that enjoyed great popularity, *The Return of Martin Guerre*. It was made in 1981 or 1982, but I probably only saw it in 1984, when I finally overcame my reluctance and got up the courage to go; several people had spoken to me about it and its subject matter filled me with terror. It was based on a true story, which happened in the south of France, very close to the Spanish border, in the sixteenth century, and also – as I found out later – on an excellent novel published in 1941, *The Wife of Martin Guerre*, written by Janet Lewis, an American writer I'd never heard of until then (despite my classes and my teaching specialism). The trials that ensued were so famous in their day that the then young Montaigne travelled to Rieux or Toulouse to attend the court sessions, to which he referred in one of his *Essays*. It told of the sudden disappearance of a well-off husband in the provinces, who left one day with no explanation, and then, after several years, came back – or, rather, a man returned who not only closely resembled him, but also had a detailed knowledge of Martin Guerre's past, and so must have been him. He was accepted as such by his sisters, his uncle, now head of the family, and also by his wife, Bertrande de Rols, to use her maiden name, who went on to have a second child by him, having had her first child by Martin before his mysterious departure. I'm not sure now whether all this is in the film, the novel of forty years before or a later book of 'micro-history' by a professor at Princeton, which I also took the trouble to read once the threshold of fear had been crossed and my curiosity aroused. Probably all three did, for none of them departed from the fundamental facts, none of them departed from the truth. After her initial reaction of joy and welcome (a reaction that lasted a long time), doubt and remorse began gradually to eat away at Bertrande, and she ended up convinced that this second Martin was an impostor, who had led her to commit adultery (or, put in the ugliest of terms, had raped her by dint of deception), to conceive and give birth to an illegitimate child and to hand over her absent husband's money to an adventurer, a swindler. Hence the denunciation and the trials, the first one in the small town of Rieux and the definitive one in Toulouse. The shocking, paradoxical aspect of the case was that the supposed impostor was kinder and more affectionate, more benevolent and harder-working than the surly, awkward, discontented young man who had abandoned her all those years before. And, yes, that story was real, it had actually happened, for alongside those artistic reconstructions or reworkings, there were chronicles from the period and even the proceedings from one of the trials; there was documentation. The sixteenth century, though, was so long ago that it was just as unreal as the story imagined by Balzac. People's memories were doubtless vaguer then, and it would have been harder to recognise someone's face, skin or smell.

And so the years passed and more years passed, and with each month that went by, I felt Tomás was even more dead, both before and after the certificates that condemned him to be dead in the eyes of the world, that confirmed his death. But you should never underestimate what you see and read and hear. We soon forget the twists and turns, let alone the details, of any story, whether real or fictional, which tend to become flattened out beneath the sheer weight of subsequent layers of time. And yet, whatever we're told remains lurking in the nooks and crannies, on the edges and boundaries of our imagination. It forms part of our knowledge and, therefore, of what's possible. And although I was sure Tomás wouldn't reappear, either like Chabert or like Martin Guerre, I couldn't help fantasising about that in a tenuous, timid way, especially when I was most alone. And I would again remember that line: 'as death resembles life, being between two lives', as I waited for my second life to begin. And I would also recite, softly or to myself, those lines so appropriate to dreams born of desperation: 'We are born with the dead: see, they return, and bring us with them.'

I didn't remain still during all those years, I didn't fall into depression or remain paralysed. I occasionally flirted with despair, but never out of choice, only because it sometimes attacks without warning; I never immersed myself in it, though, nor did it occur to me to remain faithful to someone who was never going to come back. It didn't take long for me to consider myself to all intents and purposes a widow; indeed, I felt like a widow. I drove away the mist, raised my eyes from the ground and looked around me, ready to remake my life, as people say of someone who wants to find a new partner after a loss or a bad experience, after an unhappy or imprisoning marriage, dull or tormenting or oppressive. This wasn't the case with me. I'd been settled and contented from the start, but my husband had behaved like a ghost, or like Dr Jekyll, with too large a dose of gloom and anguish, of a strange poison accumulated when he was far from me, with farewells repeated over and over until the final farewell. I would not allow my bed to become 'a woeful bed', or if it did occasionally become one, it was not of my choosing. A few men visited it, with Tupra being the first and earliest example on that one occasion, and he could have visited more often, had he not been so far away – and I've no idea if he deliberately chose to keep a distance or if it just happened – and had he not been so shrouded in what I sensed was secrecy and darkness. None of those men lasted very long, none of them, for one reason or another, stayed – who knows why – none of them replaced Tomás. A stupid colleague from university, a friend of a friend who proved too devoted and adoring, my children's paediatrician, and an Englishman from the embassy where Tomás had worked; I fully intended each of them to last, but none of them did last very long, if by 'long' we mean a year or more. I never got that far, normally it was just a few months, and the months end and succeed each other with great rapidity, both the months spent alone and those that hurt and drag and seem as if they'll never end – they, too, escape us and immediately become the past.

One of those men fled as soon as I became slightly affectionate and sentimental: he took fright, thinking I was needy and on the hunt, if I can put it like that; and he was terrified of my children, fearing he would have to take them on as well if he stayed too long by my side, even if only out of habit; and as soon as he had satisfied, or semi-satisfied, his sexual desire, he went from greeting me with enthusiasm to merely nodding when we passed each other in the corridor at the university. Idiot. Another man quickly outstayed his welcome, he was one of those silent admirers who can't believe his luck when someone suddenly takes an interest in him, and he finds himself in that longed-for, unattainable place. Such men become so afraid of losing this miracle that they grow oversensitive and possessive, expecting to be dumped at any moment, knowing how undeserving they are and living in a state of constant trepidation, seeing in everything signs that the other person has had enough and that the end is nigh. And thus, of course, they hasten it on, for no one can bear the faint-hearted, the overly insecure or the overly keen, those who have a sense of having gained access to a privileged position, to be living in a dream. I didn't want to be a dream, nor to feel myself, at all times, the object of his devoted gaze, even in the most ordinary or – if

I'd let him – banal situations. I let him go tactfully and kindly, he hadn't done anything very serious, apart from being cloying and clinging and having sex with me nervously and ceremoniously, as if I were made of cut glass or, worse, were some kind of divinity.

My children's paediatrician was a jolly, flattering man, who immediately inspired confidence: your children, you felt, were in good hands, and it was easy enough for me to transfer that feeling of confidence to myself, for there are times when one needs at least a semblance of protection. Unlike the idolater, he was easy-going and funny and, probably, a womaniser, because, more than once, I had the distinct impression that I was not the only mother of his patients with whom he'd established that cosy connection, with home visits lasting slightly longer than usual and concluding with a reward in kind, a swift, discreet reward (we never took off our clothes), swift enough for the children not to wonder where we were. They knew when he was leaving the house (I suppose he reckoned it was worth his while to make such home visits), because before he left, he always looked in again at whichever child was ill, to say goodbye with a joke or an improvised bit of doggerel (children love rhymes) and to offer reassurance. He was too elusive a man to stay anywhere for long. He had recently divorced and was keen to enjoy a period of absolute freedom. I was the one who decided to stop those brief encounters, because, as I said, I aspired to a little stability. In the end, I had to ask him to recommend a colleague, which was the only way of breaking that particular vicious circle, because whenever he visited, I would have found it hard to say 'No' to him, with his phonendoscope around his neck and his medical bag. He was disappointed, of course, but understood and accepted my decision. 'If you change your mind,' he said, 'I'm at your disposal. At any time of day or night, with a sick child or without.'

As for the Englishman, he lasted longer than any of them, a whole eleven months. He was a quiet, rather self-contained type, respectful and solicitous, but not unbearably so; he wasn't particularly interesting and not a great talker, and yet he had a strange capacity to communicate sexual passion and to make me forget, momentarily, what I'd been through, and almost to forget what had been, to make each time like the very first time. Not just with him, but in general, as if I'd gone back to the days before anyone had entered me. The problem is that, outside that terrain, he had precisely the opposite effect on me: his job was the same as Tomás's job. In fact, he had taken over his post at the embassy, a post that, in Tomás's case, had been purely nominal, because he had been away so much and had neglected his duties there in the interests of some higher service. This other Englishman did not combine both jobs, and I was sure he hadn't replaced Tomás on that other front, presumably because he didn't have the right personality or the necessary gifts, and so wouldn't have been of great use (he even struggled to learn Spanish, another reason not to recruit him). Nevertheless, he was occasionally called on to travel to London and to other places, and each time he told me he was going on one of these trips, each time I said goodbye to him – even if it was only for a weekend – it revived in me memories of all my countless farewells to Tomás when he set off to some obscure destination and with no known return date, both equally swathed in mist before and in the silence of the non-existent afterwards. This didn't help me to bury Tomás. There hadn't been nor would there ever be a body, but I needed at least to bury him in my imagination. The only way of doing this was to stop remembering, to settle into a way of life so different that it would never be troubled by the inconclusive, the lost, the before. The paediatrician could possibly have served this purpose, if he hadn't been like a strong gust of wind that slaps you in the face and then leaves. He did, however, inhabit an entirely different world. The Englishman was a constant reminder of my past life and would be of no help in shaking off the memory of Tomás. Much to my body's chagrin, I gradually distanced myself from him, gradually let him go. And so I never saw the dust in the air suspended, which, according to the poem, marks the place where a story ended.

To my parents, had they known, this would have seemed like a lot of men, especially if I'd listed them as I just have, but there weren't that many of them really, and I should know. They paraded past over the years, and there were infinitely more solitary days than days spent in company, and even more solitary nights, the paediatrician, for example, always left fairly abruptly, although the others did stay the night, or else I would go and sleep in their bed or in the bed of some hotel outside Madrid (in El Escorial, Ávila or Segovia, Aranjuez or Alcalá), but not that often, only when I could leave the kids with my or Tomás's parents, saying I had a congress to attend or a symposium for specialists in my field. These were not jolly little escapes, they were tinged with a sense of the temporary, the exceptional, and the artificial, as if we were lovers who decide occasionally to play at being lovers, almost out of duty, and to leave the city, spend the day together with no real idea as to what we should do except wander about, eat and make the most of the hotel room, to sleep together, although with no real desire to rub sleepily up against that unaccustomed and possibly invasive and bothersome body, and really just waiting for the weekend to be over so that we could return to normality and to Madrid.

And each time an affair failed or dribbled away into nothing, or when it was clear that it was going nowhere, the phantom – or was it just my fantasy? – of Tomás gained or regained strength. There's nothing strange about that, it's normal: if someone in whom we've put our trust fails us, we tend to seek refuge in what can no longer fail us because its time for failing has passed. And it doesn't even matter if, in its day, it failed disastrously, was perplexing and discouraging, brought us sorrow and frustration and incomprehension, and kept us in a permanent state of dissatisfaction. What is lost and in the past is always more comfortable than the lukewarm present and the improbable future. Any damage it caused moves off into the distance and takes on an unreal quality. What happened is no longer a threat, no longer fills us with anxiety or with the worst kind of despair – the anticipated variety. It fills us with sadness, yes, but not with fear, and fears, once appeased, once they have been and gone, can provide refuge or shelter precisely because they will not come again.

And instinctively, or, if you like, irrationally (but who doesn't sometimes resort to irrationality), after each failure, I would cling to that last doubt: no body had been found nor had I been given a definitive account of his death, and Tupra's initial predictions had proved wrong: 'You won't be left to speculate about it for the rest of your life, I promise.' The rest of my life might go on for a long time yet, but the years were passing, and I was still speculating. Not continually, but now and then, especially after some new disappointment in love. Then I would turn to his other words, the ones intended to save me from absolute pessimism and to soften the blow: 'Tom could walk through that door tomorrow, I wouldn't exclude that as a possibility either.' One tomorrow is succeeded by another, and then another, which is both good and bad: good because it encourages us to wake up and get out of bed; bad because it paralyses us and tempts us to spend our time waiting for each day to end. I even thought about his self-serving words of advice and had to acknowledge that I had been preceded by millions of women, that my case was not exceptional: I thought about the wives of those sailors who took years to return home, about the wives of soldiers who had deserted and didn't dare come back; the wives of prisoners and kidnap victims, the wives of men who were shipwrecked or the wives of lost explorers. History is full of women who sit and wait, who gaze out at the horizon every day at dusk, trying to make out a familiar figure, and who say precisely this: 'Not today, no, not today, but perhaps tomorrow, tomorrow.'

Tupra had been right about one thing: something had told those women whether they should keep hoping or should abandon hope altogether – need, perhaps, or a lack of need, or a feeling that they'd had enough, or perhaps a growing sense of detachment from or resentment towards the disappeared husband for having left like that and thus exposed himself to danger, not just like Ulysses, but like all those men who had set sail for Troy and besieged that city for years, thus signalling the start of one of literature's and real life's long absences (for only what we're told, what succeeds in being told, exists). 'So you forget when you want to forget.' And he had been right, too, when he said: 'Obviously, it's a long process, it's not like an arrow heading straight for the bullseye, there are advances and retreats and times when it wanders off down side streets.' And that was so true: whenever I grew distracted or became excited about a project, whenever some promising lover appeared, the arrow of forgetting took on a new potency and speed and seemed as if it would, unstoppably, hit the target. The memory of Tomás would fade, and resentment would grow inside me: 'Why did he choose that absurd existence, why did he opt for a double life that would take him away from me, until he became an autumn leaf that trembled and then fell?' Then I would reject him, loathe him, curse him. Then I would bury him. The arrow would stray off course as soon as the lover ceased to be promising and I would again feel alone; I would turn around and retrace my steps and set off along the other path, that of memory, nostalgia, patience and baseless hope. And I would be assailed by that final question: 'What if he isn't dead? What if he reappears one day because he's run out of hiding places and doesn't know where to go? Will he only return then, when he doesn't know where else to go?' At times like that, I would struggle to recall his face and discover, to my consternation, that the harder I tried, the vaguer his face became, and the more it eluded and resisted me, so that I had to resort to looking at photos to see his features with any clarity, the deceptive clarity of something caught in a particular light, at a particular angle and a particular moment. As soon as I closed the album, I would again be incapable of imagining him, and nothing exists without the imagination. Even when things are happening and are present, they, too, require the imagination, because it's the only thing that highlights certain events and teaches us to distinguish, while they are happening, the memorable from the unmemorable.

Out of long habit, or enduring melancholy, I would go into his study every day and look around. That was where he used to work when he was at home, where he made his notes and sketches or prepared reports or wrote things he never asked me to read; and where, with the door closed, he held phone conversations in English. Not that he used the room a lot, but he was the only one to do so. I couldn't bring myself to empty or dismantle it, and I had kept it exactly as it was the last day he was here, 3 April 1982. How remote that date sounded in 1987, 1988 or 1989 and later still – for so many years had passed already – far more remote than my memory of that date, than our actual farewell. I would give the office a peremptory tidy, remove the non-existent dust, look at the globe and wonder where in the world Tomás had stopped, then give the globe a flick to set it turning. And every morning, when I was choosing what to wear, I would see, out of the corner of my eye, his clothes hanging in the shared wardrobe in our bedroom. I'd felt incapable of throwing those out too. If I ever stopped to smell his clothes or touch them, I would, for a moment, feel quite drunk on sadness; it was like an exhalation, even though nothing smelled of him any more. If I noticed a small stain on a jacket, I would think I should take it to the dry-cleaners, only immediately to dismiss the idea, asking myself: 'Whatever for?' And if I noticed any creases, I would imagine that they reflected the way he used to move or sit; and any bulges or sagging pockets seemed to me like traces of his wallet, his keys, his pack of cigarettes, his lighter or his glasses case, for he rarely wore his glasses. Indeed, I discovered one day that they were fake, not prescription glasses at all, and I found three more pairs in a drawer in his desk, all with very different frames and the same innocent lenses, because faces do change depending on what you wear on them, and it occurred to me that these must have been elements of different disguises.

And sometimes I would sit thinking or even address him in my thoughts: 'How little I knew about you. I don't know the you in that other half of your life at all, which was perhaps the half you valued more. I don't know the faraway you, the one that went off on journeys or childish missions, and which doubtless led you to a violent death. How many hardships did you suffer that you could so easily have avoided? How much fear did you feel? How many wicked deeds did you commit, and how many people would willingly have fallen like lead upon your soul and pierced you with a sharp blade? How many watchful, sleepless nights did you spend, how many nightmares like a knee pressed into your chest, no, what am I saying, like the body of some large, dead animal – a horse, a bull – that no one could move alone? How many women loved you and how many did you deceive and disappoint? How many secrets did you pluck from those who came to trust you? How many deaths did you cause, deaths that the dead were not expecting and would have met with incredulity? What a very devious trade yours was, however much good you may have achieved with it. I know nothing about that and never will, since you won't be coming back. And even if you did come back, I don't suppose you'd tell me anything anyway. Nor where you've been all these years nor what happened to you, why you couldn't or didn't want to return, or give any signs of life, even if only to phone me and say: "I'm alive. Wait for me." I don't know why I stayed with you nor why I still haven't entirely left, when you're no longer here, neither here nor anywhere else. Your life stopped and mine continued walking, but in a rather meaningless, directionless way, or else I've contented myself with whatever direction my children, your children, point me in – they're my compass – the children you didn't know and never will. Whenever I've tried to find a direction of my own, separate from theirs and yours, the path has become blocked at some point or I left it of my own accord. Yes, I look at your empty suits and it occurs to me that if you were here and I could look at you, you would seem equally empty, complete with sagging pockets and bulges and stains and creases, you yourself would be a hollow space. Absence and silence; or, at most, the repetition of a line like the illegible inscription on a snow-covered stone. At most, a whisper in my ear that I won't understand. I've known you since we were both adolescents. And, since then, I have continued stubbornly to love you. But afterwards, in the long afterwards that I already trail along behind me and that still awaits me, how little I knew about you.'

In the space of just eleven months, both my parents died, and so did Tomás's mother, Miss Mercedes – as her students at the British Institute used to call her. It was as if they'd agreed to mark the end of a story, the end of a generation, and the only one to miss this rendez-vous was Jack Nevinson, who was left very alone and sad. His two daughters and his other son had lived away from Madrid for a long time. One of my sisters-in-law came to spend a couple of weeks here, to keep her father company for the first few days, but her home, her husband and her little girl were all in Barcelona, and she soon had to get back to them. The other daughter, who worked as a civil servant in Brussels, only came for the funeral, and her brother, Jorge, didn't even turn up for that, using distance and work commitments as an excuse: he'd never shown any interest in literature or diplomacy, and had, for years, been running a sanitation company in Canada. He had long since cast off the family, and rarely thought it worth his while to cross the Atlantic, not even for his mother's funeral. He told one sister over the phone: 'After all, it won't make any difference to Mum if I'm there or not, so don't give me that stuff about "she would have wanted the four of us to be there to say goodbye to her". She won't know anything about it, and, besides, Tom won't be there either. And my grief will be no less deeply felt in Montreal.' He was known as George there.

I had the feeling that, without his wife, Jack must, for the first time, have asked himself what the hell he was doing in a foreign country whose language he had never quite mastered, and where there was nothing to keep him any more, neither love nor work. He would still sometimes drop in at the British Council or the embassy, but hardly anyone there knew him now and the staff were not as loyal as they once had been. Returning to England, however, wasn't an option: the country would have needed to stop changing or he would have needed to stop getting older, and neither of those things ever stop, in any age or any place. We usurp the country we're unwittingly born into, and are usurped, in turn, by the adults or the old people we unwittingly become.

Guillermo and Elisa and I became, perhaps, his mainstays, the ones who provided him with company and some justification for staying in Madrid: his grandchildren, who had been fatherless almost since they were born, and his daughter-in-law, who was officially a widow and now an orphan. In his shy, modest way, he had always tried to make up for Tomás's absence from the children's lives, and, after our latest losses, he discreetly offered himself as a father to me as well. In the circumstances, he saw me as more of a daughter than his real daughters, and Guillermo and Elisa were his favourite grandchildren because he saw them most often and because they were the legacy of the son who had died doing his duty, and whom he hadn't been able to bury or to mourn openly and finally. (Another of the inconvenient things about those who leave behind no body, no trace, is that grief is gradual and happens in stages, but it's never complete, and there can be no real mourning if you advance through the process hesitantly and in instalments.) But we still weren't really part of his day-to-day life, although ever since Miss Mercedes had died, and he was left alone in the family apartment in Calle Jenner, I would phone him every day before I went off to the university or sat down to work at home, just to see how he was. It would have been indelicate to make this any more explicit, for, put bluntly, I was checking to see that he had woken up and hadn't died in the night, in his silence and solitude. There were no mobile phones then, but there were answering machines. If he didn't pick up the phone, I would leave him a message urging him to get back to me, and I wouldn't rest easy until he had done so.

Even though I wasn't really expecting Tomás to turn up for his mother's funeral, the fact that he didn't was another nail in his imaginary coffin. He was, in his fashion, very close to her (although he was more protective of his father, and had Jack been the one to die, Tomás's coffin would have been nailed even more tightly shut), and the news was made as public as possible. Jack paid for a couple of death notices in the Spanish press and another in the British press, and, a few days later, a colleague of his in England managed to persuade a newspaper to publish a brief obituary or note, full of simple, affectionate praise. If Tomás was still alive, of course, and living in some remote country, it would have been almost impossible for him to know any of this.

It was after hammering in that nail that I began a foolish, pointless enterprise: to find the young man – although he would no longer be so very young – with whom I'd had sex for the first time, with whom I'd made my debut, so to speak. It had all been pure chance and had never gone any further. I'd met him in the street in 1969, when I wasn't yet eighteen, as I was escaping from the *grises* at a student demonstration in which he didn't even take part. He'd helped me escape from a mounted policeman, had protected me and subdued both man and beast, then taken me back to his apartment, where he'd cleaned and dressed a cut to my knee, and, in doing so, had touched

375

my thigh, first accidentally (hands that heal cannot really avoid touching the person being healed), then intentionally. He was a banderillero who lived near Plaza de Las Ventas and his name was Esteban Yanes, and I've never really understood how it all happened. It was so unpremeditated that I've always put it down to the lax sexual mores of the time, to my state of shock after the incident with the policeman and to a high degree of curiosity on my part. As well as feeling a powerful, primitive attraction, of course. He had a mane of black hair, blue or brown, almost plum-coloured eyes, the thick, dark eyebrows of a southerner, enviably perfect teeth, and a calm, frank smile. Tomás had already begun his string of absences, studying at Oxford and coming back in the vacations, and little did I know that this coming and going would continue indefinitely, that it would become our way of being together: together and separate at the same time, until separation won out.

I hadn't given the banderillero my phone number and he hadn't given me his. Neither of us made any attempt to find each other; the very brief time we spent together must have been enough for us to realise how little we had in common, and I had no intention of conducting a parallel relationship, because Tomás's absence then was only a temporary thing, and I was determined, sooner or later, to become Berta Isla de Nevinson. Over the years, though, I often thought of Esteban Yanes, both when I was alone and when accompanied. It was a pleasant memory, nice, if that's an appropriate adjective to use, even if only because it belonged to a carefree, spontaneous, capricious, frivolous time in my life. A time that was clear and unclouded, before Tomás had obliged me to see the world cut in two and as though blind in one eye. It was a small memory-cum-refuge, if you like, and I didn't have too many of those. I'd known Tomás for so long that only my childhood memories remained uncontaminated by his lack of transparency. I did know where Yanes used to live, and I would still recognise the street door even though twenty years had passed since that day. What seemed unlikely, though, was that he would still be living in that well-furnished apartment, full of photos and posters from the world of bullfighting, and loads of books, for he was clearly an avid, if undisciplined reader, or so he had told me or I had inferred.

I don't quite know what took me back there. I suppose it was my eagerness not to remain still, not to be definitively widowed, not yet, or perhaps a desire to find out if, as a young woman, I had left some mark on his memory. (When you exist in a void, you need to fill it up somehow, even if that means returning to the diffuse, insignificant past.) It was ridiculous to think anything would come of that re-encounter, if it happened. Yanes was probably married and with a string of kids, or else would have moved to another city, or abandoned the profession altogether: making the rounds of the bullrings when you're twenty-something is quite different from doing so when you're in your forties. When I arrived in the street, I was immediately beset by doubts. At the time, I hadn't noticed the number of the building, and there were two very similar street doors, right next to each other. I went into the one that seemed more familiar and asked the female porter for 'Don Esteban Yanes', that's how I gave his name. 'Yanes, you say. No, there's no Yanes here,' she said brusquely. I went to the next building and asked the same question, without much hope of success. To my surprise, the porter there said: 'Don Esteban's away at the moment and won't be back until next month, although you never quite know with him. He might be away for longer.' 'Would you mind giving him a note from me when he comes back?' 'Yes, of course, I'll leave it in his postbox along with his other mail.' I hadn't foreseen having to write a note, and would have to go to a café to do so, then buy an envelope from a local stationer's, because I wouldn't want anyone else to read what I'd written – not for any particular reason, just out of habit. I first wanted to make sure that this wasn't a mere coincidence. 'We are talking about the matador, aren't we?' The man looked at me rather condescendingly. 'A matador? Well, Don Esteban's certainly in the bullfighting world, but he's not a matador. You must mean manager.' 'Yes, that's what I meant. A Freudian slip, sorry.' He looked at me rather dubiously, as if I'd wanted to make him feel small by using a term he didn't know. 'I'll go away and write him a note and bring it back,' I added. 'Thanks very much.' And I decided I would give him a tip when I returned.

This, more or less, is what I wrote to Yanes: 'Dear Esteban Yanes, You probably don't remember me. My name's Berta Isla, and twenty years ago, you saved me from a galloping horse and a policeman's truncheon, near Plaza de Manuel Becerra. Afterwards, you took me to your apartment and dressed a cut on my knee.' I thought it best not to mention what happened afterwards, some people prefer not to be reminded of such youthful escapades. 'The porter in your building says you won't be back in Madrid for a while. I happened to be in the area, and I remembered that day and you. It would be great to see you again and catch up, if you'd like to, that is, and if you have time to spare for an acquaintance you're barely acquainted with. Here's my phone number if you want to call me. I hope life has treated you well. It seems like a whole lifetime since we last met, which was, in fact, the only time we met. Best wishes, Berta Isla.' I went back to the apartment building and gave the porter the envelope and a five-hundred-peseta tip, not bad for doing very little, but my way of reassuring myself that he wouldn't throw the envelope away or tear it up, out of spite or just for the hell of it. And when I got home, I prepared myself for a long wait, but I was so used to long waits that, two days later, I'd completely forgotten about it.

That's why Esteban Yanes's phone call almost a month later caught me completely off guard. 'Of course I remember you,' he said. 'How could I forget? I've often regretted not having asked you for your number that night. Not that I would have pestered you or anything. But now that you've taken the first step, sweetheart, it would be great to meet up. Just say a time and a place and I'll be there with drasticity.' I was amused to find that he still used that non-existent word, which had caught my ear when he'd used it twenty years ago. The word 'sweetheart', though, jarred somewhat, he had been so proper then, even in our most intimate moments. 'Your porter told me that you're a very important man now,' I said. 'A manager, no less. To the uninitiated that conjures up an image of fat cigars, wads of notes and oodles of influence.' He laughed: 'No, not me. I'm just managing a few novices, no one special. Of course, if one of them were to make it big, then I'd be rolling in it, fingers crossed, eh, love.' Again that form of address grated on me, he had grown coarser. 'So you left the banderillas behind, did you?' I asked. 'Oh, a long way behind. You need to be very quick on your feet for that game.' I suggested we meet for coffee in one of the cafés in Plaza de Oriente. I couldn't be bothered to go over to his part of town again, an area I'd never liked and to which I'd only gone back once since that January in 1969, to talk to the people at Ediciones Siruela about possibly publishing an anthology of strange, fantastic English tales, a project that never came to anything. They had their offices in Plaza de Manuel Becerra itself, which was a much more interesting place than you'd expect in that otherwise soulless district. Anyway, Esteban Yanes sounded very nice, and I enjoyed imagining his big African smile. It would be fun to see him again after all that time, and who knows, afterwards we might meet up occasionally and become friends. Even if the memory is as tenuous as a static image or a painting seen once in a foreign art gallery, you never forget someone you had sex with. And even if that person turned out to be disappointing or unbearable, you still feel for them something akin to involuntary affection or loyalty. Esteban Yanes hadn't had time to become disappointing or unbearable, he was still intact.

On the appointed afternoon, though, I was overcome by a sudden sense of anticipated regret, if such a thing exists, a feeling of apprehension. I was afraid Yanes wouldn't recognise me or that I wouldn't recognise him. I was afraid, above all, that he might be disappointed, because we're never fully aware of how much we ourselves change over two decades, and a fresh, young student is quite different from a woman nearing forty, with two children clamouring for her attention, children she has to bring up alone, a woman who has led a life of uncertainty and grief and loss (the worst, most paralysing kind of loss, loss with no closure or corroboration). Mentally, I slightly shrank back from the encounter. I tried on several outfits, but none of them looked right. I experimented with various styles of make-up, some of which I found too prim and others too over the top. I viewed myself in the mirror from every angle, but none offered me a flattering aspect, which isn't how I felt most days; I still thought I looked quite good, and didn't usually feel insecure, at least not about my physical appearance.

I realised that, with a pair of binoculars, I could see the people sitting outside the café, there were quite a few, enjoying the early-May warmth. And so, five minutes before the agreed hour, I started spying from the balcony. I waited and waited. I didn't see anyone who could have been him, the man I remembered as if in an old painting, and, at first, it didn't occur to me that he could be the rather fat chap who arrived on the dot and looked all around him before taking a seat. He was wearing a broad-brimmed hat, rather unusual at the time, old-fashioned. The banderillero had been wearing a hat when I met him in 1969; I'd forgotten that, but now it came back to me; then, the brim had been too narrow. I'd been rather disparaging about the hat, and he'd immediately thrown it in a rubbish bin, saying something along the lines of: 'Well, if you don't like it, there's nothing more to be said.' And even then, he'd struck me as old-fashioned, not just because of the hat, but because of his dapper appearance, his tie, his long overcoat.

The man before me now was wearing a cream-coloured suit, with a jacket that didn't quite meet over his possibly late-onset plumpness, its one buttoned-up button clearly under considerable strain. Before sitting down at one of the tables, he undid the button and the jacket fell open to reveal a long tie, which he perhaps hoped might conceal his voluminous belly; the tie was so long that it hung down over the top of his trousers. 'That can't be him,' I thought. 'He can't have changed that much. But then twenty years is a long time, and you never know, the years can be very cruel.' He removed his hat for a moment (it matched his suit, but while his clothes were of the highest quality, they didn't flatter him in the least), took a handkerchief from his pocket and dabbed not only at his forehead and temples but at his completely bald head, which was now fully revealed. 'It can't be him,' I thought, 'he had really thick hair, but it's easy enough to lose your hair in only a short time, and you can go grey in a matter of days if you suffer great pain or shock, and twenty years allows ample time for all that to happen, for general deterioration or for some unthinkable, unfortunate evolution. Some people age, but remain perfectly recognisable until the end of their days, and others suddenly become someone else, as if another person had stolen their face and body; obesity and baldness in men can perform such miracles or, rather, metamorphoses.' If he was the banderillero, if he was the manager of novice bullfighters, I really didn't feel like going downstairs to see and talk to him. He bore no resemblance at all to the handsome young man I remembered and about whom I had often thought, with a vague feeling of nostalgia, as if seeking refuge in that memory. What would I have to say to that fat, bald stranger, whose work didn't interest me in the least and about which I knew nothing and didn't want to know anything? And I remembered a sentence I'd read in a book by a contemporary writer called Pombo: 'Going back is the very worst infidelity.' Yes, he was probably quite right. If that man was the banderillero with whom I'd gone to bed in my early youth, he'd just ruined a memory that had endured and kept me company for half my life.

I continued peering through my binoculars at the other tables and at the passers-by, in case another man appeared, one who was a better fit with my memory. It was now five minutes after the agreed hour, which was perfectly within acceptable limits, but I would soon have to decide whether or not to go downstairs, whether to abide by the arrangements I had made or leave him in the lurch. Finally, a waitress came over to him and asked what he wanted to drink, and when he smiled broadly at her, I had no doubt then that, despite the transformation, he was Esteban Yanes. The smile was identical to his smile in 1969, he hadn't lost that. His strong, slightly prominent teeth lit up his face, it was the kind of broad, generous smile that seems to have a life of its own, a bright, charming smile in the middle of those chubby cheeks. However, there was another detail that cancelled out this pleasing, positive effect: when he turned towards the waitress, I noticed on the top of his head a kind of Japanese or rather samurai bun, perched aloft like a pom-pom. A few men at the time were already beginning to wear ponytails, but the bun was an innovation (both those things subsequently proliferated ad nauseam, no longer original but hackneyed). A ghastly innovation, in my view. As far as I was concerned, any man with a ponytail was not to be trusted, and a man with a Japanese bun, well, I would simply cross the road and run away, especially if the bun was intended to compensate for and divert attention from a bald pate. We all have our frivolous, arbitrary side, and I clung to that grotesque adornment as a reason not to go downstairs. It seemed to me the height of affectation and imbecility.

Nevertheless, I continued to watch for a while longer, for quite a lot longer. The minutes passed. I saw how he kept looking around, glancing at his watch numerous times, I saw him light and smoke three cigarettes, I saw him ask for another cup of coffee, put on and take off his hat several times. And then, suddenly, I thought he'd spotted me, that he'd seen me in the distance, on my balcony. He didn't have the benefit of binoculars, of course, and so he screwed up his eyes in order to see me more clearly. He put on his hat just in case (and he did so exactly the way a bullfighter puts on his bullfighter's hat), and then stood up, his gaze fixed on me, or so I thought. Peering through those magnifying lenses made me feel that I was now being scrutinised. He waved his hands at me in greeting or as if to say: 'Hey, if you're Berta, I'm here, it's me,' or so I thought. I felt I'd been unmasked, and I blushed, filled with alarm. I stepped back from the balcony into the apartment, I hid, like a spy who suddenly knows she's been seen. I gradually calmed down, though; after all, he couldn't be sure. He hadn't even seen my face, which was covered by the binoculars. And I, too, had changed, although infinitely less than he had. I allowed a few minutes to pass before cautiously going out onto the balcony again, trying to remain as invisible as possible. He wasn't there, I couldn't see him. Then the phone rang, and I jumped. 'Perhaps he's gone into the café to phone me, I did give him my number, that was a mistake, he has it now and will continue to have it.' I decided not to answer; it rang ten times; then it rang again, five times, he had obviously lost confidence that second time. I waited a little longer before creeping out onto the balcony once more, and when I did, I saw that I'd been right: he'd returned to his table, he wasn't standing up or waving; he'd sat down and stayed sitting, tirelessly, patiently smoking, and drinking more coffee.

I looked at my watch, that man had now been waiting for forty minutes; when would he get fed up, when would he get annoyed, when would he realise that I wasn't going to appear at the rendezvous I had instigated and arranged? This thought upset and embarrassed me. 'What a fickle, unreasonable woman I am. I was the one who went to his house, asked him to call me, suggested we meet, and now I've just dumped him and all because, physically, he's changed for the worse. Nothing more. Of course, before, his looks were all he had going for him – well, that and helping me and being a real gentleman. And, more especially, sleeping with me, thus putting an end to my virginal state, of which Tomás, the silly man, was far too respectful.' Into my mind came the idea of going to bed with that fat forty-something and I recoiled. It made me feel quite sick. Although, who knows, perhaps if I went down and talked to him, if I saw again that undimmed smile, I would quickly become used to his new appearance and end up seeing through it to the person he was before. 'It's unlikely though,' I thought, telling myself: 'The other reason I'm standing him up is because he called me "love" and because of that stupid samurai bun. Poor man, it's probably just his modest way of still feeling like a bullfighter, he hasn't got enough hair

385

at the back for a pigtail, and with a belly that big, how could he possibly stick banderillas in a bull? He did say you have to be quick on your feet.'

And then I realised that I was making a kind of transposition. The last time I'd seen Tomás was far more recent – it had been seven years now – but that was long enough for him to have changed radically too; if he was still alive and if he came back, like the characters in novels or in real life, like Colonel Chabert and Martin Guerre, he might have changed even more than Esteban Yanes, if he'd suffered hardship and persecution, if he'd been constantly on the run, if he was a deserter whom everyone was out to get. I had a kind of foreshadowing of what a hypothetical meeting between him and me would be like, and this only confirmed my own misfortune: I couldn't abandon that irrational hope, because I still vaguely, dreamily believed he would come back. 'It would be better if he didn't,' I thought, in order to drive away that hope. 'It would be better if he didn't turn up looking like that manager of novice bullfighters, whom I summoned here, and who has been waiting in vain with incomprehensible tenacity; Tomás might perhaps be fat and bald like him and utterly transformed; embittered and taciturn and elusive and not interested in anything, not even in telling me what became of him; knowing that any future would seem dull in comparison with the emotions he'd experienced in his days of travelling and plotting; immersed in the long years, now consigned to the past, of suffering and danger and abominable deeds, or perhaps eaten away by remorse or, on the contrary, grown unbearably hard and proud of his exploits and of having unleashed plague and cholera wherever he went, of having sown discord and spread fires, of having led his enemies to their deaths or strangled them with his own hands or killed them with a gun or a knife, I've no idea, and I'll never know. Yes, coming back is the worst infidelity, and after too much time has passed, no one should come back. And no, I'll never find out.'

Unexpectedly, I burst into tears, although admittedly this was something that happened quite often, I just couldn't help it sometimes. A brief fit of crying would come upon me without warning, even in circumstances that were normal, or what you might call neutral. It wasn't always brought on by my own errant thoughts, as on that occasion. The tears would come unbidden, while I was at the cinema or watching the news on TV, while I was laughing with friends or teaching (and then, of course, I had to hold them back), while I was walking alone down the street doing my shopping, or playing with the children, who were not so very young now, and if I didn't manage to suppress my tears in front of them, they would look at me, greatly concerned, for it always upsets children to see their parents helpless, because then they feel there's no one to protect *them*. They never saw their father either happy or sad; as they got older and asked more questions, I gave them the official version, the version provided by Bertram Tupra, the Foreign Office or the Crown, that he'd been another casualty of the Falklands War, one more death in that small, unheroic war, another of the fallen whom almost no one remembers, in that absurd battle, which ended in ignominy for the Argentinian military and greater glory for proud Thatcher, who did very well out of it. A waste of lives, a few squandered deaths, the usual story.

When I next looked out, sixty-five minutes had passed since the banderillero's arrival at the café; I wouldn't have seen anything with my eyes full of tears, and so I waited until I'd stopped crying, which took a while, and then splashed my face with cold water. Sixty-five minutes, and he was still there. The phone had rung again, ten rings, he was presumably trying to contact me, although without wishing to be overly insistent. I was touched by such patience. Was it so very important to him to see me? Was he so very excited at the prospect? Had he thought about me often over those twenty years, after that brief, chance fuck, which wasn't even his first time, lost in the dark night of times yet to come? I hesitated for a moment. Since he was still there, I still had time to go down and meet him, to invent some excuse for my unforgivable lateness and chat with him a little. His loyalty saddened me. He couldn't have much to do if he could afford to spend more than an hour waiting for a complete stranger, a ghost from the past who might also have grown fat and worn and faded, so desperate that she'd gone to the trouble of tracking him down. I hesitated and hesitated. And I was still hesitating when I saw him ask the waitress for the bill, seventy minutes from the beginning of that failed rendezvous at which he had arrived so punctually. He paid and stood up, exchanged a few words with the young woman (perhaps he was embarrassed at having waited in vain and was making his excuses), gave one last look around, adjusted his hat, fastened the one buttonable button on his jacket and set off towards the Palacio Real, to Bailén, slowly, very slowly, feeling perhaps defeated and disappointed.

He didn't ever call me again. He didn't try to arrange another meeting, to ask if I'd forgotten or if he'd got the wrong date, hour or place. He didn't want to know, or to make things awkward for me by asking if it had been me standing on a balcony in Calle Pavía. He accepted what had happened, or understood.

Yes, 1990 and 1991 and 1992 came and went, the latter with all its Olympic Games hoo-ha and the optimism that spread throughout Spain, a country that suddenly imagined itself to be prosperous. For me, though, it marked the tenth year since Tomás's departure, since our temporary farewell at Barajas airport on 4 April. It seemed impossible to me that a whole decade had slipped by, and his leaving seemed both distant and recent, recent and distant, but when it was recent, it seemed like only yesterday or the day before. The previous September I'd turned forty, and I couldn't believe that either, I felt simultaneously much older and much younger, as if I were an ageless woman who has already experienced everything she was intended to experience, when, in reality, she's only covered a short stretch of the journey, with her life simultaneously finished and only just begun, simultaneously a spinster, a widow and a married woman, with her life suspended or interrupted or strangely postponed. It was as if time wasn't passing, even though it always, always does, even when we think it's waiting for us or has kindly offered us a moratorium. There are hundreds of thousands of people who linger in their adolescence or youth, who refuse to abandon either of those states and cling to the belief that all possibilities remain open to them and that nothing is affected by the rocky road of the past because the past has not yet arrived; as if time had obeyed them when they distractedly, quite mildly, said: 'Stop, be still, stop, I need time to think.' It's a disease so widespread that nowadays no one even thinks of it as a disease. This wasn't quite how I felt, it was more as if a parenthesis had opened in 1982 and I'd never found the right moment to close that parenthesis. I'd had to teach Faulkner in my classes (very superficially), and I learned that, on one occasion, when asked why he wrote such long-drawn-out, interminable sentences, he'd replied: 'Because I'm never sure I'll stay alive long enough to begin the next one,' or something like that. Perhaps it was the same for me and that infinite parenthesis: if I closed it, I was afraid I might die, or, rather, that I might kill, kill Tomás for good.

Now and then, I couldn't resist going out onto one of the balconies, especially at dusk, as it was growing dark, and looking out across the square – the part visible to me – hoping to spot, to discern his figure, his familiar figure, walking towards me, or getting out of a taxi next to the Iglesia de la Encarnación; and if I saw someone carrying a suitcase or a travelling bag (which was fairly common given the number of tourists in the area), I would rush to fetch the binoculars I'd used to spy on Esteban Yanes and would, absurdly, focus them on the individual in question, always thinking that if Tomás did return after all that time, he'd be sure to have some luggage with him. And like an irrational fool, I forgot that his figure – if he wasn't already under the earth or under the sea – could well be far from familiar; that he could have become as unrecognisable as the patient, accepting, loyal banderillero.

I was acting purely out of superstition, a superstition to which Jack Nevinson also contributed one morning, or towards lunchtime, for he had come to have lunch with us as he had every Sunday since his wife died. Guillermo and Elisa (Guillermo was already thirteen) had gone out to play in the Jardines de Sabatini or in Campo del Moro, and always left it to the last minute to come home. Neither of us knew it then, but Jack didn't have long to live: two months after that Sunday, he had a heart attack in the night and died. When I made my usual morning phone call to check up on him, he didn't answer. I left a message on his answering machine, and when he failed to return my call, I caught a taxi and went anxiously over to his apartment in Calle Jenner, already fearing the worst, convinced that this would be the day he would not wake up. I let myself in with the spare key, and found him lying on the floor next to his bed, in his pale pyjamas and with one hand clutching the dark silk dressing gown he hadn't managed to put on, as if he'd fallen while trying to reach it or perhaps while trying to pick up the phone on his bedside table, doubtless to warn me. The attack had been so sudden, so devastating, that he hadn't been able to get to the phone and had fallen over as he reached out. Or perhaps he was seeking the cold of the floor before dying, because coolness does offer some relief when we feel ill. Or perhaps he wanted to escape the accumulated warmth of the sheets and didn't even try to call for help, or to save himself. Some people, when the time comes, do accept it and think with their final thought that it's fine, not so bad after all, that it's enough, that there's no point resisting or struggling on for a number of weeks or months. Few people are quite so self-possessed, but they do exist, and sometimes I hoped I would be one of them, or at least I did then, when Jack died. With Jack's death, with Miss Mercedes having died some years before, and with Tomás's siblings living so far away, it was as if my long connection with the Nevinsons had finally ended, although my children bear that name and will always be Guillermo and Elisa Nevinson. On my business cards, though, I'm no longer 'Berta Isla de Nevinson', because it had long ceased to be the norm in Spain for married women to add their husband's surname to theirs in that possessive way. On my cards I went back to being 'Berta Isla'. Not, however, in my memory or my imagination.

That Sunday, Jack was fine, with no worrying symptoms. He had asked for a glass of white wine and was sitting where he usually sat; in fact, where most visitors tended to sit (not that there were many), that is, in the same place where Miguel Ruiz Kindelán had given me the fright of my life many years before. Jack was resting one hand on his latest purchase, a light walking stick with a metal handle. He proudly gave me a demonstration: the handle could be unscrewed to reveal a slender, very sharp dagger, thus transforming the cane into a kind of mini-lance or harpoon, which did actually look as if it could be thrown, in which case, of course, it could prove deadly.

'Given how dangerous the streets are these days,' he said, 'you never know when you might need some deterrent. I'm too old to defend myself with blows or to run away. They'd hunt me down like a rabbit. No, what am I saying? Like a snail.'

'But it seems to take so long to unscrew,' I said, 'that by the time you'd done that, they'd have overpowered you. Or, worse, grabbed the stick and turned it on you.'

'Oh well,' he said with a shrug. 'It could still be useful if I saw the danger coming, and I do always keep my eyes peeled. Then there would be time to unscrew the handle and show them the knife! It's quite frightening, isn't it? You could certainly inflict some damage with it.'

It took so many turns of the handle that I couldn't really see that it would ever be of much use, but if it gave him a feeling, however illusory, of being safe, then it would have served its purpose.

'Do you remember, ages ago now, how Tomás got mugged when he was in London? The muggers cut his face really badly and left him with a deep scar. And then the scar just vanished completely, as if it had never been there. Very mysterious. If I remember rightly, he said he'd had plastic surgery, courtesy of the Foreign Office. That's what he said, anyway, although who knows what really happened.'

Jack rested both hands on the metal knob of that death-dealing walking stick, then rested his dimpled chin on his hands; the cleft in his chin had grown deeper with age. He thought for a moment, then answered:

'Everything about Tom has always been very mysterious.' I noticed at once the tense he used: not 'was', which would correspond to a completed action (or, indeed, person), but 'has been'. 'At least ever since he went to Oxford or left Oxford. I sometimes wonder if I was wrong to insist on him doing his degree there. Something happened. Something happened to him and changed him, I don't know what. Has he ever told you what it was?' He was still not using the simple past, which you would normally use when speaking of someone who was dead. Jack Nevinson's Spanish was far from perfect, of course, despite having spent most of his life here. We alternated between the two languages, sometimes speaking in one and sometimes in the other, depending on how he felt. 'But how could I possibly have known that whatever it was that happened to him there would happen? Don't *you* know?' He repeated the question, as if he found it hard to believe that I wouldn't know.

'No, I don't, Jack,' I said. 'Tomás was always very secretive. His perennial excuse was that he wasn't authorised to reveal what he did or where he went, or anything. That if he told me anything, he'd be committing a crime, violating the Official Secrets Act or whatever it's called, to which he was subject, and apparently no one can do that without suffering grave consequences. Even once they've retired, they must remain silent unto death. I suppose anyone who breaks that silence could be accused of high treason, even today. Of course, he only told me this after confessing to me who it was he was working for, but, before that, he didn't tell me much either, and, to be honest, I didn't take much interest in those diplomatic matters.' I fell silent for a few seconds, thinking, then added: 'But, yes, something definitely happened to him at Oxford, towards the end. I noticed that change in him too. Even before we got married. They must have recruited him then. He took on responsibilities that would have been unimaginable when he first left. He started leading a double life, and both lives involved pretence and concealment. That would be enough to change anyone's character, don't you think?'

'Indeed, and yet, and yet . . . I've always thought there was something else. Tom is too mysterious,' he said again, and this time he didn't say 'has been' but 'is'.

'Why do you say "is"?'

Surprised, Jack looked up, but kept his hands still resting on the handle; he clearly enjoyed that posture.

'Did I say "is"?'

'Yes, you said "Tom is too mysterious".'

He looked out of the window at the trees, with his innocent, absorbed, blue eyes.

'Yes, perhaps I did. I don't know why,' he said. 'I suppose you never get used to the idea that a son, whom you saw when he was still so tiny and yet so filled with vital energy, should have ceased to be. You're convinced, from the day he's born, that your child will survive you, that you won't see him die. And bear in mind, too, I haven't seen him die, I haven't seen his dead body or buried him.' Then he added: 'That's the easy answer, but it isn't only that, Berta, I won't lie to you. I'm all for you remaking your life and forgetting about him. With another man, I mean. I don't want the slightest hint of uncertainty to bind you to him, nor for his memory to be a burden to you. But Tom really is so mysterious, so elusive and chameleon-like, so hard to pin down – he was even as a child – that I can't bring myself to believe he really is dead. Call it what you like, fatherly intuition, a hunch, suspicion, scepticism about the official version, wishful thinking (I never know how to say that in Spanish). Perhaps a desire to deny reality. But I'd be perfectly within my rights to do so, that's one of the advantages of getting old. We don't have much time left and reality tends to leave us alone, it washes its hands of us and passes us by. Almost all the cards have been dealt and very few surprises await us. And if reality turns its back on us, we can do the same and deny it if we want to. Within limits, of course, it's not an excuse for talking utter nonsense. I'm certainly not going to deny that Mercedes is dead, how could I? But I do have a feeling that Tom is still alive somewhere. A fugitive, in hiding, living under another identity. Perhaps even having undergone plastic surgery again. I don't know and I don't know why I think that. And I probably couldn't prove it, unless his body was found and then, yes, I would have to accept it. I don't think he'll turn up again before I die. If he's been in hiding for getting on for ten years, then there's no reason why he shouldn't stay hidden for fifteen or twenty years, until whatever there is to be forgotten is forgotten. Ultimately, of course, everything is forgotten, or is a matter of indifference to those who come after, those who succeed us. Obviously, I'll die without ever knowing anything for certain. On the one hand, that's a shame, but, on the other hand, it's an advantage, because that way no one can persuade me that I'm wrong, and I can still believe I'm right.'

I was both moved and startled. 'So he's been making his own conjectures too,' I thought. 'And for how many years has he been doing that?'

'Do you really believe he's alive?' I asked.

Jack looked away from the trees and at me, with his usual limpid gaze.

'Do I really, really believe that?' He paused for a moment, as if hesitating. 'Perhaps I shouldn't say this, Berta, because I have no evidence. And don't think I know something you don't, because I don't. I have something more than that, I have conviction.'

He was probably right, not just about the old, but about the living in general, we are all entitled to reject those bits of reality that cannot be proved, that leave us embittered and distressed or simply vexed, that deprive us of all hope. We can always say 'I can't be certain' about something of which we're not certain, and the truth is that there's very little we can be certain of; I mean, almost everything we know is what we've been told by other people, or by books, newspapers and encyclopaedias, or by History with its chronicles and archives and annals, which we believe because they're old and established, as if, in their day, these hadn't also distorted and lied about the facts, leaving legend to prevail. We've barely witnessed anything, barely seen anything for ourselves, we are almost incapable of affirming anything to be true, even though we do so all the time. Therefore, it's not that difficult to deny a fact or the existence of something when we choose to: a combination of the opaque nature of the world and our own shaky memory (ephemeral, uncertain, changing) usually makes that easy for us. If someone we admire or love commits a misdemeanour, we nearly always say: 'No, it wasn't him – or indeed her – he'd never do such a thing. I thought it was him, but I must have been mistaken. I couldn't quite see, it was dark and I was rather upset at the time, I was standing at an odd angle to him and wasn't wearing my glasses. I mistook him for another person who resembled him, yes, that's what must have happened.' Why, then, not believe that your disappeared son, your youngest son, is still alive somewhere. Priam saw his firstborn child, Hector, die before his eyes, slain by Achilles, which is why he went to plead with Achilles to give him Hector's poor, battered body so that he could bury him; if he chose to humble himself like that it was because he knew his son was dead. But if he hadn't seen him die, if they had merely come to tell him that Hector had fallen in single combat in some remote place, he could have waited for his return, he could have hoped the witnesses were wrong, and attributed their opinion to poor eyesight or over-hasty conclusions, and nothing would have prevented him then from awaiting his own death in a state of uncertainty. That's why all those words exist: confirm, prove, verify; ratify, corroborate, substantiate and ascertain. They're not superfluous or merely ornamental, they answer to a need.

I couldn't confirm anything to Jack Nevinson nor disprove anything either, you can't disprove feelings, still less convictions. However, I refrained from telling him what my own feelings and convictions were or had been, especially in 1988, after which they had abated. I would have had to tell him that old story about the Kindeláns, which I'd always kept from him and his wife, so as not to alarm or worry them. That incident, more than any other, had often made me suspect that Tomás had been deployed on dirty missions to Northern Ireland; and I imagined the people there to be irascible and hate-filled and more frightening than any other. Not just the members of the IRA and the armed Unionists, but the population as a whole; I imagined they were as gripped by savagery and a desire for revenge as we Spaniards were in the 1930s, in the last century, which I can't get used to calling 'last' because it's my century and I'm still here. (Or like the Basques in the 1980s, those dominated by ETA.)

The Soviet Union, Cuba and East Germany – to mention other places where, in my ignorance, I would sometimes place Tomás – did not, perhaps absurdly, provoke in me the same feelings of panic. They might be more dangerous countries, but at least their populations were, I thought, too much under the thumb of their governments to intervene.

On 19 March 1988, what became known as the Corporals Killings took place. Three days before, during the funeral in Belfast of three members of the IRA who had been caught preparing a bomb attack and were shot and killed by British troops, a member of the Ulster Defence Association, Michael Stone by name, had attacked the funeral cortège with pistols and hand grenades, killing three people, among them another member of the IRA, Caoimhín Mac Brádaigh, or Kevin Brady. Understandably, his funeral on the 19th took place in an atmosphere charged with tension, rage, fear and suspicion. In order not to inflame matters further, the police decided to stay away and leave the funeral unguarded. A large number of IRA and Provisional IRA members acted as stewards, and quite a lot of journalists were present, including a TV crew. It's believed that, either by accident or because they didn't know about or were ignoring general orders to stay away from the area, two British army corporals, in civilian clothes and driving a silver Volkswagen Passat, drove straight into the cortège, which was headed by several black cabs. The crowd assumed this was another attack and that the occupants of the car were, again, paramilitaries in the Ulster Defence Association, like that man Stone who had killed Brady three days before. Left with barely any room for manoeuvre, the corporals made various attempts to withdraw, and on one such attempt, their car mounted the pavement, provoking more fear and even more anger and scattering the mourners. Finally, the two men found themselves trapped, blocked in by the black cabs, and then the crowd hurled themselves on the car, broke the windows and tried to drag the two corporals out. One of them, twenty-four-year-old Derek Wood, produced a handgun – a pistol or a revolver – and fired a shot into the air, which briefly dispersed the crowd. However, the crowd, even angrier now, then surged back and managed to pull the two soldiers out of the car – Wood and David Howes, a year younger than his colleague – and punched and kicked them to the ground. A journalist described the moment when the corporals realised they were lost and how one of them: 'didn't cry out, just looked at us with terrified eyes, as though we were all enemies in a foreign country who wouldn't have understood what language he was speaking if he called out for help'. They were dragged to a nearby sports ground, where a group of men stripped them down to their underpants and socks. A Redemptorist Catholic priest, Father Alec Reid, attempted to stop the beating and asked for an ambulance to be called, because, according to the BBC, the soldiers were being tortured. He was pulled away from them, and told he would be shot if he tried to intervene further. The beatings continued, and, in the end, the corporals were thrown over a wall and into a waiting black cab, which drove away at high speed. Inside were the half-dead soldiers and two or three other individuals, plus the driver. One of the passengers was seen to wave an angry, triumphant fist in the air. You can see some of what happened on YouTube, the part that the TV crew were able to film before the crowd, aware of what was to come, stopped them and shoved the cameras out of the way. You can see that fist very clearly, though, the gesture of someone making off with some promising booty.

What was promised soon came to pass, or else their captors were in a great hurry to keep that promise. The taxi didn't travel very far, only about two hundred yards, to a piece of waste ground, where, once the identities of the two men had been confirmed, 'we executed them', to use the words of the communiqué issued shortly afterwards by the Belfast brigade of the IRA. The word 'execute' doesn't fit well with the state of Wood's corpse – he was the one who had fired his gun into the air when he found himself surrounded by the crowd: he had been shot twice in the head and four times in the chest, had been stabbed four times in the back of the neck and suffered multiple injuries to other parts of his body. This seemed to be the work of numerous frenzied hands, not that of one cool-headed executioner. Father Alec Reid had followed the taxi on foot, guessing what would be the corporals' final fate and hoping to prevent it. However, when he arrived at the waste ground, it was too late (the whole incident lasted only twelve minutes), and all he could do was give the last rites to the dead, the newly dead. A photographer captured the moment, and the image became so famous that *Life* magazine named it one of the best photographs of the last fifty years, that is, of the last half-century. In the picture, we see Father Reid wearing a kind of zip-up cagoule or anorak and kneeling beside the bloodstained, near-naked body of the younger of the corporals, Howes. The priest is looking at the camera, or rather at the person holding the camera (perhaps seeking another human being who might share and comprehend his desolation), with an expression of impotence or modesty, as if he knew deep down that those last rites would be of no use to the dead man. But it's the only thing he can think of to do, and some people feel a need to do something, even in the face of the irremediable.

Needless to say, when that picture was published in 1988, I couldn't help but remember the other image I mentioned earlier and which I've never found again, not even on the Internet. Just as well, really, because it was even more unbearable. When a crowd or a mob attacks someone, they always tear off his clothes first, I'm not sure why, whether to humiliate him or out of sheer rage or to make the person feel still more defenceless, or to warn him of what is to come or to brutalise him, I don't know. After seeing those images of the two corporals being slaughtered like that, I was again filled with terrible foreboding, if 'foreboding' is the right word for something that has already happened and is, therefore, already in the past, possibly the distant past. Seeing the collective rage that sometimes gripped the people of Northern Ireland, it was clear to me that, if Tomás had been there, and had passed himself off as Irish and even, for a while, as a member of the IRA, if he had won their trust with the intention of trapping or betraying them, and had been unmasked, he would have suffered something not so very different (possibly worse) from what the corporals had experienced, as had other British soldiers, and per-haps other infiltrators and, of course, informers. Except that his battered, naked body wouldn't have been left on display as a lesson or demonstration or message or show of force, and they certainly wouldn't have allowed a priest to help him on his journey into the next world. He would have been buried in secret one moonless night in the middle of a wood, he would have been thrown into the sea or into Lough Neagh, weighed down with heavy chains so that his body would never resurface; he would have been fed to the dogs or the pigs, he would have been chopped into pieces or cremated – ashes that land on an old man's sleeve for the old man then to blow them off. He would have vanished completely, he would have been snatched away as an added punishment for his superiors and his relatives, snatched away from me, his unknown, distant wife, Berta Isla. He would have been shown no pity, only vengeful rage, he would have been cast out from the universe, what was left of him, what lingered, as if he'd never trod the earth or traversed the world. Just as, through-out history, towns have been razed to the ground and their entire populations wiped out, so that they would leave no descendants, and since they couldn't be killed two or more times, as their executioners would have liked, they further punished them by destroying every last vestige, all memory obliterated. Just as there is hatred of place, spatial hatred, which leads to that place being reduced to rubble, to the land around being flattened (it's a very unhealthy thing, that loathing for place), there's also biographical hatred, personal hatred. Not only do they kill the person, they remove all trace of his pernicious existence, render him null and void as if he'd never been born or lived or died or travelled any distance; as if he'd never done anything either good or bad and was merely a blank page or an illegible inscription, someone of whom no record remains, as if he were no one. That could have been Tomás's fate, to be plunged into the mist of what happened and didn't happen, into the dark back of time, down the sea's throat. To be this: a blade of grass, a speck of dust, a thread, a lizard climbing a wall in summer, a cloud of smoke that finally disperses; snow that falls but doesn't settle.

I couldn't talk to Jack Nevinson about those fears dating from 1988 or from before, nor about the Kindeláns, nor about Northern Ireland or Éire. That might have made him doubt, might have undermined his conviction, and what would be the point of that, he was already old and alone, and you need something to hold on to when you're old and alone, even the most insignificant detail of the day's events, or, if not that, then a fantasy. When Jack died a couple of months later, I felt even gladder that I'd never said a word to him about those events, because, when he fell out of bed in his pyjamas, he could still go on thinking that his mysterious younger son was alive and would come back, even though he wouldn't be there to see him. And when, with his death, I remained a little more alone (although my children were with me all those years, as well as the occasional man who never

403

stayed), sometimes, I couldn't help but feel infected by his feeling, his conviction based on nothing at all. 1988 had dissipated by then, and with it what had happened in Belfast to Corporals Wood and Howes, half-lynched by the members of a funeral cortège and then murdered by several hands, hands so insatiable that they needed to kill each man at least ten times over, four stab wounds and six bullets. Yes, that sense of foreboding gradually faded, but what my father-in-law had said lingered on. For that reason, and out of a kind of superstition that often takes root and becomes a reflex reaction (like touching wood or, in the old days, making the sign of the cross), I would occasionally go out onto one of the balconies, especially at dusk, as it grew dark, or at dawn if I happened to be awake, in order to scan – with binoculars or without – the Plaza de Oriente, where *Las Meninas* was painted, Calle de San Quintín and Calle de Lepanto, where the Casa de las Matemáticas once stood, and Plaza de la Encarnación, and the esplanade outside the Palacio Real with its many visitors, hoping, at some point, to spot a familiar figure transformed by time and suffering. Or transformed perhaps by a better life than the one he would have had with me, with another wife and other children. Tomás had, indeed, proved too mysterious, and in the realm of chimeras anything is possible.

VII

'You can't imagine, Mr Southworth, the number of times I've thought what I thought at that moment when I had to decide what to do, it must be twenty years ago now.'

Tom Nevinson wasn't that much younger than his former tutor, but he continued to address him respectfully as Mr Southworth. Sometimes it's impossible to make that shift, for example, with one's former teacher, especially if, in between, teacher and student haven't seen each other, if there's been no continued contact.

'What was it that you thought?' asked Mr Southworth, perhaps more out of deference than out of any real curiosity. He had still not recovered from the unexpectedness of the visit, which had happened totally unannounced, with no previous phone call; from the sudden irruption into his life of this middle-aged man claiming to be Tomás Nevinson, but who was so different from the man he remembered. Mr Southworth's hair was now almost white, prematurely white, but otherwise he hadn't changed very much. He occupied the same rooms in St Peter's College, and was still very skilful at managing the waves of his black gown, the skirts of which fell around his legs in a cascade, but never became entangled, and which he still insisted on wearing at tutorials and classes, even though this was beginning to be frowned upon in the 1990s, as a sign of authority and elitism, a foretaste of a new, more rancorous century. Everything was beginning to be frowned upon then, any show of courtesy, distinction or knowledge was experienced as an affront. However, Mr Southworth was naturally courteous, distinguished and knowledgeable – as, even more so, was Professor Wheeler (who, shortly afterwards, would be made Sir Peter Wheeler) – and he wasn't willing to go against his own nature in order to content the manipulated masses brought up in a state of congenital victimism and encouraged to use an inferiority complex as the passport, alibi and engine of their existence.

'It will seem extreme to you, as if I were making a claim to clairvoyance,' said Tom Nevinson, 'but I was sure my decision would affect my whole life, as has proved to be the case, not necessarily in the days or months or even the years that followed, but I knew that, from that moment on, it would affect everything else, and yet my life had barely started; you knew me then and perhaps remember what I was like, but you have no idea what I'm like now. What I thought and have often repeated to myself was this: "What is now will be always. I will be who I am not, I will be a fiction, a spectre who comes and goes and departs and returns. And I will simply happen, I will be sea and snow and wind." I would repeat this over and over as a way of confirming it to myself.' He fell silent, his eyes intense and bewildered, looking around him at the cosy, book-lined room where, an eternity or two ago, he'd attended so many tutorials, as if he couldn't believe how unchanged it was after all his years of wandering, and, besides, he'd realised that his words meant nothing to Mr Southworth, who could have no idea what lay behind them.

Back then, he hadn't told him about his subsequent phone conversation with Wheeler, or only very briefly. Nor about his encounter with his recruiting officers, Tupra and Blakeston, nor the conditions they'd imposed on him. One condition had been that he must join them immediately, and the other, to tell no one anything. If he was going to work for the Secret Service and be trained by them, every-thing, from that very instant, would be just that – secret. Nevinson had come to say goodbye to Mr Southworth a few days later, but, as regards his problem, to which Southworth had been privy from the start, he'd merely said: 'You were right, Mr Southworth, thank you. Professor Wheeler was a great help. He gave me some sound advice, and it's all resolved now. The police won't trouble me any more, they've seen I had nothing to do with the death of that poor girl.' 'And what about that man Morse?' Southworth asked. 'He seemed a clever, painstaking fellow.' 'Don't worry, it's all cleared up with him as well. I took some legal advice, and the Professor was very persua-sive.' 'Have they found the man who did it?' 'Not that I know, but I imagine they will.' Mr Southworth was discreet and didn't want to insist, to draw him out. If necessary, he would ask Peter, as he called him, and with whom he was friends. And that's what he did a week later, when they met in Southworth's room at the Taylorian, alone, although Wheeler declined to go into detail, as if it were a trivial matter, tedious, old news. 'Ah, yes, young Nevinson,' he'd said. 'Oh, a fuss about nothing. A mistake, a misunderstanding, a nasty shock. He'll be back in Madrid by now, under Starkie's wing, or about to be.'

Yes, the no-longer-young man claiming to be Tom Nevinson and who doubtless was (why would anyone pass himself off as a former student of his after twenty years, why would he bother to lie to him like that?), the man who had turned up in his rooms at St Peter's with a febrile look in his eyes and the rather startled expression of someone who has just seen a ghost or climbed out of the hole of a long, deep deception, or undergone torture or survived an ordeal, realised that Mr Southworth knew almost nothing. He went on talking nonethe-less. He hadn't known where to begin and had found it hard to get started; once he had, however, he didn't want to lose momentum, even if that momentum was rather violent and bordering on the incoherent.

'And I recalled two lines I'd read a short while before: "Dust in the air suspended marks the place where a story ended." ' And before he could say anything more, Mr Southworth, who was a cultured, well-read man, immediately and un-pedantically gave the source of those lines, like someone recognising a passage from the Bible.

'Ah, yes, Eliot's *Little Gidding* if I remember rightly.'

'Yes, I'd just happened to read it, not the whole thing, only fragments. I know the poem by heart now, from start to finish, and have for some time. And then I thought: "Here, now, is the end of my story. But what awaits me? Because, at the same time, I'm still here, and now is always. This is the death of air. But one can survive that." That's what I thought, Mr Southworth, and it was both fortunate and unfortunate.'

'Shades of Eliot again, I believe.'

This time, Tomás didn't bother confirming the source, he was too absorbed in what he was saying, too distraught, his eyes darting about, now directed brightly at his former tutor and his surroundings, now turned dully inwards, towards some memory or a whole jumble of memories, towards the void.

'One survives that death, Mr Southworth, the death of air. I know this and can tell you it's true. I've experienced it myself.' He took a handkerchief out of his pocket and mopped his brow and temples, even though, despite his agitated state, he wasn't actually sweating. The handkerchief was clean and neatly folded, and remained so. 'It's very difficult to end a life, when life doesn't want to depart. It's even difficult to kill someone, when life decides it's not yet time to abandon that person, that it's not ready to withdraw. It's the same if someone

410

tries to kill you, if you struggle against it with all your might and, more especially, your will. You've no idea what the will is capable of if attacked. How could you know that, here in Oxford. This is a peaceful place, outside the universe.'

Mr Southworth had gradually recovered from his initial feelings of awkwardness and surprise and was trying to reconcile the brilliant young man with a gift for languages, who had attracted so much attention during his time at university, both his and that of other teachers, with the man before him now. This man was about forty, possibly more (it might well be over twenty years since he'd last seen him). He had a greying moustache and beard and both his body and face had filled out. His hair was flecked with grey and was thinner than it used to be; he wore it combed back, revealing a deeply receding hairline. The young man's pleasant features had grown coarser: it was as if his nose had become somehow broader and his square chin more like a trapezoid, the chin of an ancient cartoon character; his grey eyes had lost what spark they'd had, and seemed profoundly dull and tormented, their colour darker and their pupils wild, whereas, before, they had been piercing and restless; the one thing that hadn't changed was his full, shapely mouth, although it was slightly concealed by his moustache and seemed less red and less firm. His forehead and chin were deeply lined, horizontally and vertically, and he had a faded scar just below the left-hand corner of his mouth, very similar, thought Southworth, to Peter's scar, which had never faded, and which, according to what Peter had told him, was the result of a car accident back in 1941, during his training at Lochailort, on the west coast of Scotland. With time, Nevinson's scar would also grow whiter (pining palely away, but never entirely gone); it was odd that they should both have a scar in the same place and running in the same direction, for in both men, the scar ran diagonally down to the base of the chin.

411

The new Nevinson was talking very fast, almost gabbling, but, at the same time, he gave the impression of someone utterly resolute, who wouldn't go off at tangents once he'd calmed down, who could now think clearly and had regained his composure. Nor would he beat about the bush. There was something mutinous about him, impatient, exasperated, an inner hardness that the young Tom had lacked, so far as he could remember anyway. The younger man had been easy-going and ironic, whereas this man was grave and angry, with little time for jokes. Southworth hadn't thought about it for a long time, but now he remembered how fearful, almost terrified, Tom had been after his interview with Morse, at which Southworth had insisted on being present, as witness and protector. His panic, utter confusion and sheer horror had been due, too, to the hammer blow he'd just received, the news that the young woman he'd had sex with the night before, and on other occasions too, had been murdered shortly after they'd parted, after he'd left her flat. What was her name? Morse had mentioned her name, and, oddly, as Southworth now recalled, Tom hadn't known her surname until then. She worked in Waterfield's bookshop, and her name and her surname both began with a 'J', something like Joan Jefferson or Jane Jellicoe or perhaps Janet Jeffries. He'd read nothing about the incident in the news-papers, but that wasn't so very strange, since he didn't tend to read a daily paper, indeed, whole days would pass before he had time to cast an eye over one in college, for he was always too busy rushing from tutorial to seminar, and any remaining hours were devoted to study-ing and to his voluminous reading. It was true that Oxford and Oxonians lived outside the universe, absorbed in their own petty affairs. Tom had told him afterwards that everything was fine, and, like most of his colleagues, Southworth wasn't that curious about the world outside Congregation, as if what happened outside the university wasn't really their concern. He'd immediately forgotten about the episode, he didn't know the girl or couldn't place her, and all girls seemed rather alike to him; and since it was no longer a matter affecting one of his students, the crime might as well have been committed in Manchester or Paris or Warsaw. The man before him now wouldn't have been alarmed by a violent death, even the death of someone close, nor by a policeman's questions, even if they implicated him, or not at least in the same way. 'Perhaps,' thought E A Southworth (which was how his name appeared on the sign on his door), 'he wouldn't even have blinked. He would have accepted it as just another incident in the world, the world that was always faithful in its fashion, the world he now knows. What has this Tom seen over the last twenty years?' he wondered as he continued to observe him. 'What has he done or had done to him, to have become so heartless? He had been heading off to be a diplomat in Spain or a civil servant in the Foreign Office, which were the obvious routes open to him, given his mastery of so many languages. But this isn't the face of a diplomat or a civil servant. This is the face of someone rootless and disillusioned, and doubtless desperate. Yes, and heartless too.'

Mr Southworth took out a cigarette and offered one to Tomás, who accepted it, and they each lit their respective cigarette on his proffered lighter. Then Southworth asked:

'What's happened to you, Tom Nevinson? Where have you been all this time? I don't know what decision you're talking about, I don't understand. But what can I do to help, if I can do anything, that is? It's not that I'm not glad of your visit, but why on earth have you come to see me after all these years?'

No one ever knew what had happened to Tom Nevinson, what had become of him, not exactly, not in detail; not even in a very broad-brush way. Where he'd been or with whom, what missions he'd undertaken, what damage he'd caused, how many misfortunes he'd averted. Only he knew that – but, then, the same applies to everyone, as regards knowing him or herself – and, to a lesser degree, Tupra or Reresby or Ure or Dundas, the man with all those names and possibly more, and Blakeston, who were his immediate superiors, his recruiting officers, the ones who had stolen what he had thought his life might be. Others may have known something too, very vaguely, the various, high-up people he presumably served, ultimately and theoretically: Sir John Rennie and Sir Maurice Oldfield, Sir Dick Franks and Sir Colin Figures, Sir Christopher Curwen and Sir Colin McColl, although it's unlikely he was ever under the remote orders of Sir David Spedding, the director of the Secret Intelligence Service from 1994 to 1999. But perhaps he never saw any of them, and they knew nothing about what he actually got up to, probably preferring to know as little as possible about what happened in those different places or about the methods employed by their subordinates, whom they kept at a prudent distance. They would issue instructions from their lofty peak and hope eventually to see them carried out, without ever knowing who or how. They would be grateful to the intermediate officers for deceiving them and keeping them in the dark, thus sparing them the grim or disagreeable facts about the actions they had unleashed without ever having to soil their hands, and who acted without asking for authorisation and without consulting them. They would be grateful for being wrapped in several opaque veils of ignorance, for being exempted from all guilt if an operation or a device proved to be a resounding failure or ended in disaster. They would positively demand not to be involved. Although, who knows, perhaps one of them did deign to meet Nevinson in person, if the latter had been particularly useful or performed outstandingly well, or had risen up the ranks to become one of those intermediate officers, above Blakeston perhaps, but always below Tupra; Tupra wasn't the kind of man to allow himself to be overtaken by an inferior. And no one ever knew, either, what promotions Tomás Nevinson might have received. No one outside MI5 or MI6, that is.

Mr Southworth was the person to whom he revealed most, but he didn't answer the question Mr Southworth had asked, namely, what had happened to him and where he had been all that time. Besides, it was more of a rhetorical question really, a manner of speaking, for no one is able or, indeed, willing to give a full account of the last twenty years or more of his life just like that, and almost no one would happily listen to such an account, unless it was a fiction about someone who didn't exist, an invented character, and, even then, it's not easy to follow such a long story. And so Tomás summarised as best he could what had happened to him since he left Oxford, when he was still an undergraduate or about to cease being one.

'Of course you don't know. You don't even know the beginning.' And when he said this, when he realised how little Southworth knew, Tom Nevinson calmed down, became more composed, and, in a way, found his feet, as tends to happen to those obliged to explain

415

themselves, when they see that this is vital if they are to be understood, however minimally. 'At the time, I told you that everything had been resolved, that I was no longer a suspect in the murder of that girl, Janet Jefferys, who was strangled on the same night I'd been with her. Things looked very bad for me, do you remember? I told you I'd been ruled out as a suspect. However, I didn't tell you how this had come about, nor what I had to do in exchange, because, among the conditions imposed on me was that of absolute secrecy, by which I'm still bound today. But this much I can tell you.' And he told him how Professor Wheeler had recommended him and arranged for him to meet Bertram Tupra, whom Wheeler described as 'a very resourceful fellow', about his encounter with him and Blakeston in Blackwell's, and what they had proposed. About the decision he had taken, about that moment he could remember so clearly and to which he had kept returning in his mind ever since.

'So am I to understand that you've been working for the Secret Service all these years? I'd heard you were working at the embassy in Madrid and for the Foreign Office.' Mr Southworth's tone revealed a mixture of incredulity, amusement and shock, as if, from the haven of the university, from his post outside the universe, he considered such a thing to be inconceivable. He would have assumed that Tom was pulling his leg had it not been so painfully clear that his troubled state was utterly genuine and that he was speaking very seriously, almost dramatically. The last thing that would have occurred to him was to make a joke about his situation, about himself. It was as if, with age, his youthful frivolity had vanished without trace, and his whole character had changed. Now he was an exhausted, introspective man, burdened down by the past.

'Oh, I was there as well, combining the two jobs, but, yes, I've been working for the Secret Service all these years,' said Tomás.

416

'Although circumstances have meant that I've had to spend a number of years out of circulation, out of commission. But I don't work for them now, I've left. Even so, I still can't tell you very much, the ban on talking is for life. I can't say where I've been or what I've done. I can only talk in general terms. I've been to quite a lot of places and done quite a lot of things, some doubtless useful, but most ugly and sordid. There's very little I can feel proud of, as I once did in the helpful smugness of youth. In fact, there are some days when I can barely stand being me, living constantly in my own company. You do what's necessary, you're focused on your mission and don't really think about anything else. You have no perspective, there's no time, and that's the best way to be while you're on active service. You pass from one day to the next, and every day is full of pressing problems and dangers, for which you have to find solutions, leaving little space for anything else. You're given your orders and you never question them or even analyse them. In a way, it's quite a comfortable life, having someone telling you what to do all the time. You can understand why some people like being in prison, because then you don't ever need to ask yourself any questions. You get precise instructions: do this, that and the other, or imprecise: just get results. That's how I've lived for a long time, convinced of what I was doing and merely doing it as efficiently as possible. When you're obliged to do something, it's best to become a convert to the cause, a fanatic. I was serving my country, the Crown, in an abstract way. Obviously, the Queen knows nothing about all that, poor woman, she'd probably shoot herself if she knew the things that are done in her name.' He had finished his cigarette and now took out his own pack, offering one to his former tutor, who preferred, however, not to smoke another so soon after the first. Mr Southworth remembered the brand of cigarettes Tom Nevinson used to smoke – Marcovitch they were

417

called – and how intrigued that policeman Morse had been by them. Marcovitch were no more, but he noticed that Nevinson was now smoking an equally original, unusual brand, the Greek-sounding George Karelias and Sons. While he was lighting his Karelias, Tomás remained silent for rather longer than it took to light the cigarette. Then he went on: 'Of course, sometimes you have to choose, usually between two evils, and decide there and then. One of the things I did that most torments me is having participated in the deaths of three colleagues. Well, they weren't colleagues exactly, I didn't actually know them, but they were compatriots, British soldiers, fighting on my side. And they had to be sacrificed, that's the word that was used. I had to allow them to be killed without warning them in any way. I couldn't say anything. Worse, I had to collaborate in their execution, pretending an enthusiasm I certainly didn't feel. What mattered most was not to bring down a long-standing operation, not to arouse suspicions, not to risk giving myself away. If I'd refused to take part, if I'd even held back, if I hadn't shown a kind of savage glee at the success of the attack, they would have viewed me with distrust or, worse, hostility. And I would probably have ended up dead. And you always watch out for yourself first, before anyone else. You learn that very early on. If your own survival is at risk, you're perfectly capable of disobeying orders or not even waiting to receive them. With one eye on the consequences, of course, but you only think about them afterwards, not at the moment it's happening. Besides, if you get caught, there is no mission, nothing, so the main thing is to stay alive. And undetected. At least I wasn't the executioner, they reserved that privilege for themselves. But if they'd asked me to do it, then I suppose I would have to have pulled the trigger. What else could I do? I'm speaking figuratively, of course, because there wasn't an actual trigger, but a detonator, you can imagine the mayhem. Mr Southworth, could I have something to drink? My mouth is really dry, and I've barely slept for several nights now.'

Southworth listed what drinks he had available, and, standing up while he poured Tomás a white wine, lukewarm despite having been in his mini-fridge (it was still rather early for wine, only half past nine in the morning, but that was what Tomás Nevinson had wanted out of the rather limited choice available), he asked him a series of questions to which he already knew the answers:

'Were you an infiltrator? Were you a mole? Is that what you did? What you're talking about sounds very like the situation in Northern Ireland.' There was still a sceptical tone in his voice, as if what Tom was describing, that world so different from his own, was some absurd fairy tale. Mr Southworth didn't go to the cinema or watch television and only read novels by nineteenth- or early-twentieth-century authors like Galdós, Clarín and Pardo Bazán, Valle-Inclán and Baroja, and occasionally, for a treat, Flaubert, Balzac, Dickens and Trollope. He hadn't read any spy novels at all, and so he couldn't even resort to fiction to grasp what was involved.

Tomás avoided that last remark.

'I didn't just do that, but, yes, I've been in different places on different occasions, where exactly doesn't matter, because it's always the same thing, making friends with your enemies and, if possible, deceiving them. I'm not saying it isn't interesting, even fascinating, because you do get to know those people. And what else would they have had me do, Mr Southworth, given my wretched gift for languages? Because I speak so many and can imitate any accent. Don't you remember? That's why I was recruited, why else? Well, the main reason anyway. And the first person to suggest it was Professor Wheeler, but I don't imagine you would know that, he wouldn't talk about those things with anyone, apart from his colleagues in the SIS, or the SAS or the PWE, if that still exists. Earlier, you asked me why on earth I came to see you after all this time. I came partly to ask you to tell me to what extent the Professor was responsible. You're a friend of his. You know him well and are close to him. You admired him, almost worshipped him. You are still friends, aren't you? Even though he's retired now and no longer runs the sub-faculty. There's a Welshman in charge now, I understand. Ian Michael.'

'Responsible for what?' Mr Southworth broke in.

'For what happened to me. For what I think they did to me. Replacing my life with another life. It's too late now to recover the life I thought I would live. Parallel time also passes, yes, parallel time,' he repeated quietly, then drank down that glass of wine in one.

'I don't know what you mean, Tom, but whatever it is you're referring to, I'm afraid I'm not in a position to tell you to what extent Peter, the Professor, is responsible for anything. You'd better ask him. He's in Oxford at the moment. Then he'll be off to Austin for a few months. He often gets invited to American universities now that he's retired. He spends part of the year there. They treat him with something bordering on reverence, and it brings him in some extra money too.'

'No, I wouldn't want to go and see him unless that's absolutely necessary. I wouldn't want to turn violent with someone his age. How old is he now? Over eighty? Especially someone for whom I have a lot of respect. I wouldn't want to call him to account if you don't think I should. You would know better than me how to interpret him.'

'Violent?' Southworth couldn't help but laugh at this unlikely declaration. He decided to pour himself a glass of wine too and then sat down again, with a flourish of his gown. 'What *are* you talking about? Although I don't think he'd mind very much as long as you finished the job off and were quick about it. The last time I asked him how he was, he said: "Awaiting the visit of the Grim Reaper, preferably a painless one and with a bit of advance notice, like a ship firing a warning shot across the bow before discharging the first cannon." He's very aware of his mortality. He remains active and in good health, but he's accepted the idea that he'll gradually go downhill. He might not mind a violent death. He might be amused by the sheer unexpectedness of it.' All Oxford dons seemed to have a rather sarcastic vein.

'Laugh if you want,' said Tomás gravely. 'Besides, I meant verbal violence not physical, although I could be tempted. Look, you've always struck me as an honest man, a fair man, the kind who says what he thinks. I want you to tell me how much the Professor knew about me. He won't know anything for certain, of course, how could he, but I would value your opinion and accept it. You know Wheeler better than almost anyone, and if you think he wasn't in the know, then I won't go and see him. But if you think he was guilty, then I'll have to visit him, and I won't make do with firing a few warning shots either.'

'Guilty of what? In the know about what?' asked Southworth, half-impatient and half-confused. 'The Secret Service has made you very cryptic. Appropriately enough, I suppose.'

Tomás let this new joke pass.

'I'll come to that in a minute. One step at a time.'

'As long as the steps aren't too long,' said Mr Southworth, maintaining his humorous tone, and glancing at his watch. 'I have a lecture at midday in the Taylorian. Luckily for you, that's my only lecture this morning. I was going to use this time to prepare, but it's a lecture I give every year – I probably gave it when you were here – and Valle-Inclán is a permanent feature. I doubt it will make much difference, though, if I don't read through my notes again.'

Tom Nevinson realised that it wouldn't be easy to tear Mr Southworth away from his old habits, from his tranquil world and his routine. He thought he had done so by bursting in on him like that, by his wild appearance and his incoherence, like an angry, unrecognisable ghost. However, once he'd calmed down and begun to explain himself, Southworth had reverted to the usual courteous Oxford way of speaking, ironic, sceptical, and slightly offhand, Tom remembered it well, even among the nobler, more serious members of Congregation. Mr Southworth had been there so long now that he'd become corrupted, his natural ingenuousness and rectitude diluted; it's very hard not to be contaminated by an eight-hundred-year-old clerical institution. Tom, however, was no longer a student, but a veteran of far harsher worlds, and he cared nothing for hierarchies. He sprang to his feet, went over to Mr Southworth and, in an extraordinary act of aggression, grabbed the false lapels of his gown with both hands.

'You don't take me seriously, do you, Mr Southworth? Well, you're going to have to. You're going to listen to me now until I've said everything I have to say. This is not a game. My life has not been a game or a joke. Twenty years ago, you conspired among yourselves to take my life from me. How could you do that? My services couldn't have been that indispensable, I was hardly unique. But the State is a capricious thing and wants to get everything it can out of every citizen. Yes, you played your part too: you advised me to go and talk to Wheeler and put myself in his hands, then Wheeler sent me to Tupra, and that was that, there was no escape. I only left two weeks ago, two weeks.' He still kept a firm grip on Southworth's gown, thinking: 'Now he'll see that I can be violent, that I could even turn violent with the Professor if I needed to, if he deserved it. That would be easy enough. Age doesn't absolve him.' And then came this other contradictory thought: 'Poor Mr Southworth, he hasn't done anything, he just wanted to protect me, to help me.' Then he shamefacedly released him, took a step back and sat down again. 'Forgive me, Mr Southworth, I went too far, and I'm sure you had nothing to do with it. Please forgive me. It's just that I've wasted more than twenty years of my life, and that, I think, is quite enough to drive anyone to madness and despair. You can't imagine what those years have been like. You've spent them quietly here, year after year, with your lectures and tutorials, your Valle-Inclán and your seminars, a continuum, barely noticing the passing of time. I, on the other hand, have spent them waiting for the Grim Reaper, for Death, any day, any hour, with just occasional periods of respite, but always knowing any respite will be short-lived, and you never do truly rest. It's been years since I've known any real rest. And I wasn't waiting for that visit because of my age, like the Professor, but because I kept being sent to the places that Death most frequents, because there are some territories that Death inhabits more than others; I told you what happened to those soldiers, well, that's the kind of terrain I've been travelling in, no, trickier than that, more dangerous.'

Mr Southworth calmly adjusted his gown and smoothed his wide lapels; he didn't lose his composure for a moment and even elegantly crossed his legs. He was still holding his glass of wine and hadn't spilled a drop because he hadn't resisted. He had simply let Tomás do as he wished, and not a flicker of alarm had crossed his face, although he may perhaps have pursed his lips slightly – more out of caution than anger – while Tom had hold of him, although without going so far as to actually shake him.

'You're forgiven,' he said, 'but if you do that again, I'll throw you out and refuse to hear another word. Tell me what you need to tell me and ask me whatever questions you need to ask, and at a quarter to twelve, that will be that. At midday, I'll give my usual lecture.'

He sounded determined and slightly offended, but not angry and not autocratic either. Tom Nevinson seemed momentarily disoriented, as if he didn't know what to say now that he was being urged to say it; where to begin, or, rather, how to continue, because he'd already begun in a rather disorganised way.

'I've served in good faith, Mr Southworth,' he said at last. 'At first, I did so reluctantly, but afterwards I served in good faith for many years. I did what I was asked or ordered to do, with a greater or lesser degree of success, and to the best of my ability. As I said, I've been to a lot of places and I've done my duty. I convinced myself that my work was useful, or, more than that, crucial for the defence of the Realm. I was unwilling initially, but I became an enthusiast, and enthusiasm can justify anything.'

'Your work? As an infiltrator, you mean.'

'Yes, but not always. Quite often, but not only. I've done other work too: desk work, research, writing reports, conducting inquiries. As well as phone-tapping and monitoring and surveillance. I've spent whole nights sitting in a car, watching a door or a window. And I've watched endless video footage. Better to use the term "espionage", it's wider-ranging and encompasses everything. But, yes, it involved a lot of disguises, changes of personality and appearance, speaking like someone else, changing my voice and my accent. That's the grubby part. It's what Henry V did when he wrapped himself in a cloak and mingled with his soldiers, to chat to them and sound them out. Or perhaps draw them out.' Mr Southworth was so well read that Tom was sure he would know the reference. 'He was perhaps the highest-ranking spy ever, at least in fiction. My wife pointed it out to me one day, because I'd never really noticed it before.'

'Of course you have a wife,' said Mr Southworth. It was only natural that, at his age, Tom should be married.

'Yes, Berta. We married years ago, in 1974, in Madrid. She was already my girlfriend when I was studying here. I don't know if I ever mentioned her to you. We had two children, a boy and a girl. I haven't seen or spoken to them for twelve years now. I wouldn't let myself, for reasons of security, of survival. They believe I'm dead, assuming they believed what they were told, if Berta did, I mean. I suppose she must believe it, but I'm not dead in her thoughts, which is what counts. Because I am officially dead, Mr Southworth. I no longer exist. And I have another daughter by another woman with whom I lived for a few years and who doesn't know my real name.' This time he said 'woman', not 'wife'. 'The girl doesn't have my name, but an invented one, the one I had to adopt after my death and which still appears on my papers now. But soon I will become Tomás Nevinson again and emerge from the archives of the dead. That girl, though, will always bear a false name, I'm afraid. And I don't think I'll be able to stay in touch with her, or even know anything about her. I've missed a great chunk of my Spanish children's lives, and I'll have to miss most of my English daughter's life too. I have no choice. Her mother wouldn't want me back. We lived together until she grew tired of my mysteries, my silences, my strange, passive life. And she kept the child, of course, children do tend to belong more to their mothers. I haven't seen them for a while now either, but not for quite as long. And what about you? Are you married? Do you have children?'

'Oh, no. That's not for me,' answered a now fully recovered Mr Southworth, although without giving any further explanation. Tomás had always felt he was a man almost religiously devoted to teaching, to music and literature, which were his passions. His life outside the university was a complete mystery, assuming he had a life outside. 'And you say you know nothing about your wife, and haven't for twelve years. How extraordinary.'

'No, as I said, I haven't seen or spoken to her. But I do know something about her and about the children, who, by now, are only just still children. Tupra keeps me informed now and then. He tells me they're fine and lack for nothing. Just so that I don't worry, not too much anyway, and don't succumb to temptation. It's been like that for some years. I know that Berta is now officially a widow, both here and in Spain. And that she hasn't remarried, even though she's free to do so. That's what makes me think that perhaps she's not entirely convinced I'm dead, because, obviously, no body was ever found. The official version is that I disappeared in Argentina. And since that happened a long time ago, she ended up having me declared legally dead. And, believe me, I've been dead a long time.'

'In Argentina of all places,' murmured Mr Southworth with a touch of irony in his voice. 'A bit out-of-the-way, don't you think? A bit remote? Even Borges left, and presumably for good reasons.'

'Even you seem to have forgotten that we fought a war against Argentina. It's amazing how easily we forget. Unless there's a football match between the two teams, and then everything flares up again for a while.'

'Of course, yes, you're right. We don't think much about that war. Did you take part in it? And what do you mean "a football match"?' Mr Southworth had no idea about football either.

'Whether I did or did not take part is unimportant. The report of my disappearance says that I did, that I vanished without trace and no one has heard from me since. It's assumed I was the victim of incensed Argentinians. It doesn't much matter. As I said, I've been in a lot of places, and they had to give some explanation to my family. And to a section of the Foreign Office which tends not to know much about anything, and who are happy to be told very little.'

'Hence the twelve-year absence.'

'Yes, I said goodbye to Berta right at the very start of that war. The truth is quite different, of course, otherwise I wouldn't be here with you now. You see, we all believe that the worst will never happen, despite the evident dangers. Basically, we're all optimists, we go to bed convinced we'll get up the next day. You gain confidence as you take on missions and assignments and emerge from them unscathed. And success of all kinds breeds pride, and, unconsciously, you develop a sense of invulnerability. If it went well this time, why shouldn't it go well the next, you think. And the more obstacles you overcome, the more scrapes you get out of, the more you believe that and the more risks you take. Until, in the end, something does go wrong and you fail. Or you don't fail exactly, but you have to be removed and are written off, useless. Burned, they call it. You don't know for how long, or if it will be for ever. Anyway, I had to disappear for real, I had to hide, to be a dead man as far as everyone was concerned, especially my wife, of course, with all communication, all contact, forbidden. A couple "befriended" her years ago, people from the other camp, you understand, just trying their luck really, and they terrified the life out of her. If I was assumed to be dead, then there was far less chance that anyone would go looking for me, although our enemies do tend to be sceptical types, who won't believe someone is dead until they see the body. They'll pursue a mole and punish him, and they'll only forget about him if enough time passes and they still haven't found him, and when those he harmed die or retire, join the reserves or end up burned as well. That's why so many years have to pass, unless you get lucky and someone bumps them off or puts them in prison. It doesn't last for ever though: the clandestine life is a short one, people get replaced very quickly, and your successors won't know you from Adam and will have their own scores to settle. They have no interest in avenging their fathers or their grandfathers, that's a complete myth. You quickly become ancient history.'

'I'm not sure I'm following you, Tom. Not entirely.'

Tomás was speaking at high speed now, on the assumption perhaps that Mr Southworth would, as he said, leave for his lecture promptly.

'Of course you do, Mr Southworth. You're an intelligent man. Anyway, I erased myself from the map. I took on another identity. I was provided with papers and a work permit so that I could lead an ordinary life in the town they sent me to, I could open a bank account, rent a flat, get my National Insurance number, just like everyone else. A medium-sized provincial town where no one would come looking for me. A town inhabited only by people who were born there or whose work had brought them there. I became a modest schoolteacher.'

'Teaching Spanish or languages, I imagine.'

'No, that could have aroused suspicions, because I speak the languages I speak far too well. No, I taught history, geography, literature, depending on the needs of the school. I spent about five years there – imagine that, one loses track of time – teaching twelve- and thirteen-year-olds or fourteen- and fifteen-year-olds, who aren't interested in anything. It was lucky really that I wasn't teaching them languages, because, at that age, they can't even be bothered to speak English well. The trouble they take to mangle their own language is remarkable really. Fortunately, I didn't have to live on my teacher's salary alone, although I pretended to: I couldn't be seen to be living beyond my means, I couldn't draw attention to myself or to any aspect of my life. It was, needless to say, very tedious, being stuck there, far from home, and having to live so circumspectly. But that's what I had to do to stay alive: one false move and I could lose everything. Our enemies have their own moles. They're not as good as ours, but they exist. Every cause does the same thing: namely, recruit people with nothing to do and nowhere to go, people who need a reason to get through the day and who'll join anything; every gang has its fanatics. And so you obey orders and do what you have to, you get on with things. As Cervantes said: *paciencia y barajar.* Shuffle the pack and deal again. The trouble is that, in those circumstances, there's no pack of cards to shuffle. You're trapped, glued to the spot, until one day someone tells you: 'It's all right, the danger's pretty much past. You can leave if you like, albeit cautiously. Everyone either thinks you're dead or has forgotten all about you. No one will be concerned for you or waste their time worrying about you.' Anyway, at least I lived fairly decently and without having to economise too much, thanks to a payment I received every six months, in cash, because they couldn't risk that money appearing in my account. You have to become paranoid, you have to think you're being watched even though you're probably not and no one knows where you are. You have to assume that the tiniest little thing might be detected. Tupra would send someone with the money, always someone different, a stranger, who would also give me a brief report on how things were in Madrid. I did have a few phone conversations with Tupra, though, always from a public phone.' Tomás fell silent for a moment and looked down at the floor, as if overcome by sudden grief or by a grief briefly deferred by that visit to Mr Southworth. Then he added:

'It's funny really, ironic: when Professor Wheeler suggested to me that I could be of use, one of his arguments was that it would give me the opportunity to influence world events and decisions; I wouldn't then be an outcast from the universe, he said, as the Earth's inhabitants always have been, although every place and time has its exceptions. And yet that's precisely how I've felt for years, it's how I feel now: an outcast from the universe. The one saving grace is that people think I'm dead and no one remembers me.'

Mr Southworth got up and poured Tom another glass of wine, first interrogatively raising the bottle. Tomás Nevinson had just downed his drink in one and mechanically lit another Karelias cigarette, this time without asking his former tutor if he would care to join him. He seemed silent, abstracted, his gaze still fixed on the floor. Mr Southworth again consulted his watch; they still had quite a lot of time.

'Given what you say, yours is clearly a special case. But, yes, being presumed dead would put any of us out of danger. No one would ask or want anything from us, no one would make demands or give us orders, no one would bother to seek us out or to inflict harm,' he said, perhaps simply to say something or to draw Tom out of his melancholy. 'Speaking of Peter, what was it you wanted to ask me about him.'

Despite Tom's radically changed appearance, despite his aggressive behaviour only a few moments before, Mr Southworth realised that he was beginning to feel the superficial affection and esteem he had felt for Nevinson when the latter was an outstanding, almost dazzling student, not dazzlingly intelligent, but endowed with an extraordinary linguistic talent, a remarkable facility for learning and speaking any language, for imitating and reproducing it. He had barely given a thought to Tom for about twenty years – or perhaps once or twice just after his departure; and perhaps once or twice more

431

when someone mentioned that he was working for the Foreign Office or at the embassy – but now he could clearly recall the concern he felt for him on the morning Tom found himself caught up in the murder of that girl from Waterfield's, and that policeman Morse came to interrogate him in these very rooms. He didn't remember the matter being cleared up or the guilty party arrested, but then he had rather lost interest once Tom had ceased to be a suspect and had left Oxford. However, Southworth always felt very protective towards his students, and had now, with some difficulty, succeeded in juxtaposing the broad, weather-beaten face of that man with the beard, moustache, scar and receding hairline with the now remote face of that promising, rather charming young man. Physically, the man before him was rather nondescript, as is the case with so many Englishmen, and so many Spaniards too. And yet, even in his current state of abstraction, he sensed that Tom had a ruthless streak. Perhaps he'd fallen silent because he was plotting or pondering his revenge. He exuded a kind of resentment that was at once abstract and real, and which seemed to belong to the worst of all resentments, that of the deceived. He had spent his life deceiving others, because of the nature of his work, but probably also because he considered himself to be the victim of a great, primordial deception. And that was how Southworth understood Tom's answer:

'I want to know, in your view, to what extent he was a party to it all. I'm not going to confront him if you don't think I should, if you believe him to be innocent or ignorant. I've already confronted my immediate boss about it, insofar as that was possible, of course. Some people are impervious to such confrontations, however murderous you feel towards them. That's something you learn, it's a fact. You just have to accept the dirty tricks certain individuals play on you, or, at most, rebuke them.' And he used the Spanish word, *putadas*, for 'dirty tricks'. After all, like Wheeler, Mr Southworth was a Hispanist. 'And you can do nothing against the State, against the Crown. The Crown is always in the strongest position, it's too big, too powerful, it has laws that it can change or ignore at will, or break with impunity. And it can crush you. When there's no other way out, when there's no going back . . . The last thing you should expect from the world is justice or redress. They simply don't exist. You can try to retaliate, and feel a small, momentary sense of satisfaction, but it doesn't last. Nothing can restore what's been lost. I often used to say that to Meg, and it would drive her crazy, because I never explained what I meant exactly or why I was saying it. She would eye me curiously, fearfully, wondering what had happened to me in the past and what it was that I'd lost. She never knew anything about me, or only about my present life and a vague, invented past. She found it odd that I had no family and never spoke about them, no parents or siblings, nothing. No one ever visited me in that provincial town, no one even wrote me a letter. At first, I would sometimes pretend to go on a trip somewhere, but would immediately get bored; in fact, I would book myself into a hotel for a few nights and barely leave the room during the day, in case I had the misfortune to run into Meg in the street, when she thought I was away.'

'Meg? The other woman?'

'Yes, the mother of my little girl. I didn't intend that or anything like it to happen. I assumed I wouldn't be stuck there for very long and didn't want to form any strong bonds. I intended just to teach my classes and keep a low profile, and generally pass myself off as a drab, dull fellow. On Saturdays, I'd go and watch the local football team, who were struggling not to get relegated from the First Division, because I had to do my best not to seem odd or reclusive. Having known far worse situations, I thought I'd be able to cope with the loneliness, but the lack of things to do and the lack of tension and adrenaline didn't help, and actually became a real burden. Time drags then, and you need company, need someone to talk to. It's best not to get a reputation as a *putero* either, in small towns like that, people end up knowing everything.' Again he resorted to the Spanish term, as if all the words deriving from *puta*, 'whore', were more graphic or more uncompromising than in English. 'In the end, I didn't have to make any effort at all, she did all the work; I mean, she was the one who chatted me up and came on to me. She worked as a nurse at the dental practice I went to. That's where we met. She brushed up against me a few times, whether intentionally or not, I don't know, and briefly positioned herself so that I couldn't help but admire her bust. We'd exchange a couple of jokes when I arrived and again when I left; and she seemed to find my jokes funny, which is always flattering. I probably shouldn't say so, but she fell for me like a ton of bricks, and placed me firmly in her sights. And, well, who can resist a tight-fitting white tunic?' He stopped and wondered if Mr Southworth was sensitive to such curves, but seeing that Southworth remained unmoved, he assumed this was not something that interested him. 'Only a few months later, she was talking about getting married, or at least wanting us to live together. She was quite a lot younger than me, although not in absolute terms – that, at least, was her view. There was nothing to stop me marrying, given my new identity as a bachelor. I could have married, then vanished later on, without a goodbye or an explanation, when I was allowed to return to the world. I was used to that as well, to appearing and disappearing from the lives of others. A few months here or there, pretending to be someone else; on one such mission, I stayed in a place for two whole years, and then, once the mission was over, I was off, leaving the people I'd lived with either condemned to death or dead, and others on their way to prison.' Tomás briefly fell silent, then went on: 'There's a long tradition of husbands leaving their wives in the lurch without a word, but rather fewer examples of wives doing the same. Still, I preferred not to do anything that might attract attention, not to be a cause for celebration or become too involved with Meg's family, who lived elsewhere and never visited; she always went to see them. The fewer people who knew me, the better. Knew me well, I mean.' He paused again.

'And yet you have a child by her,' said Mr Southworth, taking advantage of that pause. 'How did that happen?' He was at least intrigued now, crossing and uncrossing his legs as a sign that he was interested, creating waves with the skirts of his gown.

'Well, after some time had passed, she played a trick on me. Yes, a trick. However careful you are, if a woman wants to become pregnant, she will. As long as she's fertile, of course, and I already knew that *I* was. And so she broke the news to me one day ("I don't know how it happened, it was an accident"), and then I had no choice but to move in with her, because of the child. It wouldn't have been fair to leave her to cope alone when we were both living in the same town. Oh, I suggested she have an abortion, but how could she possibly agree to that, when she'd deliberately wanted to get pregnant? Had planned it. I was definitely not amused, but it didn't really change anything, and, in a way, had its advantages: the more normal my life seemed to be, the less danger I was in, and what could be more normal than moving to a town, finding a girlfriend and having a child with her? What could be more commonplace, something anyone could do? I still resisted marriage, though; I fobbed her off with various excuses. She became suspicious of my silences, the absence of any concrete past, because my past remained a mystery to her. I had to improvise a little to fill in the gaps, inventing episodes I would sometimes have difficulty remembering later on. In general, though, I wasn't much of a talker, and so I got by. And she put up with it; she was forgetful and she forgot.'

'Why did you resist marriage? As you yourself said: you were someone else and you were single, and, when the time came, you could always make yourself scarce, *tomar las de Villadiego*. With no qualms, I mean.' Here Mr Southworth revealed the Hispanist in him, because all Hispanists have a liking for the kind of colloquial expressions they've read in books and which almost no one actually uses.

'I was someone else because I had to be, but I was also me. I'd been many people in those twenty years, that was, in part, my job, but I've always been me as well as all those other people, and I was married to Berta. That probably won't make much sense to you: I've been with quite a number of women, sometimes because I liked them, sometimes out of loneliness or desperation and sometimes because it suited me, because it made things easier or provided me with a cover or with certain information. But if you don't maintain some symbolic loyalty, if I can put it like that, you're entirely lost and you forget who you are, who you really are. And however many anomalous situations you may experience in your life, you always hope to go back to being that person one day. That identity can become very shaky when you pretend to be someone else for a long time and settle into a borrowed life. As I said, you need something symbolic to cling to, anything more is almost impossible. I don't know, it's like the exile who refuses to change his nationality even though, for the last thirty years, he's lived outside his own country, a country that abused him and threw him out. I know several such examples.' He raised his glass for more wine, and added, as if not wanting Mr Southworth to take him for a sentimentalist or a fool, 'Oh, I would have married Meg if I'd had to, if my survival had depended on it. It's not as if I'd vowed never to marry again. But it wasn't necessary and I didn't have to. I just preferred not to. Fortunately, no one nowadays frowns on couples who live together without getting married, even in a provincial town, even in a school. Anyway, I managed. The little girl was born and everything followed its normal course. Totally normal. I felt safer with each day that passed; each day took me one day nearer to being able to climb out of that hole, however slowly things moved. That, at least, is what I told myself.'

'But Berta was officially a widow,' said Mr Southworth. He wasn't sure whether to pour Tom any more wine, but he could hardly refuse him either. The drink seemed to have no effect on Tom, who, if he was accustomed to beginning so early in the day, was clearly a seasoned drinker, or else an alcoholic, because some alcoholics can remain completely unaffected even after several drinks. 'According to you, she could have got married whenever she liked. Your loyalty, as you call it, would have counted for nothing. Didn't that give you pause for thought?'

'I don't know. Possibly. I'm me and she is she, and she's been told that I've been dead for years, which is quite a different matter. But she hasn't got married, not as far as I know. That's what Tupra told me anyway, and he checks up on her regularly. Not that I entirely trust him. On the contrary, after what happened two weeks ago, I don't trust him an inch. He's capable of anything, but he would gain nothing by lying to me about that. He's someone who really does have no scruples, no qualms. He's better than I am at our job, at what is no longer *my* job. I bet you he's been married several times, under his many different names. Even that grotesque fellow Blakeston might have done the same when he was a field agent. There are plenty of women desperate to find a man, any man. As many as there are men desperate to find a woman, any woman. They usually end up getting together, and then no one's happy.' He was suddenly uncertain as to whether he'd already mentioned Blakeston by name, because he added: 'As I mentioned before, Blakeston was my other recruiting officer. The one disguised as Montgomery.'

Mr Southworth didn't reply, but said:

'I see. And now what? What was it that happened two weeks ago and that brought you here?'

And life did continue for the person who had been Tomás Nevinson, brought up in Madrid, and who had studied, first, at the British Institute in Calle Martínez Campos, and, later, at the Studio in Calle Miguel Ángel, a lad from Chamberí, who, now, at forty, was living in a medium-sized English town with a dental nurse called Meg and a little girl called Val or Valerie. In a way, he enjoyed that quiet, monotonous life, it was a relief after all his vicissitudes and endless wanderings, and who doesn't now and then long to retreat to one of those towns where you can feel the hours passing and become a provincial gentleman with methodical habits and no hidden secrets, plain Mr Rowland, the name he'd been given for his time in hiding and in flight, for that vital period of exile.

Tom Nevinson loved the little girl right from the start, indeed, he totally adored her, especially when she was a few months old and began to smile at him with something resembling consciousness or at least a kind of animal recognition, rather than just vaguely making a face at no one in particular. He didn't hold back his feelings either, even though he knew that, sooner or later, he would have to part with her, possibly never to see her again, or perhaps precisely because of that. 'While it lasts, I have to make the most of this,' he told himself. 'What does it matter if I leave no trace, no memory in her, that will be tomorrow, and today is today, and it's today that matters, the only thing that has ever mattered to me. I've lived my whole life from day to day and from night to night. She'll leave both trace and memory in me, I'll preserve those images and the memory of her soft, smooth touch. I had so little to do with Guillermo and Elisa, and by now they'll be really grown up; I was present so rarely in their early years, and, given that I'm marooned here now, imprisoned, I'm not going to waste the years I have with Val. And even though she won't remember, no one will be able to take her first love story from her, so that it can be said of her: "*Elle avait eu, comme une autre, son histoire d'amour*" – even if she turns out to be a stern, cold woman, or a soulless creature like me, even if she drives people away, for it's impossible to know how a child will turn out, they can prove very disappointing and it might be best not to see that, or so I tell myself as some sort of consolation. How mean-spirited it is, though, that *comme une autre* – "like anyone else". Mr Southworth had murmured those words in his almost perfect French, on my last morning of freedom, my last morning of innocence. And then he'd added: "We don't always know about other people's love stories, not even when we're the object, the goal, the aim." I've had plenty of opportunities since to find out how true that is, and to suffer the consequences.'

And so Tom would eagerly await going home after school. As soon as the child could walk, as soon as she discovered speed, she would race towards the front door the moment she heard his key in the lock, stumbling, falling, getting to her feet again with incredible determination, levering herself up on her tiny hands, until she recovered her ephemeral balance and excitedly staggered onward, to launch herself into his arms. He would pick her up and throw her into the air a couple of times and catch her, both of them laughing, while her mother stood watching, concerned that her daughter might fall, but pleased to see the two of them together. It was a pretty good life really, almost a blessing in comparison with the other lives he'd known. He sometimes wondered if, unbeknown to him, he had other children elsewhere, another girl or boy of another nationality, speaking another language, or living on that other island, brought up by his enemies, and taught to hate people like him, indoctrinated. He shrugged: if there were any children, they weren't his responsibility, even though he might have casually engendered them. Val wouldn't be his responsibility either, when he left. Children soon forget, only grown-ups remember.

At the same time, though, Tomás despaired. Patiently and silently, like people who wait hopelessly, knowing there's no escape: those who must wait to be rescued. When Val wasn't there, when she was at nursery or asleep, he felt each passing hour weighing on him. The quietness, the greyness, the repetitiveness, the slowness, the feeling of being useless and marginalised, of being cut off from what moved the world, from everything that was meaningful – of being expendable and replaceable – all these things tormented and consumed him. He didn't delude himself: he knew the day would come when he would have to retire completely, like so many of his colleagues and all his predecessors since the days of Sir Mansfield Smith Cumming, since 1909, and that day was not far off either; the clandestine life eats away at body and soul and corrodes your personality, yet it's addictive too, and almost everyone finds it hard to give up. Yes, he was tired, and had only realised just how tired when he stopped, but he also still felt young, forty is no age at all in other fields, in most fields. He didn't accept that his present enforced retirement would be definitive. He was too involved in his work to comply with an order to stop altogether. That order had not yet been given, and so, despite the indifferent passing and passing of time, he could still fantasise about leaving there and returning to his old life. Even if that meant sitting at a desk and

441

dreaming up strategies and tactics, as was doubtless increasingly the case with Tupra. He'd be quite happy planning operations, although it was true that these were fewer in number since the fall of the Berlin Wall in 1989 and the disintegration of the Soviet Union in 1991. MI6 had been left feeling somewhat vacant, in a vacuum, and certain agents were already offering their services to the private sector, to multinationals, political parties, big foreign companies. Marooned in his adoptive town, he had missed those two great historic events, but he simultaneously consoled himself with and brooded on the fact that he had in some way contributed to them, except, of course, no one would remember him now.

Alarm bells only rang once during that period of endless stability in the provinces, and that was at the beginning of his time there, before he'd even met Meg and when there was no hint of either disintegration or fall. A woman turned up at school asking for Mr James Rowland, which was how he was known there, although those who were allowed to invariably called him Jim, though not, of course, his pupils; this was before the days of false camaraderie between teacher and pupils. He was in a class at the time, and the caretaker had told her that he couldn't be disturbed. Tom had another lesson immediately after that one, and when the woman insisted, the caretaker went to his classroom as the first lot of pupils were leaving and the next lot arriving, and told him that a woman was waiting to speak to him at reception, that she hadn't wanted to come back at a more convenient hour, but had preferred to wait.

'Did she say what her name was?' asked Tom, or, rather, Mr Rowland.

'Well, that's the thing, you see. First, she said it was Vera Something-or-other, and I didn't quite catch it, because it was a foreign name. And she has an accent too.'

'What kind of accent?'

'I've no idea, Mr Rowland. I couldn't tell. She repeated the name, and when I still didn't understand, she added that now she was also Mrs Rowland. If you don't mind my saying, Mr Rowland, I was unaware that you had a wife.'

'And I don't, Will. You were quite right.'

'So she isn't your wife.'

'Of course not, Will. Tell me, what does she look like? How old is she?'

'About thirty. Pretty well dressed for a foreigner. I mean she's not like one of them immigrants. Not exactly proper, though, if you know what I mean.'

'No, I don't.'

'I mean, she could be an actress or a television presenter, that kind of thing. Not that I've ever seen one off-screen, of course. She's wearing a lot of perfume too. My room will stink of the stuff for days. It's a nice smell, mind, a bit strong, but nice.' He said this as if it were somehow Mr Rowland's responsibility. 'What shall I tell her? To wait another hour? It's a bit awkward having her perched on a stool there. I don't know what to say to her. I could give her my chair, I suppose.'

'No, tell her I've left and won't be back until tomorrow.'

'Are you sure? She seems dead set on seeing you today.'

'Yes, I'm sure. It must be some mistake. She must have got the wrong Rowland.' It wasn't an unusual surname by any means, nor was it that common either. There were thirty or so Rowlands in the London directory, and six or seven in Oxford. That's why he'd chosen it; a Smith or a Brown sounded less credible.

'I'm sorry, Mr Rowland, and I know it's none of my business, but wouldn't it be best if you spoke to her?'

'I haven't got time today. If you wouldn't mind, Will, would you just do as I ask?'

Tom didn't like the sound of this at all, he found it highly suspicious that someone should have tracked him down in that town so soon, when his new identity was known to so few. MI6 had its moles as well, they were everywhere, and, at the time, he still felt in great danger, a feeling that didn't begin to go away until a good two years of absolute, excessive peace, boredom, routine and waiting had passed, a wait that had no fixed term. At the end of the day, he went cautiously over to Will's office, and, seeing him sitting alone on his chair, he peered round the door and asked:

'Has my fake wife left? Did she say anything more?'

'She asked where you lived, so that she could visit you. "I'm not authorised to give you that information," I told her. What about a phone number? "No, sorry, no phone number either." She said she was staying at the Jarrold and asked if you'd be kind enough to drop by when you finish work.' The Jarrold wasn't the best hotel in town, but the second best, and the most traditional, comfortable and old-fashioned. 'I don't think she believed that you'd left for the day. If you don't go and see her at the hotel, she'll come back here tomorrow.'

'All right. And thanks for everything, Will.'

No, he didn't like this situation at all. Even if it was a mistake, the caretaker was now aware of that peculiar visitor, which meant that his colleagues would know about it too, possibly the head teacher and his pupils, and the first commandment was to go unnoticed, to avoid giving rise to any gossip. And since he hadn't asked Will to keep the matter to himself, because that would only have made him more curious and ask more questions, there was nothing to stop him commenting on it to someone else. Such tiny novelties and unexpected titbits were meat and drink to him.

Tomás felt he couldn't risk meeting that woman, because, for all he knew, she might shoot him dead the moment she set eyes on him, even in a public place and with witnesses, it wouldn't be the first time: a settling of accounts regardless of the consequences; what mattered was that the account was well and truly settled. It wasn't advisable to do nothing either and have that Vera Something-or-other or Mrs Rowland coming to the school day after day, when she might not always behave with such discretion, and, besides, it would be impossible to avoid her for ever. So he went back to his flat, picked up his Charter Arms Undercover – which they'd allowed him to take into exile because it was small and easy to hide – slipped it into his overcoat pocket and headed for the Jarrold. It was best to clear up that business as soon as possible, despite the uneasy feeling he had about it.

He asked for Mrs Rowland at reception. Still holding the phone, the receptionist asked who he should say was calling.

'Mr Rowland.'

'The lady says you should go straight up. Room 38, third floor.'

'No, tell her I'd rather wait down here. I'll be in that room over there.' There were two rooms, one on either side of the foyer, and he indicated the one that was busiest.

He sat down at a table, his eyes fixed on the door, but a safe distance away from it, his back against the wall, well protected. He waited for five minutes, during which time more people came in; there was only one woman on her own, but she was middle-aged and didn't look remotely like an actress. He ordered some tea, and before they brought it, he finally saw someone come in who could possibly be Mrs Rowland. She was rather well dressed, as Will had told him, but in a more frivolous style than most English women, better groomed; she was about thirty and quite striking, not pretty exactly (her nose came within a millimetre of being too long), but altogether rather good-looking. She stood in the doorway, surveying the occupied tables, clearly searching for someone in particular, someone she would recognise at once. She looked blankly at Tom, without a glimmer of recognition. Then timidly, inquiringly, he raised one hand, keeping his other hand – still gripping the wooden handle of the gun – in the pocket of his overcoat, which he had not yet taken off. He saw a look of disappointment, almost desolation cross the woman's face, a look that instantly became one of exasperation or annoyance. This wasn't a very English reaction either, too spontaneous, too blatant. She recovered enough to more or less erase that look, and came over to his table. He stood up to greet her, one hand still in his pocket.

'Mrs Rowland? I'm Jim Rowland. I understand you wanted to see me. But I don't think we know each other, do we?'

She made no move to sit down, nor to shake his hand. She remained standing, avoiding his gaze, as if in a hurry to leave. She nervously smoothed her thick straw-coloured hair. Her pale eyes were not quite prominent enough to be described as bulging, and were just a touch too pale to be the colour of white wine, that is, slightly yellowish. All her features seemed to conspire to make her rather plain, and yet, while she did border on the ugly, she nevertheless managed to be very attractive.

'I'm sorry, it's not you I wanted,' she said in what sounded to Tom like an Italian accent. He would have to hear more to know for certain, she could be Yugoslavian or from some other Eastern European country. This thought put him even more on his guard.

'Well, I'm definitely me,' he answered. 'I don't know who you were hoping to meet. You came to my school this morning.'

'I was hoping to find my husband, but you're not him. Forgive me. It was a mistake. You have exactly the same name. I'm so sorry to

446

have put you to any trouble. And I'm sorry, too, to have bothered you. Have a good afternoon.'

It occurred to Tomás that it was quite a coincidence to have chosen the name of a man being pursued by his new wife. She was in no mood to explain any further. She turned to leave, having first murmured another hasty apology. Since he wasn't her Jim Rowland, she had nothing to say to him and certainly wasn't going to tell him her life story. He still couldn't pin down her accent, which was quite marked, but not grotesquely so.

At that moment, they brought him the tea he had ordered, and the woman had to stay where she was to allow the waitress to pass.

'Wait. Now that we're here, wouldn't you like something to drink?' Tom said, then immediately realised that, in his present life, even the most elementary curiosity was forbidden to him.

Had he insisted, he was sure it wouldn't have taken much to persuade Mrs Rowland to sit with him for a few minutes and set out her case, her history and that of her husband. But he mustn't attract anyone's attention in that provincial town. If someone saw him at the hotel chatting to a foreign-looking woman, when foreigners were still a rarity, someone would notice and people would talk, he would suddenly seem less anodyne than they'd thought and they would ask him questions. And if she somehow managed to draw him in, if he got interested and felt tempted to help her find that other Jim Rowland, for example (he was, after all, an expert at finding people), he would be stepping out of his assigned role. 'I'm a drab, bland schoolteacher, who couldn't be more ordinary, and to whom nothing unexpected can ever happen,' he reminded himself. 'My adventurous life is over, at least for as long as I stay here.' Then another thought occurred to him: 'Perhaps this woman is pretending. Perhaps she's been sent here to meet me face to face and find out if I am, in fact, Tom Nevinson;

447

she'll have been shown photos of me and recognised me despite the glasses, the moustache and this stupid pseudo-intellectual beard. She won't do me any harm herself, but she might tell someone else: "Yes, that James Rowland is definitely Tom Nevinson. Over to you." Or perhaps the people who sent her, and who will turn up later, know me by another name. That's why she doesn't want to sit down for a casual chat. She's seen enough, her mission is complete, and she knows that, on the basis of her testimony, they'll do me in.' What came into his head was the Spanish term, *dar matarile*, 'to do someone in'. That's what being bilingual is like, both languages are always drifting around in your head, and sometimes emerge simultaneously.

'No, thank you,' said Vera Rowland, if that was her name. She skirted round the waitress and walked smartly out of the room. She would doubtless go straight back to room 38 and catch a train the next morning, going who knows where.

VIII

That was the only unpleasant surprise he experienced during his long, dull stay in that town, which, like so many other towns, never seemed to be fully awake. The whole business had lasted only a few hours, but it took him months to drive it from his mind, all the time expecting someone else to arrive, a man or a woman with a job to do. Or two men, like Lee Marvin and Clu Gulager at the beginning of that film from the 1960s, *The Killers*, which he seemed to recall took place somewhere similar, in a school or a boarding house, where John Cassavetes had been holed up for years, working as a teacher or something. In Spanish, it was called *Código del hampa – The Criminal Code* – and he saw it when he was about fifteen. It was loosely based on a short story by Hemingway of which all he could remember was that the victim of the paid assassins – a Swedish man called Ole Andreson, he did also remember that name – made no attempt to run away or defend himself, but simply accepted his execution – the jus-tificatory euphemism used by any group that needs to justify itself, including the SIS and, therefore, Tom too – as if he were weary of waiting or weary of being afraid and said to himself: 'At last they've found me. I shouldn't complain. I was given a little extra time. Use-less, meaningless time, but nevertheless a little extra time to spend in the universe. And since all such respites must have an end, so be it.' The assassins in the film, Marvin and Gulager, were so struck by his attitude that they set about conducting their own investigation. If something like that happened to him, thought Tom Nevinson, he wouldn't remain inert and passive like the Swede, he wouldn't allow them to gun him down in front of a blackboard without putting up a fight. During the months it took him to shake off that fear, he would always carry his gun in his pocket, even when he was teaching. He knew he would grow weary if that situation went on for much longer, but not weary of living with fear, because fear had been his constant companion since he was very young, ever since the night someone killed Janet Jefferys, shortly after he, Tom, had sex with her. He was too accustomed to fear to grow weary of it, having known fear in almost every possible form.

But time passed and no one appeared, no one came for him or tried to 'do him in'. Gradually, he began to relax, although never completely, always keeping his antennae alert: some people are in no hurry at all and will wait patiently for the one moment when you lower your guard. He would sometimes think about that woman, Mrs Rowland, and couldn't help amusing himself inventing possible stories, since he would never know the truth, and he regretted not having made her stay with him for a while at the Jarrold, so that he could question her; it would have been easy enough to persuade her: 'You owe it to me for the minor inconvenience you caused.' If she hadn't come simply in order to identify him, then she really must have been on the trail of her husband, which was very odd indeed. Perhaps she was some sort of mail-order bride. She must have moved to England, where she'd got married, or so she thought, to a certain James Rowland ('I'm also Mrs Rowland,' Will said she'd told him as a last resort, after he'd twice failed to understand her foreign surname; a shame really, because that would have provided Tom with more information), and he, for whatever reason – disappointment, regret, belated jitters, bigamy – had *tomado las de Villadiego*, to use that phrase which, in Mr Southworth's view, was still in current usage, and quite simply deserted her. Or perhaps she had been tricked into joining a prostitution ring, in which case she'd clearly managed to escape, because she certainly didn't look like an abused, submissive whore. She'd seemed very resolute, almost commanding, and certainly not helpless; she was tastefully made up; and, while her continental clothes may have been rather too frivolous for that priggish country, they were certainly not loud. Perhaps she wanted to have her revenge on that devious husband and was intent on tracking down all the existing Rowlands in Britain, ruling them out one by one. Or perhaps she merely wanted to demand an explanation, after having been so unceremoniously dumped. This all sounded very strange, but, then, imagination was not Tom Nevinson's strong point, and he could think of no other possible scenario, except that it was rather as if Berta had set off to scour the world in search of him, because he really was a disappeared husband. As far as Berta was concerned, though, he was dead, and there was no point looking for him, not even for his dead body abandoned at some remote point on the globe, and, besides, in theory, others would already have tried or would have tried and failed.

With the passing of time, the whole episode faded from his memory, or else he kept it in mind only until it took on the quality of a prediction or an omen. Later, he met Meg, unexpectedly made her pregnant, went to live with her and their daughter Valerie, whom he adored, but with whom he would spend only a few years. He sometimes felt as if he'd lived in that town all his life, had been born there and would die there an old man; that everything that had happened before, however varied and intense, was just a dream. This happens to almost everything that ceases to exist, which, precisely because it does cease to exist, always seems like a dream. What no longer exists is like ash on the sleeve.

Then, in 1993, he received the visit. Tupra informed him of this the day before, but neither he nor Blakeston deigned to come, neither did any of the various individuals, doubtless mere errand boys, who had brought him that cash payment every six months, something that had never once failed in all those years. They sent someone new, possibly a subaltern, an intern, a beginner. Despite being warned of the visit, Tomás approached the meeting with great caution and with his old Undercover in his hand, as was only right when meeting any stranger. They met in one of the visitors' lounges in the Jarrold, to which Tomás had immediately taken a fancy, and where, subsequently, he would sometimes go on his own to read the newspapers, as if he, too, were merely a visitor passing through. The messenger was a dandyish, rather pudgy young man, inoffensive in appearance and pedantic in speech, very well turned out and with an absurd Dickensian kiss-curl on his forehead, like a polychrome moulding (he had bicoloured hair, blond and brown, a style fashionable in the 1990s). He said his name was Molyneux, an apparently French surname, not uncommon in England and which had a certain cachet, and he had come to tell him that, with the fall of the Berlin Wall and the rapid break-up of the USSR, no one in those Eastern European countries was either particularly alert at the moment or very active. The Stasi and the other secret services were more worried about their own fate, about their slow dismantling and – sensing what was to come – afraid that, one day, depending on the direction taken by events, they might themselves become the object of reprisals or lynchings (after what had happened to the Ceauşescus in Romania, no one felt entirely safe). Everyone was taking up positions and, in some cases, a general stampede had already begun, along with the destruction of compromising files.

'We do not believe,' he said, using a rather grand 'we', which doubtless included Tupra, 'that they're much concerned now with settling old scores, that must be the last thing on their minds.' As for Ulster, there was real, if secret, progress being made, and it was unlikely they would want this disrupted by some extemporaneous act of revenge. It was always possible that a loose cannon, an unrepentant diehard, might try, because no one can control the individual psyche (Molyneux used the word 'psyche', for he was equally pedantic in his choice of vocabulary). 'There will still be damage done and murders committed before peace or something like it is achieved, we take that for granted; not for nothing have there been three thousand dead in the last twenty years, that's counting the casualties on both sides.' But the current tendency was towards moderation, leaving the unresolved unresolved, at least until the Last Trump sounds, and Molyneux tittered to himself, pleased with his little joke. 'In short, Mr Nevinson – sorry, Mr Rowland,' the pudgy young man went on, 'it seems to us that it's time for you to come back, to leave. Not in order to rejoin the service, not at once. That might happen one day should we need you, but, then again, it might not, we can't make any promises. You worked yourself into the ground last time, and you've been out of training for many years now.' This was his perfunctory way of announcing to Tom that he might be definitively retired. 'It will be a gradual process, but, for the moment, you can return to London and see how things develop. It's a nice central location, too, so don't worry, you won't be banished to some remote suburb, as if you were still in exile, but you'll be a safe distance from us, at least temporarily. Of the very few people who know your identity and your face, most will believe you're dead, so you shouldn't be in any danger; still, better safe than sorry. Best to maintain your current appearance and not show your face at our offices or those of the Foreign Office.'

That young whippersnapper, thought Nevinson, had the nerve to speak to him about 'us', an 'us' that excluded him; he bit his tongue, choosing not to put him firmly in his place just yet; Molyneux was, after all, an emissary from Tupra; but Tomás found that Napoleonic forelock so absurd, perched there like a cockroach, that he felt like grabbing a pair of scissors or a comb and scissoring or combing it into extinction.

At the same time, though, he couldn't help feeling touched and grateful, and even experienced a ridiculous impulse to kiss the young whippersnapper on his bulging, kiss-curled forehead, for being the bringer of such good news. During those long, slow years, there had been quite a few afternoons after school when he'd walked to the station and gone out onto the platform that bore the sign *Trains to London*. He'd watched those trains come in and stop for a couple of minutes, calling to him with their open doors, inviting him to climb aboard. He'd felt such a longing to walk over, climb on, and pay for his ticket on the train. It was so simple, so normal, and so many passengers did it without a second thought, as a matter of routine. For him, on the other hand, it had become an impossibility, as unimaginable as setting off for Java. Once in London, it was only a few stops on the Underground to the airport, where he could get a direct flight to Madrid, to Berta and his real or first children. Sometimes, when he was at a low ebb, he'd watched those trains leave with almost painful longing. He'd watched them move off much as some nineteenth-century country bumpkin standing on a footpath or in a field would have observed the trains passing in the distance.

'When can I move?' he asked Molyneux.

'In a week's time, a small flat will be ready for you in Dorset Square, which, as you know, is near Baker Street. It's pretty small, more of a garret really, but large enough for an interregnum. You just tell us when you want to move. Take as long as you like, because the flat will be there waiting for you.'

Young Molyneux would, of course, be unaware that during the Second World War, a section of the famous SOE had its headquarters at No. 1 Dorset Square. Tomás wondered if he would end up living in the same building, even if it was just for an 'interregnum', to use Molyneux's word; if, that is, it was still owned by the Secret Service after half a century. 'Crown properties probably remain the property of the Crown for ever,' he thought. 'The Crown only lets us go when it no longer needs us.'

'The flat will be ready in a week's time, you say. Well, then, I'll be there in a week's time.'

It simply wasn't an option to leave without a word, without so much as a goodbye or an explanation, as so many unscrupulous husbands, and a few wives, have done over the ages. To avoid Meg kicking up a fuss and trying to find him, to avoid her reporting his disappearance to the police, he decided to tell her the truth, or part of the truth. No one would have been able to find the James Rowland he was, because he didn't exist, but it troubled him to think of Meg vainly scouring the country, like that foreign Mrs Rowland, because you never can tell what desperate people might be capable of, that is, people who don't understand what has happened to them.

'I've been married for many years, and I have two children,' he told her. 'When our marriage ended, I came here to forget about them, because it was too painful living in such close proximity. That's why I didn't want to marry you, because I'm already married, and still am, we never divorced, you see. At least I didn't take my deception that far, and didn't break any laws. I now have the possibility of going back to my previous life, and, yes, you're quite right, I shouldn't have remained so silent about my past, it would have been better and fairer to have told you everything. My silence wasn't ill-intentioned, but it was utterly selfish, but then we all survive as best we can, taking one day at a time, defending ourselves against infinite grief and grabbing whatever comes our way, without even thinking about the consequences. Yes, I did use you, but I would remind you that I never wanted things to go this far, I didn't want us to have a child together. Not that I regret it now, on the contrary, I'm glad of it, as you well know. I can't ask you to forgive me, and I don't expect or deserve that. It breaks my heart to think I won't see you or Val every day, but you must understand that, for years now, my heart has been in pieces over my other children, whom I've known for longer.' He felt ashamed to use such expressions, to speak of his pain, his broken heart – his infinite grief, for heaven's sake – but he had to do it. Such words wouldn't make things easier, but not to trot out such clichés would be even worse; in certain circumstances, people need them, especially when someone is about to leave. They're pure window-dressing, but you have to say them; they don't help, but they soften the blow, if not at the time, then at least retrospectively. Besides, it wasn't the first occasion on which he'd had recourse to them: anyone who spends his life pretending to be someone else has to learn to use those trivial words, however ashamed they may make him feel. 'You won't lack for anything. I'll send you money every month to cover expenses, so you mustn't worry about that. I know that's the last thing on your mind right now, but later on, you'll realise how import-ant it is.'

Tomás Nevinson knew he was in for a few days of psychodrama, with alternating bouts of tears, reproaches, pleas, rages and wounded silences. It was a price he was happy to pay, because what he wanted, above all, was to get out of there, to return to the universe and not continue slowly, unfailingly, to wither and rust away. Those days and nights of pointless struggle were as nothing. They would pass and then, suddenly, he would be free, he would be in London, and after London, who knows. He found it far more painful having to leave his little girl than having to leave her mother, but then again, he was used to separations, often abandoning people to a far worse fate, some even condemned to die. He made a suggestion: 'I'd like to come and see you both from time to time, and spend a week here with you, at least until you meet someone else. Because you will meet someone else, and you know that, even if, right now, it seems impossible. I beg you, please, to allow me that. I will, of course, understand if you say no. How could I not, when I once left my other children behind so as to ease my own pain, so as not to rub salt in the wound. I've been in your shoes too. I know how much that wound hurts. I've been through it myself.'

He said nothing to her about Madrid, nor that he was half-Spanish, nor gave her his real name, he didn't tell her what he'd devoted much of his life to (besides, he wasn't authorised to do so and never would be). Best not to tempt fate, best not to encourage her to find out more, best not to let her even know the name Tom Nevinson existed, a name he still couldn't be sure he would ever be able to reclaim, given that, for those who remembered him, it was the name of a dead man. If he did manage to return to Madrid one day, he didn't want Meg turning up there with a little girl, his little girl; never give desperate people ideas, because they might put them into practice.

'No, I don't want to see you again, and I don't want our little girl to see you either,' was Meg's final answer, her verdict after those days of accusations and screams and tears and nights of fitful sleep, if they slept at all, and a lack of sleep can wear down even the most hard-hearted of men. 'If she does ever have another father, it would be best for her if she doesn't remember you. She'll be happier if she gets used to your absence as quickly as possible, and then forgets you completely, as if you'd never existed. I wish my own memory were equally malleable, but we grown-ups are not so lucky. *I'll* remember you, though, and I'll hate you until the day I die.'

Tomás Nevinson waited patiently for that week to pass. Everything comes if you wait long enough. And he waited sadly, but doubtless with a frisson of excitement too. He preferred to spare himself a final farewell, with all three of them aware that it was final, or, rather, just the two of them, because for the little girl it would be inconceivable. They'd said all they had to say, and so he didn't tell Meg the exact date he would be leaving. He took advantage of a morning when Meg and Val were both out, one at the dental practice and the other at nursery school, then he packed a few belongings into a bag, including his gun, because he wouldn't want Val to come across it by accident. Finally, he threw his keys down on the bed and left, shutting the door behind him; it seemed unnecessary to write a note. As soon as she arrived home, Meg would know he had left, she would smell it. He walked briskly to the station, where, this time, he would board that train to London; he wouldn't have to loiter on the platform watching as it moved off. He would get on and, a few hours later, would arrive in Paddington, or so he assumed, never having travelled to London from that provincial town. From there it was just three stops on the Underground to Baker Street, and Molyneux would be waiting for him outside the Dorset Square Hotel, to take him to his garret, give him the keys, and probably some instructions too. He would be free, his exile at an end. What came next, well, he would just have to wait and see, but, at that moment, he really didn't care.

When he saw the train come into the station, he didn't move, he didn't immediately stand up and move to the edge of the platform. On his occasional afternoon visits there, he used to stay sitting on a bench, and, for a moment, it occurred to him to do as he always did. Perhaps he had a moment of doubt. He looked up at the big station clock. He had two minutes, three at most, otherwise he would miss

461

the train. There was a calmness about that place, about that whole monotonous, dull, sleepy existence, which he hadn't known anywhere else. And it's a pleasant feeling having no responsibilities, or only those everyone else has. When something comes to an end, even the something you most want to end, you suddenly regret that ending and begin to miss it. He thought: 'What we leave behind us seems inoffensive, because we've successfully come through it, that is, we've emerged alive and unscathed. We'd like to go back to yesterday because yesterday is over; we know how it ended and we'd like to repeat that day. "What was to be the value of the long-looked-forward-to, long-hoped-for calm, the autumnal serenity and the wisdom of age?" I've been safe here, I've led a tranquil, orderly life. Boring, really, but I'll miss that boredom. I'll miss my classes and my pupils, the walks along the river watching the water flowing past, and I'll even miss my colleagues. I'll miss the football matches and sitting in the Jarrold's lounge drinking tea and reading the papers, like an idle provincial gentleman or someone just passing through. I'll miss Meg and her warm body, and, above all, I'll miss Valerie, her short, quick steps when she runs to greet me, her sudden bursts of laughter for no reason, which is always the freshest and most delightful of laughters, and which will, in time, disappear. "Because I know that time is always time, and that place is always and only place and what is actual is actual only for one time and only for one place." There was the train, its doors standing open, calling to him as they always did. Tomás only had to take a few steps: one, two, three, four; perhaps five. He thought or remembered: "History is a pattern of timeless moments . . . Quick now, here, now, always . . ." Those lines read distractedly in Blackwell's had accompanied him all those years. He got to his feet, picked up his suitcase, took a few steps and was inside the carriage; all it would take was one backward step to be outside again, on the platform. He looked at the platform and looked at the time on the clock. The doors closed.

As the train pulled out of the station, with him now safely in his seat, he allowed himself just one more thought, as brief as these words, before forcing himself to forget as he had so often done before: 'Farewell, river. Farewell, woman. Farewell, child. How much I continue to accumulate and how much I leave behind.'

A few months passed, bringing with them 1994. Tomás Nevinson found that things were exactly as he'd been told: he was to keep well away from MI6 and MI5 and their various scattered, semi-clandestine buildings, and from the Foreign Office too; he must make no attempt to meet Tupra or Blakeston or any former colleague, there could be no phone calls, no snooping. No attempt, either, could be made to establish contact with Madrid, nor could he succumb to the temptation of revealing to anyone that he was back in the land of the living. He was no longer James Rowland, and it would be wise to stop using the name by which he was known now by a number of people, the inhabitants of a medium-sized town where he had spent a few years, had forged rather too many bonds, and where he had left a child. Molyneux gave him new papers. He was now called David Cromer-Fytton, and he had no idea why they had given him such a strange, double-barrelled name (it made him sound like a character in a novel or an army general, or someone straight out of the Crimean War), precisely the kind of name that would attract attention and be remembered, and yet he was supposed to go unnoticed. Tom Nevinson was still officially dead, and ever fewer people would remember him; ephemeral or hurtful people are quickly dismissed once dead and equally quickly fade from view, and there's little point in keeping them in your memory or keeping their telephone numbers in your address book. However much you resist, you do end up putting a line through both. It's also true that memories are easily awoken, even by the mention of a name or the glimpse of a face. And although Tom had changed his appearance many times, it would be unfortunate if anyone from the old days were to recognise him. What lay ahead was more waiting, more passivity, more inaction, more invisibility and pretence. He was finally back in London, but it was as if he were there as a tourist or a retiree, as if he were still in exile. At least in the other place, he'd had his teaching and his little girl.

Two weeks after moving into his garret, he'd asked the pudgy young man who had become his only contact: 'What should I do?' The flat was small but comfortable, and he had everything he needed. He had lived in infinitely worse places, and there was plenty of light and he had a nice view of the square, which gave him the fascinating option of watching the comings and goings at the Dorset Square Hotel, where Molyneux and he had first arranged to meet. It wasn't in the Strand or in St James's, but it was very central: there were endless visitors to the Sherlock Holmes Museum, which was still quite new at the time, and Madame Tussauds wasn't far away either; the multitudes also made expeditions to Selfridges, while a refined few went to the Wallace Collection.

'Absolutely nothing for the moment,' said Molyneux, smoothing the polychrome moulding on his forehead; he had let said moulding grow a little longer and now it looked like a petrified lizard, doubtless heavily lacquered. 'Do whatever you like. I'm sure you've never had so much time on your hands before, so take the opportunity to explore the city, because there must be thousands of worthwhile things you haven't yet seen. You are, after all, from Spain. There's Sir John Soane's house, for example, which more and

465

more people are starting to discover. Soon you won't be able to move in there for visitors, and it's full of fascinating details. Or there's Kew Gardens.'

'Are you telling me I should buy myself a guidebook?'

'That's up to you, whether it's end-to-end films, or a theatre binge, or a porn show. You have enough money. We give you money.' He continued to use that plural 'we', with which he puffed himself up, but suddenly he shifted to the first person singular, and Tomás interpreted this as a desire to humiliate him. 'In fact, I've brought you some money today, and I'll bring more every two weeks, in cash. Spend it as you wish. What with one thing and another, you're turning out to be quite expensive for us.'

'Careful, Molyneux,' said Tom Nevinson gravely, angrily; or was it already Cromer-Fytton speaking? 'Just don't go there, all right? Who says I'm expensive? Tupra? If he does, tell him from me that however much they spend on me or my family over a lifetime, they would still have got a bargain. Don't make me list what I've done, or the money I've brought in or saved them. He's perfectly aware of that and shouldn't need reminding.'

Molyneux obviously didn't want any problems with his boss, and so he immediately corrected himself:

'I'm sorry, I just invented that. Mr Tupra has never said anything of the kind and has never complained. I'm sure he knows what he's doing. It's just that I noticed you've spent a long time in dry dock, but then again I know nothing about the remote past. Forgive me, I shouldn't have made that remark. I withdraw it.'

'I would just remind you that we do have ranks, even though we don't use them, and you, Molyneux, would be a mere corporal at most. So don't you get cheeky with me, or over-familiar, or you'll be in big trouble. And don't talk about the years I was active as the "remote past". It's not my fault you're an ignorant little squirt. I don't know why I wasn't assigned someone with more experience. The thing I want most in the world is precisely to leave this dry dock, as you call it. I haven't the slightest desire to remain out of circulation or become a retiree, or, according to you, a burden. When will I be able to talk to Bertram?'

The fatuous fool Molyneux was taken aback. He went instantly from braggart to coward. After that dressing-down, he very nearly saluted. He must have thought Nevinson was a hard man of the old school, one who had seen it all. That he would have committed unimaginable atrocities. For the younger generations, the days of the Berlin Wall and the Soviet Union were beginning to seem mythical, almost archaic, fictitious. Such is the speed with which the world moves on. He answered politely and respectfully now:

'Mr Tupra? I don't know, and he may not know either. That's the main obstacle to you rejoining the force, Mr Cromer-Fytton.' At least he had remembered the name he was supposed to call him at all times. 'We have to wait, we have to be sure it's safe, that no one is looking for you and no one's going to shoot you the moment you put your head above the parapet. I'm speaking metaphorically, but not entirely, and I'm sure you know what I mean. Try to be patient. It will take whatever time it takes, but in comparison with what you've been through, those months will pass quickly enough. That's why I suggested you make the most of it, that you spend the time as best you can. I certainly didn't intend to demean you.'

'And don't say "you're from Spain after all", as if I were a foreigner. Do I look like a foreigner, Molyneux? In what way? Do I seem any less English than you are? What accent do you want me to put on?'

'No, not at all. It's just that I've read your file, insofar as I can, of course, as far as it goes. As you can imagine, there are a lot of blanks. Again, I'm sorry if I upset you in any way.'

'And do I look like someone who wants to see porn, Molyneux? Just watch your step in future.'

During the weeks that followed, the first weeks of only a few months if he was lucky and didn't have to wait too long, Tomás Nevinson remembered that brief exchange more often than he would have expected, on one of his interminable, aimless walks or when shut up in his garret. He was not yet forty-three and yet, to a mere youth, he already belonged to the remote past, like a mammoth. That, perhaps, was the problem with having begun so early. It was true that he'd spent some of those years in dry dock. And it was true that he was from Spain, where he'd spent his childhood and early boyhood, as well as some of his adult life. He had married there, and his wife and children were Spanish. It was twelve years since he'd visited Spain, since he'd seen Berta and the children, who would hardly be children at all now. In his enforced state of inactivity, he had time to miss them intensely, perhaps more than he had during his exile in that provincial town. There he'd had to create a persona, to pass himself off as someone else, someone invented, something at which he was highly skilled and which kept him occupied and alert, even though it had nothing to do with any investigation or mission, merely with remaining hidden. In London, on the other hand, he didn't have to be anyone. In the capital, almost no one asks questions or even notices other people: you can enter and leave your house for decades without a single person taking an interest in what you do, what your job is, whether you're single or married or divorced or widowed, if you're alone in the world or have family near or far, if you're healthy or ill. In London, he was invisible, even more invisible. He would often wonder who on earth would come looking for him, who would take the trouble to station himself somewhere, wait for him to appear and then kill him. All these precautions seemed to him superfluous, a waste of time and money. He had ceased to exist for nearly everyone: his wife, his children, his parents, and, of course, his siblings, comrades and enemies. He didn't really have any friends, he realised, or perhaps a few in Madrid who would have forgotten him completely, and whom he had shamefully neglected. Who would remember him, who would ever think about him? He lived just a few stops away on the Underground from MI6 and from Tupra – the man who used to breathe life into him with his orders and commissions – and yet, at the same time, he wasn't close at all: he was living in another galaxy, until he was summoned. Now he really was a ghost. And Molyneux had been talking utter nonsense: this time of waiting didn't seem shorter at all, it seemed infinitely longer. The nearer you get to your objective, the nearer you get to the time when you can return, the less bearable any delay: there comes a point when another twenty-four hours turns into a hideous torment for someone who has already been waiting for what seems like centuries.

He wandered the streets, he strolled about like a living being who has renounced the smallest privileges most people enjoy, the most ordinary and modest of privileges: work, company, a chat over a couple of beers, the sense of beginning the day and ending it, the idea that the next day will be slightly different from the one that has just finished. For him, morning, noon and night were all the same, and he had to fill them; he had nothing to do, he barely spoke to anyone. He went to Sir John Soane's house and to all kinds of other museums, even the most obscure. He went to the theatre occasionally and saw a fair number of films. He walked so as to have some exercise and not spend all his time in his attic flat, watching TV or reading, or looking out of the window, and yet he did still spend a lot of time there. He

469

would steep himself in the crowds who traversed the city from one end to the other, some in a hurry and with things to do, others with the idleness of tourists, who, nevertheless, also seemed to be in a hurry. He liked gatherings and envied them. He drank in the excitement, the buzz, the chance phrases caught on the wing, the bad manners and the laughter. And he knew, on the other hand, that his presence had not the slightest effect on them and gave them nothing back. He was like the air. 'Yes, that's what I am,' he would think. 'Dead air.'

He wished he'd never heard that particular form of words, 'to pass yourself off as someone else', because now, with time on his hands to think, he had begun to analyse it. For years, he'd never even considered what it meant, it was simply his job to be various others and almost never himself. Mr Cromer-Fytton, though, had no characteristics, no role or behaviour had been assigned to him, he'd been given no other languages to speak, no particular diction or accent, which meant Tom was free to mould him as he wished because there were no spectators to be deceived or persuaded, and Tom realised that he found it hard to know who he really was. All those comings and goings, all those absences, had blurred his identity. Until very recently, and for some time, he'd been Jim Rowland, schoolteacher, but he had quickly buried him. Once that London train had set off, distancing him from that other self, he rarely looked back. When he was haunted by memories of Meg and Val, especially Val, he would immediately dismiss them, as he had before in other incarnations, without a thought, almost without a hint of remorse; you couldn't allow yourself to get caught in a spider's web. The only place to which his mind or memory did keep returning was Madrid, the house on Calle Pavía and the now empty apartment on Calle Jenner (he'd been kept informed of any really important news, the death of his mother first and, later on, that of his father), the streets of Miguel Ángel and Monte Esquinza

471

and Almagro and Fortuny and Martínez Campos and so many others. If he was still someone, if time and circumstance had not worn him away, transforming him into an illegible stone or inscription, then he was, despite everything, Tomás Nevinson: the youngest son of Jack Nevinson from the British Council and Miss Mercedes from the British Institute, the boyfriend and then husband of Berta Isla, and the father of Guillermo and Elisa. Jim Rowland had been just another role, an illusion, he had nothing in common with the man who had behaved so appallingly badly with that woman, getting her pregnant, fathering a little girl, and then abandoning them both. That idiot teacher wasn't him, but he, Tomás Nevinson, had done more or less the same; or worse, he had pretended to be dead and was still pretending, and hadn't yet revealed the truth to his wife. He was suddenly filled with longing for Berta and the life snatched from him when it had only just begun. Knowing full well that his missing life continued to be off limits to him and that a large part of it had already passed, he pinned all his hopes on Tupra's phone call: the one thing that could rescue him from his sorrows and his temptations would be to feel useful again and minus his own personality. Inactivity and waiting were urging him on to reclaim that missing life, and he couldn't allow himself to do that, because it undermined and confused him, provoked crazy thoughts, made him think of Madrid.

In his search for crowds and multitudes and throngs, he often went to Madame Tussauds in Marylebone Road, just around the corner from his flat, almost on his doorstep. There were always long queues, mostly foreign and British tourists, and school groups led by their teachers, whole classes on a special trip to London; in a few years' time, Val would probably be among them, transported there from the town where he'd condemned her to live, possibly for ever. Inside, you could barely take three steps without bumping into one of the hundreds of people being photographed next to the most famous of the wax figures, the current ones and the old favourites, from the Queen to the Beatles, from Churchill to Elvis Presley, from Kennedy and Cassius Clay to Marilyn Monroe. Tomás wondered if the younger visitors would know who those last three were, or when they would be withdrawn and replaced. 'The living forget the famous so quickly now,' he thought, 'and feel only impatience, scorn and resentment for those who didn't even have the courtesy to wait for them in order to exist and who are known to them only by name, or because of some irritating legend whose creation pre-dated them and should, therefore, be erased. The living feel increasingly at home in their role as barbarians, invaders and usurpers: "How did the world dare to consider itself important before we were born, when, in fact, everything begins with us and everything else is mere junk, to be crushed and tossed onto the scrap heap." I'm part of that,' he thought, 'I'm both alive and dead, and as far as almost everyone is concerned, I'm not even a dead man worth remembering, not even by those who loved me, not even by those who loathed me.'

Being there, in the queue and inside the museum, in the midst of so many fresh, young, thoroughly alive people eager to see the celebrities of yesteryear or their current idols, captive and at their mercy, available to be photographed and to be touched – although touching was forbidden – honed wax figures who were far more distinguished than him, even though he could walk and talk and see; all those things contributed to him feeling less solitary, less preterite and less spectral. He may have been alone and silent, and always an outsider, never one of the jolly groups, yet he could still share in the enthusiasm and chatter surrounding him, both jostling and jostled; he would hear their shrill exclamations when they recognised a favourite singer or footballer, and would even dare to make some superfluous comment to a fellow visitor standing next to him: 'It doesn't look much like him, does it?' for example, or 'I always thought the originals allowed their exact measurements to be taken, and I imagined Mick Jagger to be taller somehow and not so weedy, didn't you? Perhaps he's shrinking with age.' To which one clever woman replied: 'Do you think Cromwell and Henry VIII would have agreed to being measured up?'

One morning, when he was in one of the most crowded rooms, he noticed a boy and a girl, especially the girl. She would have been about eleven, and her brother a couple of years younger, and you could tell they were brother and sister because they were so alike. They barely stopped to look at any of the figures, but ran back and forth, going from one room to another, returning briefly to the first room before racing off again, coming and going all the time, too excited and overwhelmed by the superabundance of things to see, shouting to each other: 'Look, Derek, look who's here' and 'Look, Claire, they've got James Bond as well'; the sheer number of visitors prevented them from fixing on one particular figure, and they were constantly being enticed away by new discoveries. This was common enough behaviour among children at Madame Tussauds, and, for some time now, the museum has really been aimed at them and at adolescents, which is to say at the universe's great infantilised masses, who continue to grow exponentially.

What attracted him were the faces, the features of those two siblings. He had a strange feeling that he knew them, that he wasn't seeing them for the first time, especially the girl. But who could they be? Where could he have seen them? He felt a shiver – or should that be a shudder or flash? – of unequivocal recognition, followed by an irritating inability to place them, as when, in a film or TV series, we see a minor actor or actress with an unmistakable face and yet can't recall what other roles we've seen them in. And the more we try to put a name to them, the more they elude us, or we muddle them up with someone else, and our brain – having lost all interest in the plot – won't rest until we've tracked them down. His very first, irrational thought was that they could be his own children, Guillermo and Elisa, but that was just the absurd product of his perplexity. There was, of course, no reason why his children couldn't be on a visit to London, but they were different ages, Guillermo was older than Elisa, not the other way round, they wouldn't be speaking English and they wouldn't be called Derek and Claire. So who were Claire and Derek? Which part of his brain were they coming from? How did he know that attractive young girl? Because she would clearly grow up to be very attractive. In his mind, he rapidly riffled through the various children with whom he'd had some minimal contact on his travels, because he had sometimes mingled with the local population, had sometimes slept with a mother or a young woman with younger siblings, but the ages still didn't match. He'd spent the last five or more years far away from all that, cloistered in a provincial town, which he wasn't allowed to leave even in the school holidays, and, during that time, he'd known many pupils, male and female, and precisely because he'd been in such close contact with them, he could clearly recall most of their faces, although he had a rather vaguer memory of their other qualities, but none of them had ever aroused in him that mixture of unease and fascination, a feeling similar to that provoked by certain paintings or portraits, which, inexplicably, you can't take your eyes off: you think you've looked your fill and so pass on to others in the same museum, but something impels you to go back and study them again, something forces you, two or three times, sometimes four, not to part from them just yet. He realised that he couldn't take his eyes off those two children and that his gaze was becoming increasingly Spanish (in England, people tend not to look at anyone too intensely or fixedly, still less at a pre-adolescent, still less if it's an adult doing the looking), that he was captivated by the children's almost identical features, although the girl's face was the more evocative, the more unequivocally familiar from some other time in his life. That fact drew him like a magnet, and he tried to follow her through the different rooms and not lose her among the crowd. It made no sense at all, the girl would only have been born when he was already in his thirties, at the very earliest. He couldn't possibly have known her before.

Claire was very fair, with delicate features that were also somehow fierce and determined, indicating someone of a fiery nature. She had a very red mouth, typical of children and young people, with slightly downturned corners, which gave her an expression that was sometimes scornful, sometimes melancholy, suggesting a person who might one day prove rather testing, both to herself and to others. However, she often smiled too, and then the corners of her mouth lifted with excitement and joy, revealing a gap between her front teeth that would one day prove the downfall of some man or perhaps several. Her eyes were inquisitive, taking in one wax figure after another swiftly and intelligently, so swiftly that she and her brother didn't linger long before any of them: 'Look, Derek, it's Napoleon, I've studied him at school' or 'Claire, you missed Darth Vader. Go back and have a look'.

It was only a matter of time before the keen-eyed girl would notice that man who kept appearing and reappearing, following his own erratic itinerary and observing her curiously and insistently with strangely southern eyes. Far from taking fright, though, Claire kept an equally curious eye on him, shyly and modestly as befitted her age. Perhaps she could see that Tomás's espionage was not in the least unsavoury or dubious, but born of pure pleasure and sympathy.

Sympathy and mental effort, like someone deciphering an enigma. For children who have not yet reached adolescence, and who tend to be ignored by most adults, attracting the attention of a grown-up is rather flattering and comforting. They feel, for a moment, that they're important enough to be singled out. This was probably the case with Claire (Derek was more childish and distracted, and probably hadn't noticed a thing). Claire continued to rush here and there, but in each room, she would stop to check out of the corner of her eye if Tom Nevinson – or was he David Cromer-Fytton? – was still paying his kindly visual homage to her or if he had grown tired and bored. She did this discreetly and still shyly, but with no show of fear. After all, what could possibly happen in such a cheerful, busy place?

At no point did Tomás notice any accompanying parents or teachers. The two children seemed far too young to have gone to Madame Tussauds on their own. Perhaps their elders, their parents, with no interest in seeing the displays, were waiting for them in the shop or the café, or out in the street. It was a fine day, so perhaps they, the parents, were waiting for them quietly in a park or sitting outside having a drink; yes, the father and the mother, or one of them, just the mother perhaps, whose face they had inherited. And then he had a sudden flash of insight: those children, or, rather, the girl, yes, the girl was the spitting image of Janet, well, they both resembled her, but the girl was the same sex and the likeness was quite extraordinary, like a reproduction in miniature, on a reduced scale. That was where the child came from, from part of his remote past. Janet. That's the name he'd known her by during those youthful years of occasional sexual encounters; he'd only learned her surname once she was dead, and hadn't forgotten it since. That girl Claire looked like, or, rather, *was*, the daughter that poor, dead Janet Jefferys had never had.

It had been twenty or more years since he'd last thought about Janet Jefferys, and her face had become unreal to him, pining palely away until that precise moment, until he saw, or, rather, recognised, what must have been her daughter, because the resemblance really was remarkable. Then, as if someone had placed a photo before his eyes, he could clearly see Janet's delicate, fierce, determined features, her dazzling, Scandinavian-yellow hair, doubtless dyed, which some-times resembled a golden helmet lit by a hidden sun that fell like a spotlight on her through Oxford's shifting clouds, utterly unmistak-able if you saw her in the street; she had very red lips and a gap between her front teeth, which lent a childish element to her smile, just as it did to that little girl's smile, except that she still was a little girl. He could recall Janet in movement too, and her naked or semi-naked body, as he had seen it on quite a few occasions, and, on the very last occasion, when he had approached her still tumescent, still unwashed cunt with his eyes and fingers. It felt as if all that had hap-pened a million years ago. He had lived several lives since then, while her life had stopped.

He had, in fact, ceased thinking about Janet there and then. The news of her murder had shaken him, but he hadn't had time to assimi-late it, to feel the necessary shock and regret, as he would have done in different circumstances, had he not found himself directly affected and involved. He had immediately realised the danger he was in, and there is no defence against the egotism of youth: he had to look to his own needs, to confront the threat. 'I didn't kill her, I know that,' was the thought that rushed through his mind now, 'but, if I had, then my main concern would surely have been to avoid being caught and to emerge unscathed; even someone who kills another person by accident, unintentionally, is only briefly horrified, then instantly moves on to thinking how best to protect or save himself, and ensure, if he can, that his life is not ruined or merely changed, even though the person he has killed has changed so radically that he or she no longer has a life.' That murder had determined the direction his life would take; in a sense, it had robbed him of the life he'd had up until then. He'd accepted the conditions and thrown himself wholeheartedly into the cause, and since it was too upsetting to recall the origin of that catastrophe, that earthquake, he had tended to blank it out, feeling that taking on the various tasks he was assigned on each occasion, in each place, was more than enough for him to deal with. If there was anything good about the state of perpetual disquiet and endless pretence in which he lived, it was that it prevented him from going over and over the reason why he'd begun that absurd life. He had often completely forgotten about it, and thus forgotten about poor Janet too. After all, their relationship had been superficial, utilitarian, almost functional on both sides, and on Janet's part there was also perhaps a desire for revenge, one of those strange acts of reprisal purely for the avenger's own satisfaction and use, and about which the object of the reprisal would never know: Hugh Saumarez-Hill, the name came to him at once, one of those memorable double-barrelled names. An MP who, it seemed, hadn't done particularly well in the 1970s. Not that Tomás was interested in politics, and he didn't much care who was in power, given that, in his line of work, one's personal preferences were very much put to one side. He knew enough to be able to carry out his work properly, and, he assumed, that particular MP couldn't have been very prominent during that time, because he would have heard of him and his name would have appeared in the press. He hadn't been a minister of anything while his party was in government, and it's likely that his promising career had been cut short, like that of so many Labour politicians with the rise to power of Margaret Thatcher and her successor John Major, who, between them, occupied 10 Downing Street for some eighteen years. Hugh Saumarez-Hill might still be in Parliament, where he would be merely one of many, and so, in the end, he hadn't been Somebody with a capital 'S', as Janet and Tupra and Blakeston had said, yes, it had been Blakeston who told him that. Or he might well have slipped over into the more opaque world of the private sector. What a waste, though, the hundred thousand brilliant futures that come to nothing, the world is full of them and, in politics, one mistake, one foolish alliance, one miscalculation, is all it takes to fail. Unless Janet had blackmailed him and ruined or brought his career to an abrupt end, as she'd told Tomás was her intention, so as to have her revenge on his caution and his carelessness, his endless procrastination and smugness, he couldn't quite remember the details. That night had been the first and only night Janet had spoken to him about her London lover, and, indeed, the only time he'd asked her about him. Tomás Nevinson reran that thought: 'Unless Janet had . . .' But what was he thinking? Janet couldn't have done anything after that night. She couldn't see or hear or touch or feel or speak, or get angry or look or read; she'd been lying on the bed, reading *The Secret Agent*, and this struck him suddenly as an ironic warning, because isn't that more or less what he had become? Or could she have done all those things and even given birth to two children, the same two he could see there before him on that idle morning in Madame Tussauds in 1994? Weren't they far too like the young Janet Jefferys not to be hers, not to have sprung from her? The *young* Janet Jefferys? But then there had been no other.

You can't allow a suspicion to enter your mind without it taking full possession of you, invading and appropriating everything, at least until it can be roundly dismissed. Janet was three or four years older than him, and if those children were, as he reckoned, eleven or twelve and nine or ten, she would have had them quite late, when she was between thirty-three and thirty-six, which was perfectly possible. If she were alive, she would be about forty-six now. If she were alive? This jumble of ideas elbowed their way into his mind in a matter of seconds, a rapid succession of lightning flashes. Had he actually seen her dead? No, he hadn't seen her corpse, just as no one had ever found his, because it didn't exist. That policeman Morse had given him the news in Mr Southworth's rooms, and he had seemed an honest, reasonable man, but Tom knew now, and had for a long time, that a modest policeman always obeys orders, especially if his superiors have received those orders from the Secret Service, who are always above all other authorities apart from a few army chiefs and high-up civil servants, and even then, if there's no alternative, they simply sidestep those authorities. They would have forced Morse to lie, to play his part, and although Morse would have disliked having to deceive a poor, naïve student, still wet behind the ears, he wouldn't have been able to refuse, or even complain, without ruining his career or possibly losing his job.

Had Tom seen anything in the newspapers or on the television about the murder? He had barely glimpsed either at the time, being too preoccupied and anxious about himself, and, besides, since he'd been given first-hand information, why consult the media? Perhaps he'd seen a headline in the local paper somewhere, but he knew perfectly well – at least he did now – how easy it was for them, for 'us', to get a newspaper, especially one of the smaller ones, to include a bit of useful fake, even non-existent news, you had only to appeal to their sense of duty and patriotism, to mention the defence of the Realm. What he did know for sure was that the case had remained unresolved, no murderer had been found (people quickly get bored and stop asking questions). Perhaps because there had been no murderer. Not him or Hugh Saumarez-Hill or the man who arrived and rang the bell as soon as he left and while he stood smoking a cigarette on the corner of St John Street and Beaumont Street; how far away all that seemed now; how far away his all too recognisable Marcovitch cigarettes, which had ceased being manufactured eons ago, indeed, all those things had happened eons ago, so why should it come back to him with such force now, to someone so different and mutable, to Mr Rowland and Mr Cromer-Fytton, and to others who were rapidly dissolving into the mist of borrowed and abandoned identities, who had done such superfluous things, without which the world would have been no different? Yes, he had doubtless averted misfortunes, but he had doubtless caused others too, it was absurd, impossible, to try to keep a tally, he hadn't always been told what the consequences of his actions were, he had struck a match and left before the fire started. All these thoughts were coming back to Tomás Nevinson now because they were all that were left to him during that empty period of waiting; he was increasingly reverting and returning to the old Tomás Nevinson, Berta Isla's boyfriend and husband, the one from Madrid, the first one.

But how could they have known he was going to visit Janet that night? It had been entirely unplanned, as it always was: he'd gone to Waterfield's in the morning where they'd begun their fumblings, with him staring, he recalled, at the spines of some books by Kipling, and had postponed any further activities until the evening. What a fool he was, he thought. Janet would have had the whole day to warn them, Tupra, Blakeston, even perhaps Wheeler. Janet had agreed to be part of the farce; after all, she didn't earn much as a bookshop assistant, and had little hope of there being any change in the situation with her London lover, Hugh Saumarez-Hill or another Hugh entirely; she wouldn't mind leaving Oxford and living somewhere else, and those children, he thought, had a slight Yorkshire accent, although not very marked, which is only logical given that their mother was from Oxford, and it's mainly mothers who pass on accent and language, their voice being the first their children hear. Tupra and Co. would have made her a good offer: a new life, a better job and a healthy sum up front, she had nothing to lose and didn't owe Tom any debt of loyalty, he was just a pastime, a comfort and compensation for the routine solitude of certain Tuesdays, Wednesdays or Thursdays, a small dagger she could sometimes stick into the negligent Hugh, without him knowing. Tom would soon be leaving Oxford anyway and would forget all about her, he would go back to Madrid and his long-term girlfriend, so why shouldn't she set a trap for him? Tomás was transient, a speck of dust or ash on an old man's sleeve. There was no reason to blame or reproach her if she was still living, perhaps in Yorkshire, with a husband and two children, Claire and Derek, and hadn't been strangled more than twenty years before with her tights. A grotesque imagined death.

He'd lost sight of those two elusive, mercurial children, Claire and Derek; he'd become sunk in his own thoughts, distracted by those memories, conjectures and hypotheses. Cursing himself, he walked briskly through the different rooms looking for them, but in vain; he waited outside the Chamber of Horrors in case they'd gone in there, again without success; he trawled through the rooms once more, then went out into the foyer, peered into the shop and, there, to his relief, he saw them: they'd obviously finished their visit and were about to leave. He had to find out the truth, he wouldn't get another chance, he would have to ask them something, but wasn't sure what he could ask without alarming them, without arousing their suspicions, or giving rise to misunderstandings; even in 1994, approaching children in a friendly manner already constituted a problem, if not a depraved act in itself, for the age of susceptibility and hysteria was just beginning.

They were looking longingly at the plastic reproductions of some of the wax figures, about the size of old-fashioned lead soldiers, gazing with delight at the handful of figures lined up on a shelf, but without touching them, because they clearly wouldn't be able to afford them. He did actually see them counting out their few coins, doubtless calculating whether, if they pooled their funds, they would have enough to buy at least one. There was still no sign of teachers or parents or other adults keeping an eye on them; they were still alone, perhaps they were self-sufficient, or orphans living with a young, irresponsible aunt who sent them off to do whatever they liked. They were dressed quite ordinarily and seemed neither rich nor poor, just middle-class kids of which there are millions; if Janet had died, they would be motherless, but Tom immediately corrected himself, telling himself off for mixing up tenses and times: if Janet had died when she had been murdered, the children couldn't be hers, because she wouldn't have had any children.

He joined them in viewing the figures of the most popular characters: Winston Churchill was on sale, but not the Queen (perhaps out of respect), as were Indiana Jones, or Harrison Ford; James Bond, or Sean Connery (however many actors may have played the part, Connery in a dinner jacket is always the real Bond), Shakespeare and General Gordon and the diminutive Queen Victoria, Napoleon and Montgomery with his beret and moustache and stick (Blakeston would definitely have bought that one), Elvis Presley, Lawrence of Arabia on a camel (that would probably be more expensive), Sherlock Holmes and Dr Watson and Long John Silver, Oscar Wilde with cane and gloves and long hair, Alice in Wonderland, someone resembling Fagin with a goatee beard and wearing a long overcoat, Mr Pickwick and Mary Poppins and Frankenstein's monster and Dracula; fictitious characters are always more famous and more memorable than historical ones, although sometimes it's hard to tell them apart.

'Which is your favourite?' he asked after a brief pause, because this seemed the most innocent approach.

The children turned to him, and an involuntary look of recognition crossed the girl's face. She wasn't frightened or suspicious, her expression was one of natural sympathy (Janet Jefferys' lively face),

485

as it had been when she'd indicated to him that she knew he was watching her.

'Mine's Sherlock Holmes,' she said at once.

'Mine's Indiana Jones,' said the boy enthusiastically (children appreciate adults taking an interest in their tastes and opinions). 'What's yours?'

Tomás made a pretence of thinking long and hard. Then, to engage their interest, he said:

'My real favourite isn't here, alas, nor in any other museum.'

'Really? Who is he?' they asked, intrigued and almost in unison.

'Just William – William Brown.' He had named his son, Guillermo, after him, the son who would be so much older now and would assume that he was fatherless.

'Who's he?' asked Derek with a mixture of disappointment and surprise. 'It's hardly surprising he isn't here if no one's heard of him. What film was he in?'

'I've heard of him,' said Claire, 'but I don't know what he looks like, I've never seen him. He's not in any films, he's in one of those old children's books.'

'Yes, I read them when I was a child, and even then, he was quite old, so there's no reason why you should know him,' explained Tomás. 'Anyway, out of the figures here, I'd choose Sherlock Holmes too.' Claire looked pleased, her face was much easier to read than Janet Jefferys' had been. She was flattered to have a grown-up endorse her choice. 'Which one are you going to buy? I can see you're having to pool resources.'

'We were deliberating,' said the girl, and she used that particular word. 'We've only got enough money for one.' The wax figures weren't expensive, but for children everything is expensive.

'How will you get home if you spend all your money? Or do you live nearby?'

'No, we don't live in London, we're just visiting.' Claire was the spokesperson; Derek was still absorbed in gazing at that unaffordable row of dolls. 'But our father is waiting for us in a pub next door. He'll take us back to the hotel. We've only got one more night here, and we go home tomorrow.'

Tom Nevinson or David Cromer-Fytton immediately saw an opportunity to play the nice guy or the even nicer guy.

'Let me guess where you're from, and if I'm right, I'll treat you to four wax figures, two each, to reward myself for giving the correct answer.'

The boy looked as intrigued as he was sceptical:

'You'll never guess. Britain's huge and there are so many different places.'

'You're from York or thereabouts,' said Tomás confidently.

The children stared at him open-mouthed with admiration.

'How did you know? You must have learned how to do that from Sherlock Holmes.'

'Well, we've all learned from him,' said Tomás. 'But I happen to be very good at distinguishing and imitating accents. Anyway, as agreed, you can now choose four figures.'

'Really? Are you serious? Thank you very much.'

The children were so thrilled that they didn't even wait for him to confirm his offer, although Tomás did so at once ('Of course I'm serious. A wager is a wager, and wagers are sacred'). They immediately turned their backs on him and again began deliberating over which four they would choose, which two pairs, and without having to spend any money either. While they were deciding, Tom continued asking questions:

'And what about your mother? Did she not come with you?'

Claire half-turned her head to answer, but only half, because now she couldn't bring herself to look away from the figures.

'Our mother died a year and a half ago in a car accident.' She said this in a flat voice, like someone who's had to give this explanation far too often.

'So she is dead,' thought Tom, with the very briefest feeling of relief. 'But not when she should have died.'

'Oh, I'm so sorry,' he said. 'What was her name? It's just that you're the very image of a friend I had when I was young and whom I haven't heard from for years now. You could almost be her children. Almost.' And he thought: 'They're going to say Janet. And they *are* motherless. I'm sure they'll say Janet.'

'Her name was Janet,' said the girl, again half-turning her head, looking at him out of the corner of her eye, less out of curiosity than out of deference, not wanting to offer him the back of her neck when she was speaking to him, although she wasn't in the least bit interested in that supposed friendship.

'What a coincidence! That was my friend's name too,' said Tom. But there were millions of Janets in Great Britain. 'Janet what?' he asked urgently, because this would be his one chance to find out.

'Bates, like us.'

'So that was her married name,' thought Tom. 'She obviously didn't marry Saumarez-Hill; well, he was hardly likely to leave his wife for a bookshop assistant. At the time, he was an MP on his way to becoming Somebody. As far as I know, he didn't get far in politics. So she must have got married late to a man with the very ordinary name of Bates, from Yorkshire. The same name as one of Shakespeare's soldiers, one of the soldiers duped by a disguised Henry V, a mere private, I seem to recall.'

'I mean her name when she was single. My friend wasn't married when I knew her. Do you know her maiden name?' They might not know, since English wives don't usually keep their names, unlike Spanish women, unlike Berta Isla.

Derek turned and looked at him in some bewilderment, as if that were the first time he'd ever heard the expression 'maiden name', as if it had never occurred to him that his mother could possibly have been called anything other than she had always been called, *his* always that is. The girl was older, though, and she did know. Tomás read it in her eyes before she even opened her mouth. 'She's going to say Jefferys,' he thought, 'she's sure to say Jefferys.'

'I know,' Claire said. 'When she was young, she was called Janet Jeffries.' That's what it sounded like to Tom, the pronunciation of both names was very similar, almost indistinguishable. It would have been too much of a coincidence for their mother and Janet not to be one and the same. Especially given the astonishing resemblance, for they were exact replicas of her. And he wasn't going to ask them to spell her surname. 'Was she your friend?'

'No,' said Tomás Nevinson. 'My friend was called Rowland, Janet Rowland.' He preferred to leave it there and to withdraw, what would be the point of exposing himself to more questions? He didn't owe those Bates children from York the truth, he didn't even know them. For half a lifetime, almost a whole lifetime, he hadn't owed anyone the truth, not even those closest to him, and would do so even less from now on.

Derek chose his favourite, Indiana Jones, and Frankenstein's monster. Claire chose her favourite, Sherlock Holmes, and his inseparable companion, Watson, she couldn't have one in the house without the other; she understood about loyalty, unlike her mother, who was finally dead, having been a very long time dying. He, on the other hand, was not dead, or only officially, and that official verdict could be refuted and annulled if the corpse turned up alive. Tom gladly paid for the figures and handed them, neatly wrapped, to the children, then said goodbye with a handshake at the exit; after all, none of this was their fault. They didn't ask him his name. It would have made no difference if they had: he now had so many names, perhaps as many as Tupra. Or Reresby or Dundas or Ure.

'Do you think Professor Wheeler knew about the whole thing right from the start, and was in on the deception?' Tomás asked Southworth, adding: 'He was the first one to try to draw me in, and I remember you telling me that very little of what happened in Oxford escaped him, still less a murder. That he would be sure to know about what happened before I did, and would probably be better informed than I was. And that's certainly how it seemed to me when I spoke to him on the phone.'

Mr Southworth paused for a moment, as if he were examining his conscience, peering into his inner depths with his small, honest eyes. He no longer kept looking at his watch, he must have forgotten about his lecture. Then he spoke with great certainty:

'No, I'm sure he didn't know, I'm sure they deceived him too and concealed from him the fact that it was a fake death. I don't know much about the Secret Service, but I can't imagine they would be capable of killing an entirely innocent person purely in order to recruit a new agent. I can see them using pressure and blackmail, and generally putting on a farce — that would be easy enough.' He gave an ironic sigh. 'That's essentially what they do, isn't it, put on farces?'

'That much I can guarantee,' said Tom, interrupting him. 'That's par for the course, it happens every day. You'd be amazed at how many people we have at our disposal, how many unexpected, unsuspected candidates.' He realised that he was still using the first person plural, was still including himself among them. Like Tupra and Blakeston on that now distant morning. But he didn't correct himself. He would gradually learn to exclude himself, and his mind would grow accustomed to that. 'Nor how relentless those people are. Once they start, once they step up, pause for a moment to ask for instructions, they never want to stop, they need to be productive. They can put on a farce at the drop of a hat, for almost no reason at all. And it's done in a trice, because the world is full of volunteers, amateur enthusiasts or the merely venal.' And there he used the Spanish expression *en un santiamén* – in a trice – although that was already rather old-fashioned. Like the Spanish spoken by Mr Southworth, who would probably never, for example, have heard of *en un pispás*.

'I've known Peter for years and years, and I know he would never have set such a trap for you. Nor would he have allowed it, had he been told about it. That would be completely out of character, at odds with his sense of decorum. I'm convinced that he would still believe now that the girl was strangled, if, of course, he does ever think of her, which, to be honest, I very much doubt. He has far too many things in his head already. Think of what he must have accumulated there since he was born in 1913, and in the Antipodes too.'

'But he was Tupra's teacher, as he was yours and mine. Would you have played such a dirty trick on him?'

'No, I wouldn't, but then I'm a very different person and do a very different job. I wouldn't have done it to you either, and you were only my student. Have you been to see that policeman Morse yet? He might still be in Oxford, although he'll be an inspector by now, at the very least. He was the one who gave us all the details of the case, who saw Janet dead.' He raised his eyebrows in an expression of disbelief and added with what remained of his slowly disappearing innocence: 'Outrageous.'

'No, I did consider that, but I'm not going to bother. It wouldn't make sense,' said Tom. 'He wouldn't tell me or admit anything, he might even deny ever having seen me before, might deny all knowledge of that visit more than twenty years ago, and of which there will be no record. He was obviously following orders then, and wouldn't want to haul any antediluvian skeletons out of the cupboard now. He wouldn't be allowed to, what the Crown buries stays buried for all eternity. At most, he would look for the file, which probably never existed, given that there *was* no murder. And yet Janet Jefferys was even allowed to keep her name, they didn't force her to disappear from the world, to change her name, she just had to leave Oxford. And if a file does exist, for appearances' sake, it will say: "Case unresolved or open", nothing more. It would be a waste of time, and I wouldn't want to embarrass the man, because he seemed a decent enough fellow. I know what it means to obey orders, even when those orders go totally against the grain. I can understand that.'

Mr Southworth, a studious, peace-loving man, seemed troubled by such machinations, which were entirely new to him, but his strong sense of justice didn't rouse him to revolt, as if he assumed that one can do nothing to oppose the lofty, legalised justice of the State. He seemed stunned, flabbergasted.

'And what about Tupra and Blakeston? What have they told you?' he asked doubtfully. 'Haven't you spoken to them? Haven't you called them to account? It must have been their idea. I'm sure Peter had nothing to do with it. Please don't go and see him, don't upset him. He would be truly horrified to know the consequences of his advice, the irreparable consequences. He would merely have pointed out to them how useful you could be, and how was he to know they would use that information for such devious ends?' Mr Southworth was protecting his old friend with almost paternal care. Tomás had calmed down since his first wild irruption into those cosy quarters, but his former tutor had realised, too, that he was now a dangerous man, and could, if necessary, be ruthless.

'He must have made a very convincing case for my usefulness, though, for them to go to such lengths.'

'Well, your linguistic gifts *are* extraordinary, and very rare, especially among the British, who have no talent for languages at all. There are very few people like you, as you know.' He preferred to say nothing more to exonerate his teacher and friend, feeling that it would be counterproductive. 'Haven't they deigned to talk to you, Tupra and Blakeston, I mean? They're all you have left, they must have been the ones behind this whole charade.'

They hadn't, at first, deigned to speak to him, but Tom had finally managed to speak to Tupra. That was what he had burned to do, talk to Tupra, while he was leaving Madame Tussauds on the way back to Dorset Square and his garret. Except that he immediately diverged from that path and spent several hours wandering the city, even going close to the prohibited zone, where the SIS and the Foreign Office had their offices. He stood for a long time, staring at their respective front doors, wondering if Tupra would be there or away travelling. No, there was no question of going in and creating a ruckus, the bouncers or doormen would immediately have ejected him. He needed to plan his conversation and not rush things, and yet there really wasn't anything to plan: reproaches speak for themselves, just as irrefutable accusations do, they speak and are listened to, shamefaced. Also, Tupra could hardly deny that Janet Jefferys had lived in York for many years. Nevertheless, he would wait, it was best not to have it out with him on his home turf, it would be best to meet away from those buildings, one of which had no name. It would be another couple of days before his next encounter with his contact, the pudgy young man with the kiss-curl; he would tell Molyneux his demands, and Tupra wouldn't dare to refuse to see him now, even though there was almost nothing the shameless Tupra wouldn't dare to do.

Tomás Nevinson walked and walked and continued walking until night fell and he was utterly exhausted, and only when he returned to his garret, there in the square, and before again shutting himself up in his flat, did he realise that the eternal part of his life, which had become his only life, that wandering, deceiving, disparate life, was over, had reached its natural end. Whatever happened in his conversation with Tupra, he would never go back to a job for which, that very morning – before seeking out the hustle and bustle of the museum, before seeing Claire and Derek – he had felt intense nostalgia. The threat that had hung over him for more than twenty years, growing ever more diffuse and forgotten, did not exist and had never existed, or only in his ingenuous mind and his student panic, a real lamb to the slaughter. It was too late for regrets: he had put his life on hold, and other lives don't wait, and both his lives, the real and the parallel one, had escaped him. He didn't care about the other threats, the subsequent and now unlikely threats, those he had acquired under different names and in different languages and accents, and what did it matter, anyway, if those threats were carried out and he exited the world; nothing matters once you realise that a story has ended.

He saw the dust in the air suspended, he saw it with a noonday clarity in the square disfigured by his surrender, by his exhaustion, and he thought: 'You can only go back when there's no longer anywhere to go back to, when there are no more other places and the story has ended. This story has ended here, in Dorset Square, in this place and now.' He took a few seconds to absorb that thought, to

495

assimilate and accept it, and then he looked to the future, or, rather, to the past: 'I can only go back to Berta and to our apartment in Calle Pavía – if she'll let me in. That's the only thing left standing, the only thing that remains and that is perhaps waiting for me without knowing it's waiting. Berta hasn't made a fresh start, as the saying goes, she hasn't remarried despite having been a widow for years now. My only hope is that Mr Southworth's French quotation can be applied to her: *Elle avait eu, comme une autre, son histoire d'amour*, "She, like anyone else, had had her love story", and that I was that love story, dead and alive.'

'Can you remember where that quotation comes from?' he suddenly asked Mr Southworth, and repeated it; he had wanted to ask that question for ages, because those words had been in his head for far too long. 'You came out with it that morning, when you said we don't always know about other people's love stories, not even when we're the object of that love. It was when you were talking about what feelings Janet might have for me, although she obviously didn't feel anything, otherwise she wouldn't have agreed to set the trap.'

Alert and intrigued, Mr Southworth crossed and uncrossed his legs in his characteristic manner, sending a ripple through the skirts of his gown. He listened attentively to the words, mouthed them silently, trying to recall where they came from.

'No, it's impossible, I have no idea,' he replied with a touch of irritation. 'Now I won't be able to stop thinking about it. It must have been from something I'd read recently. It could be Stendhal, but it could just as easily be Flaubert or Maupassant or Balzac. Or even Dumas, who knows. And how could anyone know what she felt. Perhaps she was having her revenge on your indifference, for seeing her merely as a way of passing the time. One thing is certain, you'll never know.'

'Tell Tupra that I need to see him now, Stevie. Something urgent has come up and it can't wait. It needs to be dealt with at once, without delay,' he told Molyneux as soon as the latter sat down in the hotel lounge. He not only addressed him by his first name, when he usually called him by his surname alone – just as, on that long-ago day of decisions in Blackwell's and in The Eagle and Child, he had been addressed as plain 'Nevinson' – he also used a diminutive to belittle the young man, not Stephen or even Steve, but Stevie, which also happened to be the name of that eccentric poet, Stevie Smith, who had been fashionable when he first arrived in Oxford, and who had died quite recently. Molyneux would know none of that, but it didn't matter: being called 'Stevie' would only increase his sense that he was being given an order.

'All right, all right,' he said defensively. 'Tell me what it's about and I'll pass it on, Mr Cromer-Fytton. When I can, of course, because Mr Tupra is always very busy.' Molyneux didn't dare repay him in kind by calling him 'David' or 'Tom'. Tomás was of a higher rank and far more experienced.

'I need to see him now, and it is, I assure you, in his interest. Today or tomorrow, but no later than that. And if he's not in London, then he needs to come back from wherever he is. Someone will know where to find him. Just tell him this: I've met Janet Jefferys' children.'

Despite Tom's imperative tone, Molyneux remained his usual opinionated, inquisitive self. The kiss-curl, the lacquer and the bicoloured hair had gone, he had reverted to an earlier look, which wasn't actually any nobler, merely less ignoble.

'And who's she? And what about her children? Are they young or grown-up? I really can't see what's so urgent, especially if they're still only small.'

'Just give him the message, Stevie. He'll understand, and then you'll see how urgent it is. Do you want to bet money on him seeing me at once?'

Molyneux declined, and he would have lost the bet, for that same night, he rather resentfully phoned Tomás, on Tupra's behalf.

'Mr Tupra says he has some free time tomorrow after work. He asked if you would prefer to go to the building with no name – his words, not mine – or if he should come to the hotel or some other place nearby, whatever suits you best. At seven o'clock.' He couldn't resist asking: 'By the way, what does he mean by "the building with no name"?'

Tomás didn't answer. He decided to take with him the small revolver, his 1964 Charter Arms Undercover, which had accompanied him during his tranquil years in that provincial town, just in case he found Tupra too exasperating, too dismissive, in case he wanted, at the very least, to give him a fright, although time does take the sting out of even the most painful of wounds. They wouldn't let him into the building with no name, which he knew so well, and to which Molyneux had not yet been given access. He suggested meeting in a café close to his garret; they would be alone there, and no one would frisk them, although he never could be sure that Tupra or Reresby was alone.

Bertram Tupra didn't change. Tomás hadn't seen him for a long time and he really hadn't changed; he was one of those men who remain frozen at a certain age as if by a process of crystallisation, or else by the application of an iron will that allows them not to age more than they deem tolerable. (He may well have had that iron will when he was still an adolescent, or earlier still, for there had always been something anomalous about his manner, his clothes, his accent, his knowledge: an indefinable trace of his harsh, combative origins, plagued with difficulties.) He had hardly changed at all from the first time they'd met, in the Oxford where they had both been students, although it was hard to imagine Tupra studying Medieval History, which, if Tom remembered rightly, had been his chosen subject. He doubtless dyed the near-ringlets at his temples, but that was the only minor artifice he allowed himself. His bulbous cranium was still crowned with abundant curls, his mouth still appeared to lack consistency, like soft chewing gum. His exaggeratedly long eyelashes were still far more like those of a woman than a man, his skin was still disturbingly lustrous and the lovely golden colour of beer, his eyebrows like black smudges and with a tendency to grow together (he probably made frequent use of tweezers), his rather coarse nose still looked as if it had once been broken by a blow or by several, his all-embracing, appreciative gaze, mocking and pale, still looked at everything straight on and from an appropriately male height, probing the past and bringing it back into the present for as long as it remained under his scrutiny, endowing it with due relevance and not rejecting it as outmoded or insignificant. Unlike almost everyone else, for whom anything that is over no longer counts.

Tomás Nevinson had changed far more, and not only because of the various masks he'd been obliged to improvise or accept during his years of role-playing and usurpation; he'd reached a point where he had no idea what his real face looked like, if it was with or without a beard, with or without glasses, with or without a moustache, with short hair or long hair, fair or dark or greying, thick or sparse, if he had scars, was thin or slightly fatter, plump like Molyneux or still solidly built, if he was still attractive (he had, after all, won the heart of the dental nurse Meg some years before). Or, rather, what that face would have been like had it evolved naturally and without suffering any hardship, had he been free to lead the life he should have led. He wondered if he would be recognised by people from the past, although what people would they be? Would Berta Isla recognise him, she who had known him from their schooldays? Above all, he felt exhausted and battered, often slightly drab, and internally much older, as if, inside, he were ten or perhaps fifteen years older than the forty-three years he had not yet reached. The itinerant life wears a man down, as does the hidden, feigned, vicarious, usurped life, the life of treachery, exile and death. He had known them all for most of his life now. When he felt this most acutely, he would remember another line from Eliot, from an early poem: 'I grow old, I grow old, I shall wear the bottoms of my trousers rolled', which he wasn't quite sure how he would translate into his first or second language, something he always did, although it was never clear which language came first or second. He felt it was essential to preserve an element of rhyme, but not so much the rhythm: *'Envejezco, envejezco, llevaré los bajos de los pantalones vueltos'*; or, more colloquially and faithfully: *'Me hago viejo, me hago viejo . . .'*

That was his first thought – 'I grow old' – when he saw Tupra there untouched by time (Tupra had already arrived at the café and was waiting for him) with a serene, cordial, almost affectionate smile on his lips, as if he and Tom had been in regular contact during the long period when they hadn't seen each other at all. He was a few years older than Tom, not many – Tom wasn't sure how many exactly – but he seemed quite a lot younger, indeed Tom was convinced that he would always look both younger than him and younger than his age, which must have been rather unnerving for people being introduced to him for the first time, new recruits and the women he seduced. He looked as if he hadn't a care in the world, even though he knew what awaited him, a call to account at the very least, a past fury made present. This blatant unconcern annoyed Tomás. He hadn't taken off his raincoat and probably wouldn't (he guessed this would be a brief encounter), and he slipped his hand into his pocket as he once had in that provincial hotel, touched the butt of the gun with the tips of thumb and index finger, just to reassure himself it was there. Or else to give himself courage, you never stop feeling intimidated by someone who intimidated you from the outset.

'So you met her children. They're called Bates, I understand. Yes, you forced me to do a little homework,' said Tupra affably. 'How did that come about? I didn't even know they existed. As you can imagine, I don't follow the trail of all the people who are occasionally useful to us and to whom we extend a helping hand, each according to his or her merits. We've greatly improved the lives of some, or at least provided a solution. They certainly can't complain of any lack of generosity on our part. You yourself have benefitted from it, Nevinson. And in no small degree either, indeed, you continue to benefit.' He was still using that corporate 'we' and, as he had at the beginning, he addressed him as 'Nevinson', but then he'd never really stopped doing that, apart from on certain occasions when he'd called him 'Tom', depending on the circumstances, the pressures or the requests being made, because Tupra had more than once begged him to do something, and had, over the years, relied on him, on his patience and intelligence, on Tom's boldness and stamina and self-sacrifice, and on his own ability to make Tom overcome his scruples, something he had always succeeded in doing. He had got the first word in, and Tomás saw at once what he was up to: he wanted to turn the tables on him right from the start. It was as if he were saying: 'Don't come to me with your reproaches, you owe me a debt of gratitude. Before you accuse us, remember what we've done for you and consider your own best interests, because whether your situation proves acceptable or disastrous or, who knows, pure torment, all hangs on the outcome of this meeting.'

'Was I so very important, Bertram, for you to do what you did to me? You snatched my life from me before it had even begun, when I was only a beginner,' said Tomás with a serious, ominous look on his face. He refused to be infected by his boss's façade of light-hearted cordiality, which was already about to stop or already had stopped being quite so light-hearted, he knew that and Tupra would know it too. Tupra was no fool, and one of his great gifts was his ability to anticipate other people's reactions, to sense what was happening in their heart of hearts. Tomás was leaving and would not be taking any more orders from him. The dust in the air marking the story's end was still hanging there suspended.

Tupra took a cigarette out of his Egyptian cigarette case and lit it with the tremulous flame of his Zippo lighter. And knowing that Tomás was also a smoker, he didn't bother to blow the smoke to one side.

'Judge for yourself, Tom. How many missions have you carried out? How many were successful? How many were unmitigated failures? Only one. I checked your service record this morning. Have you been useful or superfluous? You should be flattered that we immediately saw you as a potential agent, someone who would be useful in the defence of the Realm. There aren't many men like you, as you know. Despite your long time away from operations, we're very pleased with you, and you should be too. It's been a very equitable arrangement really. We have perhaps come out more on the credit side, but both parties have gained.'

Tomás's anger grew; he again touched the butt of his gun, as a way of calming himself and containing his rage.

'What do you mean, "credit side"? And what gains are you talking about? I've spent more than twenty years reluctantly lying to my wife. I've spent twelve years dead as far as she and my children are concerned, children I don't even know any more. And dead as far as my parents were concerned; I couldn't be with them even at their funerals. I've risked my own neck and that of my family too. You forced me into a way of life I'd already rejected; no, you didn't let me choose my own life.'

'Ah, I knew it would come down to that,' said Tupra, 'The poor-little-rich-kid philosophy of our times, which is ubiquitous now, regardless of what class people come from. Since when have people chosen their own lives? Over the centuries, with very few exceptions, people's lives have been laid out for them. That was the norm, not a tragedy. Most never moved from one place, they died in the place they were born, in the country, in a village or some wretched city, or, later on, in some wretched slum. Families with a lot of children would send one son into the army, another into the Church, if they were lucky and were accepted, because at least, then, they wouldn't starve to death; and they dispatched them very early on too, lost sight of them when they were still only beginners, to use your word. If the daughters were pretty, then they'd find them husbands, sometimes an old man and often a tyrant, and if not, they would teach them some vaguely useful secondary skill, like sewing, embroidery, cooking, in the hope that someone would take them into service; or they'd pack them off to a poor girls' convent where they would be unpaid maids. And that was in families with a bit of money, so just imagine what it was like for those who had nothing. The poor little rich kid didn't choose his own life. That's how it was for all humanity until very recently indeed, and what we have now is pure illusion. It's always been considered reasonable to want to get on in life and prosper, and history is full of social climbers. But how many made it up the ladder then and how many do so now? A tiny minority. The majority accept their lives and get on with them without asking any questions, grateful for what they've been given, and that's the norm too: just dealing with life's daily difficulties and being contented with your lot. Not being able to choose isn't an affront, it's standard practice. It is in most countries, as it is in ours, despite the collective illusion. Do you think I chose my life, or Blakeston chose his, or the Queen for that matter? The Queen had less choice than anyone. So what are you talking about, Nevinson? You're describing extraordinary privileges, which you have enjoyed to the full. Did anyone put a gun to your head in that pub in Oxford? Were you forced to agree? Did Blakeston twist your arm and threaten to break it? Of course you chose. And you're not going to tell me that you haven't enjoyed it.'

'Being accused of murder is worse than having your arm broken,' Tom retorted, albeit without much conviction. How quickly Tupra had, once again, succeeded in undermining his confidence and intimidating him. He touched the butt of his gun for a third time, although this time the gesture was pure superstition, even fantasy. He could always stop talking, if talking meant he would lose. He could take out his gun, cut to the chase and silence Tupra, but that was no more than a theoretical consolation, a fantasy: now that he was so newly and justifiably free, now that he could go back to Berta if she would have him, now that he wasn't going to end up in the prison he'd avoided in that Oxford pub. Had he enjoyed that life? Perhaps he had in a way, just as an addict enjoys his addiction, and gives himself over to it entirely. But he had also hated it and found it painful. He would miss it, he would rejoice at its ending, and he would miss it. It had all sprung from a deceit, it was sullied and besmirched. He would bid it farewell for ever. And, yes, he would miss it.

Tupra looked at him coldly now. He had little patience for weakness, complaints, reproaches, or with anyone who contradicted him. He was cordial, and even pleasant, in situations in which he could instruct, enlighten, hold forth and convince. He could be chatty, and make his companion feel important and the object of his esteem; some even came to feel it an honour that he should require their services and think them valuable. Tom had sometimes felt the same, but not always. He had also seen Tupra's harsh, draconian side, and how he used that to impose his will by dint of persuasion or force, and, on one occasion, he had been witness to a near-beating, although Tupra had stopped in time or else realised that the mere threat of a beating was enough. He could see from Tupra's expression that he was bored, but not disappointed, because he was the kind of man who feels disappointed in advance of any actual reason to be disappointed. Tom, after all, was just one of many recruits, and Tupra didn't have time to attend to the troubles of each individual.

'You could have stayed and faced up to the accusation,' he said. 'And if you'd done so . . . well, if you had, you'd have discovered that the accusation couldn't possibly stand, it would have melted away like an ice cream. And you would have calmly resumed your ordinary life.' It was exasperating to Tomás that Tupra should speak so casually about that initial trick, that initial farce, as if there were nothing unusual about such a deception, nothing reprehensible. There wasn't even a hint in his voice of implicit apology, the slightest suggestion of shame. They had soured his entire existence and, to Tupra, that was simply an occupational hazard. 'What's it got to do with me if you made a bad choice, if you couldn't deal with your fear, if you gave in. That's not my responsibility, I simply get on with my job, which is to do my best by the Realm. Besides, I think it's given you a very singular life, a life out of the ordinary, which some will be able to read on your face. There's nothing at all to read on most people's faces.' 'An illegible stone,' thought Tomás Nevinson. There was no point in getting angry or arguing with that man, he was like the sea's throat that swallows everything without a thought.

'I'm leaving, Bertram. I'm resigning. I'm going back to Madrid. I've finished here.'

'There's nothing to stop you, Nevinson, there never has been. Besides, you've been out of the loop for a long time now. We won't miss you as much as we would have years ago. If you'll forgive the expression, we feel we've recouped our investment, you've performed well for us.' He lit another cigarette, and Tomás lit one of his own, a way of keeping his feelings under control. 'But you be careful.' Tupra shifted in an instant from the official to the friendly. 'If you go back to Madrid and stay there quietly, you shouldn't be at too great a risk. But the danger is still there, you know, so don't completely lower your guard. Even if years pass without anything happening.' He clicked his fingers to summon the waitress, a Latin, very un-English gesture. 'For us there's always a risk, until we die.' It was kind of him to include himself in this, to share that sentence.

'I'll take the risk, which really isn't that great,' said Tom. 'Every day is full of risks: illness, an accident, a mugging. It would be arrogant to think that anyone would remember me. Everyone's too caught up in his or her own present, and I belong to another age. The new generations get on with their lives and don't care about the past, they don't feel it's their concern. And I am the past now.'

'That's usually the case,' said Tupra. 'But there could always be someone still anchored in the past, who does remember. There's usually at least one person who does. It's quite another matter for that one person to actually bother to do anything about it. The tendency is just to let it go, water under the bridge. They put away their resentment and move on. But while that's true, don't rely on it. Resentment can sometimes make people get up from their chair and take the few necessary steps. Just enough.'

'One more question, Tupra.' Despite the concern Tupra was showing for him now, he couldn't bring himself to revert to calling him by his first name. Tomás had decided not to pursue his complaints, given that Tupra was immune to them, but his feelings of resentment were growing, resentment towards Tupra and someone else. 'How much did Professor Wheeler have to do with my recruitment, with the whole business?'

Tupra responded at once, without a moment's hesitation, and he sounded sincere, but who knows.

'Absolutely nothing. Wheeler didn't know a thing. He merely discovered you and recommended you, that's all. He did sound you out, but he obviously wasn't persuasive enough. We did the rest. He, like you, believed that the young woman was dead. He remarked on the coincidence, of course, on that stroke of luck, but he accepted it as precisely that, or so he said. Or, rather, he said nothing.' Tupra gave a half-smile. 'We couldn't tell him the truth, because with Wheeler you can never be sure. He's far more decent than we are; he really is from another age. He might well have ruined everything. He would certainly have objected. And would certainly have alerted you.'

'So, according to you, it was better to deceive him too. I find that pretty hard to believe. He took part in the war, where you have to lose all scruples, and I don't know if you recover them later on.' Tupra did not respond. There was no need. 'And what about that policeman Morse? He did know the truth. He'd examined the corpse.'

'Don't think too badly of Enfield Morse. I remember the name because it's the name of a gun, like being called Winchester or Remington or Smith & Wesson. Being a man of conscience, he did put up some resistance, and his superiors had to come down really hard to make him do what he had to – orders from above and all that. He'll be an inspector by now, if not some still higher rank. His career will have made up for that unfortunate incident, because I imagine that, if he'd dug in his heels, his career would have been finished. Was there anything else, Nevinson?'

To Tupra, these were all mere anecdotes, he had millions of them and sometimes he liked to bring them out. He had taken out his wallet to pay, but there was only one waitress and she didn't come.

'I don't know. I don't think so.' Tomás sat staring down at the table either pensively or as if he suddenly felt completely empty. 'The fact is it's too late for everything.'

'Not too late to go back perhaps,' said Mr Southworth, trying to cheer him up, to draw him out of his stupor. 'Have you spoken to your wife yet, have you phoned her?'

'No, it's not something I can say over the phone,' said Tomás, his gaze still unfocused, fixed but not focused on one spot. 'Nor in a letter either. I'm not sure, I need to think about it still. The fact is, though, I have nowhere to go. I can't go back to Valerie and Meg and shut myself up there again. However much I love my little girl, they're both part of my long exile, my days without a name or a face, I don't even know which is my real face. But I wonder if going back might be the worst thing I could do to Berta, and I would hate to upset her.

She wouldn't know what to do with me, where to put me or how to talk to me. If, that is, she would take me back. I'd have to see. And as for my children, well . . .'

'I see the difficulty – well, "difficulty" is hardly the word for it. I certainly wouldn't want to be in your shoes. And what about Tupra? Was that the end of the conversation?' asked Mr Southworth.

'I do have something else to say,' said Tupra, and he waved his wallet around in front of his eyes, to draw Tomás out of his abstraction, at least a little. 'Even though you won't be on active service, you will remain subject to us. Nothing too onerous, so don't get alarmed. Keep us informed of your movements and whereabouts, of course. Molyneux will probably continue to be your contact, until he's moved on, if he is, of course. Consider him an appendage of mine. The Crown is very grateful, but you know that already. You have given good service, which is why we've spent years subsidising your family.' That was the word he used, 'subsidising', no beating about the bush. He didn't say 'helping' or 'taking care of'. 'And now you've acquired another family. Whatever were you thinking of? Without our contribution, you'll have a hard time trying to maintain both. Anyway, if you do go back to Madrid, we'll find a slot for you back at the embassy or the British Council or, at worst, the British Institute, where there are always vacancies, and with your skills, you'd make an excellent teacher. Unless you want to find another job under your own steam, which you're perfectly free to do, always assuming you're lucky enough to find one. If not, we'll pay you your salary anyway, just as we've been paying your wife for some years now. We never abandon those who have worked to defend the Realm, you can be sure of that. However, we will abandon anyone who lets the Realm down or allows his tongue to run away with him or reveals things he shouldn't and cannot reveal. Your wife is sure to ask you questions when you reappear, how could she not? And others might too, your children, for example, who won't understand a thing, but will want to hear all kinds of tales of derring-do; but since she knows more, she'll be the one to ask more. Tell her whatever you like, that the dead wouldn't let you in, that you've had amnesia, which, of course, she won't believe, but it doesn't matter. However, don't tell her the truth whatever you do, unless you want us to withdraw your maintenance payments and all financial help.' And again he used a rather offensively bureaucratic term – 'maintenance payments', no less. 'That would happen immediately, but it wouldn't be the only thing. We could even prosecute you. You're still bound by the Official Secrets Act and will be for the rest of your life, so don't forget that. By the 1911 Act and the revised 1989 Act, which are essentially the same if you take the trouble to compare them.' The waitress finally came over, and Tupra handed her a note. While he was waiting for his change, he added: 'In short, just to make things clear: it's exactly as if you'd been part of Sefton Delmer's PWE.'

This advice was unnecessary. Tomás was now a veteran and unlikely to forget. He was no longer the terrified, impressionable young man he had been at that first meeting with Tupra. Besides, what Ted Reresby had said to him all those years ago – Tupra, he recalled, had been Ted Reresby to that striking lecturer from Somerville, Carolyn Beckwith by name (and had probably slept with her that night) – had remained engraved on his memory: 'We don't really belong anywhere, neither officially nor officiously. We are simultaneously somebody and nobody. We both exist and don't exist. We both act and don't act, Nevinson, or, rather, we don't carry out the actions we carry out, or the things we do are done by nobody. We simply happen.' Those words had sounded like something out of Beckett and he had barely understood them. Now, they no longer sounded like Beckett and he could understand them, because he, too, had been through the same thing, he had 'happened' several times. Now, though, he would stop.

Tupra or Reresby didn't leave a tip, not even a penny. He was usually very generous, even extravagant compared with his thrifty compatriots. It was his way of punishing the waitress for her delay in attending to him. As Tom well knew, he always dished out rewards and punishments. They both stood up and, once out in the street, Tupra offered him his hand, as the English tend to do when they say goodbye for some time or for ever; they don't usually shake hands willy-nilly. Tomás took his own hand out of his raincoat pocket – a reflex reaction more Spanish than British, he who had always been so careful not to let such trivial details give him away. However, to go from stroking the butt of his gun to shaking Tupra's hand seemed excessive, as did shaking the hand of someone who had done him harm, irreparable, irreversible, prehistoric harm. And so he put his hand back in his pocket, without even touching Tupra's proffered hand, which Tupra elegantly diverted to lighting another cigarette with the fluctuating flame of his lighter. He wasn't in the least offended. He probably didn't care, and wouldn't punish him for it.

'Goodbye, Tupra.' Tomás wouldn't have many opportunities to speak to Tupra in the future, but, he thought, he would never again call him by his first name as he often had, as if he were a comrade in arms, which he couldn't deny he had been on occasion.

'Goodbye, Nevinson, and good luck. Give my regards to your wife, once you're back in Madrid with her. She's a very nice woman, and intelligent too.' A thought crossed Tomás's mind, but he immediately dismissed it: 'I hope he didn't take too much of a liking to her.' But this was no time for pointless, retrospective questions. Tupra added with an encouraging smile: 'I think that, although, over time, she's got used to the idea, she'll be very glad you're not dead.'

IX

For a while, I wasn't sure my husband was my husband, or perhaps I only needed to feel that and was merely playing at being unsure. Sometimes I thought he was, sometimes not, and at others, I decided to believe nothing and simply continue living my life with him, or with that man so similar to him, albeit older, and who had emerged from a mist somewhere and had never been counted among the dead, which meant that while it couldn't be said of him: 'We die with the dying: see, they depart, and we go with them', it could be said: 'We are born with the dead: see, they return, and bring us with them'. And I, too, had grown older in his absence.

As long as I decided to believe nothing and to carry on regardless, I felt safe in a way. It was as if I'd returned to that state of waiting and uncertainty that benefits us all and helps us make the transition from day to day, because there's nothing worse than the feeling that everything is fixed and certain, or set firmly on the right path; that what should have happened has happened or is in the slow process of happening, that there will be no anxieties or surprises until we reach the conclusion, or only phoney anxieties or surprises, which we could have safely predicted, if that isn't a contradiction in terms. Most of the Earth's inhabitants settle into their daily lives and merely watch the days begin and see how they trace an arc as they pass and then end: that's how I would like to have lived when I was young and there was only the future stretching out before me, and no potholed present or past. However, since my experience was quite different and I became used to that, it's the latter experience I still want now: anyone who grows accustomed to a state of constant waiting never entirely allows it to end, it's as if half your air had been taken away. And so, for a time, Tomás both was and wasn't him. I observed him with a mixture of suspicion and satisfaction, and, absurd though it may seem, the one contributed to the other, or, rather, they were mutually dependent and fed each other reciprocally, and the suspicion was the waiting, its prolongation or survival.

I didn't recognise him when he appeared in the square. As so often before, I'd gone out onto one of the balconies very early one morning, a Sunday when Guillermo and Elisa had both stayed over with friends the previous night. It was still getting light or almost, because the clocks had just gone forward an hour, an hour stolen from the previous night for what is known as 'summer time', a theft that takes place at the beginning of April or even the end of March. Twelve years had passed since Tomás had said goodbye to me at Barajas airport, on his way to the Falklands according to my conjectures, and that war was now as remote as Britain's two Afghanistan wars or the Crimean War, or our war in Morocco or that of the soldier beloved by women, Luis Noval, he of the ugly statue. Who can ever properly remember their dead: it's as if they'd never existed, erased just a little sooner than those who managed to survive the wars.

It was a cold day lit by a yellowish light that presaged snow, which is why I went out onto the balcony in my coat, thinking I wouldn't stay long. I had to revisit *Moby-Dick* for one of my repeated courses, although I knew the book inside out; I'd gone to bed vainly going over and over in my head a sentence from the first chapter which may or may not be mysterious, but then we teachers always like to scrutinise each and every word: 'Yes, as every one knows, meditation and water are wedded for ever.' Why 'every one'? With that superfluous question I managed to fall asleep, but woke up later feeling ill at ease, and far too early for a relaxing Sunday, perhaps it was the sudden drop in temperature or the unease brought on by that arbitrary change of the clocks. And sure enough, just a couple of minutes after I stepped out onto the balcony, some flakes of snow began to fall, slow and lacklustre to begin with, and not enough to bother me. Nevertheless, I felt a shudder run through me, more psychological than physical, and I drew my coat around me, without buttoning it up; I leaned on the balustrade and looked to right and left; there were very few people about at that precarious hour, so few that I could count the number of passers-by. And as I did – one, two, three, four, five, six; and seven – I saw a figure approaching from the direction of the Teatro Real, carrying a small suitcase in one hand; every few steps, he rather half-heartedly raised his other hand as if he were timidly greeting someone. He would take those few steps, then stop, put down his case, look around, and again raise one hand before advancing a little further. I couldn't see his face until he was quite close, or, rather, I could see only part of his face, and what I saw I didn't recognise at all. He was middle-aged, rather heavily built, and with a grey beard, the kind of beard worn by submariners in films, at once thick and well trimmed, or perhaps kept in check. He was wearing a dark, belted raincoat, black or navy blue, and a rather old-fashioned peaked cap – more French or Dutch than Spanish, and worn perhaps as protection against the coming snow – which made it hard to discern his features. He looked rather like a sailor home from the sea, which, in Madrid, was a distinctly incongruous image. I had the impression that he was waving at me, that he'd seen me on the balcony, which is why he kept raising his hand now and then, only to lower it at once – it was a matter of seconds – as if he wanted

517

both to attract my attention and not attract it, as if he regretted the gesture, as if it were quite involuntary and to be suppressed the moment it occurred. Or perhaps he lowered it because there was no response from me, but then I wasn't going to wave to a complete stranger carrying a suitcase – he was probably drunk – on a morning of unexpected snow and with so few people around. I just wanted to savour briefly those first flakes of snow before submerging myself in Melville's November of the soul, before those flakes grew heavier and thicker and more energetic, if, that is, they did.

And they did, but I didn't realise quickly enough to close the balcony window and take shelter indoors, because that man had distracted me. He approached the street door below, then abruptly moved away and walked into the little park containing the statue of the soldier, and there he sat down on a bench. He took out a cigarette and lit it, and I watched him smoking, sideways on to me now, although I could barely see him through the trees. I heard the sound of horses' hooves, and he did too, and both he and I looked round to see where the sound was coming from; a couple of mounted policemen were riding along Calle de San Quintín on their way to Plaza de la Encarnación, one white horse and one black, on the former the snowflakes were invisible, and on the latter they really stood out, momentarily turning it into a piebald. When they reached Calle Pavía, they turned and headed off towards the Teatro Real; it was odd that they should be out patrolling so early, in the middle of all that silence and with the square almost empty. I couldn't take my eyes off them as they rode past, I followed them until they were out of sight, leaving behind them a trail of dung, at my feet so to speak. Then I looked again for the flying Dutchman, but couldn't see him, he had vanished while I was watching those two snowy horses. My coat was spattered with snowflakes, as was I, and I imagined my hair must be too, half white. Before I returned to that 'substitute for pistol and ball', I needed to dry myself off.

Then the bell rang, which was the last thing I was expecting. I closed the balcony window and tiptoed over to the front door, cautiously peering through the spyhole; it was too early for visitors or deliveries, and, besides, it was Sunday. There was the sailor, with his cap still on. He kept his eyes lowered, whether out of modesty or patience, I couldn't tell, and with his head bowed like that, the peaked cap concealed his whole face, apart from his chin. I was tempted not to answer, to pretend no one was at home. He must have come to the wrong apartment. I couldn't understand how he'd got into the building, because the street door was locked, and he hadn't rung my entryphone; the neighbour he was visiting or staying with must have opened the door and he'd then mistaken the apartment number or the floor. I still don't know why I revealed my presence.

'Who is it?' I asked. 'Who are you looking for? I think you've got the wrong apartment.' And I added irrelevantly: 'It's very early.'

He then doffed his cap with a respectful, gentlemanly gesture, as if I were standing there before him. I saw his receding hair, which was darker than his beard. He looked up. The glass of the spyhole does tend to distort, but even so there was something familiar about that face, although only vaguely. You never expect a dead man to reappear, even if his body has never been found. And you don't expect the disappeared or the fugitive or the exiled either.

'It's anything but early, Berta,' said the man. 'You don't recognise me, do you? I'm not surprised. I barely recognise myself. I'm Tomás, and it's anything but early. In fact, it's probably too late.'

I believed him and I didn't believe him, both things at once, how could I know. But what could I do, what could I do but open the door to him.

A year and a half has passed since that ghost reappeared on a cold Sunday morning in early spring. Tomás Nevinson, or the person who is beginning to resemble or replace him, the one who has memories that could only be his and who perhaps has no one else in the world, doesn't live with me and the children, not exactly. He was the first to reject the idea, to give up all claim to that privilege; indeed, he thought it best for us to live apart, felt it wouldn't be right to share the same living space permanently. He gave various reasons, all of which were eminently sensible and coincided with my own: Guillermo and Elisa would have to get used to him and accept him, if they could; I had, for years, been leading an independent life as a singleton or widow, and he didn't expect me to welcome him back with open arms unless and until I wanted to; and although he didn't say as much, not openly at least, I sensed that he still didn't feel entirely safe, and the last thing he would have wanted was to put us in any danger. After many months had passed, the most explicit comment he made on the subject was this: 'I think I can live in peace now, despite all those years of playing dirty tricks on people, because that's what the job involved; circumstances change, though, your enemies stop being your enemies, time passes, those people withdraw, go into hiding, grow old and tired; some of them die, and almost everything is forgotten. But you never know. There could still

520

be someone who stays anchored in the past and neither forgets nor forgives.'

As in the past, as always, I didn't receive any concrete answers to my questions, and I soon stopped asking them; I've never found out what he did during those twelve years of absence, of absence and death, or, rather, of pretending to be dead. 'I'm still not authorised to tell you anything,' he said and says. 'Even less than before, because, in order to bring my activities to an end and still receive their financial aid, I signed an additional absolute confidentiality agreement. We would lose the money they pay me if I were to talk; worse than that, they would prosecute me, and I'd be sent to prison.' I myself no longer received my 'salary' from the Organización Mundial del Turismo. It was deemed unnecessary once Tomás went back to working at the embassy – in a higher and better-paid position – and would have been tantamount to paying two salaries.

Tomás rented a small apartment, almost a garret really, just near us, on the other side of Plaza de Oriente, in Calle de Lepanto, more or less where the Casa de las Matemáticas once stood a few centuries before. And so while he doesn't exactly live with us, he's only a stone's throw away and visits often, more and more often in fact, with my consent and that of the children. He can't recount any of his own adventures – something which, at their still-idealistic age, they would probably love – but he has won them over with his pitch-perfect imitations of all kinds of people, people they know. Just as he used to do at school. They were very wary of him at first: Elisa was shy and stand-offish, Guillermo clearly cross and upset. Their father, though, has been so discreet, so sensitive, during this year and a half, asking them questions without seeming to probe too deeply, taking an interest in them, but not in an ingratiating way, almost asking their permission to talk to them, as if he really were a totally unexpected intruder and not the person who, indirectly and in large measure, provides for and has provided for them (even when he was thought to be dead), that they've gradually taken him to their hearts, even asking him to come and see them. They find him amusing with his different voices and accents and mimicry, and they sense that he's someone who has led a far from ordinary life; they take it for granted that he's had some strange, possibly mysterious experiences (he sometimes drops hints, as discreet as they are intriguing), and that he will one day reveal these to them. That's where they're wrong, of course, but they don't know that, so it doesn't matter: they look at him expectantly, that is, with sustained curiosity. They find his presence stimulating, at least for the moment. They're coming to depend on him more and more as they grow accustomed to him being around, and if he has nothing else to entertain them with, Tomás will come up with some invented story, since he has more than enough material to draw on. I sometimes think it must be child's play for him, winning over his still young children, because, in the past, he must have had to win over all kinds of cruel, vicious people, guarded and suspicious, whose main companion and shield was distrust. He's been trained to break down people's resistance.

He soon lost the weight he'd gained and was no longer the burly figure who came to the door with his Dutch hat still on, a hat he hasn't worn since. He shaved off his Captain Nemo beard and looked much younger once he'd divested himself of all that grizzled hair, thus revealing a scar on his chin, one I hadn't seen before, but it didn't even occur to me to ask him about it. As soon as he resumed work at the embassy, he went back to wearing a suit and tie, and he sometimes dons a hideous pinstripe affair, complete with ridiculous waistcoat, perhaps to emphasise his English half. He goes to work every day, and fulfils his tasks brilliantly, or so he tells me, boasting slightly, as if he expects me to be impressed. He's invited me to a few receptions and suppers, to keep up appearances, and, after resisting for months, I have accepted on a few occasions, as I did in the old days. After all, we never divorced, and I was only his widow by mistake, and the mistake has been put right.

He found me much harder work than the children, because for them he was a novelty, whereas for me, he was a returning ghost. He was always very respectful and careful and never tried to force anything, but, initially, I eyed him reproachfully whenever he came to visit and still kept asking myself if he really was him or if he possibly could be after all those years, during which he hadn't once phoned to say: 'Berta, I'm alive.' 'You have to understand, Berta, I simply couldn't. It was essential that, during that time, no one should know I was alive, because if anyone found out, I would probably be dead. Besides, those were my orders,' he said to justify his silence. I understood this intellectually, but I would still look at him and think: 'How utterly unimportant I've been to you during our life together. What a tiny role I've played in your life, a life that was always happening elsewhere.' Resentment is inevitable, and I know I'll feel it until I die. Even if he dies first, I'll still feel it, because there are some posthumous resentments that continue to seethe away even when the person who caused them has disappeared.

But I hated seeing myself turning into this mean-spirited wretch, and, besides, I hadn't, as the saying goes, made a fresh start, and nothing can be deemed to be over and done with until it's been buried and replaced by something else. And you realise – not with any great surprise – that there are such things as undeserved loyalties and inexplicable fidelities, people whom you chose with a youthful or, rather, primitive resolve or determination, and that choice prevails over maturity and logic, over resentment and the feelings of loathing felt by the deceived. I began allowing him to spend more time with us, he sometimes stayed for supper and, one night, he didn't leave after supper nor when the children had gone to bed. I let him into my sometimes woeful, sometimes dull bed, through which other men had passed and barely rumpled the sheets, and there I found that he *was* him or a part of him, that he hadn't changed very much on his journey to the block, to the fire; that he'd come very close, but hadn't quite reached them: his way of making love was the same as it had been in his now distant bouts of insomnia or wakefulness, the same almost animal-ish way of entering me, albeit with slightly less vigour (we are, after all, in our forties now), as if he wanted his body temporarily to deceive or confuse his mind, or silence it. He didn't talk about what he'd done, but his thoughts were doubtless constantly filled with his memories and experiences, whether he was alone or at work or with us, and he needed to empty his mind through that physical act, even if it lasted only a few minutes. I couldn't help holding out my arms to him not so much to welcome him as to keep him there, as if, rather than coming back to stay, he were about to leave. And afterwards, I would run my index finger over his lips, which, though less firm and smooth, were as clearly drawn as ever.

Uncertainty and waiting, as well as irrational expectation and fantasy, can become essential to the human heart, and prove impossible to relinquish. Even grief and sorrow and spite can become essential, and end up shaping the way you live your life. That neither is nor was the case with me. However, letting him into my bed was an expression of hope that was unrealistic, but which survived nonetheless, because that night and the nights that followed and that continue still, as and when I choose – although they are and have been few and far between – I treat as exceptions that won't necessarily be repeated, rather than a return to normality. We'll see, and will continue to see, because everything remains as uncertain as when Tomás hovered between the world of the living and the world of the dead, and had even inclined towards the latter. And it's of absolutely no significance that, when he's in my arms, this recurring thought flashes through my mind: 'How utterly unimportant I've been to you during our life together. What a tiny role I've played in your life, a life that was always happening elsewhere. But here you are now, inside me.' As I say, it's only a flash, which is gone the next instant.

There's been a change in Tomás during this year and a half, in some aspects at least. He appeared to adapt very quickly to living in Madrid again, and to his distinguished post at the embassy; he met new people, made a few superficial friendships, recovered a couple of old friends insofar as that was possible, given the long gap in time. But behind that apparently normal existence, I could see that he was permanently on edge, ill at ease. He would jump at the slightest noise, and he reacted to crowds as if he feared they were about to turn on him, that someone still anchored in the past might have come from afar to find him or sent someone more local to do the job.

One summer night, while we were sitting outside a café in Rosales, drinking and not talking (initially, we still found it hard to sustain a conversation), a fight broke out that had nothing to do with us, except that we happened to be sitting quite close to the two men arguing and exchanging insults and blows and generally getting worked up, to the extent that one of them smashed a beer bottle and, wielding the bottle as a weapon, hurled himself on the other man. For a second, I saw fear in Tomás's eyes, as if he imagined that the man with the bottle was about to slit *his* throat rather than the man's opponent, who, meanwhile, had snatched up a wicker chair as a somewhat flimsy shield. Once that second had passed, though, the look in Tomás's eyes hardened and, without further thought, he sprang to his feet, went over to the attacker and, before the latter was even aware of his presence, grabbed the arm holding the weapon and, with his other hand, punched the man, delivered one short, sharp punch; I didn't see where exactly he punched him, but the man slumped to the ground. He fell like a sack suspended from a beam when someone suddenly cuts the rope. He lay there crumpled and unconscious, as if felled by that single blow. I sensed that Tomás must have done this or something similar before. Then, in 1994 (I'm rereading and revising and recalling these notes after two decades or more, notes I stopped taking ages ago), such altercations could still be resolved with no need for formal complaints, without even getting the police involved. Tomás himself helped revive the man a little, making sure he hadn't sustained any serious injury, and handed him over to the care of the other drunks accompanying him (although the shock had instantly sobered them all up), and then we left. I was slightly alarmed by his violent reaction, but also felt glad to know that he could, if necessary, defend himself and, therefore, us.

Yet now, a year and a half later, I see that he's shrugged off that continual state of tension and alert. On the contrary, he often seems melancholy and passive. When he comes to our apartment, and I'm busy and the children are out, he spends ages standing on one of the balconies, his gaze fixed on the trees that, for years and years, were mine alone. Or he sits on the sofa deep in thought, while I'm in my study preparing my classes. And when I go back into the living room, and it's grown dark, there he still is, as if, for him, time hadn't passed. I don't know what he's thinking or remembering, I don't know what inner depths he plumbs and never will. I tell myself that we all have our secret sadnesses. Even those of us who have stayed quietly at home and never experienced any drama, any turbulence. Or to quote Dickens – at least I think it was him – who I sometimes have to teach:

'. . . every human creature is destined to be a profound secret and mystery to every other creature. A solemn thought comes to me whenever I enter a great city by night: that every one of those darkly clustered houses and every room in every house contains its own secret; that every beating heart in the hundreds of thousands of breasts hidden there, is, in some of its imaginings, a secret to the heart nearest it, the one that drowses and beats by its side. And there is in all of that something akin to awe . . .'

When I see Tomás sitting there, pensive and weary or perhaps lost in remembrance of things past, I'm assailed by the unpleasant memory of Miguel Ruiz Kindelán's words on that worst of mornings: 'No one ever emerges from that business well,' he told me, the lighter still open in his hand, and referring to the 'business' in which Tomás was involved. 'I've known a couple of men like him, and they usually come out either mad or dead. And those who survive end up not knowing who they are. They lose their life or it splits in two, and those two parts are irreconcilable, mutually repellent. Some try to return to normality years later and just can't do it, they don't know how to reintegrate themselves into civilian life, or else enforced retirement simply finishes them off. It makes no difference what age they are. If they're no good any more or are burned out, they're withdrawn from service, just like that, sent home or left to vegetate in an office, and some individuals don't even reach thirty before feeling that their time has passed. They miss their days of action, of villainy, deceit and falsehood. They remain attached to their murky past, and are sometimes overwhelmed by remorse: when they stop, they realise that what they did achieved little or nothing; that they weren't indispensable; that anyone could have done what they did and with the same result. They also discover that no one will thank them for their efforts or their talent, their astuteness or their patience or their sacrifices, that they will receive no gratitude, no admiration, not in those invisible worlds. What was important for them is of no importance to anyone else, but merely an unknown past . . .'

He's not always like that, far from it. He has very busy, active days too, he's learned to enjoy his new or old job, and every few months, he travels to England as he did before, but now he's only ever away for a week at most, and he phones me almost every day, as dusk is falling, when he's finished work. When he's in Madrid, though, these ruminative moods come upon him more frequently, or perhaps they're moments of surrender, as if, unlike his state of mind before he returned to normal life, when everything was so tentative and uncertain, he had now accepted that he would be defenceless if confronted by someone who did remember him, someone who hadn't mellowed over time and who had come to settle some distant account with him; as if he were no longer prepared to run away or defend himself if it came to it; as if he were tired of waiting or tired of feeling afraid, and had said to himself: 'At last they've found me. I shouldn't complain. I was given a lot of extra time. Useless, meaningless time, but nevertheless time to spend in the universe. And since all such respites must have an end, so be it.'

I don't know, though, because, one night, we went to the cinema together. When the film ended and the lights went up, and as he was unfolding the raincoat he'd placed on his lap, a small revolver fell to the floor, the sound muffled by the carpet. I stared at him in astonishment before he'd realised what had happened and swiftly picked up the gun and put it back in his pocket. Fortunately, no one else noticed.

'What's that gun for?'

'Oh, nothing, don't worry. I've just been used to carrying it around, and have been for years.'

'Do you always have it with you?'

'No, not always, and less and less now.'

So I don't know if this means he *would* defend himself if he had to or if he hasn't discounted the possibility that he might shoot himself one day, if he turns out to be the one anchored in the past, the one who remembers and can't bear his own continued existence on Earth. When he sits looking at the trees from his place on the sofa, I wonder vaguely what horrors he must have accumulated over the years, while I was playing no part in his life, neither his living nor his dead life. It's a blessing really not to know, it's good that he's not authorised to say anything; after all, why make a story out of something that simply happens. Most people would insist that the opposite is true, that nothing simply happens. They're the kind who revisit and repeat what happened until the end of days, and never let it stop happening.

I often tell myself that there's nothing so very odd about the fact that I don't really know my husband, just as I don't really know anyone else. Dickens also wrote, if the words that surface in my memory are indeed his: 'My friend is dead, my neighbour is dead, my love, my heart's darling, is dead, and that means the inexorable consolidation and perpetuation of the secret that was always there in them . . . In any of this city's cemeteries through which I walk, is there a sleeper more inscrutable to me than its busy inhabitants are in their innermost selves, or than I am to them?' Even as a boy, an adolescent, Tomás was never interested in knowing or deciphering himself, in finding out what kind of person he was. This seemed to him a job for narcissists and a waste of time. Perhaps he hasn't changed in that respect, despite all he's been through, or perhaps he's always known this ever since his consciousness took its first steps. So why should I struggle to understand someone who doesn't even bother to observe himself. We expect a lot of ourselves, we think we can get to the bottom of people, especially the person who lies dozing and breathing beside us in bed.

He does occasionally spend the night in my bed, but not often, or else I stay with him in his garret in Calle Lepanto; if the children need me, I'm very near, they just have to phone or run across the square, where there are no cars, and, besides, they're older now. Tomás still doesn't sleep deeply; he's restless and anxious and mumbles in his sleep, but he does sleep. When I look at him, I feel like softly stroking the back of his neck and whispering: 'Lie very still, my love. Don't move or turn around, that way sleep will come upon you without you realising it and gradually, in your nightmares, you'll stop thinking. It's just as well you don't tell me what it is you think about for hours and hours, at all hours, sleeping and awake. You're always thinking something, and, luckily, I don't know what that something is. I'm far better off with the blank page. I know you have your reasons, and you're fated now to have a brain that never stops thinking.' But I resist the temptation and say nothing, nor will I say it however long I live. I keep it to myself and simply think those words. Saying it to him would be a gift too far, even if he didn't hear me: he was away from me for far too long, he even declared himself dead, left his body on some distant shore.

Sometimes, when he's standing on the balcony, looking out, absorbed in thought, he runs his thumbnail over the scar on his cheek, a scar that hasn't existed for ages, and which was swiftly erased by surgery. Then I speculate about what he might be thinking when he recalls an invisible mark that only he remembers and whose origin he alone knows, probably not the result of a mugging, but something more premeditated, an act of revenge or a punishment. And he may be thinking that, basically, he belongs to the category of people who don't see themselves as protagonists, not even of their own story, their lives shaken and shaped by others from the very start; who discover halfway through that, regardless of the uniqueness of each individual's story, their story will not merit being told by anyone, or only as a fleeting reference when recounting another person's more eventful and interesting life. Not even as a way of passing the time during some prolonged after-dinner conversation, or sitting beside the fire one sleepless night. That is what usually happens to lives which, like mine and his, and like so many, many others, simply exist and wait.

Acknowledgements

The translator would like to thank Javier Marías for all his help and advice, and, as always, Annella McDermott and Ben Sherriff for their unfailing support.